TAROT FOR TWO

Book One - Alone

ELLA HAMILTON

Tarot For Two

Tarot for Two Book One – Alone

ISBN (ebook): 978-1-9193044-1-0
ISBN (paperback – version 1): 978-1-9193044-4-1
ISBN (paperback – version 2): 978-1-9193044-7-2

Cover design courtesy of Tarot For Two
First published in the United Kingdom by Tarot For Two

To all the people who feel – or have heard – they're *too much* or *not enough*.
To anyone with a "normal" or "boring" job, or who isn't physically fit or muscly.
To anyone who's heard that showing feelings is a weakness or unmanly.
To the divine spark who ignited this story within me.
To the neurodivergent community (hey, family!).

Be yourself.

I see you. I encourage you. I accept you as you are.
I hope my words help you shine brightly.
The world needs your light.

I wish you all happiness.

PROLOGUE

It's enough to drive you nuts. You read tarot for a living, and you keep getting emails from people thanking you: they've found their happily ever after, dream career, yadda yadda yadda.

And it's amazing, and gratifying, and you feel you're helping people find happiness.

And you can't do it for yourself.

Oh, I'm not saying that I can't read for myself. I can. No problem. But there's no sign of anything love-related in my readings for me. No "tall, dark, handsome stranger", no "Mr Right", or even "Mr Right Now".

It's a right royal pain in the arse.

And it's not something you can force or forge either. The ol' intuition won't come if you try and twist it to your own ends. Trying to get a prediction of something that isn't there is a guaranteed one-way path to "I'm not getting anything that makes sense, sorry".

That's not good enough for the people I read for. They're paying for my time, my connection to the larger world. The world that others often can't see or communicate with and, with some practice, I can.

I've been reading tarot since I was seventeen. I was with an older friend browsing a shop window, and my eye was drawn to a brightly-coloured box. That was the first time I saw a tarot deck, and I was hooked on what it could do.

I started out reading for myself, for my friends and family, and word got round. I hadn't ever spent much

time in conventional jobs but that suited me fine. I didn't class myself as a conventional person.
Tarot was a little extra thing I did on the side for a few years, until the early 2010s when it became more mainstream. It wasn't long before I had a website up, offering short readings on love, careers, or life paths, and it went from there.
Most of my clients are women. More than 95%, I'd say. I guess men either don't believe in it or don't feel they need help with the same things that women do. And the few requests I've had from guys tend to be more sceptical, less open-minded.
I need to be able to tune in to the person's energy to find out what's going on with them, so the readings for men are more surface-level compared to most of the women's ones.

Usually, anyway.

AUTHOR'S NOTE

PLEASE READ – 18+ CONTENT AND TRIGGER WARNINGS

Dear Reader,
This is an adult story. If any of the content below is triggering or traumatising for you, please don't read on unless you're in a safe place and you feel able to take that risk. Your wellbeing matters hugely – I'd hate to cause you distress.
I'm not a mental health professional, and I can't take responsibility for how the story makes you feel. Your emotional safety is in your own hands, always.
Please get support if you need it, my love.
If you choose to continue, I hope this book helps you feel seen, understood, and – most importantly – never alone.

The *Tarot For Two* series contains the following:
• Sexual abuse (descriptive, not graphic – forced kiss / masturbatory, no penetration)
• Psychological abuse (gaslighting, coercion, manipulation)
• Physical violence (one incident against a person, one between two people)
• Suicide attempts and ideation (descriptive, not graphic – water-based, no blood)
• Emotionally traumatic recounting of events (past and present)
• Explicit language throughout
• Explicit sex scenes

PS: This story is dual Point of View (POV). Lori is the main POV narrator.
I've marked the starts and ends of the other POV as
*** **enable(altPOV)** *** and
*** **suspend(altPOV)** *** for a reason which will become clear soon after you start the book, but I wanted something that looked like it belonged in a computer program.

PPS: This is a **SERIES** not a standalone novel.

I hope you fall in love with the story the way I did!

Love,
Ella
x

CONTENTS

PROLOGUE

It's enough to drive you nuts. You read tarot for a living, and you keep getting emails from people thanking you: they've found their happily ever after, dream career, yadda yadda yadda.

And it's amazing, and gratifying, and you feel you're helping people find happiness.

And you can't do it for yourself.

Oh, I'm not saying that I can't read for myself. I can. No problem. But there's no sign of anything love-related in my readings for me. No "tall, dark, handsome stranger", no "Mr Right", or even "Mr Right Now".

It's a right royal pain in the arse.

And it's not something you can force or forge either. The ol' intuition won't come if you try and twist it to your own ends. Trying to get a prediction of something that isn't there is a guaranteed one-way path to "I'm not getting anything that makes sense, sorry".

That's not good enough for the people I read for. They're paying for my time, my connection to the larger world. The world that others often can't see or communicate with and, with some practice, I can.

I've been reading tarot since I was seventeen. I was with an older friend browsing a shop window, and my eye was drawn to a brightly-coloured box. That was the first time I saw a tarot deck, and I was hooked on what it could do.

I started out reading for myself, for my friends and family, and word got round. I hadn't ever spent much time in conventional jobs but that suited me fine. I didn't class myself as a conventional person.

Tarot was a little extra thing I did on the side for a few years, until the early 2010s when it became more mainstream. It wasn't long before I had a website up, offering short readings on love, careers, or life paths, and it went from there.

Most of my clients are women. More than 95%, I'd say. I guess men either don't believe in it or don't feel they need help with the same things that women do. And the few requests I've had from guys tend to be more sceptical, less open-minded.

I need to be able to tune in to the person's energy to find out what's going on with them, so the readings for men are more surface-level compared to most of the women's ones.

Usually, anyway.

CHAPTER ONE

10th September 2021

The email came in as they normally did: a reading request through the website, payment had been made, and it should've been straightforward. Signed with the initial "J", there were very few clues about the client. He or she had had a few strange dreams which eventually led them to my website, and they wanted to know what was going on in their life.

I replied and said that was a little general; did they have anything particular they wanted to know? As we emailed back and forth, trying to clarify what "J" wanted to learn, I began to get a feel for their energy. "J" was a sensitive man who'd had a bad break-up. He was OK in his career, but his home life was a chaotic mess. His sister kept trying to set him up on blind dates he didn't want to go on, his parents were dropping hints about grandkids, and he was at the stage of cutting himself off from everyone just so they'd leave him alone.

He didn't feel ready for all that dating stuff, and he didn't know how to tell them to sod off without hurting their feelings. The last thing he wanted to do was cause pain to others.

He'd decided to get a reading, after the weird dreams, to see if there was any hope of someone, or something, coming his way – to get his family to stop badgering him. They meant well, he thought, but it was all too much, too soon.

Finding this out took a couple of weeks of coaxing via email, and I was glad I'd studied a little psychology in

my spare time. "J" wanted to turn round to his interfering family and give them something to gain himself space to breathe.
My empathy kicked in, and I felt for him. He'd been through enough already, from what I gathered.
When I got to the stage of pulling cards for him, the situation clarified yet mystified. Yes, someone was out there for him, but getting a read on her proved tricky.
I emailed him that she had a varied career which involved helping others, but I couldn't discover any more about her work. She was an animal lover, cared about the planet, loved to read and paint, and she liked to laugh.
I rolled my eyes at what I was typing. There were probably hundreds of women who matched the description I was giving. He was as likely to meet someone on the train as walking down the street.
But when he pressed me for more details of their meeting, things got fuzzy. It appeared he already knew her, although not well. I shrugged, saved what I'd done, and turned to another client for a while. I knew better than to try and push when things weren't clear.
The next client was a breeze to read for. There was no lack of clarity in the reading. The woman wanted insights into her spirit guides as she was drawn to Native American lore. I was able to give her a name she could call her guide, describe him to her, and give her enough clues that she could, if she wished, find some history about his tribe.
I was relieved. At least I wasn't blocked from getting information through from Spirit. That would've been a nightmare.

The reading for "J" niggled at me, though. It was like an aching tooth that kept drawing my attention. I concentrated on his lady friend's physical appearance to see if it helped him identify her.

The cards "told" me she was mid-height with long mousy brown hair that she liked to wear down but didn't often. Blue-eyed, she liked wearing bright colours and dancing, and loved the water. I was thrilled with the information coming through. Hopefully it'd help him narrow it down.

Except it didn't. When presented with the new insights, "J" denied knowing anyone like that at all. He didn't have many female friends, and the ones he did were nothing like the woman I'd described.

It was perplexing for us both.

I put the information aside and did some chores instead. It didn't help, but at least it took my mind off it. The longer "J" was without his lady friend, the more his family would pressurise him, and I felt he was getting closer to snapping at them.

Perhaps that was why I suggested a phone consultation, where I'd "tune in" while "J" and I talked, to see if there was anything further that "them upstairs", Spirit, or whoever could tell me. I didn't do them as a rule, because I couldn't always get into the right frame of mind, but it was worth a go and we sorted out a time to speak.

I was as nervous as an actress on the first night of a performance. What if I couldn't get through? What if nothing was forthcoming? I was starting to feel like "J" had to be feeling himself: fast heading towards the point of giving up. I'd never failed a client before, and as I meditated before the phone call, I told “them upstairs” I wouldn’t fail this time, either.

They had other ideas.

CHAPTER TWO

"J" or, rather, Jamie, to use his proper name, had a pleasant voice. He spoke typical Estuary English which didn't surprise me, as he was from the Home Counties. As I'd never lived outside South East England, there were no accent barriers or peculiar words to contend with on either side.

We chatted for a few minutes. He did something in IT which I didn't fully understand but, as we discovered a common love for some English literature classics, my nerves diminished and I became more at ease with trying a reading while I spoke to him.

I often shied away from reading in-person for someone I didn't know well, as their emotional state and energy could jar with mine. I'd learnt that quite early.

"I'm going to put you on loudspeaker while I shuffle the cards, OK?" I told Jamie, placing my phone on the low table in what I called my "reading room". It was the box room in my one-slash-two-bedroom flat, but it was separate space from the everyday rooms and no-one went in there except me.

Candles and crystals rubbed wax-to-rock on every shelf in a large bookcase, along with my many tarot decks which were lined up like they were ready to clock in before work. I wasn't someone who believed in things being tucked away when they should be enjoyed and available for use at any moment.

"OK Lori," Jamie's voice came from the tinny speaker of my phone, and I felt a moment's dissatisfaction that it didn't sound like him.

Never mind. On to the job at hand.

I chose a deck, worn at the edges from use, and lit a fat pink candle for affection, waving the cards through the smoke to cleanse it of any past perceptions. My decks didn't need clearing often, but I wanted to be extra-thorough for the patient man at the other end of the phone.

"Choose a number between one and ten."

"Seven."

I grinned, although he couldn't see it. "My lucky number."

"Huh, mine too."

"You seem pretty uncommon for someone in a science-based career, having lucky numbers and consulting a tarot reader," I teased, and he rewarded me with a chuckle. At least he seemed relaxed.

I shuffled the deck, thinking specifically about Jamie and his future lady. Who was she? Where had they met? What else could the cards tell me about her? Diddly squat, it appeared. No matter how I tried to interpret the seven cards I pulled, whatever parts of the images I pored over, I couldn't get more than I already had in the previous readings. He knew the brunette who enjoyed dancing and had a sense of humour. I mentally grouched that if they ever did meet, she could have a bloody good laugh over how much of a runaround the cards had given me.

I even called Jamie back partway through to see if I could get a clearer psychic signal, but to no avail.

I admitted defeat. "I'm really sorry, Jamie, I'm still getting nowhere. I think I'll have to send you a refund. Maybe you should try someone else? They might have

better luck."
Silence followed, and I guessed he was considering it, but he finally spoke.
"Call it a hunch, but I don't feel we should give up yet."
Perhaps he didn't, but I was getting a headache and I wasn't in the frame of mind to keep going. Once you get irritated, the flow of intuition is disrupted and you get nowhere.
"OK, I'll try again, but not tonight. I'm exhausted."
"I'm sorry it's so difficult for you. I hope all your clients aren't this hard to read for." Apology softened his voice.
I managed a laugh. "No, if they were, I wouldn't still be doing it. I've never come across a situation like this before. I'll have a think about what else we can try. Give me a couple of days, and I'll email you to let you know what I come up with. OK?"
"Yeah, that's great. Thanks."
"Goodnight, Jamie."
"Bye Lori."
We ended the call, and I leaned back on my hands, puzzled and pissed off. I didn't understand why it was proving so hard to get a handle on the situation, but couldn't settle enough mentally to ask my guides.
I did something unusual for me instead and opened a bottle of wine. Two glasses later, I was ready to sleep. *I'm done*, I thought. *I can't help him. It's not fair to keep stringing him along.*
*
The next day was busy with readings, all new enquiries and all successful, so I tried not to think about Jamie and his problem reading. I still didn't have a solution

for him. It irked me that I couldn't help, but I consoled myself that he was the exception that proved the rule. I was a highly accurate reader, and I helped many people.

Everyone except him, that was. He seemed such a nice guy when we'd spoken. Why couldn't I help him? Why was I falling at this hurdle? I calmed my thoughts and became reflective as I stood in front of my bookshelf.

I was drawn to an oracle deck instead of tarot, which surprised me. I didn't read oracle cards for specific purposes. They were my go-to for the general 'what does today bring' type questions.

The oracle deck told me I was doing things the wrong way, and the timing was off, too. I blew a raspberry at it.

Really?? Not helpful.

But there were hints of a possible stronger connection, and waiting for the right phase of the moon.

Great. How on earth was I going to communicate that to Jamie, who worked in a purely logical field, and who hadn't had much success with this tarot reader? Would he think it was a step too far? I resigned myself to giving him a refund once he'd finished laughing at me, and I sat on making the decision for most of the afternoon while I did other stuff.

Then he texted me:

Hi Lori, hope you're well. Your website doesn't mention in-person readings, but I wondered if you'd consider it for me? Still really want your help. Thanks, Jamie

I read it through twice. Whatever I felt, he still had faith in me. That both eased and added pressure. He was right, I didn't advertise phone or face-to-face readings, but that was because I liked my privacy. I wouldn't read in a public place for fear of judgement or interruption, which meant I'd have to allow him into my personal space.

I automatically shied away from the idea, but the more I thought about it, the more I wondered if I didn't owe it to him to try. It'd be a one-off, and nobody said I had to let him into my reading room. We could work at the table in the living room.

I thought back to the oracle reading, which said I'd been trying to do it the wrong way. Maybe this was what it'd meant?

I returned his text, and we arranged to meet later in the week, on Saturday afternoon. It'd be just after the new moon too, which was perfect for new beginnings. Once I'd made the decision, a calmness came over me and all my stress released, which surprised me. I expected to feel more tense, knowing I was going to let someone into my flat. And I didn't know the guy that well.

I wasn't completely naïve, so I made sure a neighbour knew as much as I could tell them about Jamie – aside from confidential things. When and where we were meeting, as well as how long I expected him to be at my place.

Two hours should cover it easily, especially as I'd already spent a good few hours trying to get information. Just as well I was OK money-wise, because my pay rate for the reading averaged well below minimum wage. But it wasn't like I was going to make a habit of it, so I shrugged it off.

CHAPTER THREE

9th October 2021

Saturday came, and as the time approached, nervous anticipation flooded me with nausea. We were to meet at a coffee shop near Littlehampton station, then walk back. That'd give me plenty of time to see how comfortable I felt with him, or whether I was sufficiently ill-at-ease to call it off there and then.

I nearly did, before we met, and apprehension nibbled at me. But my guides and guardian angels made sure I turned up.

I needn't have worried. Jamie was six feet tall, with sandy brown tousled hair, hazel eyes, and a ready smile. Not a bad-looking guy, and certainly with nice manners. He insisted on buying my coffee, even though I had a free one on my loyalty card, and we talked about everyday life as we walked to the flat.

He played football most Sundays, and Saturdays were for laundry and housework. He had his work shirts collected, ironed and returned on a weekly basis, with a week's worth in hand.

I pulled a face. "I hate ironing," I stated. "It's utterly dull and I'd rather have my nose in a book."

"Why do you think I pay someone to do it?" he replied. "I can do it myself, but what's the point? I can think of loads more fun things to do."

"What like?" I asked as I slowed to sip my coffee.

"Well we—" He stopped speaking and shook his head before continuing. "We used to find different places that did afternoon tea and try them out. I'd pick her up from her place. If it was close we'd walk or get the bus,

but if it was further away we'd dress up like we were going to the theatre and make an event of it."
A shadow crossed his face, and I touched his arm with my free hand. "I'm sorry."
He squared his shoulders. "No matter. If she's happier with someone else, good for her." He'd revealed during our email exchange that he'd popped the question but, instead of accepting, she'd told him she was seeing another man. She'd always intended to tell him that night.
They hadn't parted friends.
"Do you have a romantic streak, then?" I smiled up at him.
He hunched forward, slightly embarrassed. "Maybe a little. It's not a cool thing to admit."
"Are you kidding? A lot of my girlfriends would be over the moon if their guys did romantic things for them, or with them."
"What about you?"
I waved my free hand in dismissal. "We're not talking about me. We're talking about Jamie-the-romantic-IT-guy, who's broad-minded enough to get a tarot reading. Even if it's a crap one that tells him pretty much naff all."
He laughed with me, and as we reached the front door of the converted house, I handed him my coffee.
"Hope you don't mind holding that, it's a two-handed job."
"No, course not." He watched as I turned the key and handle at the same time, then followed me inside, pushing the door shut with his shoulder. "Lead on."
My upstairs flat looked over some green space at the

front from the living room. The kitchen and main bedroom both overlooked the tiny garden, but the bedroom door was closed. Instead, I led him through to the living room and offered him a seat.

"You don't work in here, do you?" he commented, and I shook my head.

"Not often, no. It's a nice enough room for when I have friends over. We always sit in here. I don't let anyone in my reading room, it's private space, like my bedroom. All my decks and most of my crystals are in the reading room, but my bedroom's just for sleeping."

He nodded and leaned back on the sofa, his coffee cup on his knee. "How many decks do you have?"

"More than I'd care to admit, probably. Maybe fifty."

"Fifty?" He sounded surprised.

"They all have a different feel to them. And that's not including my oracle decks, I have a good few of those too. In fact it was an oracle deck that showed me I was doing something wrong with you and I had to try a different approach."

"Really? That's interesting." He smiled, and I thought he was humouring me, but it appeared to be a genuine reaction.

"We'll get started. I'll bring in a few decks and you can choose one. Hopefully that'll get things moving along."

I selected half a dozen different tarot decks and laid them out in front of him.

"How do I choose?"

"What are you drawn to?"

He shifted forward, letting his eyes roam over each deck in turn, before he shook his head. "I don't know. None of them are standing out."

Bloody hell. We were having the same trouble in person that we'd had via email and phone.
"Hold your hand over each in turn, see if one feels warmer than the others."
Again, nothing. I was starting to feel uneasy about the whole thing.
"Are you sure you still want to try this? We're not getting very far. These are the decks I let people handle."
"You said you had about fifty. What about the others?"
"No-one's ever touched them but me."
"Can I see them?"
"Do you want to see me naked while you're at it?" I flared, and the instant hurt in his eyes struck me. "I'm sorry. That was a bit over-dramatic."
He shook his head. "It doesn't matter. But what do we do?"
"How open-minded are you?"
"I thought you knew that by now."
"OK, we'll try something."
I sat in the middle of the floor and slowed my breathing, closing my eyes. "Spirit, if Jamie is supposed to have his reading from one of my other decks, please give me a sign." I paused, then repeated the sentence twice more.
Nothing.
I was about to give up when there was a noise from the next room: a soft thump as if something had fallen. I peeped at the wide-eyed man on the sofa. "Did you hear that?"
"Yeah. What was it?"
I brought myself to my feet and beckoned to him.

“Let’s go see.” I wouldn’t ignore what sounded like a deliberate effort from “them upstairs” to do something in the physical world.

“Had you better look first?” It was the first time that Jamie had sounded anything less than confident. “Just in case...”

I grinned. “In case what, there’s something scary in there, like a demon? Don’t believe in them. Suck it up, buttercup. You didn’t want any of my other decks, now you deal with the consequences.”

I flung the door to my reading room wide open. A squat silver candle lay in the middle of the floor, and I wondered how the room appeared to him.

It was tidy, but I could feel the presence of something. All the hours of tarot readings had created an aura of energy so layered it was almost tangible.

“Do you want to come in?” I scooped up the candle: silver for the moon, which was three days past new, and divination, symbolic of psychic awareness, and for connecting with the divine. I knew it was the sign showing me how to proceed, and I turned to Jamie as he edged into the room with something like reverence on his face.

“Wow.” His gaze swept over my crystals and candles, and he ran a cautious finger along the edge of the shelf with my oracle decks on.

“The tools of my trade,” I waved my hand. “Take your pick.”

He moved unerringly towards a carved wooden box sitting on a velvet square and pointed at it. “That one.”

He was kidding me. That was my private deck. No one ever saw it, or touched it, or even knew I had it. It hadn't been out of the reading room since I'd bought it. I'd whispered my secret questions to it, my hopes and desires. It "knew" how much I yearned for a partner to share my life with, and had refused to give me anything. I'd tried other decks for my own readings, but I always came back to that one.

The Gilded Tarot.

The imagery had drawn me the moment I'd set eyes on it. I'd had to stretch a bit initially to shuffle it, but my fingers grew accustomed to its size the more I used it. And it was imbued with so much of my energy it practically glowed.

None of that was visible outside of the box, and it rattled me that Jamie had gone for it.

"Why that one?" I asked, trying to conceal how it affected me. "You can't even see there's a deck in there."

He shrugged. "I don't know, it's like it's pulling my attention. I can almost feel it."

That was pretty odd. This guy was practical as they came, a computer nerd, and he could almost feel the energy of a tarot deck? But who was I to argue with whatever Spirit had planned? I reached for the box and cradled it almost protectively against my chest.

"How does this room feel to you?" I asked Jamie, curious as to his sensitivities. Perhaps they were awakening because of the atmosphere in the flat.

His reply came slowly. "I can't describe it easily. I can feel something in here but I don't know what it is."

"Good or bad?"

"Neither. It's just present."

"Do you want me to read in here? The space is

limited."
"Is this where you did my other readings?"
I nodded.
"Well didn't 'they' tell you to try a different approach?"
"Yeah. So, not in here. I guess the living room will have to do. At least you can sit in a comfy chair."
"And you?"
"Oh I'll sit on the floor like I usually do. It always helps me to feel grounded."
Jamie was studying the decks with interest. "Can I look at some?"
"Yeah, course. Feel free. I'll go clear the table."
"I still want that one though..." he asserted, although his voice was distant, as if he wasn't entirely focused on what he was saying. I glanced back over my shoulder at him but I wasn't worried. He could look at the cards if he liked. I was still off-kilter with him choosing my personal deck.
As I moved our coffee cups and other assorted bits off the table, I tried to get into the right mindset to do the reading. I sat on the floor with my hands in my lap, breathing slowly, waiting for the usual calming and reflective routine to kick in. It took a while to work, but that was OK.
I accepted that, for whatever reason, the deck Jamie had chosen had an important message for him. Hopefully, it'd give him what he wanted: enough information that he could use to keep his family happy. And, if not, at least he could honestly tell them he'd spent the afternoon with a woman at her place.
Gradually my thoughts steadied as my breathing slowed, and I felt the emotional exhale that came with

regular practice. I unfolded the silk square that the deck lived in and laid it out flat.

"What's this one?" Jamie called, waving the Tarot of Sexual Magic at me through the doorway. I turned a smile on him.

"Have a look... if you're brave enough!"

"Oh? Dirty pictures?" He jerked his eyebrows up and down a couple of times, and I laughed at him.

"Don't say I didn't warn you."

He brought the deck out of my reading room and sat on the sofa, sliding the cards out to rifle through them for a few minutes. When he put them back in the box, he cleared his throat.

"Um... there does seem to be rather a lot of sex depicted in the pictures."

I fidgeted on the floor, stretching one leg out to get the blood flowing again from where it was numb. "What did you expect, with a deck called Sexual Magic?"

"They seem rather unused."

I sniggered. "There aren't many people that want me to give a reading on what their sex life's like. Most would rather hear about romance and 'lurve', not getting down and dirty." I massaged my ankle. "Are you ready to get started?"

He seemed distracted. "What? Oh... Yeah, I guess."

"What's the matter? Changed your mind?"

"No, but..." He scratched his cheek with a fingertip. "Can I ask you something?"

"Yeah, course."

He looked embarrassed but blurted his question out. "Have you done all of those things? In that deck?"

I rolled my eyes. "No."

"Oh thank Christ, I thought it was just me and I was being—" He stopped, and I guessed he was searching for the right word.

"Prudish?"

"Yeah, that."

We both laughed.

"Some of them I've looked at and thought 'why would you do that?'," I admitted, "And others I've thought, maybe with the right partner..." My voice tailed off and I looked away. I steered clear of that tarot deck because the energy portrayed in it was absent from my life, and looking at the imagery made me feel like time moved on without me.

"Are you single?"

I made a derisive noise. "You may as well know the truth, before you finally give up on my skills as a tarot reader. There's only one other person in all my years of reading I've had as much trouble with predicting their love life as I have with yours."

"Who's that?"

"Me."

He stared at me. "Seriously?"

I raised then dropped one shoulder.

"So, no special someone in the picture?"

"Nope. Been by myself for... well, ages." Eight years, five months, thirteen days. And every day that passed with no change sank me a little deeper into a pit of despondency, especially when the tarot kept telling me, *not yet. Not yet.*

"So you're a tarot reader who can't see anything romantic for herself. That must suck." His voice sounded kind rather than scornful. I risked looking at

him – he was leaning forward, his arms on his knees.
"It sucks donkey balls," I agreed, trying to lighten my mood and getting a smile from him in response. "It doesn't matter. You're the client. It's only my skills under the spotlight, not my private life."
"I didn't mean to pry."
"It's fine. I wanted to be honest with you, in case I still need to give you that refund after we're done today."
An odd expression came over his face, but he said nothing, only nodded.
"What is it?"
"Never mind. Shall we get started?"
"If there's something on your mind, we need to get it out of the way first. It could hinder what we're trying to do if we don't."
His sigh was sharp, more like a huff. "OK fine. Maybe I shouldn't have looked at those cards. Now all I can think about is sex."
I smirked up at him. "No, we're not really looking for information on one-night stands and the like, are we? Let me find you something to take your mind off it." I rose and scowled at the offending deck, but as I stepped past him he caught my sleeve.
"Lori?"
"Mmm?"
"I feel I should apologise."
I tilted my head to regard him. "What for?"
"I don't know... just that I should say sorry."
"I can't think of anything that warrants it, but I forgive you. Does that help?"
He released me. "Yeah, I think it does."
Odd. I didn't know anyone who could see far below my

surface feelings, but that was mostly on purpose. You get hurt, you go more carefully. Simple. And Jamie didn't know I'd been hurt, it was the first time we'd discussed my personal life. My focus was on the client, and I was the channel the information came through. That was it.

I pulled the Romantic Tarot from the shelf and dropped it into his hands. "Here, flick through this. It's more the energy I want to embody."

He smiled as he glanced at a few of the cards. "I can see you doing some of these."

"Not yourself?"

"Yes, but... you're a romantic at heart too."

No shit, Sherlock.

I gave him a few minutes with the deck then tapped him on the knee. "Better?"

He jumped. "Oh, sorry. I was daydreaming."

"Happy thoughts, I hope."

Nodding, he put the cards on the table, away from where I had the cloth spread out. "Yeah, all good."

I sat straighter, adopting what I classed as my professional persona and drawing it around me like a cloak. "So, concentrate on the things you'd like to do with a partner. Trips out, romantic dinners, lazy Sunday mornings in bed with coffee, stuff like that. Things on your bucket list. Don't try and visualise her, but you doing those things and a female presence by your side. OK?"

He closed his eyes, nodding at my instructions. I shuffled the cards and murmured my customary blessing over them, both for protection and so the reading was for the highest good of all involved. I let

Jamie cut the cards and dealt six out into three sets of two.
"So before I turn these over, I'll explain the positions. These two represent you: who you are and where you're at. These two are for her, and these last ones are hopefully going to give us some clues for the two of you together."
He leaned forward to study the backs intently. I smiled.
"Don't bother, they won't give you any clues. I'm careful not to mark these ones because my subconscious can make me pick the right cards for the result I want."
"You can do that?"
"Well yes, but it's not an accurate reading at that point, it's manipulated. And who am I trying to fool, except myself? This is my personal deck – I don't read it for other people. I could draw all the cards that make it look like I've found the love of my life but if I've 'cheated' it won't come to pass because at a higher level I don't believe the truth of the reading."
"Do you read ethically for everyone, then?"
"Of course. I wouldn't have much of a reputation otherwise. Didn't you read the testimonials on my website?"
"I glanced at them," he said, "But I felt you were the right person to trust for this sort of thing."
"Those feeling things again," I teased, "IT genius with a bucketful of hunches."
"Sometimes it helps with the job," He raised one shoulder and let it drop again. "Nobody said I have to do it by the book."

I'd nearly given up because of the same thing.
"I threw the manual away pretty quickly too, it was holding me back. But it took a while before I trusted how I felt about the cards. So, let's see what we've got."
I flipped the cards that represented Jamie over first.
"King of Pentacles. Strong earth energy, very grounded. But with the Page of Cups, water energy, there's a fluidity, an ability to roll with whatever life's throwing at you. And also giving a small nod to the more mystical side of things." All very similar to how I'd first read for him.
He cocked his head. "Can I look at the cards?"
"Sure." I handed them over, noting his introspective look. "What do you get from them?"
"Why is the King the more pronounced energy?"
"A Page is always subservient to a King, but in your case I'm going to guess that your birthday's either the end of April or the beginning of May."
"Didn't I tell you that?"
"Not that I remember. So when is it?"
"The eighth."
I grinned. "OK then, Mr Taurus-earth-sign. I got that right, anyway. Let's see if we can get a read on her." I turned over the Queen of Swords. "So, what have I given you before?"
He listed a few things. "She's a creative woman, she paints, loves to help others. Loves the outdoors, especially the water. And she's environmentally conscious. There's other bits but that's what comes to mind."
"We have the Queen of Swords here as her primary significator. Chances are she's an air sign, which would

be Gemini, Libra or Aquarius. The other card is the Eight of Swords, so as it's not another court card she's pretty typical of her sun sign. But the Eight..." I shook my head. "She's well and truly stuck in whatever she's got going on. Look."

I angled the card towards him. "Her hands are chained together and she's blindfolded. She can't see a way out. If someone was to free her hands, or take the blindfold off for her, she'd find that she's not hemmed in at all. It's all her perception. She needs a bit of help." I glanced up at Jamie. "You up for that? Rescuing a damsel in distress?"

He grinned. "Isn't that more of a Knight's job than a King's?"

"If it was a Princess I'd agree with you. But what if it's *his* Queen? Would he leave her to be stuck, if she'd got herself into a situation? I think not. Besides, she's probably not a young woman. I'd guess she's in her thirties, so she's able to do stuff for herself most of the time."

Jamie nodded slowly, his eyes focused on the Queen's card. "So how do I know what she needs rescuing from? And where are we supposed to have met?"

The Ace and Four of Cups turned up as cards for them together. "You've known her... Well, this shows a lunar cycle, so it's indicating periods of four weeks. One or two. Maybe three, but not more. You've met within the last three months, but I can't tell where."

I waved the Ace at him. "This is a very positive card. Like finding the Holy Grail or something magical and awesome. And there's water indicated again, under the cup. But we already knew about her connection with

water locations."
I turned the Four of Cups round so Jamie could see it.
"Look, she's got something to offer you. So she could be a longer-term prospect rather than a few months. Drink from her cup and..."
"It's not a poisoned chalice?" There was a hint of wariness in his tone, and I glanced up at him. He narrowed his eyes as he looked at the card. I touched his wrist, conscious that negative energy could mess with how I interpreted the cards, even if it was unintentional.
"They all look the same to begin with, don't they?" I murmured, staring off into space, "It's only later...true colours come out."
Jamie turned to stare at me, and I started, coming back to myself in surprise.
"Was that your thought or mine?" I said with a nervous laugh. He shook his head.
"I'm not sure. Were you cheated on, too?"
I shrugged noncommittally. He didn't need to know.
"There are four cups for her to choose from. She knows which one is right. It's not like all the animals on the card are dead, is it?" I tried to lighten things, but he continued to stare at me. "What?"
"You were." Like he was stating a fact.
"It was a long time ago. Can we get back to the cards?" It was a plea for him to change the subject before it got too painful.
He checked the time on his phone and showed me it. We'd been working on the reading for well over an hour.
"I need some coffee," he told me, "Or something to eat.

Can we go for a walk and get something?"
"Yeah, course. I could do with some fresh air anyway."
I stretched down towards one ankle, then the other, before rising, and he watched my every move.
"Something the matter?"
"No, but you doing that reminds me of my sister. She stretches that way if she's been sitting still for a while. She said it's a dancer's move."
"Did she do ballet as a kid?"
"Yeah. Maybe it's that. Did you?"
"Oh, a couple of years. I got bored of it." I grinned, and he seemed to relax. I picked up the cards and put them away. "We got a bit further, didn't we? Maybe we'll try something else when we get back."
On the walk between my flat and the seafront, things continued to evolve from the client-reader relationship it'd started out as, to a more comfortable, almost-friendly rapport. I was pleased, because he was a nice guy and I didn't have any male friends, but it'd also help any other methods we tried when we returned.
We walked along the beach near the high tide mark, talking, and when he discovered I had a sea glass collection, he scoured the shingle for any bits that caught his eye. There was hardly anyone around as it was a cool afternoon and the sun was setting, and I perched on a breakwater while he poked through the odds and sods he'd picked up.
As he neared me, his phone rang, and he shoved what he'd collected into his pocket.
"Sorry, it's probably my sister. I'd better answer it."
"Take your time." I smiled and leaned back on my hands, enjoying the feel of the weak sunshine on the

back of my neck. He took a few steps away and frowned at his phone before moving out of earshot. He was only gone a few minutes, but it seemed like the warmth of the sunlight drained away in the interim, because when he returned he had a serious look on his face.

"Lori, I have to go. Something's come up at work and I'm on call. Sorry."

My face must've shown my disappointment because he pulled a tenner from his wallet.

"Here, get yourself pizza or something for dinner. My treat." He offered me a smile. "I'd rather have stayed, maybe we could've shared it, but..." He pulled a face. "Comes with the job. At least I haven't got to go home and get all dressed up first, as it's Saturday."

"Does it happen often? That you get called in?"

"No, it's the first time in a couple of years. And it's also the first time in months I've actually had plans for a Saturday, so the timing's shit." He sounded put out. Whatever information we had or hadn't been able to get on his future lady, at least he acted like he'd enjoyed the change of scenery.

"I'll give you a call and we'll sort something out. OK?" He stuffed the tenner into my jacket pocket and headed off without another word. I figured his smart brain was already trying to work out what had gone wrong at the office and he didn't need any distractions, but as he reached the foot of the lighthouse he looked back and waved, and I waved back until he turned away.

I sat in contemplation for a few minutes until my glum mood lifted, then went in search of food and something to drink. Not everywhere was open at that time of year, and I got a bottle of wine before I bought some hot pizza slices to scoff.

I found a bench out of the wind with the sunset behind me and took a selfie, with the caption "Pizza for now, wine for next time", and sent it to him. I didn't get a reply, but he might have been stuck for a signal where he was, so I didn't worry.

The walk home seemed longer than usual. Part of me wondered if he'd dump all the bits from the beach into a bin as soon as he could, or whether he'd ditch them later.

As I let myself into the flat I could smell something unfamiliar, which had to be his cologne: a nice scent for a nice guy. I put all my usual things back onto the table and sat in the middle of the floor to re-balance my energy, before I hopped onto my website to look for new enquiries.

They were just the distraction I needed.

*

Days went past. Jamie didn't call or text or get in touch by any method. The days turned into weeks, the readings I'd done for him faded away, and the bottle of wine I'd bought for us to share gathered dust on the worktop in my kitchen. It sat almost accusingly next to my mug tree, which held two mugs, and reminded me daily that I was human, and therefore fallible. I'd failed to channel a proper reading for that client.

About a month later, I put the bottle away in a cupboard and focused on my new and existing clients. Business was good, my confidence rose again, and I returned to enjoying life through the help I gave other people.

CHAPTER FOUR

18th December 2021

I finally dragged myself away from work on the last Saturday before Christmas. So many people had wanted to know whether they'd find their one special person in time for the festive season that I'd barely had a minute to myself.

To celebrate my temporary freedom, as I always took time off for the last two weeks of the year, I headed to my favourite place for chilling out amongst fellow humans: Creative Heart, a community hub and arts café in Beach Road. I could people-watch a little, as I didn't feel like sitting outside or strolling on the seafront.

I paid for my gingerbread mocha and aimed for a table in the window. There were people walking past, stopping to chat to one another, some of them bundled up against the cool air. It never got dreadfully cold in my town because the sea made sure of that, and we hardly ever saw snow, but it was still definitely winter.

I savoured my coffee, relishing the mix of spices and chocolate that I only ordered in this season, barely noticing the comings and goings of other customers.

Until one.

I could see he walked with a limp, which was unexpected. As was he. His nose was pink with cold, and he wore a grey beanie and a red scarf, plus a thick coat which looked like it was one of those with duck or goose feathers in it. He didn't see me.

What had brought him down to the south coast when I knew he lived the other side of London? It was Jamie, the client I'd messed up with. My failure to give him a decent reading had made me doubt my abilities for a while.

What reason could he have for being here?

He collected his drink and turned to view the room, his gaze moving from face to face as if looking for someone. Our eyes met for a moment, his moved on, and I considered sliding down in my seat to become less visible. But he looked again and made his way hesitantly through the crowded café. It was too late to escape and, much as it was awkward seeing him, part of me was curious. Was he going to speak to me, or simply come over to say hi then go to a different table? Had he met his new lady friend on his way back to the station, or through some other twist of fate I was unaware of?

He stopped and smiled a little shyly. “Hey Lori,” he said.

“Hello Jamie,” I responded, but didn't know what else to say. I'd let him lead the conversation.

“Is anyone sitting here?” He gestured to the seat opposite mine, and I shook my head. “Mind if I do?”

Did I mind? Well, that implied he wasn't sure of his welcome. And perhaps he wasn't, given the two months of no contact between us, and him suddenly appearing in my favourite coffee shop. I wasn't sure how I felt about it, but I didn't want to be rude, so I extended my hand.

“Please.”

He sat, and I heard him sigh before he took a sip of his coffee. He didn't take his coat off, and I wondered why – it was pretty warm in the café. I'd be roasting in something like that.

"How've you been?" he asked in a conversational tone, like we were friends catching up.

"OK, you?"

"Eh, you know."

Not the answer I was expecting. And not much in common with the lighter-mooded man I'd met before either. I gave him an opening.

"Oh?"

He shrugged, an eloquent gesture that spoke volumes about... what, I didn't exactly know. But there was something underlying it.

"Come on," I said with a smile, "You can't just shrug and leave it at that, not after this amount of time."

"What do you want me to say?"

"How about you start where we left off? You were going to call me."

"Yeah, I was."

"So when you didn't, I figured you'd given up on me, and I expected an email asking for a refund. But you didn't do that either. So..." I held up my hands, palms upwards. "And now you turn up here and I have no idea why."

He took off his hat and ran his hand through his hair. I noticed a scar on his wrist, which I didn't think had been there before.

"OK, yeah, I owe you an explanation. But you never emailed me either."

"What, to tell you I'd sent your money back? Or to check in and say hey, are you OK? That'd be the sort of thing friends would do. I thought this was a professional relationship between client and reader."

A look crossed his face, and I could've sworn I'd hurt his feelings, but he picked up his drink to hide his expression and took a long swallow.

"I left you money for pizza and whatever, do your clients generally do that?"

We were fencing, both cautious rather than open, and I didn't like it one bit. I didn't think it was his style, and it certainly wasn't mine.

"Tell me what happened."

"I... wow. This is harder than I thought it'd be. I had it all planned out in my head, on the way down." He laughed a little. "I don't know if you'll believe it anyway."

I sat back in my chair and put my hands in my lap. "Try me." At least he was willing to talk.

He put his cup down and fidgeted. "It's going to sound stupid, but here goes. I left here, went to work, as you know, and it was only after I got there I found out the big bosses had set it up as a practice attack. It wasn't a real security threat at all."

I nodded once. "Go on."

"I was pretty pissed off, as you can imagine, and when I went home I wasn't really paying attention and some guy snatched my phone and took off with it. I'm normally more careful than that, but I was distracted." He stopped for a moment, then continued, "Anyway I ran after him, nearly caught him, but I—well, I tripped over something. A paving slab maybe, or something like that. And I fell hard, and he got away."

"Oh Jamie!" I hoped I sounded as sympathetic as I felt. "What a horrid thing to happen."

His mouth twitched. "It's not too common in London,

not as much as people think, and like I said I had my phone out so I was a target. It was only when I went to get up that I realised I'd hurt myself."

"Badly?"

"A twisted ankle..." A grim smile followed, "And a broken wrist: a distal radius fracture. So that's one of the arm bones, to be accurate, but most people would call it a broken wrist."

I pointed at the scar. "Did you have to have an operation?"

"Yeah, they had to pin it. I'll be getting full use of it back soon, so I'm returning to work after the New Year, in about a month's time. Not much use when I can't do any of the normal two-handed work things."

"Couldn't you type one-handed?"

"Work's Occ Health signed me off with stress, too. So I've been sat at home waiting for everything to get better. I'm not back playing football yet either. I tried last weekend, but..."

"But it probably still hurt, right?"

"Yeah it did. I couldn't even get through the warm-up."

"So what did you do with yourself?"

"Oh I read all of Dickens' works again for the hell of it. I wasn't bored. I could've emailed my friends, but I didn't want to bother them all the time. They have their own lives."

And he hadn't thought to email me? I raised my eyebrows at him.

"What about me?"

His smile was a little embarrassed. "You just said we weren't friends. And, to be truthful... I was a bit pissed off with you."

My eyes widened. “Why?”
He squirmed in his chair. “Because I was looking at that pic you sent me when my phone got nicked.”
“Really?” I laughed shortly.
“It was the first chance I got. If I hadn’t been intrigued by the cloud behind you I’d have seen how that guy was looking at me,” He glanced away. “Then maybe it wouldn’t have happened at all.”
“So it’s my fault?” It was my turn to be defensive.
“No, but... have you looked at it?”
I shook my head. “I took it and ate my pizza, I didn’t notice the clouds.”
“Got your phone with you?”
I pulled it from my pocket and waved it at him.
“Have a look. You’ve still got it, haven’t you?”
I scrolled through my pictures to find the selfie. Studying the clouds behind me rather than thinking about pizza, I frowned in concentration. “What am I looking for?”
“You can’t see it?” He held his hand out for the phone.
I looked at him for a moment, debating whether to give it to him, but I had nothing to hide. Handing it over, I wondered what he’d seen that I hadn’t, or couldn’t.
“You remember the Four of Cups card?”
Duh, of course I did. It was my personal deck. I could visualise every single card in my head.
“You can’t see the chalice in the clouds?” He zoomed in to the picture and handed it back. I looked, but couldn’t see what he meant.
“If you say so. I’ve seen shapes in clouds before but no-one has seen the same thing when they’ve looked.

Maybe it's a difference in perspective."
He didn't sound convinced. "Maybe it's some sort of sign but I don't understand it."
"I think there's something neither of us understand about stuff. Like, what are you doing down here, causing yourself ankle strain when you should be resting it, but you say you're pissed off with me?"
Jamie's sudden grin reminded me how easily we'd chatted when we'd spent time together before. It made him look younger, more carefree, more like the guy I'd met back in October. I relaxed. That side was still in there somewhere. Whatever his reason was, it wouldn't be unpleasant to spend some time with him.
"You're my alibi," he told me, and I stared at him.
"With whom? What are you supposed to be doing?"
"Resting it, like you said," he retorted, "But I got fed up of my sister's surveillance so I said I had a date. Funnily enough, she let me go."
We both laughed.
"And have you?"
"Not yet," he winked at me.
"So what type of woman are you looking for, to spend your date with?"
"Well I was sort of thinking something would turn up. And I didn't set out to come down here on purpose, but when I got to the station I sort of thought 'why not?'. Then I wandered round, ended up in here, and there you were. I sort of hoped I could buy you coffee, and I wondered if it might be a sort of date."
"That's a lot of 'sort of'," I laughed. "Are you trying to 'sort of' ask me out?"
"No," he answered with a brilliant smile, "I *am* asking

you out. As friends. I'd say let's go for a coffee but we're already here. So, Lori, tarot reader extraordinaire, with saintly patience towards a guy who's hard to read for, will you spend the afternoon with me and show me round your town?" Then he stopped, and his face fell. "But maybe you're waiting for someone? I didn't think to ask, sorry. We've not been in touch and I just assumed..."

I reached over the table and touched his hand with a smile. "Jamie, stop. I'm not here to meet anyone. I'm here as a break from work and to watch the world go by."

"Is that a yes or a no? Because I'm not sure." He drew his brows together in puzzlement.

I finished my coffee and put down the mug, wiping the froth off my top lip. "I said earlier that we weren't friends, but we could be. I don't have sisterly surveillance so I can please myself, but if you think you'd like to spend the afternoon with me, I'm happy to." It gratified me he wanted to spend time together because, if quizzed, I could use him as an alibi for the same reason.

Not that anyone cared what I did with my free time except my friends, as I had no immediate family, but it'd feel nice to pretend I actually had a male friend.

"Great!" He didn't hide his excitement. "What is there to do in the depths of winter?"

"Well I'm not taking you ice skating, that's asking for trouble. Have you done all your Christmas shopping? We've plenty of shops and there's a Christmas market up the road."

"I did it all online, but we can wander round the

market if you like. Maybe there'll be a few bits and pieces I like the look of."

"Who for?"

"My sister's expecting her second child next month, so maybe something for the baby."

I nodded slowly. "Mmm, no wonder she wanted to keep an eye on you. Is she nesting yet?"

"Dunno, but she's always been a bit mother hen to me anyway."

"Wait, you've not left her when she's about to pop, have you?"

Jamie laughed. "No, of course not. She's with her husband. They live about five minutes from my place." He drained his cup and set it on the table.

"That's OK then."

"Shall we go?" He stood and limped round the table to help me on with my coat.

"Are you sure you want to walk around?" I asked tentatively, "I don't want you hurting yourself."

He scoffed. "I'm an adult, I don't need you to mother me. If it hurts too much, I'll tell you."

"I bet you will," I mumbled, not believing him, but he pulled on my shoulder so I had to face him.

"Seriously, Lori. I want to get back to playing football on Sundays. I'm not going to screw it up."

I had to take him at his word. But I made a mental note that he might actually be a guy who knew his limitations, or at least some of them. God knew, those types of men were few and far between in my experience.

"So where to, first?"

"The market?"

"OK then." He held his arm out to me, I took it, and we ambled up the road towards the brightly-lit market with red and white striped awnings above the stalls. The first stall we came to had handmade wreaths for front doors and fireplaces, but Jamie shook his head and we moved on.

"Nobody would see it on my door."

"Have you got a house or flat, then?"

"It's a loft apartment so nobody but me comes up that high."

"Is it your own?"

"No, I haven't got that sort of money," he laughed. "I can barely afford the rent!"

"Wouldn't it be cheaper to buy?"

"Massively, but I don't have enough for a deposit, and it's hard trying to save when you're paying rent every month."

"Don't I know it."

"Isn't it cheaper down here?"

"Yeah, but... self-employed means there are so many hoops to jump through to get a mortgage. And that's even if I could find a company that'd lend to someone like me." I wrinkled my nose. "Tarot reading isn't exactly what most people would class as a normal occupation."

"I guess not." He seemed thoughtful.

"I have some cash, proper money, in the bank, but it won't go very far, even here."

"We could look..."

I laughed up at him. "Don't be silly, what could possibly be more boring for you than looking in estate agents' windows?"

"Oh, I don't know, sitting in my flat with my sister hovering over me? Besides, we're only looking aren't we? Unless you're serious about finding somewhere."
"I am, but..." I paused, thinking it over, "Not yet, anyway. Not before the spring."
"Let's do a bit of daydreaming—oh look! Pancakes!" He pulled me towards a crêpe stall, and I had to laugh at him. It was clear he was eager for different things in his life to his usual routine. If being in a small seaside town brought him this much vitality, however temporary, what was he doing living so far inland?
"Crêpes, dear, crêpes," I corrected him, and he flapped a hand in dismissal.
"Yeah whatever. You hungry?"
We ordered: sliced banana and chocolate spread for me, peanut butter, chocolate sauce and pretzel pieces for him. Mine had squirty cream on, and I secretly wished for mini marshmallows, but they didn't have any so I had to go without. We wandered along, occasionally brushing together as we tried not to get too messy with our crêpes. I was more intent on eating than noticing what was going on around me.
"Estate agent!" Jamie exclaimed and bounded off, then looked back at me and beckoned with his head. "Come on, let's look!"
"Jamie!" I called after him, trying to catch up and lick my fingers at the same time. Even with a limp, his long legs had taken him away fast. "Why are we doing this? I'm not ready to buy somewhere."
"What if the right place is waiting here for you? I know you said spring, but if you put an offer in now..."
"Stop!" I laughed. "I'll find the right place when I'm

meant to, and not a minute before. There's nothing on the market..." My words tailed off as I looked past his arm to the estate agent's window display. It wouldn't hurt to look. And although I wasn't ready to buy it didn't mean that I wasn't keeping tabs on houses that came up for sale.

Jamie pulled me in closer to see.

"What sort of thing are you after?"

"I don't know." I hadn't got my house-hunting head on, I'd been too busy thinking that I was out with a guy. The practicality of looking for a house wasn't on my agenda for the afternoon.

"No, come on, we're just daydreaming. Have a look."

"There's nothing I like under half a mil," I mumbled, but he heard me and whistled.

"Wow, expensive taste for a tarot reader," he commented with a chuckle. "So if money was no object, what would you go for?"

I played along. "It has to have character. Be something a bit different, not boring. And I don't like modern houses."

"Hmm," Jamie perused the details in the window. "How about... something like that?" He pointed at a halls-adjoining Victorian semi at £400,000.

"It's alright, but there are plenty of houses round here like that."

"OK, let me try again." He rubbed his chin. "Nothing under half a mil, she said."

I smirked. "Good luck. You think you know me."

He turned to assess me, an intent expression in his eyes, and I had to look away fast. It felt like he was seeing into my soul, and it was unnerving.

"Look *with* me," he smiled, and draped his arm round my shoulders. "There has to be something here."
There was, because I'd just seen it. Money no object, he'd said, and it was 700-odd thousand. I knew there was no way on earth I could reach it, but I couldn't help but gaze at it with longing. It was unusual, much too big for one person, and its upside-down layout would probably drive me nuts, but I liked it.
Jamie pointed at its listing. "That's more like it, right Lori?" It sounded like a rhetorical question. He didn't need my confirmation, but he looked my way and I nodded.
"Yeah, like that. But I can't afford it so what's the point?" I shoved my hands into my pockets. "That house deserves a family, Jamie, look at it. The turret's perfect for a teen wanting their own space but still being part of the usual noise of a family. Somewhere they can get away from younger siblings, but close enough to be shouted for dinner. It's not for a thirty-four-year-old spinster who may never end up having kids the way her life's going."
"Do you feel like time's running out, then?" He posed the question gently, as if he didn't want to cause offence.
"Yeah, a bit. I'd want to get to know someone properly before we even talked about a family. And that means dating, spending time together, maybe even living together first." I turned my back on the estate agent's window and tried to smile. "It's not the house for me."
"OK," He squeezed my shoulders for a moment and then released me. "Let's go do something else." He seemed more subdued, and I felt bad that I'd spoilt his

game, but as we walked along chatting, his mood lightened.
"I need a drink," I eventually said, and steered him into a bar in the town centre. "What's your poison?"
"Uh-uh," he grinned at me. "You choose something for me, and I'll choose something for you. And get what you actually want as well, right? Then we'll see what we've picked for each other."
"Oh God, this could be a disaster," I giggled. "Just so you know, I'm not much of a drinker."
"Nor me, but let's let our hair down. Ready? Go!"
The place was packed. We separated and went to opposite ends of the bar. I frowned in thought. What would Jamie drink? Did he have sophisticated taste? Would he prefer shorts rather than pints? He worked in the City, so he might drink wine... No. I dismissed that. He'd drink a pint, I was sure. But a pint of what? I mulled over the choices while I waited to be served, deliberately not looking his way so I couldn't see what he'd got for me. By the time I turned round to see where he was, he was at a table off to the side, waving. I manoeuvred my way over, trying not to get jostled. As I put our drinks on the table, I looked over at what he'd bought and chuckled.
"What've you got?"
"Strongbow Dark Fruit for me, pink gin and lemonade for you."
"Not bad," I nodded in approval. "I do drink pink gin on occasion, but I prefer Bombay Bramble and cream soda. They don't have that here."
He smiled and pushed the gin across the table. "What did you get?"

I turned the bottle of Kopparberg mixed fruit to face him and passed it over with the pint glass. "Strawberry daiquiri for me. I'll probably be tipsy later."

"We both did OK, didn't we?" He smiled and lifted the bottle to clink against my glass. "Cheers!"

I took a large sip of my pink gin, then another. It was a nice one, not some cheap crap, and I wondered which one it was. "What brand's this?"

"I don't remember, but it's wild berry flavour."

"So even closer to what I'd choose for myself. Well done."

"It seems we're pretty in tune with each other. That's good."

I looked at him over the top of my glass, one eyebrow raised quizzically. "Good?" I ventured, hoping he'd elaborate.

"Well, you know, first dates are all about getting to know each other. Aren't they?"

"It's been so long since I went on one that the rules might have changed. Don't people jump straight into bed these days?"

He settled more comfortably in his chair. "Seriously? Why don't you date?"

"Jamie."

"No, I want to know. You're a very attractive woman. You have an interesting career, and you're obviously a people person. Why don't you date?"

"I *was* a people person." I shifted and looked away with a bit of a frown.

"What happened?"

"Oh... life happened," I shrugged. "People change, or they're not who they first appear. I got burnt."

He leaned forward. "Want to talk about it? You can say no, but you already know my story."
The gin kicked in. "My ex. I used to live up town. London, I mean. We often went to parties at the weekends, and I usually drove because I'm not a big drinker. He didn't drink a lot but it was enough to loosen his inhibitions one night and—" I pulled a face. "You can guess the rest."
"Was it only the once? Not that it makes it any better."
"I thought so, but after we'd split up my best friend said it hadn't been the first time. She'd seen him in a bar with his arm round some woman, when he'd told me he'd had a late meeting. I'm grateful we weren't living together. That was when I moved back down here, to be near my parents. I can work from anywhere as long as I have the net. Then some time later my dad got ill and I recognised that everything happens in divine timing whether I like it or not. So I was here when he died, and helped my mum through that, then she started going downhill because she missed him so much. You know how it can be, when people have been together for a long time." I took a deep breath and smiled. "And now you know why I don't drink very much, because I spill my life story all over the table! Bet you wish you hadn't asked now."
Jamie's eyes were soft. "You've no siblings?"
"No, and what friends I do have are still up town so I don't see them. But they're all doing their own thing anyway, families and stuff, so it's just me."
"Is your mum still around?"
"No, she passed a year ago. Left me the house but it didn't feel like the family home any more and I was

already renting, so I sold it."
"I can understand that. So you're sitting on a load of cash?"
"Well not a load, as such, but it might be enough. It depends if I want to stay local or not."
"Gotcha. So you'd stay here if you could?"
"I could move further along the coast. Eastbourne, for example, where money goes a bit further. But I wouldn't want to live inland, I like having the sea within walking distance. It calms me even when I can't see it." I sat back in my chair. "I've always been the same. Mother used to say the tides ran deep in my veins, and I think that's a great way to describe it. She'd tell me stories of when I was teething or fractious, she'd put me in the pushchair and walk along the seafront with me, and apparently it always stopped me crying."
"Do you miss her?"
"Some days," I replied. "I'm not convinced she fully accepted my choice of career but she didn't hassle me about it, and eventually she saw that I could make a living from it so she worried less. What about you, are your parents still about?"
"Yeah, they moved up north when they retired."
"Is that where they're from?"
"No, but they met when they were both holidaying in Blackpool in the 70s. Kiss me quick hats and donkey rides, or some such." Jamie laughed a little.
"So do you not see them?"
"We video call a couple of times a month and I sometimes go up for Christmas, but not this year."
"Because of your ankle?"

"No, because my sister Emily is staying at home in case she has the baby early. It's thought a second baby's more likely to come sooner, so she's not taking the chance."

"That's fair enough, I guess," I felt a pang of resentment. Everyone around me, including Jamie's sister and most of my friends, seemed to be popping babies out left, right and centre. Almost like the universe was laughing in my face at my single status. I ruthlessly suppressed that thought.

"So do you have any weird Christmas traditions in your family?" I asked Jamie.

"Not weird ones as such. We always try and give each other a completely useless present but a good one, too. What about your family?"

"I used to get a CD on Christmas Eve instead of having to wait for Christmas Day, but that was about it. We'd have a little gift each then, too, when Dad was still here. Mother continued the CD tradition but we kept other presents back for Christmas Day after he went. I don't know whether to buy myself a CD this year or not, now she's gone too."

Jamie looked thoughtful. "I think you should. It's carrying on a family thing until you have one of your own, and it honours her memory too."

"Yeah, maybe. I've listened to loads of music this year on the radio and online, but not bought myself anything."

"There's still time. Is there anywhere in town that sells CDs?"

"Don't know, with so many places going bust. I'll get it off Amazon."

"Let me buy you one."
I laughed. "No, Jamie. Don't be silly."
"Come on, you know you'd like that."
I fixed him with a look. "We're supposed to be on a 'date'. You could buy me dinner, not a CD for Christmas."
He frowned, then a mischievous smile crept over his face. "Can I do both?"
I rolled my eyes. "Seriously, you're impossible."
"Impossibly cute?" He laughed and leaned forward with his chin on his hands, eyes wide and innocent, elbows on the table. "You know you like me."
"Jamie, stop it," I couldn't help but laugh at him, and it was fantastic to be so light-hearted for a change.
It was dark by the time he walked me back to my flat. He hadn't complained about his ankle, but I'd seen him frown a little more often as the evening went on. Luckily, it wasn't more than a few minutes from my place to the station, or I might have called him a cab. But as we stood on the pavement outside my front door, I realised the temperature had dropped and our breath, as we talked, flowed around us like fog.
"Do you want to come up for coffee?"
"Thanks, but I think I'd better head back. I might've overdone it a bit today." He gave a rueful shrug. "It's the longest I've been out and about since I was injured."
"OK, well, I won't take it personally," I smiled, and stepped forward to hug him. I was surprised when he brushed a kiss over my cheek, but not displeased. "I had a great time today. Thanks for coming down."
"Yeah it was good, wasn't it? Maybe we'll do it again

some time."

"Don't be a stranger, OK?" I didn't have any expectations of a repeat, but quality time spent with a guy after years without it felt so good it'd keep me going for ages.

"Nor you. Let me know when you find a house. I'll come view it with you and give you a second opinion."

"I'd like that. Safe journey, Jamie."

"Goodnight Lori, take care."

I watched him walk away, thinking that I probably wouldn't bother him if I did find a house, but it was nice to have a friend. A man friend. Even though he lived the other side of London I'd still seen him more, and spoken to him more, than I had any of my friends up town all year. They all had their own lives. Travelling up to the city was too much effort, just to watch them play "happy families", when nothing about it made me feel happy – it highlighted my single status even more acutely.

Hoping I had squirty cream in the fridge, and marshmallows in the cupboard, I headed inside to meet my friend for the rest of the night: hot chocolate.

*

A CD arrived the next day: Harry Styles' *Fine Line*, via Amazon. The note that came with it said:

Merry Christmas Lori, we crossed a 'Fine Line' yesterday into friendship. Hope you like the CD. Best wishes from Jamie.

I emailed him back to thank him and to tell him I'd got myself Dua Lipa's *Future Nostalgia* too, so it looked like the family tradition was going to carry on.

CHAPTER FIVE

2022

Jamie and I emailed and texted sporadically after that, checking on each other every couple of weeks, and he went back to work and playing football on Sundays. His fitness returned but whenever I asked him about it he didn't seem to have the enthusiasm I expected, given how much he'd said he missed it.

I did wonder if he had something else on his mind, but he didn't volunteer any information, and it felt like a breach of trust to ask the tarot without his permission. His sister had her baby with no issues, and I hoped they were getting on well.

It seemed our friendship was continuing on a fairly low-key basis, which was OK. It was still nice to have a guy to talk to, even if it wasn't on a more personal level. But an email came through from him towards the end of February that completely threw me. It said, "Saw this and thought of you" and had the full details of a house for sale attached to it.

How had I missed this one in my continuous search since the start of the year? And what was Jamie doing, looking for houses for me?

It was Victorian or maybe Edwardian, with a roof extension that reminded me of a boat's wheelhouse. It needed full modernisation, decorating inside and out, and pretty much everything doing to it. There was a master suite in the roof extension that even had a bit of a kitchenette. On paper it looked perfect, but when I enquired about a viewing, I was told it'd already sold. There'd been an offer put in the same day it'd gone on the market. I ended the call and threw myself down onto the sofa in frustration.

"Come on Spirit, help me out a bit, please. We both know things aren't right here and I need my own space."

But the oracle and tarot cards told me the same thing about a house that they had about my love life: *be patient, everything's coming along, all in good time.*

I was sick of it.

I thought that was it, but a couple of weeks later the estate agent called me. The offer on the "boat house", as I termed it, had fallen through, and the sellers wanted a cash buyer. Was I interested in a viewing? Damn right I was! But I was one of many people who had expressed an interest in the house, and the agent wanted to set up multiple viewings over the following two days. They said the vendors weren't desperate, but it didn't feel that way.

The fact that it'd come back on the market was screaming at me. Although Jamie had sent me the house details initially, I wasn't going to risk missing it by waiting until he could view it. I didn't even text him to say I was going, because the viewing was half an hour after the agents called me and I was in a bit of a tizzy. I tried to calm myself but when you get something that excites you, and scares you at the same time, it's not easy.

Needless to say, the house felt like a good fit. I went home and checked my sums. It was on the market at £290,000 and I had £350,000, plus a little extra stashed away. It'd probably need about £20,000 spending on it, there'd be my legal fees to consider,

and there were plenty of other people interested.
I offered £325,000. I also offered exchange and completion on the same day, in 4 weeks' time, and crossed my fingers.
The offer was accepted, but the sellers decided to exchange in two weeks and complete four weeks later. In six weeks' time, I'd own a house. I was excited to tell Jamie but wanted to wait until the exchange took place, so I kept things a secret.
And he definitely had something he wasn't telling me, because his texts and emails had become short and to the point rather than chatty. I wondered what was going on and suggested he come down on Easter Saturday for the day, if he wanted to, which was two days after I was due to exchange contracts on the house.
We met at the station, and I hugged him. He seemed quiet and looked shattered. Never mind, the sea air would soon blow away any cobwebs – or so I hoped.
"Are you up for a little walk?" I asked, smiling brightly up at him.
"Is there coffee?"
It was barely 10am, and it would've taken him at least two and a half hours on the train to get down here, so he'd had an early start. I looped my arm through his.
"We'll get some on the way, come on."
After collecting coffee from somewhere in town, I turned our steps along Arundel Road. The caffeine quickly worked on Jamie's brain.
"We're not going to the beach, are we?" he observed, and I shook my head.
"No, but maybe later. I have something to show you

first."
We took a few side roads, and shortly afterwards stood outside the "boat house".
"I know this place," Jamie said, taking more interest in his surroundings. "Isn't this the house I sent you details of?"
"Yep."
"But you said it'd sold."
"It had," I shrugged, "Then something happened and it went back on the market." I took the keys from my pocket and shook them in front of his face. "You're here to give me your opinion on it." Not that it mattered, as I'd committed myself, but I wanted to share it with him. Hopefully it'd gain his approval. And once I'd shared my secret, maybe he'd open up about what was going on with him.
"How've you got the keys?" he asked, frowning down at me. I gave him my best winsome smile.
"I pulled a few strings, OK?" It wasn't precisely a fib. The vendors had given permission for me to measure up for carpets, even though it wouldn't be the first thing I did once it was my house. I'd get it safe first, with central heating and rewiring, knock through between the shower room and toilet on the first floor and put a bath in, and then I'd see what sort of money I had left for carpets and decoration. I'd probably reinstate the wall between the living room and dining room, in case I ever did in-person readings at home, although that was pretty unlikely. But that was all for the future.
"Shall we go in?" I unlocked the door and pushed it open, letting him go past me. I could hear him sniffing

as I closed the door behind us.
"It smells damp."
"Yeah, I think it's been empty a while, because the vendors were waiting for probate. It's not been properly aired out. It needs living in." I pointed out the mouldy corners where cooler air had condensed on the walls, and Jamie nodded.
"It needs a lot of work, doesn't it?" he observed as we wandered from room to room.
"Nothing structural, which is a bonus. It's all modernising and decorating. But what do you think of it?"
"It seems OK. Would you get a survey done?"
"Yeah, of course." The previous week, but nothing had come up in it to alarm me. It was going to be enough of a financial stretch as it was to get everything done.
The post arrived while we were upstairs, and as we came back down the stairs, I tried to nab a letter addressed to me before Jamie saw it.
"Bloody council tax bill already?" I muttered, and he gave me a sharp look.
"Lori, show me that."
I put it behind my back. "Uh-uh. You can't make me."
"It's illegal to interfere with someone else's post," he pointed out. "You can't steal people's letters."
"I'm not stealing it. Putting it up here, OK?" I placed it on the little shelf in the hallway, facing away so the addressee wasn't visible. "I haven't opened it."
Jamie darted past me and snatched up the envelope, turning it round so he could read who it was to. It was addressed to Miss Lorelei Archer.
Well, that was me rumbled.

"Lori!" Jamie turned incredulous eyes my way. "You've *bought* the house?"
"Might have done?" I twisted this way and that with my hands behind my back, trying to look innocent and not succeeding.
"You've already completed on it?"
"No, not yet, we only exchanged contracts on Thursday. Completion's end of the month." I peeped at him through lowered lashes. "Are you annoyed that I didn't ask you to come and view it when I first did?"
"Well no, but... it's your life, your money. I just thought..." He sounded a bit hurt.
"I'm sorry," I said earnestly, "The estate agent gave me half an hour's notice on the viewing. There were loads of people disappointed when they missed it first time round. I felt I had to see it straight away. Besides, you found it so I took that to mean you already approved."
"I did. I do. But..." He shrugged. "You didn't even tell me you'd viewed it."
"Because I wanted to wait until we'd exchanged contracts on it, in case something went wrong or the survey showed something up that I couldn't afford to deal with. I'm sharing it with you now. Nobody else knows." Or cares, was the thought that crossed my mind, but I didn't voice it. I had other friends apart from him, but hearing from any of them was becoming rarer with every month that went past.
Jamie was quiet as we went round the back garden and I pointed out shrubs I was keeping and what would be for the tip, but as we walked back into the kitchen, he put a hand on my arm to stop me.
"Lori, I'm really happy that you've got the house, it

seems like it's everything you were looking for. I'm sorry I'm not more enthusiastic, I've got some stuff going on at the minute that's causing me some problems."

"Do you want to talk about it?"

"No... well, I don't know."

"We're only five minutes' walk from the flat. We could put the kettle on and maybe you'll tell me?"

He looked mutinous, like he was going to refuse, but he exhaled slowly and nodded. "Yeah, let's go to the flat." But he didn't say he'd tell me, and I left it for the moment. He would if he wanted to, and not if not.

I let him choose the conversation as we walked, and he was happy to tell me about his new nephew Rory. I listened with half an ear to what he was saying and the other half attuned to the emotions behind everything. I was sure it was surface cover for some deep concern. I'd already thought so, but I was more accurate "reading" him in-person than via phone, text, or email.

As I made us both coffee and sat on the sofa next to him, I smiled in encouragement. "OK, spill it. What's happening with you? Or do I have to get the cards out and ask them?"

He gave a short laugh. "You haven't already?"

"No, Jamie. Because reading something that feels pretty big without your permission is plain rude, and me poking my nose in. Yeah, I want to know, but not like that. I'd rather we talked."

"I appreciate your discretion," he said dryly. "I have some work stuff to deal with, that's all."

"Do you want to tell me about it, or is it too technical for a simple tarot reader?" I asked. He shook his head.

"It's not technical, they're restructuring. I might be out of a job."

I gawped at him. "Shit."

"Yeah, that. A mate of mine said about going contracting rather than working for one company the whole time. Do a few months here, six months somewhere else, that sort of thing. I've been thinking about it."

"Would you get redundancy money?"

"Yeah I would, but it's the whole hassle of do I get another job before I'm pushed, or not? I'm finding it hard to make the decision."

"Is there more money in contracting?"

"Probably, but there's no stability. So there's little chance of a mortgage, especially as my savings are lacking." He shrugged. "Dunno what to do."

"Could you do it remotely?"

"Yeah, so?"

"Well, potentially you could move somewhere cheaper, earn more money, and have more to stash away into savings. Would that work?"

He sipped his coffee, thinking. "It might."

"I guess it'd depend on how quickly you wanted to buy somewhere, but if you kept the contracting going for a few years, built up some cash, then maybe went back permanent some time in the future when you've got a deposit saved up... I mean you're what, early thirties? So there's no rush."

"Thirty three. Yeah, I see your point. It's a risk though."

"What does your mate do? Couldn't he give you some pointers on how to pitch yourself to clients?"

"Maybe," Jamie smiled, "He's got a race coming up that I might go to, pick his brains at the same time perhaps."
"What distance does he do?"
A laugh followed my question. "It's a boat race on a lake, not running."
"Oh, OK," I nodded. "Well you can ask him, anyway."
"And I could ask my friend the tarot reader to see if anything comes up, too."
"Be serious, I'm completely rubbish when it's for you."
"Are you?" Jamie angled his head to regard me, a slight smile twitching the corner of his mouth. "We've only tried asking about romance. Maybe you're OK with work stuff."
I shook my head. "You really want me to have a go?"
He pulled his wallet from his pocket and threw two twenties at me. "What'll that get me?"
A mischievous smile crossed my face. "With a prostitute, probably sex and maybe something you didn't want."
We laughed heartily for a moment. Jamie took the money back, folded the notes into a little roll and offered them to me.
"Try."
"Keep your money, you're a friend. I'll try, but no promises."
"I didn't think we were friendly enough for me to be on a promise," Jamie winked, and I slapped at him with a grin.
"Gilded Tarot? Or something else?"
"I'm not sure. You pick."
I gave a slow smile. "I have just the thing. I've not used

it yet, so we'll see how it reads straight out of the box."
"What is it?"
I fetched the brand new deck from my reading room. "Gilded Tarot Royale."
"What's the difference between them?"
"The artwork's been redone. Similar, but done with different techniques I believe. The artist chose to reimagine the pictures."
Jamie turned the deck over in his hands. "I feel it needs a special occasion before you open it. Maybe save it until completion goes through?" He handed it back, and I shrugged.
"OK, whatever you want. Come and choose something, then."
"You've not started packing them?" Jamie smiled at me, and I shook my head.
"I never know which deck's going to be needed from one day to the next, so there's no point until the very last minute." I opened the door to my reading room, and Jamie stepped in. As before, his expression turned to something like reverence as he ran his fingers along the shelf, trying to choose.
"Is there anything specific that usually gives a good reading for work situations?"
"No," I answered, "I choose the deck based on the person's energy at the time. What works well for one reading won't necessarily talk another time if the client's in a different frame of mind. It's one reason I have so many decks."
"What are the other reasons?"
"I enjoy having them around," I said almost shyly. "They're like friends after I've read with them a few

times. Because they feel different in terms of energy, it's as if they have individual personalities. And it's not solely the subject of the deck that influences that, either."

"No?"

"No. I mean, you might expect angel or fairy decks to be light and fluffy, almost, but they're definitely not. Fairies can be blunt to the point of rudeness, especially that one," I pointed to the Faeries Oracle.

"And the angels are strong. So strong. They're warriors, because they have to be. That's their thing. And that's what some of us are here for too, to be warriors and fight for what we believe in. Metaphorically, of course, because violence isn't the answer to anything. But if we each had enough faith to stand up and say 'this is my truth, and it's right for me, and your truth is right for you too, whatever it is', the world might be a nicer place." I rubbed my nose in embarrassment. "Um... sorry about that. I didn't mean to come across all preachy."

Jamie was looking at me with a thoughtful expression on his face.

"I've never heard it expressed like that before," he said, "So each person's truth and perspective is unique."

"Exactly."

"So doesn't it matter if two people believe two completely different things?"

"Not at all. I believe everyone can do good, no matter what they have faith in. Even those who believe in violence as a means to get their message across – is that their own, real, belief, or what they've been indoctrinated with over the years? Do they ever stop long enough to listen to their hearts and see what they really believe?"

"Hmm."

"But maybe we should shelve that for another day," I suggested. "Pick a deck."

"Let's pick together." Jamie was unfazed by the sudden change of subject and stretched out his hand.

"How are we going to do that?"

"I'll hold your wrist, and you move your hand along the shelf until you feel something."

I laughed. "But they all feel like something to me, so it won't work."

"Well damn," Jamie laughed with me.

"Close your eyes, and reach out in front of you with both hands. Be willing to feel something calling your attention."

He did as he was told, but somehow turned slightly towards me. His grasping hands looked like they were heading straight for my boobs, so I took a step backwards.

"Careful, you're venturing into uncharted territory there," I told him with a giggle and turned his shoulders so he faced the shelves. "You're supposed to be choosing a deck, not trying to... well, whatever you were trying to do."

"Oh, sorry." But he didn't look very sorry, even with his eyes shut. I sighed and wondered briefly what it'd be like to have someone in my life who actually wanted to touch me. I couldn't remember how it felt, no matter how hard I tried. Even my memories of the ex were fuzzy – but they weren't worth remembering, anyway.

"This one will do," Jamie's voice startled me from my thoughts. He pulled the Arcanum Tarot from the shelf and held it out to me, his expression shifting to puzzlement. "Where did you drift off to?"
"What?"
"Well, it was like you weren't quite here for a minute. Like you'd gone somewhere else."
"Oh. Memory Lane, I guess," A very lonely place, but I didn't see the point in telling him that. "Let's go get set up."
We took the deck into the other room, and I moved my papers off the table. Jamie pointed at one bundle.
"Is that a survey?"
"Yeah, have a look. I didn't spot anything worrying." I gave it to him. "Do you understand much of the jargon?"
"A bit. Emily's husband Matt is a surveyor, so we've talked about stuff over the years." He skimmed through it, nodding in places, before handing it back. "You're right, nothing that living in won't fix."
"OK so are you ready, then?" I shuffled the deck and handed it over. "We're going to do a simple four card spread. Where you are now, what's going on with work and two options for you. How's that?"
"Let's do it."
"Cut the deck into four piles, and I'll take one from each."
The first card up was the Magician.
"So here you are," I said with a smile. "You've got all the tools you need at your fingertips and you know what you're capable of. You're able to focus and bring your attention squarely onto whatever it is you're

working on in that moment. See how he's using his power to levitate the wand and sword? It looks like it's only a matter of time before the other two objects join in and he's successfully juggling all aspects of his life. Mind and soul are in balance, with body and heart to follow."

I showed Jamie the card. "But if you look behind him, there's a doorway. Anyone comes through that, he's in for a surprise. He's so focused that it'd be a shock. Not necessarily a bad one, but a shock nevertheless. I'm seeing this panelling on the right as shelves of books, so there's learning going on. And see the caduceus? I think it's supposed to indicate there's healing happening too, but it's the wrong symbol." I frowned at it. "The caduceus is more to indicate communication and things associated with the Gods Hermes and Mercury, such as business and commerce, but that's not how I'm seeing it. It's healing wings to me. So he's learning and healing, and he's vulnerable to surprises or shocks from behind. Something unexpected."

Jamie took the card. "OK, fair enough. I can see what you're getting at. So the work thing could've been the surprise?"

"Yeah, it could've. Or it could be something that hasn't happened yet, but is imminent."

"What's the next card?"

"Your current work situation." I picked up the card. "Five of Pentacles. She's begging, barefoot, in the snow. The bowl's empty. It's a challenging situation to do with money and work. We know this. There's light behind the window so it's not all doom and gloom, but it definitely isn't easy. She could have someone come along and offer her a warm place to sleep for the night, or someone could come along and steal her bowl, leaving her with nothing. It could go either way. But I think you already had some inkling of that when you said, should you find a new job before you're pushed, or wait for redundancy, right?"

Jamie rubbed his chin with a hand, brow furrowed in thought. "Yeah. That's pretty much where I am."

"So it's not telling us anything we don't know yet. That makes these last two cards all the more important." I turned them both over together: Death and The Tower. I laughed. "Oh you're in for some changes alright, Jamie."

He didn't look happy to see either card. His hands bunched into fists on the table, and I could see from the tension in his jaw that he was clenching his teeth.

"Jamie."

He ignored me so I laid my hand upon one of his fists. "Jamie, look at me."

He glared at me but held my gaze.

"It never means the end of life, Jamie," I told him softly, "It's always the end of a cycle. A metaphorical death. Giving room for new beginnings. That's all."

Jamie let out a slow breath and uncurled his fingers. "You sure?"

"Absolutely. And The Tower usually means tearing something down and starting again. Going right back to foundations for a new direction. So it doesn't seem to matter which path you choose, things are not going to stay the same. It's going to be entirely up to you which path you take, and it'll be a different direction to

what's going on now."
I patted his hand gently. "You might decide to retrain as something else, the contract stuff that your friend knows about might come off, your company could offer you something else... You're a man with skills. When one door closes, another opens."
He shook his head. "I'll have to take your word for it. I almost wish I hadn't asked you to do the reading."
I grinned. "Well, it's too late for me to go back and not do it, but everyone has free will. What you do with the information is entirely up to you. It's your life and decisions."
"Let's change the subject," he suggested. "What are you most looking forward to about getting the house?"
"Hmm." I pondered for a moment. "I think being able to decorate it the way I want, with colours, is a big one. I've had some great ideas for the master suite, and I've started looking at wallpaper. There's a silver one I've seen with trees on it that I like, but it's probably more suitable for downstairs. I thought I might keep the other bedrooms fairly neutral, but they need to be cheery. The entire house needs love and attention." I knew the feeling, but pouring my heart into the house was a good way to make me feel better. Self-care practices were critical for someone like me. "What about you, have you thought at all about what you'd want for your own place?"
"I don't need a lot of space," Jamie answered, "I'd probably be perfectly happy in an apartment as long as I had separate space to work from home if I wanted, and I'm not a frequent cook so I don't need a massive kitchen. But the issue with flats is they're leasehold, so

you have to be careful what you're agreeing to when you take on the lease."
"Yeah, that makes sense. But what about decorating it?"
"Something bright, I guess. After all these years of renting I'm sick of beige and magnolia."
We laughed, and I put the cards away. It was going to be interesting to see what decisions Jamie made regarding his work.

CHAPTER SIX

I couldn't remember ever being as nervous as I was on the day of completion. I couldn't settle to anything, so it was just as well I'd made sure I didn't have any readings to do. There was a brisk wind and light drizzle, but it wasn't going to stop me doing the thing that had the best chance of calming me in a situation like this: a walk by the sea.

I recognised, as I strolled along the beach, that without too much thought Jamie had found a house for me that could be my forever home. I could see myself having a family there, maybe two kids. They could share a room to start with, then when they were older, I could move up to the top floor and have private adult space.

I'd definitely want to re-partition the ground floor so there could be a family room, but it'd make sense to decorate the ground floor last to see how the budget went. I didn't want to spend loads on paint and wallpaper, only to find there was something in the wiring or plumbing that was more important but I didn't have enough money left for.

God, there I was, mentally decorating already, and I hadn't yet completed. But I'd been so eager for everything to do with the house that I hadn't been able to stop myself choosing paint colours and interior furnishings. I laughed at myself, and stooped to pick up a small green piece of sea glass to go in my large collection jar at home.

I'd started collecting because I thought I would make jewellery from it, but I'd never got round to it. As my house had a garden, it might be nice to create a table top in a sort of mosaic. I could do it all indoors until I finished it and could protect it from the elements with a glass top. Glass wasn't exactly child-friendly, especially with younger ones around, but I could make it and enjoy using it in the stages leading up to children.

I walked for a few hours until I was almost stressed enough to take up smoking. It got to 2pm, and I'd still heard nothing from the solicitors. I decided to wait until 3pm, then chase them to see what was going on. They rang me at 2:57. There'd been a small hitch, they said. There'd been a signature missed on the paperwork. We couldn't complete until it'd been done. And it was on the vendors' side, so it wasn't even something I could get fixed myself. It was probably going to be another week.

I flopped onto the shingle, a breakwater at my back, and wondered what to do. I felt deflated, like a blow-up beach ball that'd had all the air let out of it – I'd collapsed inwards until I was flat on the ground. I mugged a sad face and took a selfie, and was about to send it to Jamie when my phone rang.

It was him.

"Lori?"

I stifled a sob. "We're not completing today."

"Aww sweetheart, I'm sorry. Why not, what's happened?"

I shed a few tears as I told Jamie what the solicitors had told me, and he said various things which were probably supposed to soothe me, but my mood went the other way instead.

"No, stop it with the platitudes, please, Jamie. I'm utterly fucked off and I know you're trying to help, but it's not working."

There was silence at the other end of the call for a little while, and I tried to breathe through my anger. Eventually, he spoke.

"I've never heard you swear before."

"I've never tried to buy a house before, either." I snapped.

"No, I've heard it's pretty stressful." There was heavy irony in his voice, and I felt bad for biting his head off.

"I didn't need this today."

"No, I know," His voice softened into its more usual tones. "It's a shame you don't have any friends nearby. You sound in need of a hug. Hugs make so many things better."

"Yeah, they do."

"Where are you?"

"At the beach, but I'll go home now. I've been out all day and I didn't bring any lunch with me."

"Is it a hot chocolate night?"

I sighed. "No," I told him, "I think it's a tequila night. Because that way I won't remember anything tomorrow."

He gave a short bark of laughter. "Trust me, you don't want to drink that stuff."

"Probably not, but I don't have many options."

"Get yourself something nice on the way home."

"What like, meths?"

"Wow, you're being over-dramatic about it, aren't you? It's a week's delay. Go pick wallpaper or something."

"I've already done all that," I told him. "Anyway, what

did you call me for? I've been horrible to you and not asked how you are or anything. Rubbish friend I am."

"Don't worry about it," Jamie answered in a kind tone. "I only rang to see if it was going ahead today. I wanted to... share your excitement if it was all done, and to talk you through it if not. We've done that."

"Thank you Jamie," His thoughtfulness touched me. "That was really sweet of you. I'm sad it hasn't gone as planned, that's all."

"And knowing you, you won't let it out properly until you're back inside your safe four walls."

That was pretty astute, but he didn't need to know that. I wanted to shut the world out and retreat to my private space, but that'd also involve switching my phone off, and I wasn't quite ready to end the call.

"Jamie?"

"Yeah?"

"Will you call me next week? When they tell me what day it'll be."

"I'm tied up Wednesday, Thursday, Friday with meetings, but I can call you in the evening?"

"OK, that'll be good."

"Are you going to be OK now?"

"Yeah, probably. In a while."

"Good, because I've got some stuff I need to do before I leave for the day."

"You're in the office?"

"Yeah, but it's fine. I have to go, though."

"Well, chat soon then. Next week."

"Next week will be good. Bye Lori."

"Bye."

A short time later I enclosed myself in the flat with a

bottle of wine and a large glass, which somehow emptied itself regularly. The boxes that I'd already packed looked forlorn in the middle of the floor. I kicked disconsolately at the nearest one. At least I hadn't packed any breakables or perishables, but my foot connected with a large saucepan and made a thunk.

I wanted someone in my life to cook for, or with. I desperately hoped that the new house would bring in everything I wanted. Low vibrations swirled around me, pulling at my aura, trying to drag me further down. I was determined not to let it.

"Furniture! I can look over my shortlist." With renewed interest in everything to do with the house, I checked that the perfect pieces to complement my new life were still available.

CHAPTER SEVEN
30th April 2022

*** enable(altPOV) ***
Jamie's weekend hadn't started out brilliantly. He had the whole work scenario hanging over his head, and he'd got up late, so he'd probably miss the train he wanted. He scrubbed his hand over his face. There wasn't enough time to shave but it wasn't a problem – he didn't expect to meet any women while he was out. Besides, his thoughts were enticing him in the direction of a certain tarot reader. Maybe sometime in the future they could discuss it, but catching up with Rod and getting something sorted regarding work was far more important.

He grabbed a coffee from the kiosk at the station, headed into London, and boarded the train to Poole half an hour later than planned. He didn't know Dorset particularly well, nor what Rod's connection was with it, but it seemed like a pleasant enough choice of a venue. Even if it meant a good few hours' travelling for Jamie, there was a high chance it'd be worth the trip. He hadn't seen his friend for some time, and it'd be good to reminisce about their old haunts and acquaintances.

Of course, three and a half hours on a train was a bit of a downer, but it gave Jamie time to think about where his life was heading. He was about to take redundancy, having worked for that company for seven years, and had no idea what to do next.

His skills as a network security analyst were in demand, but he'd started seeing the industry in a new light since learning of the restructuring plans at his place. Situations were temporary. Things could change almost overnight, and you could find yourself out of a job. And that was no time to be thinking of taking on a mortgage for the best part of forty years.

Either he found something that'd earn him more money than a regular job, or he'd have to wave goodbye to any chance of getting on the property ladder before his parents passed away. And even then their estate would be split between him and Emily.

Thinking about his parents dying turned his mind to Lori. Again. She'd lost both her parents already, in her thirties. He'd been thinking about her frequently of late, like she'd taken up residence in a little daydreamy bit of his mind where his thoughts flittered off to now and again. He could hear her voice in his head and, although they'd only met a few times, he felt quite close to her.

Almost as close as to his sister and he used to tell Emily everything, until she got together with Matt and had a family.

Jamie looked out of the window as the train sped down through Surrey and Hampshire. He wondered what Lori was doing and thumbed out a quick text to her:

Hope you're feeling better today.

He didn't expect a reply, but when she texted back and said she was looking at cushions and rugs online and had a hangover he was secretly pleased. Not about the hangover, but about getting a reply. And again he wondered at himself, and whether he was trying to read too much into things between them. He knew she didn't have many close friends, but it was still kind of nice. Special, almost.

Poole station came into view at last, and he got off the train. Rod's instructions had been to meet him in the station car park. Would Jamie recognise him? People could change a lot in a few years... even in the blink of an eye, he mused, thinking back over the past year or two.

He didn't have to think about it for long. There was a guy in a baseball cap with a ponytail standing next to a silver 4x4 in the first row of the station car park. Rod didn't look any different to Jamie's eyes, apart from the baseball cap, and as he approached his friend Rod threw his arms wide.

"Jay! If I'd got a parking ticket because you're so sodding late, you'd be paying for it. I've been here frigging ages." He punched Jamie on the arm, grinning hugely.

"Sorry man," Jamie grinned back. "Had trouble sleeping last night, so I got up late this morning."

"Oh? Some lass kept you up all night, yeh?"

Jamie started to laugh, then stopped short. "Well, no, not really." He *had* thought quite a bit about Lori, but he'd put it down to her dreadful disappointment over failing to complete, not to anything more erotic. Although, come to think of it... He shook his head. "More like the whole work stuff, you know."

Rod eyed him suspiciously for a moment. "You said not really, but you didn't sound like you meant it. You seeing anyone?"

"Nah, not like that." It wasn't like that, was it? He pushed the thought aside. "So what's the plan?"

"Racing starts at 11. You're gonna have to help me get set up, because you're late. I should've registered half an hour ago."
"Shit, sorry. I'll do whatever you want."
"Yeah, damn right you will. Get in."
As they pulled out of the car park, Jamie looked over his shoulder. A model boat with a keel was strapped onto the back seat and a flat bag nestled in behind it.
"What's that?" He jerked his thumb backwards.
"Ahhh," Rod replied with a satisfied smile, "That's the reason I'm here today. It's my racing yacht."
"It's a toy boat."
"Fuck off, Jamie. It's a Dragonflite 95 radio-controlled yacht, and it's a highly competitive sport. It's *not* a toy."
"You keep telling yourself that!" Jamie laughed.
"No, seriously. You wait and see. There's loads of us race them. It's an open event today so it'll be a fun day."
"How long have you been doing it?"
"About six months. It's easy to get into and all the boats are the same, so who wins comes down to skill and practice. And you need to know the rules, as well. But it's a good day out, some of us bring beers and some of us stick to coffee, and sometimes we get all the way to the venue and find there's no wind, so if there's a clubhouse we all pile in there and chat shit. It's great."
Jamie was sceptical, but it'd been more than a few years since his friend had been enthusiastic about anything, so he decided to reserve judgement. "OK, we'll see."

As they pulled into Poole Park, and Rod looked for somewhere to leave the car, Jamie glanced around. It seemed Rod was right, and it was a popular event – there were lots of people. Mostly men of middle age and upwards, but there were a few around Jamie and Rod's age or younger. And Jamie had been right too: not many women, and none that seemed unattached.

"OK you grab that bag, carefully mind, and the boat stand out of the boot. I'll carry the boat and my race bag."

"What's in the race bag?"

"Spares – so rigging, glue, scissors, that sort of thing. And a packed lunch. Did you bring one?"

"No, I thought we'd go to a pub or something."

"Mate, we won't finish racing until four o'clock or thereabouts, unless I'm dog-shite and go out early." Rod rolled his eyes. "Lucky for you I thought of that and brought enough sarnies for both of us. You've not gone veggie since last time, have you?"

"No chance of that," Jamie returned with a grin, "I've always been far too fond of a steak to go down that road." He wondered briefly if Lori was a vegetarian but dismissed the idea quickly. He'd seen the pepperoni on the pizza slice in her selfie from months ago, so unless it was some kind of imitation, she was a meat-eater too.

"Here we are!" Rod dragged Jamie from his thoughts as they got to the edge of the lake where everyone else had their kit set up. People were milling about chatting, comparing sails and new paint jobs, and there seemed to be plenty of camaraderie. As Rod unzipped the sail bag, a couple of guys came over to say hello, and Jamie was introduced round. Everyone seemed friendly.

"Right, I need to get registered. You wait here." Rod instructed and disappeared into the throng of people.

Jamie looked at the boats all trying to get into a line on the lake and realised, as the one-minute warning sounded, that Rod would probably miss the first race and it was Jamie's fault. The beer would be on him later, then.

After Rod returned and began to set up his yacht, Jamie wandered down to the edge of the lake. One guy, who introduced himself as Gerry, asked him if he'd sailed before.

"No, but it looks fun," Jamie answered. It seemed this was some kind of code word because within about a minute he had a controller in his hands, and Gerry was holding up a boat and explaining how it worked.

"Your right control, left and right, is for the rudder. See? And the left control pulls in the sails or lets them out. Like that. Off you go, then." And Gerry dropped the boat into the water with a grin.

"But—" Jamie floundered, unsure what to do. Then the wind caught the sails of the little boat, and it was away.

"You'll be fine!" Gerry said as he walked off.

"What if I crash it?" Jamie called after him. Another guy looked over and chuckled.

"Don't worry about it. The boats themselves are quite tough. It's not cheque book racing where you spend loads of money and keep upgrading, it's a restricted class. The only differences are experience and how you set up your rig, which is the sails. Have a go."

Jamie initially found it quite hard to get the boat

sailing well. It was much easier to go with the wind than against it. There was a thing called "tacking" which was how you made progress going upwind, and he stalled the boat a few times before it became a little easier.

"Not bad for a first-timer," Rod said approvingly as he walked down to the lake's edge with his own boat in his hands. "The Dragonforce 65 is a nice little boat. That's what that is. Nippy, very responsive, and a lot of fun. I've got one at home that I don't sail much now. I've moved on to this bigger one: the Dragonflite 95."

"Are they much different?" Jamie asked, watching his craft flying down the lake with the wind behind it.

"Only in size. They're made by the same company, as restricted classes, so you can't make much in the way of changes."

"Yeah, that guy over there said that. It must make it easier for newbies."

"Yeah you can get set up with a DF65 for under £400. The 95 is a bit more expensive, but still affordable as model yachts go. People spend five grand upwards in some of the other classes, on all the different kit."

Jamie whistled. "Yeah I don't think that'd be for me."

"So," Rod said, "Do you reckon you can talk and sail at the same time? Only I tweaked my rig after my last time out and I need to see how it's going to perform in these winds before the first race."

Jamie realised that the boats racing currently were all smaller than the one Rod had in his hands. As he looked closer, he could see that some yachts had a number 65 at the top of the bigger sail. So Rod hadn't missed the first race of the 95s. Maybe Jamie wouldn't have to buy the beer later after all.

"Can I have my boat back, please?" The guy named Gerry asked, reaching out a hand for the controller. "I want to make some changes before my heat starts."

"Sure," Jamie quickly shrugged out of the carry strap and handed it over. "Thanks for letting me try it. It's really great!"

"You can have another go later," Gerry said, and steered his boat in to the edge of the lake.

Jamie walked alongside Rod as his friend put the little yacht through its paces.

"So have you decided what you're doing about work yet?" Rod asked.

Jamie nodded. "Yeah, I think so. They've not offered a great redundancy package but it's better than a kick in the teeth. I want to talk to you about the contracting stuff. How would I get started?"

"Well if you were going into the open market you'd need to make some pretty drastic changes to your CV. You'd emphasise how you were able to think on your feet, make decisions by yourself and carry them out, prove you can work without being told what to do. Stuff like that."

"OK, I'd probably need a bit of help with that."

"Yeah, probably. But I've been talking to Tiger, remember him? Asian guy?"

Jamie recalled that this was one of Rod's buddies from some years back. They'd met a few times. "Yeah."

"He's got a project on," Rod looked around to make sure no-one was near them. "It's seriously hush-hush. Some new security protocol in the experimental stages. All very GCHQ top-secret bollocks. It might be

right up your street."
"Oh?"
"Quantum something or other. Tiger needs smart guys like yesterday. If I put your name forward it could be pretty lucrative."
"Pays well, then?"
"You'd have to ask him. But I'd be surprised if it was running at less than £40k for six months."
"Travelling? Where's it based?"
"Again, you'd have to ask him. But I may have mentioned to him that you were in limbo career-wise."
"What's this, one of your little brown envelope deals?" Jamie laughed. "What am I going to have to pay you out of my first wages?"
"Really? That hurts!" Rod tried to place one hand dramatically over his heart but couldn't quite manage it without the radio controller dropping loose. Fortunately, it was on one of those carry strap things that Jamie had had on earlier, so it didn't fall to the ground.
Jamie started to understand why everyone either had some sort of muff-type arrangement or a carry strap attached to the controller. The last thing you needed to do while racing was drop the controller and break it.
"So do you want me to set up a meeting, you and Tiger?" Rod called, and Jamie followed him along the bank of the lake.
"Yeah, that'd be great. Cheers."
"I know he's pretty busy with the project. It might have to be an evening or a weekend. That a problem?"
Jamie thought about the fact that he'd said he'd call Lori one evening and hoped it wouldn't clash. "Nah

that'll be fine. Whenever he can fit me in. If it's in London I can do an evening and, if not, I can do the weekend."

"Cool, leave it with me, then. I think you'd be a good fit for the project, but it'll be his decision at the end of the day. No bitching to me if he says no, OK?"

Jamie grinned. "Nah, you'll have to help me with my CV in that case. I might even manage to pay you in beer for your time."

"Fuck me," Rod groaned, "The things I have to do for a mate!" He elbowed Jamie in the ribs, and it sparked them into going over some of their old sayings and catching up on each other's lives until the first race of the 95s. Jamie didn't mention anything about Lori to Rod, as there wasn't really anything to say, and equally Rod didn't offer information about his private life. Jamie didn't even know where he was living – it could've been some luxurious mansion for all he knew. Rod kept his cards close to his chest most of the time, unless he'd had a few too many. And as he was driving, that wasn't happening.

"Is there anywhere to get coffee?" Jamie asked a bit later, and he was directed to The Hutch because, allegedly, The Pantry was a bit too much like a restaurant and their cappuccinos weren't as generous, although the ice cream was good, according to some of the guys.

"Anyone want one?" Jamie was foolish enough to ask, and had to scrabble in his bag for pen and paper as half a dozen separate orders were shouted at him while Rod looked on, laughing and shaking his head.

"You mug. You do realise it's right round the other side

of the duck pond, don't you?"

"Oh well," Jamie shrugged and grinned. "Won't do me any harm. What're you having?"

"Flat white with four sugars, ta."

"Four sugars? You greedy bastard!"

"You wait 'til you see the size of the cups!"

And again, Jamie was going to have to take Rod's word for it. But as he carefully manoeuvred the tray with the takeaway cups on it back to the racing, he acknowledged that Rod seemed to know what he was on about. Jamie's own mocha, which was a medium, was bigger than some larges he'd had in London cafés. Come to think of it, the coffees he'd had with Lori in her town were pretty big too. He wondered if her hangover had gone yet, and if she'd cured it with a greasy fry-up in a café.

After he'd handed out the coffees and returned the tray, he took a photo of the model boats racing and sent it to her with a caption:

Not quite the racing boats I'd expected LOL

He waited to see if she'd reply, and shortly after, his phone rang with a WhatsApp video call.

"Show me, show me!" Lori's phone camera was pointing away from her initially, but as she switched it, Jamie got a glimpse of her face. Her hair was untidy and she looked half-asleep, and Jamie wanted to tuck her under his arm and hold her close.

Enough of that.

"Here, look at this." He switched cameras, so the race was visible to her, and let her watch the race. Once it'd finished, he switched the cameras back so they could see each other.

"Did you have a late one?"
She yawned, masking her mouth with her hand. "I was up until four. I couldn't settle to sleep. I thought wine would do the trick, but no. My brain had other ideas. And after I got up and had my morning coffee, I fell asleep on the sofa. You woke me up – I'm still in my 'jamas." She waved the phone, and Jamie caught a glimpse of her candy floss pink pyjama top and sleep shorts. Her legs were nicely toned, and a faded-suntan shade.
"Sorry," Jamie grinned at her, "I didn't expect you to be asleep."
"Well never mind," she answered. "There's stuff I need to be doing anyway. Packing and things. But how are things going with your friend, with the work stuff?"
"He's going to set up a meeting with someone he knows that's got a complex project on."
"Does it sound interesting?"
"I don't know anything about it yet." Jamie stopped and considered his next words. Should he tell Lori that he was having to move out of his flat in a couple of months' time? He'd had the letter over a month and hadn't said anything to her about it yet. His landlord was choosing to cash in and was selling the flat with vacant possession, and there'd already been a couple of viewings.
He dismissed the idea of telling Lori for now. Maybe the meeting with Tiger would help him out there, depending on where the project was based.
"Lori, I'd better go. Rod will start asking me questions about you and making assumptions about us."
She let out an amused snort. "Ah, if he only knew the

truth about us two sad sacks. Go play with the boats, Jamie. We'll talk soon." And with the brightest Cheshire cat-type smile he'd ever seen on her face, she ended the call.

Jamie rubbed his chin. Clearly, Lori didn't consider the coffee shop meeting as a proper date, yet he did. He'd even specified that he was asking her out, albeit on a friendly basis. He thought about it some more while Rod tinkered with minor adjustments on the rig of his boat. They were definitely friends – they'd both acknowledged that.

But for Jamie, it felt like it went a little further. He cast his mind back over all the things Lori had told him about his future lady friend: she had a varied career that helped people, she loved animals, the planet, reading and dancing. She liked bright colours and had a sense of humour, and probably had brown hair and blue eyes. She loved the outdoors but was especially attuned to the water.

Miss Lorelei Archer had every single attribute.

Except one. Jamie didn't know when her birthday was to know whether she was an air sign. And if she was, that made her a potential candidate for–Jamie wasn't sure what to make of the realisation and, as he thought about it, goosebumps rose across his entire body and he shivered. He was certain that Lori herself hadn't connected the dots.

Did he want that sort of relationship with her? As well as the friendship they already had?

"Jamie! Come and hold this a minute!" Rod called, and Jamie's speculation slid away.

*

The day arrived for Jamie's meeting with Tiger, and he found himself in central London in the evening. He was slightly less confident in himself "up town" after dark since the incident last year when his phone was stolen. But he didn't let it deter him from heading over to Victoria for the meeting, and as he exited the station he recalled the other times he'd come to Victoria station: to catch a train to Littlehampton to see Lori. He thought about what she might be doing, but he knew he needed to focus on the meeting. It could make the difference between having some regular money coming in right from when he left his current job, and having to eke out his savings while he found something else. He very much hoped it wouldn't be the latter.

It was a short walk from the station to where he'd agreed to meet Tiger, and he experienced a sudden burst of nerves. He hadn't had an interview for seven years and, although he knew Tiger, it wasn't anything more than as an acquaintance and one of Rod's buddies. And Rod had some pretty weird friends.

Tiger seemed friendly enough, yet professional. They talked for a couple of hours about the quantum security project that Tiger and his team were working on, and it sounded as complex and engrossing as Jamie had hoped. Being at the forefront of a new method of cybersecurity would be exhilarating for him, compared to the bare maintenance and test attacks he'd been used to.

And Rod had been right about the pay. Jamie was going to be paying a hefty amount in income tax for six months' work, and the likelihood of longer. If it went to a year, he'd be hovering close to losing some of his personal tax allowance.

He shrugged. It'd add to his deposit for a house purchase further down the line and, if he could reduce his living expenses by renting somewhere cheaper, he'd be quids in. Except where would he rent? Tiger had said he'd only need to go into the office for major testing, as the whole point of the project was network security, so most of the work was via the internet. Which meant that as long as Jamie could get into London within a few hours, he could live anywhere. He'd mentioned moving and needing to get a phone line and internet put in, and Tiger had said it'd count as work expenses, it wouldn't be a problem, and Jamie could work in the office until he had a permanent remote connection.

He checked the time. It was too late to call Lori, and Tiger had said he'd make a decision over the weekend and call Jamie Monday morning. If he got the job, he'd be starting as soon as he could leave his current role.

With his head still spinning a little from all the quantum talk, Jamie headed home. But as he neared the front door of his block, there was an unexpected sound. He wasn't sure if he'd imagined it, but as he stopped with his key in the door, it came again.

It sounded like a kitten. But what would it be doing outside at this time of night?

He looked round but couldn't see anything, although he could definitely hear it. It was low down, coming from somewhere near the bushes to the right of the porch. He knelt slowly, trying to adjust his eyesight to the gloom to have a look, but nothing was visible although the squeaking noise was still audible. It sounded very young, if it was a kitten.

He reached forward with careful hands as he crawled towards the bushes, but the sound was coming less often and it was hard to pinpoint. Right as he expected to go headfirst into the bush, his fingertips encountered something soft, small, and moving. It certainly felt like a kitten, and it squeaked as he touched it. He brought it up to eye level and peered at it in the dark.

A tiny black face with enormous eyes looked back at him. It was obvious what it was. And so young, it shouldn't be away from its mother. He glanced around. Maybe the mother cat was close by somewhere, and he was interfering. He should put it back and leave it there. Other kittens might be near it, and he was jeopardising its survival by handling it. Reluctantly, he put the kitten back under the bush and went indoors. He could check in the morning if it was still there.

As soon as it was light, Jamie dressed and went outside. For a moment he thought the kitten had gone, but as he bent over to look under the bush, he saw it. It was curled up in a tight ball as if cold. He could see in the daylight that it was thin, and it didn't even lift its head.

Jamie's heart wrenched as he realised that, by doing the "right" thing and leaving the kitten there, it might have been alone and cold all night. He couldn't leave it there any longer. Scooping it up in his hands, he could feel that its fur was chilly to the touch, but its blue eyes opened and regarded him as if pleading with him to

give it a chance.
Jamie's tenancy didn't allow him to have a pet.
He couldn't leave it there. It might die.
Not happening. He was leaving the flat anyway – he might as well make sure he had a good reason. Lori had said he was in for some major changes. Becoming responsible for another living creature was a pretty major change in Jamie's book, let alone the work stuff.
"OK, you're coming with me," he murmured to the kitten as he made a little carry pouch at the hem of his t-shirt. He tucked the kitten into it and let himself back into the building. He had no idea how old it was, but the internet would know. Just as well it was Saturday – he had a lot to learn, and fast.
Once inside his flat, he emptied a box of printer paper and put one of his jumpers in the bottom, making a cosy bed that the kitten couldn't get out of easily. It purred briefly as he settled it in the box, then curled up into a ball and went to sleep. He hoped it wasn't so weak that it was going to pass out on him.
As his research progressed, Jamie realised he was going to have to feed the kitten probably every couple of hours. He made a guess at it being around three weeks old as its eyes were open, and it should've still been with its mother. He needed two things as soon as possible, literally: something for the kitten to drink that was as good as mama's milk, and a vet to check the little mite over to make sure it was well.
As soon as the nearest vet clinics opened, he called to see if they could fit him in, but it was Saturday and the one within walking distance was fully booked. Jamie wasn't daunted and looked further afield, with more

urgency. Christ knew how long it'd been since the kitten had had a meal, and it already appeared thin. Thinking about work could wait, as could any obligations like laundry and chores. The tiny bundle of black fur in the paper box was the most important thing. He didn't want to leave it alone while he bought some formula and the other bits he'd need, but the longer he left it without food, the weaker it'd get. He made sure he had a list, money, and his keys, and called an Uber.

An hour later he was back, with a better idea of what he was facing if he was going to rear the kitten himself. The people at the shop had recommended he see if the local Cats Protection branch could take it and raise it, as they had experience and he didn't.

Jamie had taken what they'd said on board, but the kitten had come to him. He already felt that there was a reason behind things. He couldn't have been the only one out late on a Friday night in his apartment block, but maybe everyone else had ignored the squeaking noises. Maybe the kitten had only mewed for him. Whatever the reason, it had drawn Jamie's attention, and he'd done the only thing his heart would let him: he'd taken it in.

As he made some formula in the tiny bottle, he knew enough to understand the kitten needed to be warm before it could eat. He'd finally got a vet appointment, but it wasn't until Monday, and he had two days to get through until then. He really hoped he'd be able to keep it alive, and that started with warmth.

He'd done the right thing by making a nest in his jumper, and he reached into the paper box to feel

whether the kitten was cold. It was certainly warmer than when he'd brought it in, but he didn't think it was there yet.
Jamie lifted it carefully, still on the jumper, onto his lap and moved to a more comfortable position to cradle the little body against his. He'd read about using his own body heat to help it until the foot pads were warm, before he could feed it. He might as well be relaxed while he did it.
It took a little while, but eventually he persuaded the kitten into accepting some formula from the bottle. It wasn't very strong but, as it fell back asleep afterwards, at least Jamie knew it wasn't likely to starve. And to keep kitty warm, he rigged up a sling so he could carry it around while he did chores.
It was Jamie's strangest weekend ever. And he hadn't called Lori either, between work, the meeting with Tiger and finding the kitten. He wondered briefly if she'd completed on the house purchase, but wouldn't she have let him know? He contemplated ringing her but, as he was carrying the kitten around with him most of the time, it wasn't easy to juggle a wiggly bundle of fur and a phone. How did parents do anything when they had a newborn baby? But Jamie only had to get through until Monday morning when he could get some proper advice from the vet about what to do for the kitten, and maybe he'd get the use of his hands back.
*

The vet's examination confirmed some of what Jamie already knew: that the kitten, now named Sid, was too young to be away from its mother and if Jamie wanted

to keep it, he'd have to be the surrogate parent. Overall, it was thin but quite healthy, with no sign of fleas or other parasites.
The vet told Jamie that the kitten was male and, had he not taken it in, it would've become sick soon from the cold of being away from the mother cat. It couldn't have been abandoned for long, or it wouldn't have lasted. In about another week, Jamie wouldn't have to carry it around in his homemade sling, as it could regulate its own body temperature then.
The relief Jamie felt at having done the right thing was pretty intense, even if he was going to have to work from home all week to make sure the kitten stayed warm. He had holiday to use anyway and, as he'd already agreed to take the redundancy package, he was pretty sure his company would let him juggle his days around.
Shortly after Jamie got back to his apartment with Sid the kitten, Rod's friend Tiger called. It was good news – Tiger wanted him on the quantum security project as soon as he was available. And somewhere over the weekend, the salary had increased by another 10k for the initial 6-month contract period, which started after satisfactory completion of 3 months' probation: 9 months' work in total.
Hoping he didn't sound too eager, Jamie accepted, but with the proviso that he could have some time off when he moved, although it would be pretty soon after starting. It wasn't an issue, and Tiger said that if Jamie needed any stuff shifting, he knew a few guys in and around the M25 area who'd be glad to help.
It was then that Jamie realised his new job would put

him into a circle of people who'd look out for each other a lot more than he was used to. It sounded almost like a family, but without the bickering, and with a bomb load of money thrown in for good measure.

"Well, Sid," Jamie said to the little black face peeping out of the pocket of his hoodie, "Maybe it's time we found ourselves somewhere else to live. Just us boys together, yeah?"

The kitten yawned widely as if he was happy to let Jamie get on with it without Sid's involvement, and snuggled down for a nap.

After a frustrating couple of hours, Jamie gave up. Maybe his favourite tarot reader could help him. Assuming he hadn't upset her too much by not doing more than texting the previous week, he sent her a WhatsApp message asking if he could call her. Ten minutes later he received an emoji back with its tongue sticking out and 'Jamie who?' next to it. Figuring he was safe enough, he rang her. She didn't answer straight away, which was unusual, and she sounded out of breath.

"Hi Jamie!"

"What are you doing? You sound winded."

"Carrying buckets of water up the stairs. I hadn't realised how dirty this place had got."

"Upstairs? Where are you?"

"I," Lori paused for dramatic effect, "Am at the new house. And the builders have already started, so there's no upstairs water. I'm cleaning from the top downwards."

"So you're all completed and everything? Have you

moved in?" Jamie was pleased for her.
"Well not yet, because it's all a bit chaotic, but I'm pretty much all packed. Anyway, how are you? How was your meeting? I didn't want to ring in case you hadn't heard anything and were stressing about it. I thought I'd let you ring me first."
Jamie was sure he could hear a smile in her voice. "It went really well. Tiger wants me on the project."
"That's great news! When do you start?"
"Whenever I'm ready, the sooner the better for him. There is a slight problem that I need your help with, though."
"Sure, what is it?"
"I need to find somewhere to live. My landlord's got this place on the market and I've got to move out."
There was silence at the other end, and Jamie wasn't sure if he'd lost the connection. "Lori, you still there?"
"Yeah, I'm here." She sounded thoughtful. "I did see big life changes, but I didn't get any hint of this when I was looking. But never mind that now. What do you need me to do? Do you have to stay local, for your new role?"
"That's the thing. As long as I'm relatively close to London in case I have to go in, I can work from anywhere. I need a permanent internet connection though. I've been browsing around for the last two hours but not found anything."
"How urgently do you need somewhere?"
Jamie looked down at the sleeping kitten. He knew if there was another viewing on the apartment, the cat would literally be out of the bag. At that point he'd have very limited time to get somewhere else. Sid was

depending on him. “Within a month?”
“Hmm, OK. Well, you found me my house, maybe the universe has it in mind for me to return the favour. What’s your definition of ‘relatively close to London’?”
“A couple of hours. South East, definitely.”
“And what are you looking for?”
“Only a one-bed flat, I guess. Top floor so there’s no-one above me, and if it’s above third floor I’ll want there to be a lift to get furniture up there.”
“Budget?”
“Let me worry about the budget. And I don’t know if you actually need to spend time looking for me, I guess I wanted your insight on whether it was going to work out alright.”
“Oh it will,” Lori assured him. “This is going to be just what you need, I can feel it. Anyway,” She rattled a bucket handle. “I’d better get on, because the water’s getting cold and I’m not done with the second floor yet. Ring me soon? Let me know whether you find anything, and I’ll do some meditation on where you can look and things like that.”
“Yeah that’d be great. And Lori?”
“Yes?”
“I’m really happy you got your house.”
“Me too. Thanks Jamie.”
As she ended the call, Jamie realised he hadn’t questioned how she knew things were going to work out, nor had he mentioned the furry flat rental complication that currently slept in his pocket. But if anyone could bring him guidance on where to look for a flat, he had faith in Lori being that person.
*** suspend(altPOV) ***

CHAPTER EIGHT

20th May 2022

It'd been a manic two weeks. The weather had been unpredictable, which did me a favour because it meant the builders hadn't been able to work on any outside projects. As a result, they'd bumped my job to the top of the list.

But I hadn't realised how much dust would come up by having central heating put in and, as I carried on lugging clean water upstairs and dirty water downstairs, I felt like my arms had grown by about six inches.

Jamie seemed in good spirits when I spoke to him, which was comforting. I'd worried that he'd take the company restructuring too much to heart, but I thought he was dealing with it OK.

As for my new house, it was a work in progress. The morning after completion, the builders had called at 7am and said they could start in an hour. Was that convenient? Less than two weeks later, working radiators ticked throughout the entire house, and there was a new luxury bathroom.

It was the only fully done room in the house, but after all the scrubbing and dusting and clearing up, it was the most important one. I was desperately looking forward to having the space to myself. New carpets were arriving at the end of the week, even though decoration wasn't complete.

I left some rooms plain until I knew what I was going to use them for, but everything had a base coat or lining paper. And the top floor, with its own shower room and kitchenette, was a pale blue-grey for the main space and royal blue and white for the shower room. It was all very smart-looking, even if it ate into my budget.

As I closed the door behind the builders for the last time, with a grateful sigh, I wandered through the house. My *home. Mine.* Yes, I was possessive about it, but it'd been an emotional road to get here, losing first my father and then my mother in relatively quick succession. It still didn't seem real sometimes, any of it: the house, or that I had no immediate family to share it with. I had Jamie as a friend, but he was the other side of London and hadn't mentioned when he might next be down. He had plenty of his own stuff to deal with, what with the new job and looking for a new place to live.

I sat on the bottom stair, put my face in my hands and shed a few tears.

"Thank you Mum and Dad," I whispered. "I hope you'll be proud of where my life goes from here." I was a firm believer in the afterlife, and I was sure that, wherever they were, they'd hear me. As I collected a towel from the large bag of items I'd brought from the flat, I glanced out of the window – just in time to see a white feather drift past. I smiled, knowing that at least someone was watching over me, and went to try out my brand new bathtub.

I was still backwards and forwards between the flat and the house, but I'd given notice I was moving out and had transported a few things. I wasn't sleeping at the house yet, but my new bed would arrive the week after the carpets went down. I hoped there'd be no timing cock-ups that'd mess with my carefully-laid plans.

But it seemed after all the hassle of finding the house, viewing it, exchanging, completing, and all the building works, there'd be a period of smooth sailing. The carpets went in. The decorating was finished for the time being. The house was done well enough to live in.

I packed all my stuff and bid farewell to the flat that had been my home for a few years. It was the place that had seen my internet business grow and my friendship with Jamie come about, and the unsuccessful readings that accompanied that part of my life. I closed the door on it all and gave back the keys.

It was time for a new start.

*

A few weeks went by. Jamie still hadn't found a place, but he said he loved his new job. At least that was a plus. I hadn't seen him either, which he seemed a little tetchy about, but I put it down to him being stressed about his living arrangements. Each time I mentioned it, he put me off. But that was okay, as I was pretty busy with reading requests and trying to learn how best to heat the house and cope with a three-floor living space.

I wasn't sure what I was going to do with the two downstairs rooms at the front, which were still knocked through into one, but I wasn't in a rush. It was more important to build on the remnants of my savings. Fortunately business was good, and it wasn't all that long before I had a few grand back in the bank

and I could breathe again.
I didn't really know what my bills would be but I overestimated everything as I went along, especially as my luxury bath was large and had extra features of coloured lights and jacuzzi jets. The only thing that hadn't changed was my food bill. It felt peculiar to go upstairs to sleep, after I'd spent so long with everything on one floor, but it made it easier to commit to my daily meditation. That had slid a little while everything was in moving turmoil, but I soon settled back into it.
There was room for a massive floor cushion near the foot of my bed, and I could face the window if I wanted to and the sun was out. I often found myself there around 5am every day. I was an early riser, but knowing the sun was going to stream through my window more frequently with summer coming was an extra incentive. Feeling the sun's rays on my closed eyelids as I sat quietly in contemplation was a tranquil way to begin my day.
And the evening, when I drew my dusky pink curtains, had a similar yet slower quality to it. I was far more likely to meditate in bed after dark, as it allowed me to skim over the day's events from a distance, let go of any frenetic thoughts, and then drift off into sleep.
The only slight fly in the ointment was that I, too, was getting The Tower in my personal readings. I asked the cards for more information, but all they could, or would, give me was the standard 'major upheaval' that The Tower usually indicated.
Then I got a phone call, and everything became as clear as my largest crystal.

"Hey Lori," Jamie sounded tired and fed up. He'd called me without turning the camera on, which had become more common of late, but I gave him his privacy. If he had a reason, he hadn't told me it. I could wait.
"Hi Jamie, how are you? Any luck finding a place?"
"No, and Sunday's my deadline. I'm stuck. Have you come up with anything in your searches, or your insight?"
"No I haven't. What's the problem, money?"
"No, there's plenty of that. But I need access to a bit of garden and I didn't before."
"Oh? You've decided you absolutely must grow fruit and veg?" I tried to be light-hearted, but it fell flat and he didn't laugh.
"Not exactly, but I haven't been able to find a flat with use of the garden. Ground floor flats tend to have that and there aren't many in great locations."
"Can't you compromise about being an upper flat?"
"I don't really want people above me. I like my quiet loft space."
I stopped the questions and deliberated for such a long time that Jamie queried whether the call had dropped.
"Lori?"
"I'm thinking. Give me a minute."
There was a noise in the background, and I wondered if he had someone there with him.
"Can I call you back, Lori? I have to... deal with something."
"Yeah, sure. Speak to you in a minute."
In the ten minutes that followed before he rang back, I walked round the house multiple times. I had an entire

floor not being used, and every major room had network access. Jamie had become a close enough friend that it wouldn't bother me to share my space with him until he could find somewhere more permanent. If he was that stuck, he could stay with me.

And it'd be quite nice to have the company, I mused. It was a big house to rattle around in by myself. It was large enough for a family, but they showed no sign of materialising. I might as well share it with someone who needed their own space.

"Sorry about that," Jamie sounded flustered. "I had to sort something out."

There might have been a hint of laughter in his voice, but I wasn't sure and I debated asking him what was going on. I chose not to.

"No problem," I replied, "But I've been thinking. How much stuff do you have? Big furniture and things?"

"About a van load, transit size at a guess. No, nothing big. My desk and chair are the biggest items. Everything else large goes with the flat."

"Do you have any way to move stuff?"

"Yeah a couple of Tiger's guys, work colleagues, are on standby in case anything comes up. Why? It's such short notice now it's not funny."

"Jamie... I have an entire second floor not being used. It's only as big as a studio flat, but it's there if you need it. Even if it's for a month or two while you find something else."

There was dead silence at the other end of the line.

"Jamie?"

More silence, then a cautious, low voice. "You'd do

that for me? Share your house?"
I laughed. "Yeah, I know. I get it exactly how I want it and I'm offering you the top floor. I'm shrugging my shoulders here, but it feels like the right thing to do. If you want it, anyway."
"There's a complication."
"Look, I'm pretty broad-minded, but no sex dungeon stuff, OK?" A snigger escaped.
Jamie managed a short laugh. "No, it's nothing like that. But you're fairly tolerant aren't you?"
I raised my eyebrows, even though he couldn't see through the voice call. "If you don't know that by now, perhaps you're not the right sort of person to come share my house."
"No no, it's OK. But we'll need to agree rent costs and stuff."
"Jamie, move in first. Get settled. There's plenty of time, I'm in no rush. And I'll know where you live, won't I?"
We exchanged a few more comments and agreed that he'd move his stuff in on Saturday, which meant I only had a few days to organise things like a bed, chest of drawers, wardrobe and curtains.
I'd have to get my skates on.

CHAPTER NINE

12th June 2022

I'd seen little of Jamie when he'd dropped his things off because I'd been busy with readings but, even though I'd given him his own key, he knocked at 11am Sunday morning. When I opened the door, I looked him up and down in surprise.

"What are you doing? This is your front door now, too."

He cleared his throat. "Well, yeah. But, you see, I've brought a friend with me and I can't just bring him in without your say so."

"A friend?" I looked past Jamie but couldn't see anyone else except the guy currently unloading Jamie's things onto the pavement. Jamie gave a sheepish grin and reached behind him, lifting a pet carrier into view.

"Lori, this is Sid. He and I are room mates."

I peered into the carrier and smiled as I realised there was a black kitten inside. "You've got a pet? And you never told me?"

"I didn't know what was happening with moving," Jamie shrugged. "He's the other reason I had to find somewhere else to live."

"You're kidding! How did that come about?"

"No pets allowed in my tenancy," Jamie retorted, "And I didn't adopt him on purpose. He um... well, came into my life unexpectedly."

And as Jamie relayed the story of the kitten, I chuckled mentally. It was totally in keeping with what the cards had shown me: a new direction for Jamie's life,

massive change, and the work outcome.
We took Sid indoors and placed him out of the way while we moved the last of Jamie's stuff up to the top floor, then took the carrier upstairs too and set up the kitten's things.
"So are you going to keep him up here? Or are you going to let him roam round the house?" I sat on the floor next to the carrier, letting Sid get used to my presence. Jamie shook his head.
"That's your decision."
"I don't know a lot about kittens, but I don't have a problem with it. Unless he's going to have toilet accidents all over the house."
"Well, let's get him used to living up here first, until he gets confident wandering around, then we'll see?"
"Yeah, sounds good to me." I smiled. "What do you want for dinner?"
*

We soon settled into a routine. We took it in turns to cook, which was enjoyable, and we frequently ate together. Jamie's work hours seemed a little strange as I'd occasionally hear him speaking to someone in the middle of the night, but it didn't keep me awake, so it didn't bother me. And Sid, whose full name was Obsidian, was no trouble, and we let him have the run of the house apart from the kitchen, where we kept close watch on him. As he grew bigger, his fur bushed out until he was a black longhair, but his meow remained a squeaky little noise, which I thought was cute. And it also seemed that now I had a man living with me, I was meeting more guys to potentially date. How did that work?

Maybe because I was no longer focused on the lack of a partner, because I had a housemate, I was more open to a man smiling at me in a coffee shop. More aware of it. So when Jamie pulled an overnight shift, and I needed a change of scenery, I found myself at Creative Heart, sat by the window. I was people-watching again, although it was a Tuesday and raining, so there weren't that many people about.

And... a guy approached me. Said he'd seen me in there a few times. Sat at my table. Struck up a conversation. I wasn't expecting any of it, and he came across as nice enough. I agreed to meet him later.

When I told Jamie, after he'd slept and just before I went out, he shrugged and murmured that he guessed I wouldn't want dinner that night. I'd forgotten it was his turn to cook and felt mean, but it was a date.

A DATE! A real one. And I was excited.

It was a fiasco.

Eric had asked me to meet him at a bar. No big deal, as I thought being surrounded by people would be better than meeting him alone, except when I arrived he was with a load of his friends and their partners. That made me an outsider. And my usual smart attire of velvet skirt and silk blouse clearly wasn't in the same league as the designer suits and skirts of the people Eric knew. It seemed they were a bunch of people who lived in London and were down on a "jolly" for a few days. I had little in common with any of them and, when they asked me what I did for a living, it caused such hilarity that I was insulted.

I rose to leave.

"Oh no, don't go! Read our cards!" they said, still

laughing.
"Sorry, all bookings have to be done through my website." I said, trying to keep some dignity, and got out of there as swiftly as I could. It was still light, and as I neared home my façade crumbled. I was in tears by the time I got through the front door.
How could people dismiss other people's life choices so easily? It hurt badly enough that I swore off dating. The universe would have to find some other way if it expected me to have a family any time.
As I went in, I could see through to the kitchen and noticed the light was on. I wanted to sneak upstairs to my room and have a meltdown in private, but Jamie heard the door and came to meet me in the hall.
"Lori, what happened? Are you hurt?" He put his hands on my shoulders, turning me towards the light, but I shrugged him off.
"No, just... not my sort of people," I answered and headed up the stairs, but not before I saw a heavy frown settle over his face. He clearly wasn't happy about something, but whether it was me giving him the brush-off or the situation I'd found myself in, I couldn't tell.
I hung up my nice clothes and pulled on what I called my "sad" pyjamas. I always wore them when I was feeling down. They were years old and faded, but you could still make out the teddy bear shapes on the long legs and sleeves. They made me think of my childhood and a period of happiness in my life.
Flopping onto my bed, I felt it was a pity Sid was somewhere else in the house because I could've done with some company to sniffle onto, and the young cat

was friendly and occasionally slept on my bed. But he probably wouldn't have wanted to be around me while I was in that mood. I knew I wouldn't have either.

A little while later, there was a tap on the door.

"Lori? I've made some popcorn and I'm going to watch a film, do you want to come down?" Jamie called softly.

I wiped the last remnants of my tears off my cheeks and went to peep round the door. Jamie wafted the bowl of popcorn at me so I could smell it was still warm. I thought about saying no, but his gentle smile encouraged me. We'd only moved his massive TV downstairs the previous weekend, after we'd found a second-hand sofa on eBay a couple of streets away and had wrestled it home. It gave us a living room of sorts, but we hadn't yet used it as such. I still didn't have the money to partition the rooms back apart, but I was on the lookout for a screen that'd do the job in the meantime.

Jamie fussed round me once I was on the sofa, tucking me into a fleecy throw with my feet up, making sure I had enough cushions and a bowl of popcorn in my lap, then settled himself at my side with his arm along the sofa back.

"Do you want to talk about it before I start the film?"

"Not really... " I was facing away from him, obscuring my expression.

"Yeah you do. You can't internalise negative stuff like that, it festers."

I sighed. "OK fine, whatever. He was there with a load of his friends, and when they found out that I was a tarot reader they all took the piss. Like it wasn't a genuine profession at all. Like nobody could, or should, make a living at it, it was either total shit or a hobby at best. And they were all dolled up in expensive gear like they were straight out of fashion magazines, and they made me feel... inferior and inadequate." I took a deep breath. "Nobody gets to make me feel like that except me."

"When do you ever feel inadequate?" Jamie asked with a short laugh. I turned my head to look at him out of the corner of my eye.

"When I can't do what I call a proper reading. If something stops me from passing on information I know a person has to receive. When I read for you." I said the last sentence much quieter because I didn't want him to feel like it was his fault.

"You've said many times that there's always a reason for not getting the info, Lori. It's not being inadequate."

"It always feels like it, like I'm not giving my best."

"Times and places though. You can't control how the universe is going to bring things about, nor when. You're great at your job. Hundreds of people round the world have used your skills. Lots of them have told you how accurate you were. Why are you letting a few people that you'll probably never see again drag you down?"

I waved a hand. "Because. It makes me feel like if I wanted a normal life with a partner and kids and all that comes with it, I should've had a normal profession like an office job. Not something that most normal people think is weird."

"I don't think it's a weird job."

"I don't mean you, Jamie. You're not like most people."

"Are you saying I'm not normal?" He bumped his shoulder against my back, and it made me smile.

"Yeah, you're normal. But you're open-minded. Not like those... blinkered souls."

Jamie's arm came down from the back of the sofa to rest on my shoulder for a moment.

"Aww Lori, come here." He slid his arm around my waist and drew me back against his side, leaning his cheek against the top of my head. "You're normal too, you know. You have unusual abilities compared to a lot of people, but that doesn't make you strange. It makes you unique in the very best way. But you're very normal. Trust me."

Until he said it, I hadn't realised how much I needed to hear it.

I let out a slow sigh. "Thank you."

He kissed the top of my head lightly. "Any time. Now, what shall we watch?"

And as we bickered over the type of film to watch, I became aware his arm was still round my waist. And it felt... nice. Comforting. But before I could overthink what was happening, Sid jumped into my lap and spilt my popcorn everywhere. I tried to pick it up but bits stuck in his long fur, and I had a fit of the giggles, so I was no help. By the time I sobered Jamie was picking the popcorn out of Sid's fur, and the throw was on the floor. We looked at each other and rolled our eyes.

"Fur kids eh? Who'd have 'em?" I grinned as Sid, finally popcorn-free, jumped back down to settle on the throw at our feet and Jamie went to wash his

hands.
"Here, we can share." He returned and offered me the big bowl, and as I pulled a handful from it to stuff into my mouth, everything seemed mostly OK with the world again.

CHAPTER TEN

As we edged further into summer, my bank account was still in recovery mode but much healthier. Jamie contributed towards all the bills and frequently paid for the food shopping, which we often had delivered, and Sid was no trouble and had supervised access to the garden. We were sat outside having coffee one weekday morning when Jamie brought up a subject that hadn't really crossed my mind much in the past.

"Lori, can you drive?"

"Yeah, why?"

"Why don't you have a car then?"

I stretched my arms over my head, yawning, and considered. "Everything's within walking distance, and until you moved in I was happy to carry my shopping home or get a taxi if I had heavy stuff like washing powder."

"We use liquid," he reminded me.

"Yeah I know, but I still sometimes call it powder. But that was the bulkiest thing I ever had to carry, so I guess I never bothered. I haven't driven for a few years. You?"

"I can drive, but I've always used public transport for work, and didn't need a car for the social stuff."

I knew him well enough by then. "You've obviously got a reason for bringing it up, so spill it."

He crossed his legs and leaned back in his chair. "Rod said something last week about an open meeting for those yachts he sails. It would've been easy to get to from the other side of London because I could jump on the train, but it's a bit of a pig to get to from here."

"I was thinking about transport the other day," I answered, "But a car would be a lot of money and I'm only just starting to get on my feet again after the house stuff. Something for the future perhaps."

Jamie steepled his fingers, elbows on the table, clearly in thought. "Why not get one on finance?"

I levelled a stare at him. "Seriously? You want me to get myself into debt for something as frivolous as a car? We don't even have a garage."

"What's wrong with a bit of debt for something that useful?"

"Useful? I've managed without one for years."

"How do you go on holiday?"

I sniggered. "What's one of those? Besides, we have a cat. Not many places will take pets."

"He'd probably be alright overnight."

"Am I getting manipulated or something here? Are you asking me out on an *overnight stay*?" We'd gone out a few times, as friends, to the cinema to see the latest whatever-it-was. I didn't consider it dating as such. We weren't like that.

Did Jamie think we were?

I frowned a little. There'd been a couple of occasions when I'd wondered if Jamie felt a little more for me than friendship, but I'd dismissed it. He didn't. He couldn't. There was no—

He interrupted my train of thought. "Well, it depends. It's driveable in a day, but it'd be a bloody early start and the meetings are over two days."

"Would you want to go for both days?" I scrambled a few words together, trying to pick the conversation back up.

“I don’t know. But it’d be nice to have the option. Rod doesn’t have many friends and I’d like to give him moral support.”
“Hmm.”
“It could be,” Jamie continued, “That he’s not good enough to go through to the second day or if he doesn’t do really well he chooses to withdraw. So it might only be one day.”
“When is it?”
“About three months away, the third week of October I think.”
“Mmm, OK, so I don’t need to make a decision about the car right now then.”
“No no, you can take a while to think about it.” But he sounded a bit disappointed and, when he was working later, I had a little browse around on the net.
Maybe I could afford a car. Maybe he’d consider chipping in so I didn’t have to take out a loan. We didn’t need a people carrier, but if we were going to do any motorway driving, I’d want something larger and more solid than a city-type car. Maybe some sort of small hatchback. I shut the browser down and went off for a bath, relaxing amongst the pretty lights and scented candles while I considered whether it was a good idea.
I decided to sleep on it, not having made up my mind. As was often the case, “them upstairs” had a hand in it. Poor Sid got a thorn in his paw one day while Jamie was away for work, and I was late getting to the vet’s for the appointment because there weren’t any cabs or Ubers available. As we sat in the waiting room for the vet to try and fit us in around the other appointments,

who were all on time, I muttered quietly to the young black cat in his carrier.
"Well, kitten, it looks like that's decided, whether or not I'm fully in favour. I'm not putting you through the waiting again, or me through the stress. We'll get a car."
Sid took no notice of me, being more concerned with hiding at the back of the carrier so he wasn't near any of the dogs, but when we were safely back at home – me lighter of pocket because of the consultation and shot of antibiotics for Sid, and him with a lightly bandaged paw – I went onto the net to look deeper into getting some transport.
That was when I found it: a metallic light blue Fiesta. It hadn't even had its first MOT, but it had a high enough mileage to knock the price down to something more acceptable to my mind. And what made me want it, covet it, and know it was the right car, was the first part of the number plate: LO21.
Hello synchronicity.
I messaged Jamie in case he was in a meeting and asked if he'd be willing to put five grand into the budget.
Ten minutes later, he rang me.
"How much do you need, specifically? I know you said you didn't want finance, and you weren't sold on the idea of a car, so what's changed?"
I explained about Sid's visit, and Jamie sighed.
"Poor little guy. I'll pick him up something nice on my way home. I'll be back tonight."
"Are you cooking?"
"Yeah alright, I'll pick us up something nice as well."

I smiled to myself that he'd taken the hint. "That'd be good, thanks."
"We'll talk about the car then, OK?"
"Sure."
We pored over the advert after dinner and made an appointment to view it. It was a done deal from that point on, and we both felt good about it when we saw it. I'd hoped Jamie would throw £5000 in for the car, but he did better than that, splitting all the costs with me 50/50 including the insurance. That was fair, he said, as we'd both drive it.
It seemed pretty strange looking out of the front window and seeing a car there, knowing it was mine. We took it in turns pottering around town in it as we were both rusty in the driving department. I grew in confidence pretty quickly, as learning how to drive initially hadn't been too hard, but Jamie was more reluctant. In his eyes, it was solely my car, and he was only happy to drive it if I insisted.
And nothing I said would make him change his opinion.
*
As the race weekend came closer, uneasy feelings grew in my stomach about the whole thing. I wasn't sure if it was the thought of leaving Sid by himself all day, maybe overnight, or something else that I hadn't worked out what it was yet. But Jamie seemed excited to see his friend, and I didn't rush to make a decision about going or not.
My feeling of foreboding became stronger and stronger, though, in the last two weeks leading up to it.
"Jamie," I broached the subject carefully, "Are you

sure you still want to go to Three Tumps?" The venue's name came from some old munitions storage in the lake where the sailing took place.

"Course I do," Jamie responded, barely even glancing up from his laptop. "Why?"

I wondered how best to answer, but decided honesty was best. "I'd rather not go."

That got his attention.

"Why not?" he quizzed.

"Well... I have a bad feeling about it. Like something unpleasant's going to happen."

"Such as?"

I didn't normally get that level of scrutiny from him, he was usually happy to listen to my feelings and hunches, as he termed my intuition.

"Rod's been messaging me," I admitted in a low voice, "And he seems to be getting too friendly. It's making me uncomfortable."

Jamie's eyes met mine across the table. "Give me your phone."

I handed it over. I had nothing to hide from him, after all, and I waited for his reactions as he navigated to my WhatsApp messages, scrolling through the ones from his friend. Eventually he handed it back and rolled his eyes.

"Yeah, I see. Looks like he's a bit..."

"Obsessed?"

"Well at least he's not sending you dick pics," Jamie grinned, and I managed a little laugh.

"Thank God for that!"

"I'll go by myself, and have a word with him. If he won't stop, block his number. OK?"

"Thanks. You'll take the car though, won't you?"
"Nah," he dismissed my suggestion with a wave of his hand, "I'll hire one. In case you need it, then I know you're covered. Remember what happened with Sid?"
I nodded, recalling it all too well.
"Besides, it'll do me good to get some more driving experience. If I get an automatic it won't be too bad." he concluded.
"Are you sure?"
"Yeah. Like I said, I'll have a word with Rod and tell him to back off."
I breathed a sigh of relief. I hadn't enjoyed the hassle of trying to dissuade Rod from messaging me, but I'd felt it was a difficult subject to broach with Jamie as Rod was his friend. I was relieved at having it out in the open.
"I'll do you both a decent packed lunch, and you can decide for yourself when to tell him."
"Sounds good to me."
We said no more about it. When the time came, I made soup and sandwiches for both of them, and waved Jamie off in the hire car, before heading back indoors to work on a craft project I wanted to tackle.
*
Jamie was away overnight, as I'd expected, but he reported in the evening that Rod hadn't had a good day's sailing. He hadn't yet had "the talk" with him, as he called it.
I didn't hear from Jamie all Sunday, but Sid and I kept each other company so I thought nothing of it, although Sunday evening I became intensely cold and shivery, and kept checking the time.

Shouldn't he have been back by now?
It got to 8pm, and I was worried enough to call his mobile. It went straight to voicemail, so I left a message. Maybe he'd be back any minute. Three Tumps was only a few hours away and, even if they'd stayed until the end for prize giving and suchlike, he wouldn't be really late.
9pm came and went, and then 10. There was still no sign of Jamie. I tried his mobile again but, as before, it went to voicemail.
Nausea swept over me. Something had happened, I was sure. And there wasn't a lot I could do right then, except ask "them upstairs" to take care of him.
Fifteen minutes later my phone rang, but it wasn't Jamie. I didn't know the number.
"Hello?"
"Is that Lori?"
"Yes, who's this?"
"It's Emily," the female voice at the other end said, "Jamie's sister."
I was out of my chair like a shot. "Is he alright?"
There was a pause. "He will be," Emily said, "But he's a bit shaken up at the minute. He's been in an accident. I'm at the hospital with him."
I gasped, my free hand flying to my mouth. "Is he... badly hurt?"
"No, it's concussion," Emily reassured me, "But they're keeping him in for a day or two just in case. The airbag went off and the cover hit him. The rest of him is mostly fine apart from some bumps and bruises."
I sensed she was holding something back. "What aren't you telling me?" I asked with a cautious note in my

voice.
Emily sighed. "He told me a while back you were perceptive, but I didn't pay attention."
"So, what's going on?"
"He's... having trouble remembering things. Like where he lives. He keeps saying his flat's in Hemel Hempstead, but he gave that up months ago."
"And does he remember he has a job? A cat? A housemate?"
"The job, yes." Emily stopped, and I knew what she left out. Jamie didn't remember me, or Sid.
"Does he have his phone? There are pictures of us on there, and Sid the cat."
"No, it's missing. It wasn't in the car, and it's not in his bag."
I squared my shoulders. It was only a phone, albeit the second one he'd lost since we'd known each other. All our photos were backed up automatically once a week. Maybe he'd remember what happened to it at a later date, but without pictures it'd be harder to jog his memory.
"What do you want to do, Emily? How do you want to play this? I know you're busy with Matt and the kids."
"I'm going home in a few minutes. Don't worry about me. But it's half term holiday, so the boys are about all day and I think Jamie's going to need peace and quiet. The police said he got off lightly and he was lucky to walk away from the crash."
I shuddered. In theory that could've been both of us in the car, and me the one in hospital with concussion – or worse.
"I'll drive up first thing tomorrow."

"No, that won't work, they won't let him out for at least 24 hours."
"OK, I'll come Tuesday."
"Come to ours first, then you can follow me to the hospital. We'll go in together, and I can hopefully explain to him who you are."
We said our goodbyes and hung up.
Jamie didn't remember me – the woman he lived with. That was going to be weird.

CHAPTER ELEVEN

25th October 2022

I didn't sleep well Sunday or Monday night, and Sid wasn't impressed at the way I tossed and turned in the bed, but he refused to leave his favourite bottom corner. Every time I turned over to try and get comfortable, he'd raise his head to check on me and then lie back down. If cats could roll their eyes, he'd have done exactly that.

Tuesday morning at about 5am, I gave sleeping up as a bad job and went downstairs. Sid, of course, wanted his breakfast, so I was happy to do that while I had a coffee. Then I had a second one, as I wanted to be sharp for dealing with whatever came when I got to the hospital.

Emily had texted me their address and a few directions, but I looked it all up on Google Maps anyway. I didn't trust sat navs much, so I used Maps on my phone if I got stuck while I was out and about. I made sure Sid had plenty of biscuits and fresh water before leaving the house, and he jumped up to headbutt me before I left.

"Don't worry, Sid," I told the black cat softly. "I'll fetch him home and we'll see what we can do for him together, alright?"

He made a brief chirrup, which might have meant 'OK then', then headed upstairs to do cat things.

Four hours later I arrived at Luton Hospital, having followed Emily, Jamie's sister, from her home in Hemel Hempstead.

"I won't be able to stay long," Emily advised me.

"We've got park tour tickets booked for 12:00 and I have to make sure I get back for that."
"OK, I'm sure I can cope... if we can convince him who I am!"
"The doctor last night seemed to think it'd come back in time. In fact, he might even remember this morning."
We went in, Emily leading me quickly through the warren of the hospital to the ward where Jamie was. After a brief conversation with the nurse at reception we were allowed onto the ward, and I saw first hand what damage the airbag cover had done.
Jamie sat dressed on the edge of the bed, a plaster across his nose and with two very obvious black eyes, but the thing that concerned me most was the large goose egg of a swelling immediately above his left eye. I drew a deep breath as Emily stepped forward.
"Morning Jamie!" She spoke in a bright, cheerful voice as if he'd spent the night in a hotel, not a hospital bed.
"Hey Emily," he replied with a weary note in his voice. I imagined he hadn't slept much either, with all the beeps and other equipment noises in the ward that I could hear. It was just as well he couldn't also feel other people's pain and suffering, and I was glad that my empathy wasn't off the scale at that point. It felt muffled somehow, like I was wrapped in a thick blanket, and I was grateful to my guides and angels for the insulation.
"Who's your friend?"
My heart sank. No progress with that yet, obviously.
"Jamie, this is Lori. You live in her house, on the top floor. Remember?"

"No, my flat's in Hemel. I reminded you last night, because you'd forgotten."
"You left the flat months ago, Jamie, soon after you got the new job. You know about the new job, don't you?"
"Yeah, Rod got me talking to someone he knew... wait, what is it about Rod that's... No, it's gone."
I watched him struggle with trying to remember what it was, and my heart went out to him. I stepped forward and touched his hand.
"What's the last thing you remember, Jamie?"
He shook his head. "I don't know. One minute there's something about a boat, then it goes, the next I'm having a drink with a load of guys I don't know and wishing I was at home... Which is funny, because you're telling me I don't live in a flat any more, I live in some strange woman's house?" He turned pleading eyes to Emily for an explanation.
"I don't know that I'm all that strange, am I?" I too looked at Emily, who shrugged.
"Well you know what I mean. I don't remember you at all."
"OK, well how about I show you some pictures of the house? See if it helps?"
"Wait, where's my wallet? My driving licence is in it."
I breathed a sigh of relief that we'd changed all that sort of thing as soon as we'd spoken about buying a car. Jamie had protested, feeling it was cutting the last link to his former life in Hemel Hempstead, but I'd persuaded him that if we were both going to drive, it was better to be legal right from the get-go.
I watched Jamie scrutinise the address on his driving licence, following it with his finger while he read it

under his breath. I wondered what he was thinking for a moment before producing my licence and showing it to him. The addresses were clearly identical.

"Isn't Littlehampton on the south coast?"

"Yes, we're about twenty minutes walk from the beach."

"And I live with you?"

"Yes, you do. We're housemates. And friends. We take turns cooking, and we, actually you, have a black cat." I confirmed in a gentle tone.

Jamie snorted. "Can't be very lucky, can it?"

"I think he'd disagree. He's very lucky indeed. You found him when he was a tiny kitten and took him in."

Emily chuckled softly then. "Sounds like you, Jam. Some things don't change." She took a quick glance at the clipboard at the end of the bed. "Doctor not been round yet today, then?"

"No... some time in the next half hour, the nurse said."

Emily checked the time. "I probably can't wait that long. I need to be off in a minute."

"What am I meant to do?" Jamie asked plaintively, and Emily patted him on the shoulder.

"Go home with Lori. Rest. I'll call this evening and check on you, OK?"

"But—"

"I can't take you home with me, Jamie. You're going to have a monster headache when the painkillers wear off. It's half term, and Daniel's made Rory scream five times so far this morning. Trust me, going home with Lori is the right thing to do."

His shoulders slumped, and I was glad that Emily was the elder of the two. The big sister vibe worked a treat

right then.
He mumbled his assent, and she kissed him on the cheek. As she hugged me goodbye, she whispered, "good luck" in my ear and smiled at me. I smiled half-heartedly back and watched her leave the room before I pulled a chair up to the side of the bed and seated myself.
"Do you want to see where we live?" I took my phone from my pocket.
A shrug was his only response.
"OK, how about pictures of Sid? He came with you from the flat in Hemel." I opened the folder with the cat photos in it and handed it over, watching Jamie's expression soften as he scrolled through them.
"He's cute."
"Remember him yet?"
"No... wait, maybe? I think he was under a bush...? And I thought the mother cat might come back for him so I left him there. Overnight. Alone." Jamie broke into quiet tears. "He was so small... and all alone!"
I was out of my chair in an instant, my hands on his shoulders, and I squeezed gently.
"You saved him, Jamie. He's safe. He's at home waiting for us to come back. I'm sure he's missed you. He didn't leave my side the last two nights because you weren't home." I passed him a tissue, and he dabbed carefully at his face with it.
That was one out of two on the way back into his memory, then. So that only left me, and I could suck it up for a while if I had to.
The doctor came into the ward then, and Jamie and I waited until it was his turn.

"Ah, Jamie Brightfield. How are you feeling today?"
"Well my head still hurts, but some of my memory's come back."
"Mmm." The doctor turned Jamie's head this way and that, then shone a light in his eyes to watch how his pupils reacted. "Yes, it looks like there's some improvement there. I think the bruises will continue to come out, so nothing too adventurous for a couple of weeks, OK?"
He turned to me then. "Are you his transport, Miss...?"
"Lori Archer," I supplied. "We're housemates, so yes, I've come to take him home if you're happy he's well enough."
"I don't see any reason to keep him longer, and to be honest we really need the bed for another patient." The doctor signed Jamie's release notes, gave him a script for painkillers and wished him well.
"Guess that's that, then," Jamie said and picked up his bag. "Which way's the pharmacy?"
The journey home was pretty silent, and I left Jamie to his own devices. I wanted to see his reaction to the house when we got there, and I think he dozed a little against the window. I risked a glance across at him a few times, and his eyes were shut, but whether that was to avoid conversation I didn't know.
The traffic was fortunately lighter on the way back, and it was shortly after three o'clock when I pulled into the end of our road.
Jamie rubbed his eyes, winced at what had obviously been a painful movement, then glanced out of the window. "Are we here?"
He didn't recognise the area either. That was a pity.

"Yes, we're here. Come on, I'll put some coffee on."
I wondered if after the blow to the head, he'd change what he liked to eat or drink. Not that it mattered, but if he didn't remember me fairly quickly and he'd changed his tastes, it'd be like two strangers living in the same house. That'd be bloody hard.
Jamie leaned against the car for a moment, looking wide-eyed around him.
"It doesn't feel like the seaside."
I smiled. "Maybe not to you, but I grew up round here. You could blindfold me and spin me round a few times, and I'd still be able to tell you the beach is that way." I pointed back over my shoulder.
He nodded and picked up his bag, bringing it up the path to stand behind me.
"Where are your keys?" I asked and stepped aside as I watched him fumble them from his pocket.
Interestingly, out of the four on the keyring, he chose the right one to put into the door. I hid a smile. Maybe he'd regain his memory easily enough.
"Oh," he said in surprise, "How did I know it was that one?"
"Lucky guess?" I flashed a saccharine smile at him, and he rolled his eyes.
There he was: the Jamie I knew. He was in there somewhere – I just had to work out how to reach him.
"Let's have some coffee, and I'm sure Sid will want some food. Especially now you're home."
We went in, and Jamie settled himself at the kitchen table. I set up some filter coffee and got it started, watching Jamie's face as his brow furrowed.
"Some of these things are from the flat," he said

eventually.
"Yep, you didn't bring much with you because a lot of the furniture was your landlord's."
Jamie nodded slowly. "OK, I think I remember that. But where had I been before the accident, and what day is it?"
"It's Tuesday. You went to a meeting of those model yachts that Rod sails. It was all weekend. I guess you were coming home when it happened."
"That'd explain being around a load of guys I didn't know. And Rod..." Jamie stopped, and pressed his hand to his forehead. "Rod said something..."
"It can wait. Take some painkillers, you look like you need them." I placed a mug of coffee in front of him, but I'd deliberately not added sugar, to see his reaction.
As he took a sip, I saw his nose wrinkle up and I laughed softly.
"Give it back here. I was testing you."
"You didn't sugar it?"
"No, on purpose. Sometimes people change when they get a blow to the head." I quickly stirred in his normal one and a half teaspoons and handed it back, drinking deeply from my mug.
"That was unkind... wait." Jamie closed his eyes for a moment. "We've done this before, haven't we?"
"What, sat here and drunk coffee? Many a time."
"No... We've drunk coffee elsewhere, I think? At least, I remember drinking coffee with a woman, so I guess it's you. Unless I have a girlfriend I don't know about."
I blinked in surprise. "If you do, I don't know about her either."

"Oh well, it'll come to me."
The cat flap clicked and Sid slunk into the kitchen, his tail low, but when he saw Jamie his entire posture changed. He trotted across the room, and I watched as Jamie instinctively half-turned in his chair to allow Sid to jump onto his knee. The black cat wound his bushy tail around Jamie's neck once with a chirp and then settled down on Jamie's lap, his purr audible from across the table.
I grabbed both empty mugs and busied myself at the sink, hiding my face, feeling both unnecessary and unwanted in my own house. This was going to be harder than I thought. I hadn't realised how much I'd come to rely on Jamie's steady, warm friendship in my life... until it was gone.
Perhaps forever.
No, that was stupid, wasn't it? The doctor said there was every chance Jamie's memory would come back of its own accord.
But sometimes doctors say things like that to make you feel better, my inner critic hissed. *And they've been wrong before. Remember what happened with Mother? They said she wouldn't die of a broken heart but she did, and you had to stand there and watch. And there was nothing you could do to stop it, or keep her with you. They were wrong. And then you were alone.*
I sniffed, holding in a sudden sob. "Be right back!" I told Jamie and fled to the safety of my bedroom before he could see the tears in my eyes.
After a minute or two of deep breathing to calm myself, I was composed enough to return downstairs.

I'd left Jamie sitting at the kitchen table in a house he didn't remember, and I hadn't reminded him where the bathroom was or where the stairs led to, or even how to get up to his own top floor.

Fantastic, Lori. Way to go.

I plastered a bright smile on my face as I entered the kitchen. Jamie hadn't moved from the table, and he barely looked up. I cursed inwardly. Normal Jamie would've at least asked if I was alright, but this man was completely indifferent to me. I was sharing my house with someone who had become a stranger.

"Sorry about that," I said. "Putting my hands in the water to wash the mugs reminded me that I hadn't been to the loo since before I left this morning to come and collect you. I had to go right then, or else. You know how it is."

He set the cat carefully on the floor and stood. "Yeah." I could almost hear the silent "whatever" at the end of his sentence.

"I think I need a lie down. Do I just go up?" he asked, strain apparent in his voice.

"Yes, go up, then up again. There's only the one door. I'll bring your bag."

"No it's OK, I can do it. Thanks."

I watched his retreating back and wondered whether he felt as awkward and unsettled as I did.

*** enable(altPOV) ***

Jamie's hand gripped the rail tightly as he ascended the two flights. He hadn't noticed the headache creeping on until a sledgehammer pounded behind his eyes, and he wished he'd had something like water instead of coffee to drink – maybe the caffeine hadn't been a good idea. He reached the top, and his heart thumped in his chest as he faced the door. Would it feel like his space? Would he remember how it was laid out? What if, even surrounded by his own things, he was still this lost?

Taking a deep breath, he put his hand on the doorknob and twisted. It opened easily and Jamie wondered if the woman had been in here while he was away. Was there any reason for her to have been? Had she touched things? Had she moved anything around? How would he even know?

Sighing heavily, knowing he had no answers, he entered the room and put his bag down. It felt familiar yet not, with some things he recalled from the flat, like his bed linen and massive desk, but other things – the wardrobe and chest of drawers, and the shape of the room with its odd window recess – completely alien. He closed the door behind him then, as something pushed at his memory, he opened it again. Sid might want to come up, and the cat wouldn't be impressed at a closed door. Jamie managed a smile at that. He remembered Sid wasn't great with doors that didn't open when he wanted them to. He *remembered* that specific thing. Maybe in time things would be OK.

But that still left the problem of the woman, Lori. Who was she to him? How had they met? How had he ended up here, living in her house, on the complete opposite side of London to his flat? Had they been – Jamie's mind recoiled at the thought – lovers? He shuddered. He didn't think so, yet something about that fleeting query teased at a part of his memory he couldn't access.

As he moved around the space, touching items with careful fingers, trying to force his head to piece together the bits of his life, the pounding inside his skull intensified. He could think about it later. What he needed right then was a drink of water and the painkillers from the hospital.

He found the en-suite shower room easily – it was the only other door in the room – and discovered a glass on the vanity unit. Filling it, he went to sit on the bed while he rummaged in his bag for the painkillers. With the pain acted on, Jamie evaluated the wisdom of a nap and pushed his shoes off, lying back against the pillows. He folded the duvet over himself, and tried to relax.

That was easier said than done. His mind returned to what bits of the weekend he could remember. He'd left Littlehampton fairly early Saturday morning, according to Emily. Had he gone from here? He must have. He couldn't remember much at all.

But he'd got the right one, hadn't he, when the woman had asked him about his keys? He supposed he should try and remember to refer to her by name in his head. Lori obviously knew him well enough that he had his own set to the house. And Emily had said Jamie gave up the Hemel flat months ago. So he must've been here some time.

But that still left a whacking great gap in his timeline. And, of course, there was still the Lori situation to wonder about. How did he know her? And thinking about her, he questioned whether she'd been upset earlier in the kitchen. He wasn't sure but, in hindsight, he thought it was possible and that was why she'd run off for a few minutes.

What was that about?

Nothing was forthcoming, and he'd drive himself nuts if he couldn't work it out, but right then his pain was receding, and he was warm and comfortable on the bed, so he'd make the most of it.

A couple of hours later, the pervasive smell of food stirred Jamie from his nap. He wondered how long he'd slept and automatically reached for his phone to check, but recalled that he hadn't been able to find it in his bag at the hospital.

Frustrated, he rose and dumped everything out of the bag onto the bed. It had to be there somewhere, surely? But as he sorted his toiletries and dirty laundry from the clean clothes he hadn't used, he found there was no sign of it. The charger, yes, but not the phone.

Where was his phone?

Screw this, he needed answers, and he needed them right away.

As he descended the stairs full-pelt, his headache threatened to resume, and he slowed his pace to a walk. The woman – Lori – might not know where his phone was, and there was no point getting pissed off at her when there was still the possibility he'd need her help to put his life back together. He had to be calm and, at the very least, polite.

If he upset her, she might well tell him to 'do one' and to move out. He couldn't risk that happening, not while he was like this. He had be sensible. And there was Sid to think of, too. It wasn't only Jamie who'd be out of a home if he went off half-cocked.

By the time all this occurred to Jamie he'd reached the ground floor, and he made his way along the hall to the kitchen. It still felt unfamiliar, but not as strange as it had when they'd first arrived. Maybe he was starting to remember things, and his missing memories were returning.
But first things first: WHERE THE BLOODY HELL WAS HIS PHONE?
*** suspend(altPOV) ***

I figured Jamie had got some sleep, so I'd spent the intervening time doing a couple of client readings and preparing dinner. It was easy enough, and I'd waited as long as I could before cooking the spaghetti to go with the bolognese. I was ready to serve myself but had paused at the heavy footfalls on the stairs. When they slowed to a walk, I deduced Jamie was feeling quite fragile, and might not actually *want* anything to eat. But there was plenty if he did.
As he came through the door, I sucked in a sharp breath. His hazel eyes, already deeply shadowed with bruising from the accident, were burning with intensity. And I had no clue why.
"Do you want some dinner?" I ventured and watched him grit his teeth.
"Not just yet," he said. "Do you know where my phone is...Lori?"
Ouch. It was the first time he'd used my name since I'd arrived at the hospital that morning, and it sounded like he'd had to force himself to do it, but at least he'd used it. And this was a Jamie I hadn't seen before – like he might hit someone, or was out for revenge. A

hushed part of my mind might have said she liked that intensity and it looked good on him, but I quelled it. Something was up.

"No, I don't," I answered in as calm a tone as I could. "I guess you've been through your bag and your pockets, otherwise you wouldn't be asking."

"Yep. I have the charger, but not the phone."

"I haven't seen it since you took it with you on Saturday. When did you last have it?"

He turned red in the face, and I thought he was going to explode.

"Never mind," I rushed the words out. "It doesn't matter. The point is, you had it Saturday and now you don't. So in between, you and it have gone separate ways. It's just a phone, right? Your laptop's in the front room, go and order a new one."

"But Tiger will be expecting—" He still looked like he was about to burst, probably with frustration but it could've been rage. I'd never seen him properly angry so I wasn't convinced I'd recognise it. He'd always been very easy-tempered. This was noticeably bothering him, though, so I did the only sensible thing I could think of: I pulled a chair out and pointed at it.

"Sit down," I said firmly. "You've been through a lot, you missed lunch, and hospital food is normally horrible so I doubt you ate anything much yesterday either. You need to eat, then we can talk and see if we can work out when you last had it. Tiger knows you've been in an accident, so he won't be on your case about work. Now sit." I gentled my tone at the last part, hoping that the softness would persuade him, and mentally sighed with relief when he did as he was told.

"You told Tiger?"
"Of course I did, first thing yesterday morning. He was fine about it, but he wants you recovered ASAP. You're not allowed to work until you're rested and not having headaches. Tiger's orders."
Jamie mumbled something under his breath, but I didn't quite catch it. Maybe just as well. He might have used the word 'interfering', but I chose to let it go instead of asking him to repeat it.
I served up two smaller-than-usual plates of the spag bol, and we ate in silence. I didn't know where I stood with him right then, but eating usually grounded us both. I could wait to discover what was next, although my throat was tight because of the tension between us. I'd thought I could deal with him not remembering me, but I was finding it much harder than I'd expected. When we'd both finished – Jamie demolishing his, and me only picking at mine – I cleared the table and got a notepad and pen out of a drawer.
"You ready to do this?" I asked, and he nodded, exhaling loudly.
"I need to order a new phone tonight, though. Then I'll have it by Thursday."
"And a new SIM card."
"Obviously." The reply was terse, but not unexpected. I wondered if I'd get a sighting of "normal" Jamie during the evening, but the way he'd shovelled his dinner down and not even spoken to me showed that it'd be unlikely. I steeled myself, and we began.
"So... you had your phone with you when you left here Saturday. Did you take any pictures at Three Tumps?"
He scrunched up his face, his eyes shut as he tried to

recall. "I can't remember."
"OK, not a problem. What *can* you remember about the weekend, if anything?"
"I don't know. It's all jumbled. Bits and pieces."
"Tell me those bits and pieces." I suggested, and the lid burst off his frustration.
"What's the bloody point?? *I* can't bloody fit them together! I don't know when I last had the bloody phone and that's that! You say I had it Saturday? Well, get this straight in your head! I can't even remember leaving *here* on Saturday! I can't remember this house! And, most of all, I can't remember *you*! I have no damn clue who, or what, you are to me, if *anything*. You said at the hospital we're friends. Well, while I can't remember shit, we're *not* friends! So give me the bloody pen and paper, and I'll try and work it out for myself. I don't need *you*!"
I bit my lip hard, tears welling in my eyes much as I fought for them not to. He'd never spoken to me like that before and, shocked by the outburst as I was, I didn't get the chance to cover it up like I often would when I was hurt.
"OK," I forced out, and pushed the notepad and pen across the table to him, "Do it yourself."
I scrubbed my hands over my face and rose out of my seat, stepping towards the door. "But in case it helps you, you called me on Saturday evening so you still had it then. Goodnight, I'm going to bed." And I left him to it.
As I walked up the stairs to my room, I heard a crash and a yelled expletive from the kitchen, but I wasn't going to go back and investigate. I needed some alone

time with headphones and soothing music. Or maybe even a nice bubble bath. Perhaps that'd work. Because unless I shifted what I felt right then, which was a lead-weighted devastation perched on my ribs, I wouldn't be able to sleep.

CHAPTER TWELVE

The next morning I came downstairs, fully expecting the kitchen to be a total wreck, but apart from one obviously dented saucepan there was no sign of the previous evening's outburst. The leftover bolognese was in the fridge, and the leftover spaghetti was in the bin. Our plates were dry in the draining rack, and the cutlery was all put away. I heaved a soft, grateful sigh that Jamie had at least not completely trashed the room, but my relief was short-lived as the front door banged shut and he stormed in.

"What the hell is all that stuff in the front room?" He demanded, eyes flashing.

"What stuff?"

"All that weird whatever-the-hell-it-is kind of stuff!"

"Weird? What on earth are you on about?"

Jamie caught my sleeve, pulling me along before I could react. He dragged me into the front room and gesticulated at the bookshelves lined with my tarot and oracle decks, and my crystals.

"All this! All this bizarre stuff! What's it for?"

My heart sank into my slippers. I hadn't even had coffee, and I knew that whatever followed was going to hurt.

"I'm a tarot reader." I replied evenly. It appeared there were no noticeable memory improvements so far.

"A what?" He sounded stunned.

"A tarot card reader. People come to me for help. They ask if I can give them some guidance with their lives. Like with work, or their love life, or something else."

He scoffed. "That's a load of crap. Do people really

believe in all that? You're fiddling people out of money, aren't you? How long have you been doing it? Because I don't think I'd have put up with it, if I'd known."

I stared at him. My mouth opened, initially in horror, but then words tumbled out and I wasn't able to stop.

"You don't? Am I hearing you right? Wow. Seriously?? Can you even hear what you're saying? I've been reading tarot since I was *seventeen*. That's *half* of my lifetime. And yes, people believe it. They pay for it, and they're *grateful* I can help them."

"That's how you and I met, Jamie," I continued, "You booked a reading with me. You *trusted* me. You don't remember that either, I bet. How bloody convenient!"

I paced back and forth in front of the bookshelves.

"This is *my* house, that *my* skills helped pay for, and you have the audacity to disparage my intuition, my psychic ability, the things that make me *me*?"

"I certainly *don't* remember booking a tarot reading! Why would I do something odd like that? Someone must've put me up to it, right? I don't *do* weird shit." He raised his voice in response.

"Weird shit?? I don't believe this! You've even *defended* me against people that don't believe my work has any value!" I stamped my foot. "You do *not* get to dictate my life or what I do for a job! We're friends, and that's it. Or at least, we *were*! If the Jamie that I'm friends with ever comes back, he'll need a bloody JCB to dig himself out of this hole!"

"Yeah, whatever. You're a con artist and a charlatan!" Jamie sneered, and something inside me snapped.

"FUCK YOU!" I screamed, and threw my phone at his

face. "Go talk to your fucking creepy friend Rod, on *my* fucking phone because you've *lost* yours, and *both* you fucking arseholes can laugh about me and my 'weird shit' that I do for a living behind my back! I'm *done* with you!"

I realised, as I was about to run out of the front door, that I was still in my pyjamas. I had enough presence of mind to go upstairs and pull a tracksuit on over the top of them before fleeing from the house like I was being chased. And in a way, I was. By the ugly monster called insecurity that, in the past, had devoured chunks of my contented life.

This time it'd be having an entire banquet.

*** enable(altPOV) ***

Jamie stared down at the phone in his hand. He'd caught it without conscious thought when Lori had launched it at his head, and he almost missed the slam of the door. He turned his head towards the window in time to see her fly past, white-faced.

She'd run away. From her own house. Because of him.

He sank onto the sofa. He didn't recognise any of the furniture in here, but that was his massive TV over on the stand, and the remote control lay on the right arm of the sofa in the same place that he would've put it in his flat.

There were touches of him in this room, as he took the time to notice: his laptop on the table. A pad of sticky notes in his favourite colour, and his preferred type of pen on the right-hand side. Lori had thrown her phone with her left hand.

Unless she'd staged the whole thing, Jamie had used

this room. So he'd known, in what was starting to feel like a life that hadn't been real, that she read tarot cards for a living.

He'd shit all over her life choices and accused her of conning people. Whatever his opinion was, he had no right to do that. And she said he'd booked a reading with her?

But before he could think any more about what he'd said, the phone rang with a plaintive tune. It tugged at something deep inside Jamie, something visceral, something pained and distraught. The tune repeated once, then the call disconnected.

Leaving Jamie transfixed on the photo that Lori had as her background: a picture of the two of them laughing outside a cinema. It was a selfie, with them making bunny ears behind each other's heads, and Jamie's arm was outstretched towards the front of the shot. He'd taken the picture. And he couldn't remember it at all.

The phone buzzed with an incoming WhatsApp message, and he caught sight of the name and the first part of the message. It was from Rod.

Hey babe, it said, *I can't get hold—* and the preview cut off.

Jamie's curiosity ate at him like a shoal of piranhas. Should he read it? It was Lori's phone, so the message was for her, but... something about Rod tickled at Jamie's mind. Lori had, a few minutes before, referred to Rod as an arsehole and said he was creepy. It could be important.

But it was *Lori's* phone. It wouldn't be right for Jamie to open the message, would it? Yet what was Rod

doing calling Lori "babe", when she clearly had a low opinion of him? Before he could stop himself, Jamie had thumbed open the message.
To see a long line of other messages from the previous couple of weeks. Ones Lori hadn't replied to. They all carried the same sort of tone, which was pointing towards Rod being interested in Lori as much more than the friend of a friend.
Jamie scrolled, feeling more and more uneasy, until a new message popped in. And he realised he had, unintentionally, marked the entire WhatsApp thread as read. He hurriedly exited the thread, but as he tapped out of it, he glimpsed the new message:
See, babe? I knew u couldn't resist me forever. Message me when u r free, and alone, and maybe we can do a little sexting xxx
A hollow feeling settled into Jamie's stomach as the words burned themselves into his retinas. He'd inadvertently let Rod think Lori had read the messages when she hadn't, because she didn't want to. The messages weren't friendly. They were—Well, Lori had said it: they were creepy. Jamie had no idea what to do about it.
Could the day get any worse? Apparently so, because the next message said:
R u busy? Or just shy? Are you a sexting virgin?
An emoji of a cherry followed by an aubergine ended the message.
Nausea gripped Jamie like a fist. He had no idea how long Lori was going to be, or how he was going to explain to her what had happened. And would she even believe him, when the last thing he'd done was

call her a charlatan and a con artist?
She'd been wrong. It wasn't going to take Jamie recovering his memories before he realised he needed the JCB – he needed it right that minute.
He hurriedly put the phone on the table and sat on his hands while he debated what to do, paralysed by indecision, but the longer he was immobile, the stronger an odd feeling came to him. Lori's phone was here, but his was missing. He snatched up the phone again and, acting on a hunch, dialled his own number.
It rang three times, then went to voicemail.
And outside, ominous grey clouds infiltrated the pale blue October sky.
*** suspend(altPOV) ***

My headlong dash through the streets had taken me unfailingly to the one place left to me that felt safe: the beach. As I slipped and skidded down the pebbles I fell full-length, a wail of despair and anguish tearing from my lungs, as I gave in to the tears I'd suppressed from the second I'd shut the front door behind me.
My guides and guardian angels drew close to me, wanting to offer comfort and support, but I couldn't tolerate their presence.
I'm sorry, I told them mentally, *I can't do this right now.*
I felt their regret and sorrow as they withdrew, and heard in my mind their whispered promise that they'd be there when I was ready, but I wasn't open to it.
Blinded by tears, I covered my face with my hands and curled into a ball. My only friend, someone I'd trusted intimately, who knew me at a near-soul-deep level

after the four months we'd been sharing a house, had turned on me.

He'd become a sceptic.

And, worse than that, he'd accused me of conning people. He'd gone over to the other camp – the people I tried to avoid because they dragged my energy down, they ridiculed my lifestyle, and they made me feel less than the person I was, because I was different to them. Jamie had become my enemy – a knife thrust deep into my heart and twisted until I thought the pain would choke me.

I was alone.

Time meant nothing, and I didn't even notice when waves threw spray over me. It was salty water running down my face, the same way my emotions were running out of my eyes, and I was already sweaty and damp because of my precipitous flight from the house. I wasn't unfit, but I'd pushed myself harder than I ever had before, to get some distance between Jamie and me. Before my heart broke open and he saw how vulnerable his words made me.

I wouldn't give him the chance to hurt me further.

A touch on the top of my head made me look up. A man stood in front of me, dressed in a simple red robe, with fair hair, but his eyes were so dark they seemed to glow from within. I didn't recognise him, but he smiled at me, and I heard his voice in my mind.

I am Uriel, he said, *And you are in the depths of the crucible now, child. I bring you a message of hope from the Divine: Do not despair, for you will arise like a phoenix from this. Wiser, stronger, and better able to serve.*

But you will need all of your strength soon, for the man who lives with you needs you far more than either of you realise. You are both being broken apart to be made again new, as you agreed before you came to this Earth. I feel your pain, dear one, but it will pass, I promise you.

He smiled again, extending a hand to me, which I took. It felt like a perfectly normal hand, warm and solid.

Will you accept the blessing of the Divine, beloved child of Spirit? He asked and, as I nodded, he placed his other hand on the top of my head, murmuring a few soft words. Then he disappeared.

I sat utterly still, stunned into immobility. Archangel Uriel, the Angel of Transformation, knew who I was, what I was going through, and had come to speak to me, to reassure me I'd be OK.

Wow!

Take that, Jamie-the-sceptic, and all the others who thought I was a charlatan. Uriel had called me a beloved child of Spirit, and I felt that knowledge re-settling deep inside me like the warmth of a hug. My resolve stiffened, and I raised my head. Come what may, no-one could take that away from me. And with that thought, my guardian angels and guides crowded round me, patting me lightly on the arm or the hair, swirling around me in joy as I embraced my internal Divine spark once more.

A footstep behind me made me stiffen, but I didn't look round. Jamie edged into my field of view, an odd look on his face.

"Hey," he spoke softly, "I need to talk to you about

my—"

"Have you packed?" I interrupted sharply.

"No, I—"

"Why not?" I narrowed my eyes at him, and it was then I realised how close the sea was to my position. During the visit from Archangel Uriel, I'd been oblivious to my surroundings, but I was swiftly reminded the tide usually came over the pebbles I was sitting on. My light jacket hung over Jamie's arm.

"Give me that!" I snatched it off him and struggled into it, finding it harder than usual as the sleeves clung to my damp sweatshirt.

Jamie looked pretty haggard. Good. I almost smiled at that, gloating, but Uriel's words came back to me: *He needs you far more than either of you realise.*

Yet whatever happened, whatever he said, I wouldn't allow myself to be belittled by him, or anyone else, again. I'd rediscovered my balance.

"Can we get off the beach? We need to talk."

I wiped some of the spray from my face and gestured for him to lead the way. I'd let him speak, then see how I felt. He'd torn the wings off the butterfly of our friendship and left it dying, in agony. I had no idea whether there was a way back from that. It didn't matter right then. Uriel had said Jamie needed me, and I speculated briefly if Jamie had realised that himself.

Walking behind him, I could see the stiff way he held himself, and I remembered the doctor at the hospital had said there'd be more bruising to come out. He was probably experiencing major discomfort, on top of the memory loss and everything else. I mentally shrugged.

It didn't excuse or forgive what he'd said, and I didn't know what would. But I was fair-minded enough to take it into consideration. We'd *been* friends.

He led me in a roundabout way to my favourite place to go for coffee and treats, Creative Heart on Beach Road. I was vaguely curious about how he was navigating. The concussion had badly affected his memory, and he seemed to remember nothing about either my town or me, but when he held the door open, I ducked under his arm like I usually would.

This wonderful arts café was where we'd met for the second time, after he'd fallen off the planet and I thought he'd given up on me doing a successful reading for him. Deep within his subconscious, there was something drawing him back here. It was, and I got goosebumps at the thought, the origin of our proper friendship. He'd brought us here, when we were on the far side of it and heading for the exit. Significant? I wasn't sure.

Jamie bought us each a mocha, and I chose a corner table not too far from the door, in case I needed an escape route or the paramedics needed to get to him after I'd finished with him. Whichever. I pulled a tissue from the pocket of my coat and dried the top part of my hair with it, then folded my hands in my lap.

"Well?"

"I need to—"

I cut him off. "Why haven't you packed?"

"This is more—"

"If what I do for a job is so distasteful and 'con artist-y', as you so delicately put it, I have to assume you don't want to continue our living arrangement. In

which case, why haven't you packed?"
"But I—"
I interrupted again. "I don't see how you can expect me to even *want* to share my space with you after what you called me. How can you possibly *ever*—"
He interrupted me this time. "Lori! Rod sent you a message."
I eyed him suspiciously. "And?"
"I—I read it." Jamie looked down into his coffee.
I choked on my coffee, spraying scalding liquid onto my hands. "You *what*?"
"It—it rang first, and I didn't answer it. But then it buzzed while I was holding it and—I saw it was from Rod." He proffered his napkin to me and, as I took it, I caught the look in his eyes: fear.
Jamie was afraid. Of me, or of what the message said?
"You read the message," I spoke slowly, trying to get my head round it, "You read a message sent to me. On my phone. The phone that belongs to someone you can't remember, so you don't know her." I laid my hands flat on the table, and it was obvious from the bright pink spots on my skin where the hot coffee had spattered. "In what crazy, fucked-up world do you think that this is in any way OK?" My voice was fairly low, but it had a wobble to it and I hadn't yet worked out which emotion was causing it.
"I—I saw the other ones too."
"You—" I stopped in horror and I felt colour drain from my face. "The unread ones?"
"They're... not unread any more." Jamie looked at the table.
I couldn't halt the soft moan that escaped my lips. This

was disastrous! I'd been avoiding Rod's messages for some time, but they'd become more intense over the weekend while Jamie was away. Almost like Rod found it easier, or more fun, to message me when he knew I was alone.

"What did it—they—say?" I whispered, not wanting to know, but needing desperately to discover how much lower things could sink. Uriel's words flashed into my head: *You will need all of your strength soon.* He'd given no sign it would be this soon, but time meant little to the spirit realm.

Jamie pulled my phone from his pocket and pressed the button on the side to wake the screen. As he tapped on the WhatsApp icon, I reached out and grabbed at the phone.

"Haven't you stomped on enough of my boundaries for one lifetime? Give me my damn phone!" I ground out. He looked like he was going to protest but, smart man, actually kept his mouth shut, and handed it over.

"Wait!" he blurted as he let go.

"What *now*?" I raised my voice sufficiently that people nearby turned to look.

"It's not good."

"I *know* that, dummy. Why did you think I hadn't read them? Oh, that's right, you *didn't* think. You just read them. Because that's what people do to each other, isn't it?" My voice held unrelenting sarcasm.

"You don't remember who I am, yet you stuck your nose somewhere it wasn't wanted. The Jamie I knew wouldn't have done that, he'd have asked first, no matter what. He was my friend. You're *not* him. You *don't* have the right to read my stuff. And don't think

for one fraction of a second I have forgotten, or forgiven, what you called me earlier. I have had it up to here—" and I chopped my hand above my head, "With you and the things you don't remember and your attitude to my career. Cross me again and I *swear* you'll wish you hadn't come round from that accident." I glared at him again for good measure before looking down at the phone.
And immediately wished I hadn't.
If the written word doesn't do it for u, the most recent message said, *maybe we should hop on a video chat and I can show u exactly how I feel when I think about u.* And three emojis followed: a fist, a smirking face, and water droplets.
My jaw dropped open. Was he actually suggesting that he would—? No, I didn't want to think about it. That was disgusting and perverted and so many levels beyond what I found acceptable, that seeing it made me feel like I was in a bad dream.
"Nonononononono," I whispered, trying to deny what I'd read. But it was there in front of me, and I squeezed my eyes shut as I tasted bile in the back of my throat.
"Lor—Lori?" Jamie sounded hesitant, but right then I couldn't even open my eyes. I could only shake my head.
"Lori, may I read it? The last one I saw—well, it had a cherry and an aubergine. Is it that one?"
I shook my head again, and kept shaking it, eyes tight shut.
"Lori, stop it. You'll make yourself dizzy."
"Can't." I replied as my teeth began to chatter and my entire body shivered. I felt a warm hand on mine and

forced my eyes open for a second. "Jamie—get me home. Please?"

"Yeah... yeah. Of course." Jamie stood slowly, not wanting to jostle the table and spill more coffee on it, but as he moved round to help me out of my seat, my knees weakened to buckling point.

"It's OK, I've got you," he whispered, and slid an arm round my waist. "We'll go slowly, OK?"

An elderly gent at the next table chuckled, leaning over to say, "Perhaps too early in the day for an Irish coffee, right girl?"

Jamie forced a grin and answered, "You're probably right. See you later!"

We made snail's-pace progress. My legs were unsteady, and I couldn't stop shaking, but the more I used Jamie to support myself, the whiter his face became. I realised that my added weight was putting pressure on his bruised ribs and stopped walking. The clouds scudding across the sky looked like they were threatening rain.

"Jamie..." We were both panting from the exertion. "This isn't working."

He attempted to catch his breath. "Come on Lori, I know you can do this." He tried to pull my arm, but nothing happened.

"No, I'm going to have to walk myself somehow. You can't support me, your injuries—"

"Screw my injuries," he growled, "I'm doing what you asked."

"But it's hurting you—"

The haunted look he threw me stopped my words and brought tears to my eyes.

"Probably not as much as I hurt you earlier!" he burst out, and I shook my head.
"Leave that for now. We're not home yet."
"It's not far. I know you can make it. You're stronger than this. You'll do it, just to prove you can."
The thought floated across my mind that he sounded more like the Jamie that *knew* me than anything he'd said since Tuesday morning, but it was so damn hard to get walking again that the thought slipped away before I could examine it. With my head down to try and hide my face from his gaze, I tried to step forward again, but my body simply wasn't having it, and I sank to my knees on the pavement.
"Lori... please get up," Jamie beseeched, "You know it's not far now. We need to get indoors."
"I don't think I can. Just leave me here. I'll probably be fine." I was shivering convulsively, freezing cold from the shock, but I couldn't get my legs to listen to me and push me up again.
"You've been out for hours and haven't eaten all day, you won't be fine. Get up. Get up now."
"No, I'm OK here. I'm tired and I've had enough. Go home, I'll be back later."
Jamie turned his back, and I thought for a moment he'd continue without me, but he spun back around and brought his face in close to mine, his eyes blazing.
"Lori, get the fuck *up*!" he shouted. "Are you going to let someone else win? Now? After everything? Where's your spirit, your courage? Your backbone? Where's the woman that screamed at me earlier when I tore her life to fucking shreds and threw it in her face? Is she hiding? Or is she really a fucking *coward*?"

I stared at him, my mouth open in surprise, before I shook my head. "I'm not a coward."
"Yes you are," he jeered. "You're weak and spineless and can't do things for yourself. You're pathetic."
"*I'm* pathetic?" My voice rose with outrage. "*I'm* a coward? Did you even do what you promised you would, on Sunday? *Did* you speak to Rod and tell him to back off, or did you chicken out because you didn't want to upset your friend? Who's the coward now? You're all 'I can't remember' whiny little bitch because of a bang on the head and it's turned you into a complete stranger. I've been living with this shit from Rod for *weeks* and you dare to call me a coward??" I was so incensed I staggered to my feet and lunged at him, ready to punch him. He danced back a couple of steps.
"Come on then," he jeered again. "Think you can? Think anything your puny little fists can do will match the headache I already have? Bring it on!"
I was so irate that I was oblivious to him moving carefully back a few steps every time I tried to swing at him, and after a few minutes I saw, with a massive jolt, my next step would take me through the front gate. Jamie stopped jeering and taunting at that exact moment, the last of the colour draining from his face as he clutched at the wall.
"Told you you could do it," he croaked with a weak smile, and passed out.
Fortunately, he landed in the flower bed, so there was no harm done. Although I was still furious and, in addition, incredulous of what he'd done, I couldn't leave him there. I sent up a quick prayer for help to

Archangels Uriel and Michael, and clung to the gatepost.

The front door of the next house in the terrace opened and shut, and my neighbour came out, armed with an umbrella and a shopping bag. He exclaimed in surprise, seeing first me, then Jamie in the flower bed.

"Good grief!" he said. "What's been going on? Can I ring for an ambulance? The paramedics? What can I do to help?"

I sighed softly and sent up silent thanks to the angels. "It's been a bit of a morning. I'm exhausted, but if you can help me get Jamie inside I'd be so grateful. He's over-exerted himself. I don't think he needs a paramedic, but I can't move him by myself."

"No problem!" my neighbour said. "You get the front door open and I'll get him in."

I fumbled in my coat pockets for the spare key, thankful that it was there, and opened the door. My neighbour hoisted Jamie over his shoulder like a sack of potatoes and brought him straight in.

"Where?"

"In here." I pushed the living room door open and pointed at the sofa. "On there will be perfect, thank you."

He placed Jamie with great care on the sofa, and I bowed my head. I was home in relative safely and could start to deal with the aftermath of the morning. And there was a lot to get my head round.

"Are you OK to handle things from here?" my neighbour asked.

"Oh, yes, thank you so much! Sorry, I don't even know your name. We haven't crossed paths since I moved

in."
"It's Michael. And you are...?"
"I'm Lori, pleased to meet you." Of *course* it'd be Michael. I wanted to laugh. The angels were always helping where they could.
"I'll be off then. Look after yourself."
"You too, take care. And thanks again!"
I didn't have the energy to push the front door shut behind Michael, so I turned away and leant my shoulder against it, taking minuscule steps to close it. When the latch clicked, I knew it was done and I could relax.
Well, a girl could hope. But realistically, my life had turned into a complete shitshow, and I had no idea how to tackle any of it. I dragged myself up the stairs and ran a hot bath, peeling off my clothes and dumping them on the floor, before immersing myself in the water. I allowed myself a few minutes of luxuriating in the heat, watching the colours from the lights below the waterline fade in and out, then set the jets on their lowest setting and stopped the colours at yellow. There was some hard thinking to do.
First, there was an unconscious man in my house. Not only that, he'd been a friend before his accident. Now, not only could he not remember me, he also despised what I did for a living. Which meant, if I was honest, he wouldn't be able to carry on living with me unless he got his memory back. And I didn't know when, or if, that would happen. In the meantime, things were going to be uncomfortable at the least, and intolerable at the worst. I'd need answers from him before I could make any decisions about that myself. Like, could he

ignore my job enough to be civil, or was he going to tip straight back into arsehole mode as soon as he woke up? Not an easy subject to broach, but it had to be done.

Second, whether Jamie had spoken to Rod before the accident was irrelevant. The creep had upped his game into full-blown sicko mode, and as far as I was concerned, it'd take very little from here before I went to the police. His messages left me feeling unclean and vulnerable.

And that led me to another thought: if Jamie moved out, would Rod actually turn up here to see me?

That was such a distressing idea that I sat bolt upright in the bath, splashing water onto the floor. No, he wouldn't dare, would he? But without the situation being resolved, it was a possibility I had to consider.

Shit.

My safest option was to get along with Jamie and hope that his memory came back. I'd noticed, whether by design or accident, that Rod was more likely to message me when Jamie was working in the London office. As if Rod knew there was no-one with me. What was his purpose in doing that? To unsettle me more? To wear down my resistance? Whatever it was, it made me uneasy.

I shivered, and slid my shoulders back under the water, but this time it failed to warm me. I needed to get dry and put some thick clothes on to get my body temperature back up to normal. Sid probably wanted feeding, as well.

The cat gave me another reason to keep Jamie around. I loved how he'd grown and developed a character

since Jamie had moved in, and I realised I'd miss him terribly if they left. And a soft voice in my head said I'd miss Jamie too.
Hold on, what was *that*? I already missed Jamie. The Jamie who'd gone off to Three Tumps on Saturday had never come home. That revelation stabbed me deep in the heart and stole the breath from my lungs.
Someone – something – had taken that Jamie away, and left a cynical, nasty-tongued bastard in his place. Jamie might not know what had happened, why the car had left the road, but Bedfordshire police force might. Should I ask his permission before I approached them or do it off my own bat? Spirit knew he'd trampled over all of my boundaries since he'd come out of hospital, but did that give me the right to do it in return?
I let that thought sit in my mind while I dried off and dressed, going back downstairs to make myself some green tea with jasmine. I was too wired to have more coffee, and I hoped the tea might ease some of the physical tension I could still feel in my shoulders and neck. What I really needed was a full-body massage, but I didn't want to leave the safety of my house. Bad stuff happened "out there".
Like car accidents.
Emily might have more info about what had happened. I could message her and ask. That was acceptable to my ethics, wasn't it? We'd spoken occasionally over the past few days since it'd happened, and it seemed like we got along OK. She wouldn't mind telling me if the police had said something to her, I was pretty sure. So where was my

phone?
Oh God, did *neither* of us have a phone??
No, I could vaguely remember Jamie slipping it into his pocket as we were leaving the coffee shop. I knew where it was, but that led me off on a tangent – had the police recovered Jamie's phone from the wreckage of the car?
Emily would've said something if they had, probably. She knew what her brother was like with his phone: he never went anywhere without it. If it wasn't with him, or in the car, or thrown out of the window at the moment of impact, and I shuddered at that thought... Then Jamie couldn't have had it on him when he left Three Tumps.

*** enable(altPOV) ***
Jamie's first conscious thought was that he must have been in a railway station, as well as a car accident, because he felt like a freight train had hit him. He wasn't sure he could even move. His head pounded, the lump on his forehead throbbed, there was a high-pitched sound in his ears, and his chest was so tight he even considered whether his ribcage would burst open if he breathed. So, prudence said to keep still and try to assemble what had happened.
No surprise, Lori came to the forefront of his mind. He'd ripped her apart over her life choices, driven her out of her own home, and had compounded the situation by reading her messages. She'd already been on the brink after what he'd said to her, and Rod's last message had finished her. She'd either had a meltdown or a breakdown then, and Jamie died a little

inside at the recognition of it, he'd had to provoke her fury to lure her back to the house. He'd taunted her so much that on top of what had already been said, she wanted to punch him.

Her words in the coffee shop came back to him: that he'd wish he hadn't come round from the accident if he crossed her again. Jamie had to confront the stark truth that he'd done exactly that, because he hadn't had the strength to carry her. He'd found another way to motivate her to walk: rage.

Rage layered on top of shock and disgust at the messages and his behaviour, plus distress and broken trust. Jamie bitterly acknowledged that he'd caused most of those. No wonder she'd wanted to get home, to a space she'd believed safe. But he'd taken that from her as much as given her the negative stuff, leaving her with nowhere to turn. And somehow, although he didn't know how, he knew she had no-one to turn to, either.

On top of everything, he'd read her personal messages without her consent, something no-one involved in computer security should *ever* have done. He was appalled at himself. What had he been thinking? He'd never cross that line again.

He couldn't believe how monumentally he'd fucked up.

In the time it took to process all this, Jamie became aware that his hair and face were damp. Wherever he'd keeled over had been outside, and a fuzzy recollection of the front garden came to mind. However he'd done it, and he was pretty sure Lori would hate him for it and maybe even do him physical harm, he thought he'd got her home.

Had she inflicted further injury on him while he'd been unconscious? That was a troublesome thought. Or was she waiting for him to come round so she could sink him back into unconsciousness with one good punch to the face? What if she was *really* vindictive and went for somewhere... more personal? Jamie instinctively tried to move his hand to cover that area, but his arm was a leaden weight, and the only outcome was a stabbing pain sufficient to draw a sharp breath from his lungs.

He cracked his eyes open and realised the room was mostly dark. But he didn't know if that meant it was late, or that the curtains were closed. The feel of the sofa beneath him was comforting and familiar. Thank Christ, something seemed normal.

His mind sharpened as he registered that feeling He *knew* this sofa. There was so much that still didn't make sense, wouldn't come clear, including anything to do with Lori and the house in general, but this sofa was a touchstone. He'd wrangled it from somewhere to somewhere else, helped by some woman he didn't know. He couldn't even picture her face, but he knew she'd helped him. Had it been at the flat in Hemel? No, it couldn't have been. Lori had said that a lot of the furniture belonged to the landlord. He didn't remember carrying it up to the top floor, and the Hemel flat was a loft apartment. Which meant... it had to have been at Lori's house.

That felt momentous.

As the tiny instance of recall sank deep into Jamie's bones, a noise came from the other side of the room.

"Hey," said a voice, and he wondered how someone

could be alive yet sound so dead. He tried to turn his head, but his neck wasn't cooperating.

"Catch," the voice said, and in the next second something thick and smothering covered Jamie's entire face and head.

Instinctively he panicked, scrabbling at his face and trying to breathe, a strange set of noises coming from his mouth which were part scream, part grunt. It was like the airbag going off again, which threw him back into the moment of the accident, and he was unable to function as it gripped him.

"No! No!" He grabbed hold of whatever was suffocating him and pushed it away from his face, his breath coming in ragged gasps. He forced his eyes open and found Lori kneeling next to the sofa, her eyes wide and her face twisted with remorse.

"Sorry," said the voice again, and he realised it was Lori who sounded so lifeless. The thought that he'd had a hand in quenching her bright spirit punched him harder than she ever could have.

"I meant for you to catch it. What happened?"

"Accident flashback," Jamie muttered, moving his hand to his sternum where his heart was threatening to escape from his chest.

"Oh. It's just a towel." She got up, moving away to an armchair, and as his eyes tracked her across the room, he saw empty bookshelves. There were no tarot decks, no crystals, no god or goddess statues. She'd wiped the room clean of her presence while he'd been unconscious. It no longer resembled her workspace, but was dark, barren and devoid of life. Like her voice. Jamie had a wisp of epiphany about how much the two things intertwined... and knew he'd crushed them both.

"Can I have my phone please?" her dead voice said. "I need to send a text."

He still couldn't believe she was speaking like that.

"What time is it?"

"I don't know. You've got my phone. Maybe seven."

"Do you want me to check first to see if Rod's sent any more messages?"

"No. Just give it here." Lori reached a hand out for her phone, and he retrieved it from his coat pocket and offered it to her. She took it without a word and exited the room, leaving him alone.

And Jamie, drying moisture from his hair and face with the towel she'd thrown at him, didn't understand how it could be raining indoors.

*** suspend(altPOV) ***

CHAPTER THIRTEEN

*** enable(altPOV) ***

The following morning, after yet another restless night of pain, plus a side order of torment for good measure, Jamie dragged himself downstairs. There was no sign of Lori, although Sid didn't want feeding, so Jamie assumed that he'd been tended to. However Lori felt about Jamie, and he surmised she probably hated him, he didn't think she was the sort of person who'd neglect a pet.

The kitchen clock showed 10:00 when the doorbell rang, and Jamie was relieved to discover the postman had brought his new phone and a replacement SIM card. He signed for them and debated which room to use while he did the setup. He stuck his head briefly into the living room and immediately discounted it. The curtains were still closed, and his heart raced again at the panic he'd gone through when the towel had fallen across his face the previous night. His laptop was in there, but Jamie didn't need it – his main PC was upstairs in his room.

He didn't need the razor-sharp guilt from seeing the empty shelves in there, either. The physical injuries were heavy enough by themselves.

It was time to plug his life back in.

An hour later, with his phone still charging but fully activated and connected to the phone network, Jamie checked his voicemails. The first was from Lori, received on Sunday:

Hey you, it's me. It's 8 o'clock. I thought you'd be back by now. Are you still at Three Tumps? If you're staying away another night can you drop me a text and I'll go to bed? Thanks, see you soon. Drive carefully!

8 on Sunday night? Jamie groaned and pressed his fingers to his temples. He'd *been* on his way back. But that idiot had swerved into his lane, and Jamie had overreacted, sending the car over the verge and down the bank. He'd left Three Tumps at—he didn't remember what time. He *knew* the police had come to the scene, and he *knew* the ambulance had taken him to the hospital, but the rest was fuzzy and difficult to recall.

He compared Lori's voice from Sunday with the previous evening's lifeless responses, and grieved. He knew he'd played a big part in that change, but so had Rod. He needed to speak to him, but the other voicemails had to come first, as he'd been incommunicado since Sunday night.

The next one was from Emily on Wednesday:

Hey Jamie, hope you're on the mend. Lori hasn't updated me today. The police are trying to get hold of you. They thought you might've changed your number, but I told them you'd lost your phone. Call me as soon as you've got a new one, OK? Love you.

The police? Emily could wait. If the other voicemail was from the police, Jamie needed to hear it first before he spoke to his sister. But it struck him that Emily had said Lori hadn't updated her on Wednesday. Did that imply that Lori had spoken to Emily on Tuesday after they'd got home from the hospital?

Wait, Emily had called Lori's phone late Tuesday

evening, and they'd both spoken to her, although Lori had kept the call short. And she'd not been in touch with Emily on Wednesday because—

Duh. Because Jamie had insulted her and dismissed her profession as being con artistry, and driven her out of the house. But that hadn't been the entirety of it, because there'd been the messages from Rod, and Jamie trying to get Lori home when she was on the verge of a breakdown – and he'd collapsed with her phone in his pocket. So she couldn't have updated Emily until the evening when Jamie gave her the phone back. And Lori had said something about needing to send a text. Had she texted Emily then?

Never mind. Jamie had to get his head on straight. He checked the final voicemail:

Hello there. This is PC Rah Gwel, I'm an officer with Bedfordshire Police.

The male voice added the officer's ID number.

This is a message for Jamie Brightfield. Can you please call me back urgently about our investigation into your RTC on Sunday 23rd October? Thank you.

PC Gwel had added his phone number, which Jamie wrote down. He'd call the police officer first before he spoke to anyone else, but coffee was a smarter initial idea, and he left his phone charging while he went downstairs to make one.

In the kitchen he found there was a fresh jug keeping warm on the filter coffee machine, and a mug with the initial J on it out on the worktop with a teaspoon beside it.

Jamie's throat tightened. He'd neither seen nor heard Lori since the previous evening when he'd handed her phone back, but it was clear she was aware of him. He whispered a thank you and poured the coffee, adding milk and sugar to his liking, before taking it back up the first flight of stairs.

He paused outside Lori's bedroom door, noticing it was slightly ajar, probably for Sid's benefit, and indecision tore at him. Did he peep in? If she was in there and caught him, he'd probably lose his nuts. But what if she'd done something stupid? Maybe he could—

It was a foolish idea. Hadn't he already caused enough damage? He'd likely regret it for months, possibly forever, but he had to make sure she was OK, and he pushed the door slowly enough that it opened without a squeak. He could get his head round it without going in or even stepping over the threshold if he was careful.

The scene held him motionless for a moment. Lori lay on her side facing towards the door, eyes closed in a tear-stained face, her long hair unkempt. She shifted a little in her sleep, and her skimpy pyjama top edged up from her ribs, exposing the lower curves of her pert breasts.

Jamie gawped at the sight for way longer than he should have, given that he still didn't remember her from before the accident, but he couldn't avert his eyes. It was only when he realised that another part of his anatomy was paying close attention that he knew he ought to pull back before she woke. And he still had the police to deal with. He'd better get on with that. But the mental image of her breasts stayed with him for some time while he lingered over his coffee,

interspersed with the haunting sight of her tear-streaked face.
Eventually Jamie couldn't put it off any longer, and dialled the number PC Gwel had left him.
"Hi, this is Jamie Brightfield," he said after the officer had answered and given his name. "You left me a voicemail about your investigation? Into my accident on Sunday night?"
"Oh Jamie, hi," PC Gwel's voice seemed cheerful, but Jamie had no idea yet what the officer was going to say. "Thanks for calling me back. Your sister Emily explained you'd lost your phone. I guess you've got a new one now?"
"Yes, it arrived this morning, so I could get my messages. I've kept my number the same. What's this about?"
"How's your memory of Sunday, Jamie? You were pretty dazed when we attended the scene."
"It's not very clear," Jamie admitted. "I remember telling you a car had swerved into my lane, but very little else."
"Not to worry," PC Gwel assured him, "I'll give you a little recap and then I'll tell you what else we know. OK?"
"Sure, go ahead." Jamie heard the rustling of paper in the background: report notes, he concluded.
"OK so your car left the motorway at 18:50, travelling at 68 miles per hour. It impacted with a number of trees at the bottom of the bank, the airbags all went off, and you were injured. With me so far?"
"Yeah, I remember that but I didn't know the exact time."

"A fellow motorist saw your tail lights disappear over the bank and pulled off at junction 9 to call the emergency services. We attended on scene at 19:25 with the paramedics arriving at 19:47, followed by an ambulance. We breathalysed you at the time and you registered 20 micrograms of alcohol per 100 millilitres of breath. You were under the legal limit. The paramedics—"

"Wait, WHAT?" Jamie interrupted, aghast. "I hadn't *had* a drink! I had a four hour drive ahead of me, I wouldn't have..." He shook his head, wincing at the sharp stab it caused. "Sorry, I don't understand how that's possible."

"Yes, you said that at the time as well. But you consented to a blood test at the hospital and it showed the same, although a lower reading as it was a couple of hours later. You'd definitely had a drink."

"Shit," Jamie muttered. "It'd be bloody useful if I could remember more of the evening!"

"I'm sure it would," the officer agreed. "However, when we reviewed the dashcam footage from the car, we didn't see any erratic driving before the accident, and it confirmed that a silver Mercedes came across into your lane and you swerved hard to avoid hitting it. So you weren't at fault, and as you were under the legal limit we're not going any further with it."

"What about the silver Merc? Could you get the registration off it?"

"False plates," PC Gwel answered with a disapproving tone. "There's nothing else we can do, unfortunately. How are you getting on with everything?"

"My life's a mess and my next insurance bill will

probably be colossal."
"Well, at least you're alive. Our other callout Sunday night had a very different outcome."
Jamie thought about that for a moment. "Someone must've been watching out for me that night, if you believe in all that sort of stuff."
"Oh I do," PC Gwel chuckled. "My wife sometimes goes to a psychic medium so I don't get a lot of choice in the matter. She believes, so I go along with it and I've seen odd things too many times to dismiss it any more. But if we come up with anything else we'll let you know, and from our point of view the investigation's closed with no further action to be taken. Thanks for your time, and I hope your memory comes back. And when you next drive, make sure you don't have a drink. Take care now. Bye."
Jamie said goodbye and hung up, staring at the phone in his hand, barely seeing it. He'd had a drink? He'd *never* drunk alcohol before driving before. To do it knowing he had a four-hour drive, in an unfamiliar hire car, in the dark, seemed... unlike him.
He sighed. He'd better call Emily next. If she knew about the alcohol, she'd be furious.
"Jamie?"
"Hey Emily—"
"Jamie, have you spoken to the police yet?"
"Yeah, I called them just now."
"And?"
"I don't know what to say. I don't understand."
"*You* don't understand? Jamie, how could you?? You've *never* been that stupid before!"
"Emily, I don't remember having a drink!"

"And what's going on with Lori? She was supposed to keep me updated and I heard nothing from her until gone seven last night!"

"It's... complicated." Jamie shut his eyes, not really wanting to discuss it with his sister.

"And does she know about the alcohol? What's she said? What did the police say, are they prosecuting you?"

"No, and no. Stop shouting, you're hurting my ears."

"You don't think I have the right to shout at my baby brother for being so stupidly reckless as to drink and drive??" Emily's agitation battered at him and Jamie held the phone away from his ear, but not before he heard Matt, his brother-in-law, in the background telling her to calm down.

"I don't *know* what happened, Em. I don't remember having a drink. Didn't you hear me say that bit?"

"Oh, well, alcohol causes memory loss anyway, doesn't it? Not to mention concussion on top. Of *course* you can't remember!" Emily was bitingly sarcastic.

"Emily, however it happened, I was under the limit. The police aren't taking it any further."

She was silent for a while and then let out a long breath. "You're lucky, Jamie. You could've killed someone."

"Yeah, myself."

"That's not funny!"

"What am I meant to say, Emily? The police have proof that I'd had a drink. One drink, or my levels would've been higher. And I don't know how it could've happened. I had *coffee* before I left Three Tumps. Rod was drinking, I wasn't."

Emily was quiet again, processing what he'd told her. "And what about Lori, are you going to tell her?"
Jamie knew he should, but he didn't know how to even begin a conversation with her right then. "Yes, but... we're not talking right now."
"You're not talking? And you live in the same house?" Emily's voice escalated again. "Jamie, what have you done?"
"Said something in the heat of the moment that perhaps I shouldn't."
"You idiot! She's basically your landlord. You've got no contract, no written agreement with her. She could throw you out and you'd be stuck."
"I don't think she'd do that..." Would she? Jamie's mind went back to the previous day, when Lori had asked him if he'd packed. Oh shit, was she expecting him to move out?
"Have you got somewhere else you can stay?" Emily's voice cut through Jamie's introspection.
"No." he admitted.
"Then you need to fix it. Whatever you said, whatever you did. Fix it today. And maybe she'll forgive you."
"It's not that simple, Emily. How did she sound when you spoke to her last night?"
"I didn't. She sent me a text."
"What did it say?"
"I don't see why I should tell you, you're in my bad books. I didn't know you could be such an idiot! Drink driving *and* upsetting your landlord?"
Jamie spoke urgently. "Emily, what did it say? You want me to fix this, and I know I need to, you have to tell me what she said in the text."

"OK hold on," Emily's phone beeped a few times, then she came back on the line. "It says 'Sorry for the late update, it's been one thing after another today. Jamie's new phone should be here tomorrow, I'm sure he'll call you then. I'm going to bed.' That's it. No mention of how you were getting on, or whether your headaches had stopped. And certainly no mention that you'd had a falling-out!"

Jamie wasn't sure whether he felt relief that Lori had been discreet, or sorrow. The phrase 'one thing after another' hit him squarely in the chest. First, he'd hurt her, then he'd broken her trust with the messages from Rod, then her reaction to those, and finally the tactics he'd employed to get her home... One thing after another. He didn't see how he could repair any of it, let alone all of it, yet something in his gut told him he had to.

"Emily, I've got to go. I've got other calls to make. I'll ring you tomorrow."

"But Lori—"

"Emily, we're adults. You have to let us sort it out between us."

"You better had, and quick." Emily's voice was darkly threatening, and Jamie sighed, rolling his eyes. His sister was giving him more of a headache than the police report had.

"I'll do my best, OK? Love you, bye." He ended the call, sinking onto the bed and putting the phone aside.

He didn't know what to do next. He knew he had to talk to Rod and tell him to stop messaging Lori, because it was distressing her and had already tipped over into harassment. But he also knew that Rod was

the last person who saw him before he'd left Three Tumps, and would know if he'd had a drink.
He had to play it carefully, had to be amenable, maybe pretend there was nothing wrong – apart from the accident – and see what information he could extract.
He rubbed his forehead, trying to think, and regretted it as his fingers caught the large lump still prominent there, although it'd shrunk a bit more.
Good job he had such a hard head, they'd told him at the hospital. The CT scan had shown no bleeding on the brain, but the accident had rattled it around inside his skull, and his memories still weren't any clearer.
He'd need to be on top of his game to deal with Rod. More coffee was required.
Jamie took his mug downstairs in time to see Lori slip out of the front door.
"Lori, wait!" he called to her retreating back, but if she heard him, she didn't respond. He sighed and turned his steps towards the kitchen. Maybe just as well, as he had no clue yet what to say to her.
Sid was happily munching from one of his bowls, and there was a travel mug with a J on it on the table. He opened it to find hot chicken and vegetable soup inside, and there was a buttered roll in a ziplock bag.
She couldn't help herself. After everything that'd happened, she was still the same caring soul underneath, and it occurred to Jamie that although he didn't remember her, he knew that information from somewhere.
Well duh, she reads tarot for people. Of course she's caring.
But Jamie's heart said there was more to it than that.

As he took his mug of soup and roll out into the hall, he could hear his phone ringing and he flew up the stairs, reaching the top stair at the exact second it stopped. He cursed softly, his head pounding from running, and reached for the phone as a text rolled in. It was from Tiger:

Jamie, please call me when you can.

Dealing with Rod had to wait. He needed to speak to his boss. If Jamie was going to be out of somewhere to live, mostly through his own actions, he'd need all the money he could earn. He called him straight back.

"Jamie. Back in the land of the living, are you?" Tiger's measured voice relaxed Jamie somewhat.

"Yeah, pretty much."

"Good to hear. Do you know what happened? Your housemate didn't give me much information, except you were having memory issues after the accident. That still the case?"

"Yes... no... not with work."

"OK, with...?" Tiger waited patiently for Jamie to fill in the missing information.

It was funny how Jamie had always found it easy to open up to his boss. The entire story spilled out: from leaving Three Tumps on Sunday to the memory loss around Lori, the untraceable silver car and the police report, the creepy messages Lori was receiving, although Jamie didn't mention they were from Rod. All the way through Jamie's character assassination of Lori, how he'd hunted her down and got her home the only way he could think of, to the current afternoon and not knowing where she was, although she'd left him lunch.

Tiger prompted him with the occasional question, and when Jamie concluded, he found himself pacing the room in agitation with damp eyes.

"I fucked up, Tiger, and I don't know how to make things better from here. I don't even remember her."

Tiger's answering sigh led Jamie to think his boss would make it all worse.

"Well, you're right, you have. You're in so deep you must be swimming by now." Tiger actually chuckled.

Jamie shook his head, not that Tiger could see it. "I don't see anything funny about it, Tiger."

"Of course not, lad, you're in it." He was only a few years older than Jamie, but it was a subtle reminder that he was the senior, in age and responsibilities, as well as being Jamie's boss.

"Do you *want* to fix things with Lori?"

"I must. Emily said I need to do it today."

"Emily's another woman, of course she'd say that. Leave aside what she said for now. What do *you* want?"

"There's something in me that's driving me to it, something in my gut. I know I hurt her, but it's more than that." Jamie bit his lip. "You don't happen to know if we were... more than friends, do you?"

Tiger laughed. "No, man. That's between you and her. But do you want my opinion?"

"Sure."

"You never spoke of her like you were together. But you had a picture of the two of you on your phone, which I saw once. Rabbit ears and a windmill ring any bells?"

"She has one on her phone like that, too."

"Chances are it's the same picture, lad."
He could hear Tiger's smile.
"Jamie, you've got backups of everything, I know you have, including pictures. Follow those breadcrumbs. You make leaps and jumps with the quantum project that none of the rest of us have even thought of, let alone worked out how to do. You're my best worker."
"They're just hunches and gut feelings..." Jamie shrugged.
"I bet Lori works the same way, but in her field of expertise it's called intuition and psychic ability."
Jamie swallowed hard and abruptly had to sit down.
"You didn't think of that? She makes a living from tarot, did you think she was a rank beginner?" Tiger chuckled again. "Man, you're a mess. She obviously means something to you, lad, and you to her. Maybe she knows you didn't mean what you said, or maybe not and she still thinks you're an arsehole. But if you can unlock one seemingly-irrelevant memory of her, the rest might follow."
He paused, to let his words sink in. "And then you'll be able to see if she's willing to forgive, because you can be sure, having called her what you did, she won't forget. But I know you, Jamie. You'll go to the ends of the earth to get to where you want to be. That's why you're the best."
Jamie was stunned into speechlessness. "Thanks, Tiger," he finally managed.
"Sure. Back to work Monday?"
"I hope so. I'll message you."
"Do that." Tiger disconnected, leaving Jamie with his thoughts.

Breadcrumbs. Pictures. Clues. All on his PC, waiting for him to look and then, hopefully, he'd remember.
An hour later, Jamie was shattered. His head was still thumping, and his eyes were gritty like they had sand in them. The pictures were there on his PC. So many moments of them laughing together, of Lori laughing, of Sid being silly and doing kitten things. So much to take in. And there was that selfie, too, with the bunny ears. He couldn't remember what they'd been to see, even, but it looked like the summer, which put it in July or August. He checked the date: yes, 25th July. None of it was lost, but there was a disconnect between the past and Jamie's present.
He debated whether to research techniques to improve memory, but it seemed warm in the room and he was out of energy. Maybe he should take some painkillers. He didn't want to be dependent on them, but if he took a nap he should feel better after. He stripped off and got into bed, dropping quickly into sleep.
The dream happened almost immediately, or so it seemed. Jamie's glimpse earlier of the undersides of Lori's breasts featured heavily, and he could almost feel them in his hands. Then, as dreams do, it morphed into something else, with him laughing and Lori shrieking at him:
Jamie, if you're videoing this, I'm going to kill you!
She didn't look like she was angry, though, she seemed frustrated, and she was completely bare at the rear, with a white towel held up over her front half.
Don't just stand there, do something!
Dream-Jamie was laughing so hard he was crying, and he choked out a few words: *Turn round and show me*

your pussy!
Sleeping-Jamie let out a soft groan. He was a dead man. But in the dream Lori turned to reveal that Sid, barely four months old, was hanging off the front of the towel - right in front of Lori's private area.
Fine, I'll deal with him myself, said dream-Lori, and unhooked Sid's claws carefully from the towel one-handed, her right arm desperately clinging to the towel so she didn't lose all her modesty.
Dream-Jamie by then was leaning against the wall, gasping for breath, and couldn't respond as dream-Lori stalked past him, minus kitten.
You owe me big time for that, she said, *No help at all!*
And as he tracked her into her bedroom with the camera, dream-Jamie called out, *Perfect peach!*
She turned briefly, stuck her tongue out at him, and slammed the door shut.
The bang of the door in the dream startled Jamie awake, and he wondered if it'd been a real door slam that had woken him. He listened, but the house was silent. As he became more aware of his surroundings, he realised—oh no. A certain part of his anatomy had got *way* too interested in the dream.
But there was something more, something tugging at him. Where was the dream set? He snatched up his boxers and pulled them on, creeping down the stairs in case Lori was home. He didn't want to encounter her like this, with his arousal from the dream clearly on display.
Luckily her bedroom door was shut, but as Jamie turned away from it to look along the landing, the dream-memory caught up with him. There were the

two bedroom doors. The bathroom door was ajar, like in the dream, and as he tiptoed along the landing, he could see large fluffy white towels, stacked neatly on the side. Like the one dream-Lori had held in front of her.

Jamie tripped over his feet trying to get back up the stairs. He had to know. It'd started as a dream, but was his imagination that good at conjuring up her rear view from a glimpse or two of boobs? With shaking hands, he moused over to the folder on his PC with videos in it, double-clicked it open, and—

Oh shit.

There it was. Named 'BHW-PP' and dated 28-08-22. BHW? Oh – Bank Holiday Weekend. And the PP...

Jamie thought perhaps he'd better not watch it, because as he couldn't actually remember Lori, seeing her half-naked felt a bit voyeur-like. But how would he know if it was a genuine memory if he didn't?

The faint click of the front door saved him, at least temporarily. He leapt up, intent on going down to see her, but realised that, first, he was still only in his boxers, and second, he had no idea what he was going to say to her yet. He needed a plan, and he still hadn't spoken to Rod.

He'd put things together first, then phone Rod, in that order. Pulling an A3 notepad towards him, he picked up a pen ready, but the ping of an email diverted his attention before he could start. He opened it without thinking, and a message plus an attachment burned themselves into his mind:

Hi Jamie, the two parts of the pendant are complete now, ready to solder together. Have a look at the attached mock-up. I hope you're happy with the placement, but please say if not. Also, you were going to let me know about the inscription? I need you to either pick a typeface or send over a sample of your handwriting, then I can get on with the engraving. It should be ready by Christmas, as you asked, but things get pretty busy this time of year. The sooner you let me know, the higher up the queue you'll be. No pressure! Best wishes, Stella.

Pendant? Inscription? Now what had he got himself into? He double-clicked on the attached image and stared in awe at the delicate silver flower with brilliant blue petals and a black centre, perched proud of a round-cornered, hammered, enamelled silver triangle. It was stunningly intricate.

But who was it for, and why did the blue petals make him shiver? The shade seemed to draw him in, and he fell deeper into the petals as they called, but where did he know that colour from? He shook his head vigorously. It was hypnotic and, therefore, dangerous right then. He was supposed to be mapping out what he knew, not getting distracted again. He could come back to the pendant later.

Mind-mapping had always been something Jamie enjoyed, but it'd never been this important or complex before. Where did he even start?

He sighed and put pen to paper. The first thing was to get out everything he knew for definite and link it all together. That done, he began adding in the extra bits that he couldn't explain, like the alcohol in his system and how he remembered Sid when prompted but Lori... still nothing, really. He couldn't include the

video yet. Maybe later, when it wasn't likely to get a rise out of him, and he was struggling to concentrate as it was.
Had he even had the soup that Lori had left him for lunch?
He checked the travel mug: no, but it was still slightly warm, so he necked it and reached for the roll, tearing a huge bite out of it. Great, he wanted a drink. Perhaps there was some fruit juice in the fridge downstairs. He dragged on some grey joggers and a t-shirt and padded down the stairs, soup mug in hand, to the kitchen.
Evening was creeping in, and without conscious thought of where the switch was, he snapped on the light.
And came face-to-face with someone he wanted to speak to, yet had no words to even begin the conversation.
*** suspend(altPOV) ***

CHAPTER FOURTEEN

God, that was bright. I raised my head from the table – when had I fallen asleep? Blinking a few times, I rubbed my eyes. Jamie was hovering just inside the kitchen doorway, his hand still on the light switch. He was between me and the safety of my bedroom, the only truly safe space left to me.

He'd forced me from the house the day before with his slanderous, hurtful words, and then hunted me down at the beach. Even my favourite coffee shop felt almost tainted by the memory of what had happened there. It was all too much to deal with.

I rose from the chair and flipped my book shut, sweeping it up and hoping he hadn't seen the cover.

"Let me past."

"Lori—"

"Please, Jamie."

He still looked like my friend, still sounded like him, yet I knew it wasn't him. My friend was gone.

"In a minute. There's something I have to tell you."

"Tell someone who cares."

"I want to, that's why I'm asking. Stay a minute, then I'll let you go. Please?"

I didn't want to care, but I couldn't switch it off. It wasn't that easy. And by accepting the blessing from Uriel the day before, I'd committed myself to helping this stranger, this enemy in my own home.

I glanced up at his face. I could see he was tired, the bruises livid against his pale skin, but he pulled out the chair nearest to him and gestured me into it. I complied, but he didn't join me at the table. Instead, he stood behind me, slightly off to my right. I didn't understand why, but I felt his hand gripping the back of the chair.

"Make it quick." I was pretty much running on empty as it was.

"I—I spoke to the police today." He stopped, and I heard him shift his bare feet on the floor. "I—they—" He paused, and his grip on the chair tightened, as if he was trying to hold himself up. "They – said – I'd – had – a – drink." The effort to state the words aloud was audible.

My breath caught in my throat, and my book clattered to the floor, but the words that came out of my mouth took even me by surprise. "Jesus, you killed him."

"I—what?" It sounded like Jamie was choking. "Lori, no-one was hurt in the accident but me. I didn't kill anyone."

I turned in the chair to face him, rising slowly and in more agony than I'd ever experienced before. "That's not correct, Jamie. You—" I pointed at him, my hand shaking, "You had a drink. You had an accident. My friend died that night. He never came home. And instead there's you. Someone I don't know and I can't trust, who's hurt me so deeply I can't even—" I had to stop, because the tears were starting, but I grabbed my book off the floor and brandished it in his face. "You see? See what you've done?"

The book was titled, "When There's No Time To Say Goodbye: A Guide To Sudden Loss".

Jamie stared, horror-struck for a moment, before his legs gave way, and I was able to escape by stepping over his prone frame.

Uriel hadn't said I had to make it easy for Jamie, but I'd shocked myself with my words, and I was going to be sick.

*** enable(altPOV) ***
Jamie heard Lori's retreating footsteps and the bang of the bathroom door, but didn't even attempt to get up. He didn't think he had it in him to do anything, and as he leaned his head back against the wall, tears sprang free from his closed eyes.
Lori had warned him that if he crossed her again, he'd wish he hadn't come round from the accident. He'd reached that place almost without her help. He didn't want to be here, sitting on a cold floor in a strange house, with someone he didn't remember accusing him of killing himself, or at least, a part of himself. He didn't want to be anywhere right then.
The cat flap clicked, and a weight settled gently into his lap. Without opening his eyes, his hand automatically began to stroke Sid's soft coat, and the young cat started purring, pushing his face into Jamie's hand. As if to say, *Hey, you're not alone. I'm here.*
A long while later, when Jamie's devastation had receded a minuscule amount, he was able to open his eyes. There, on the ground next to him, was a large white feather. Jamie knew enough to recognise it was an angelic sign. Someone else was watching over him, too.
*** suspend(altPOV) ***

I didn't think I had anything left in my stomach from

the last couple of days, let alone the small amount I'd eaten for lunch, but the retching and feelings of nausea kept me hanging over the toilet for what felt like hours. And when I finally stopped vomiting, I sank to the floor, lying on my side in a curled position and holding my stomach, and I began shivering violently.

"Oh God, what have I done?" I whispered, unable to accept that I'd scored such a low blow on a man who'd already been through so much: the accident itself, the memory loss, and finding out about the alcohol... and then I'd kicked him again. What sort of cruel, twisted person was I underneath, that I could do such a thing? I was meant to help people, not hurt them when they were already at their lowest.

I felt more unclean and revolted than Rod's messages had *ever* made me feel – even one about pale pink lingerie. And this time, it was all on me. I had to shower to try and get the layer of filth off. I scrubbed and abraded and scoured my skin until it was raw, but I still didn't feel clean.

It was no use trying anything else. I was going to have to live with it.

I folded myself into one of the bath sheets and made my way, my feet dragging, to my bedroom. But as I opened the door, I smelt sandalwood, and something made the hairs on the back of my neck rise. Then I saw him.

Archangel Uriel was sitting on my bed.

Come here, child, His voice sounded in my mind, as it had before, but there was no tone of judgement, only gentle empathy. I cried out and threw myself at his feet.

"Uriel – I don't understand! Why did I say that? Where did those words come from? What am I going to do?"

The angel shook his head sadly. *I am sorry, child. You must let him go.*

"What? But—"

No, child. There is nothing more you can do. It is time. He has to move on.

I was floored by his words. "Can I not—speak to him once more? Before I let him go?"

No, child. It is not permitted.

"Can't I give... anything, just for one more moment?"

Do you not remember my words to you, child? I said you would need all your strength soon. Now is that time. Uriel chided me.

"Can't I even... go instead? And give my life for his? He is—was—my best friend," I pleaded.

Uriel's eyes grew darker, and I shivered at the sudden coldness in the room.

You would throw away your gift, which helps so many, for a man you cannot save?

His words hit me like a slap. No, I couldn't do that.

It is the will of the Divine, child. All part of the grand plan, your soul contract. He must walk a different path now.

I bowed my head in acknowledgement, but inwardly I raged and railed and stormed. My version of Jamie, my best and only friend, was gone, and there was no way back. The pinprick of hope I'd carried with me all week – that he'd remember me, that we'd be friends again and move on with life as it had been before – vanished. Uriel waited in silence, implacable, while I

struggled with it all, until finally I raised my head and looked directly into his dark eyes.
"What must I do?"
Go to your cards, dear one. You will know what to do.
And the angel was gone.
I rose unsteadily to my feet, leaving the towel behind me on the floor as I walked carefully over to the desk. My skin was broken and bleeding in places where I'd scrubbed repeatedly at myself, trying to get clean, but I ignored the discomfort.
I had work to do.
A song came to mind, and I set my MP3 player softly on repeat: Imagine Dragons' track "Wrecked", off their album *Mercury - Act One* from the previous year. The words fit rather too well. I searched my storage boxes for a new pink candle, for the affection and friendship I held for Jamie, and set it in a holder next to my favourite picture of him.
The photo was a simple, candid shot, and I remembered the moment in incredible detail. Early September. Jamie had been up all night working, and he'd drifted downstairs around 8am, exhausted, barefoot and unkempt. His shirt was rumpled, and he needed coffee intravenously, so he said, but he'd taken the time to scoop Sid up and cuddle him to make amends for having shut the kitten out of the room while he worked. Not that he'd needed an excuse – he loved the little cat, as I well knew.
I'd smiled, and fetched him the biggest mug we had, topped up to the brim with strong coffee, plenty of milk, and extra sugar. He'd nodded at the side table and I'd placed it down, grabbing my phone from my

pocket, wanting to capture the look in his eyes of weariness, immense pride in what he'd achieved, and a fleeting touch of something else: vulnerability. I'd seen the real Jamie then and tapped, hoping the photo would capture what I saw.

Thanks, peach, he'd said, and I'd laughed.

You still owe me for that.

I won't forget. The warmth of his smile, barely there a moment before, had flowed around me and made me feel safe and protected.

But all I had left was the photo.

I lit the candle and started drawing cards. Not from my favourite deck, because it wasn't right for this, but from Archangel Power Tarot. Uriel had said I had to let Jamie go.

The first card out was The World, represented by Archangel Michael. It would keep spinning, but it'd never be the same. I uttered a soft invocation.

"Michael, great protector, please cut the cords of attachment between myself and Jamie. Thank you, and so it is."

The next card was Strength.

"Ariel, please give me the strength to get through this night and do what must be done, as the Divine wills it. Thank you, and so it is."

On and on I went, each card with a different archangel, until all fifteen archangels I worked with were laid out in a semi-circle around the photo and the candle. Most of the Major Arcana was out, and I knew that was unprecedented in itself, but the cost was incomparably high.

I could feel the room behind me filled with my guides,

my guardian angels, and other ethereal beings come to bear silent witness, as I sat all night in vigil, my eyes never wavering from the photo, while the candle burned lower.

It was time. The first fingers of pearly grey dawn were beginning to streak across the eastern sky, but I had never felt the world so dark. I had nothing left to give except one solitary tear that still clung tight to my cheek: my last gift to him before release. I scooped the tear up with my fingertip and touched it to Jamie's photo's mouth, then pressed my lips to the glass directly over his forehead.

"Goodbye, Jamie. Sleep well, dear friend." I murmured, and placed the photo gently, face-down, in the left-hand drawer of my desk.

And as I closed the drawer, on the photo and that part of my life, the pink candle's flame gave one last flickering sputter, and went out.

*** enable(altPOV) ***

Jamie was still at a loss over how he got back up to his room, white feather in hand. Lori had cut him to ribbons with her words, then stepped over him and disappeared without looking back. Jamie's shoulders still trembled on and off as he tried to process what had happened, the odd convulsive sob breaking free from his chest as he fought, and mostly failed, to regain his composure.

It was too late.

Too late to get his memories back, too late to find out what had happened, why the alcohol had shown up in his system when he was sure he hadn't had a drink.

Fuck.

Even with all this pressing on him, tearing him into fragments, he still needed answers. And that meant he had to call Rod. He didn't want to, with the messages that Lori had been getting, but there was no-one else to ask so he tapped Rod's number into his phone.

"Jay?"

"Yeah, hey Rod."

"Jamie, what sort of a fucking friend are you? I thought you'd call me after the weekend's fuck-awful performance to commiserate, but not a word."

"Yeah, about that..."

"I mean, I got shit-faced at the hotel, so it didn't really matter, but still."

"You didn't go home Sunday?"

"No, some dickhead had a crash on the M1 and caused hours' long tailbacks when they closed the road to recover the car, so I said fuck it and hit the bar."

Jamie was silent.

"Jay? You still there?"

"Yeah, man. It was me."

"What was you?"

"The—the accident. I'm the dickhead."

"Fuck!" Rod exclaimed. "Shit, mate, you OK? You weren't hurt, right? I mean, cars are really safe these days. You're not in hospital, are you?"

"No, not now." Jamie answered.

"Not *now*? What the fuck *happened*, man?" Rod sounded genuinely shocked, and Jamie wondered how this could be the same person sending creepy texts to Lori. He pushed the thought away.

"Nothing dreadful. Someone cut into my lane and I

swerved to avoid them. Came off the road. Police said I was lucky to walk away."

"So, what, you hit something? Did you roll the car?"

"Hit a few trees, set the airbags off. Probably would've rolled it if the trees hadn't been there."

"Fuck, man, sounds like you *were* lucky."

"Yeah, but there's a bit of a puzzle."

"What, false plates on the car that cut you up?"

Jamie was stunned. "How did you know that?" He heard his friend sigh at the other end in response.

"It's not uncommon, 'specially at weekends, so I've heard. Wankers go out, get tanked up, stick false plates on and go scaring the shit out of people for kicks. They'll kill someone one of these days."

"Christ..." Jamie rubbed his forehead carefully. "But that wasn't the only puzzle."

"I'll solve whatever it is," Rod said confidently. "You know I love a puzzle."

"Rod... did I have a drink while I was still there with you?"

"Hang on," It sounded like Rod turned his head away from the phone, calling to someone in the background. Jamie could just hear what he said.

"Yeah babe, it's my mate. I'll be with you in a sec."

Rod came back on the line. "Sorry man, got someone here and she's keen, y'know?"

"Yeah, I know it's late. Sorry. But do you remember if I had a drink?"

"What, you? You used to get pissed off getting IDed in the Students' Union bar, I remember that, but did you have a drink Sunday night? Dunno, man. I got ratted, can't remember shit." Rod paused. "Why?"

"The police said I had alcohol in my system. But I can't remember having a drink, amongst other things..."
"What other things?" Rod's voice sharpened a touch from his usual laid-back manner.
"Oh, where I live, who with, stuff like that. All normal for concussion, apparently."
"Concussion? So... what's the last thing you remember, then? Before the accident?"
"Nothing's come clear yet. I think we were talking, you and I, but I can't remember what about."
"Nor me, man. Soz. Anyway, I gotta go. Little blue pill's gonna kick in any minute, and the lass is already licking her lips ready for me. Glad you weren't badly hurt, mate. Laters!" Rod ended the call.
Leaving Jamie fuming that he still had no answers, and a vague uneasy feeling. He swore and banged his phone down onto the desk, catching the computer mouse with the corner. The mouse clicked, the monitor lit up, and Jamie was confronted with the video he'd found earlier, after his dream. He leaned forward, transfixed by the clip. Lori... the rear view... Sid and the towel... it was all there. And right near the end, video-Jamie called out after Lori *Perfect—*
Jamie in the present, actually remembering what came next, finished the sentence in unison with video-Jamie: "Peach."
And wept.
*

It was futile. He couldn't stay where everything was pulling at him, telling him how much of a fuck-up he was. How much hurt he'd caused, the devastation he'd inflicted. He needed an escape and his only possible

refuge was the office. He could escape into work, Tiger was already eager for his return. He texted his boss: *I'm going into the office Saturday early. Make sure security don't shoot me on arrival.*
Tiger texted back almost immediately: *Something up?*
Need some space.
Sure, man, whatever you want. I'm out on site until Weds, then it's the team catch-up meet at 1600. See you then.
Jamie couldn't wait to pack.
On Saturday, the train left Littlehampton before 6:00, with Jamie tucked into the corner of a carriage cradling a large coffee. It was barely-adequate quality that early in the morning, but it'd do until he could fire up the machine at work. He'd ruffled Sid's fur, fed him, and placed a gentle kiss on top of his head. Sid had sat on the table and blinked enormous green eyes at him, and Jamie hadn't been inclined to shoo him off like usual.
"You stay safe, OK?" he'd whispered to Sid, and emptied his coat pocket onto the table.
*** suspend(altPOV) ***

He'd left his keys. That meant...
I made my way slowly back to the bottom of the stairs, where he kept a packed bag in case he got called into work. I already knew in my heart what I'd find or, rather, not. Yes, the bag and his coat were gone. And even though my bedroom was right above the front door, he'd left quietly enough that I hadn't heard him. Maybe he hadn't wanted to wake me.
Maybe HE was the coward he'd called ME the other

day, and couldn't face what he'd done, the voice inside my head flared in defence.

I lowered myself to the bottom stair and tried to breathe. Archangel Uriel told me I had to let Jamie go, but I hadn't realised it'd be like this. I'd thought—I no longer knew what I thought.

Stupid girl, I threw at myself, *Did you really think he'd want to spend time with you ever again, when you accused him of destroying a part of himself by drink-driving and having an accident? He didn't even know how it happened, and you didn't give him the benefit of the doubt. You just cut him down. And you wonder why he's gone?*

The ritual from Thursday into Friday, for releasing Jamie, had been enacted. We'd gone our separate ways.

CHAPTER FIFTEEN

I must've sat there for a couple of hours, eyes unfocused, wondering what came next. Everything had been torn apart by one freak car accident. And I still couldn't see any path on which I could be happy again. Not truly carefree, happy like in the summer. Opening myself up enough to let someone into my life, even as a friend, still backfired. Every. Single. Time. Nothing had changed.

I couldn't help myself with that, but I could still help others. I had my work, my clients, and that had to be enough. I pulled myself up, rubbing my legs to get the blood flowing properly again, and heard the buzzing of a text from my pocket. Eagerly I grabbed at my phone, hoping against hope... and as quickly the hope dissipated. It was from Rod:

Hey Lori, how's Jamie doing? He's not answering his phone.

Last time that had happened, Jamie had been in the hospital.

I didn't really want to text Rod back. I didn't think a few days of him not texting me creepy stuff excused him, but Jamie was his friend. I struggled briefly between politeness and full-on ignore mode. Politeness won.

He's not here, I sent back.

Oh? Should I be worried?

It seemed like there was genuine concern behind the text. Reluctantly, I conceded that Jamie was probably as fine as he got, right then.

No, I sent, then added quickly, *Not yet.*

OK, LMK when he gets back.
I didn't bother answering, because I had no clue when that might be.
Sunday morning, around 8:30, Rod texted me again:
Hey Lori, heard anything yet?
No, I sent, and left it at that.
I had to get out of the house. I'd got so used to having Jamie around, even if he was working, that the silence was stifling me. I needed some time at the beach. To completely disconnect, to just exist in nature, with no expectations and no purpose. I hung Jamie's keys on the hook in the kitchen, checked my coat pocket for the single spare, put some food down for Sid, who'd disappeared, and left my phone on charge. There was no room to breathe within the walls of my house.
I eventually returned home after dark. Sid was pleased to see me, and I made a fuss of him, giving him supper, before reaching for my phone. One new message, from Rod:
Still nothing?
I knew he'd see I'd read it, but I didn't reply.
Another message came in:
Ghosting you too, huh? Thought you guys were close. That's gotta sting.
I hadn't seen or spoken to Jamie since Thursday evening, when I'd left him in the kitchen. I didn't know if he'd spoken to Rod or not, either to get information about last Sunday or to tell him to leave me alone. I wavered. Rod had no idea of the size of the hole left in me by following what Archangel Uriel had said, nor how much pain and regret it was rapidly filling with.
Don't go there, I typed, and my finger hovered over the

send button.
Courage, child, Uriel whispered in my ear, *Remember the Divine Plan,* and I gritted my teeth. I couldn't let Rod see how it was affecting me, and deleted my words.
I'm fine, I sent back, and switched off my phone.

*** enable(altPOV) ***
Jamie was at his desk on Monday morning before any of the rest of the team arrived. He had nowhere else, in between his hotel room and the office, that he needed or wanted to spend any time. His life outside of work had spiralled out of control, but he could still deal with this.
As the other guys and the occasional woman drifted in, they noted his presence. A couple waved, and one or two came over to clap him on the shoulder in greeting, or to exchange a few words. Jamie knew he was appreciated, and it eased his stress about everything else down a notch.
"'Bout time you came back," one of his workmates groused. "We've got a bitch of a job on and it needs your magic touch. It's been stalling us for over a week."
"Send me the link," Jamie offered, "And I'll get straight on it."
By lunchtime, he was up to his ears in code. A small knot of people watched from the other side of the office, chatting amongst themselves.
"How does he stay in the zone so long?"
"Dunno... Don't think he's got much of a home life."
"Have you seen how much coffee he drinks?"

"Who cares how he works his magic? We need it fixed and working by the end of the week. Tiger said the contract's on the line."

"Anyone spoken to him in the last three hours?"

"Barry tried – says he's like a bear with a sore head."

"He's probably *got* a sore head. You see that lump? It's from the accident..."

"Evie, pop out and get some doughnuts. I think we're all going to need the extra sugar to keep up."

The young intern grinned and headed for the stairs.

By four o'clock, the observers had changed, but Jamie's intense focus hadn't.

"I reckon Meg could walk past him naked and he wouldn't even notice!" someone said, and the busty redhead in question smirked, her gaze thoughtful.

There was one doughnut left from the box of twelve, and they discussed drawing straws for who'd take it to him.

Evie, her eyes dancing behind her thick glasses, squared her shoulders. "Interns get all the shit jobs, right? I'll do it."

"Go on, Evie! Good girl!"

"If you get him to eat it, I'll transfer you a day of my holiday!"

And as she walked away, the teasing banter quietened in anticipation.

"What's going on?" someone walking past whispered.

"Watch. Evie's going into the lion's den."

"God, she'll get mauled. Where's the first aid kit?"

Evie stopped by Jamie's elbow, doughnut box balanced on one hand, and tugged lightly at Jamie's sleeve. "J—Jamie?"

The entire office held its breath.
"Jamie?" she ventured again timidly, pulling a little harder.
"WHAT???" he exploded, and everyone else's faces mirrored the same collective 'oh shit' moment, followed by blurs of motion as people scrambled at top speed for their desks. Nobody wanted to see the intern actually get hurt. It'd only been meant as a bit of fun, but Evie was about to cop the fallout.
"We—we saved you a doughnut." And she laid the box on the desk, carefully away from his pages of scribbled notes.
He scowled at her as if she'd said something so thick that he couldn't understand. "What?"
"D—doughnut."
All the past week's frustrations, the unanswered questions, the physical pain, the emotional torment and agony, his lost sense of self, and his personal revulsion at how poorly he'd handled everything erupted at once. He burst out of his chair, looming over the startled tiny intern, and bellowed, "HOW FUCKING *DARE* YOU CALL ME A DOUGHNUT!"
Only after he'd said it did he notice her outstretched arm, pointing at the box.
Evie's mouth hung open in astonishment as the red rage faded from Jamie's face, and her eyes glistened with unshed tears. Jamie immediately recognised that if he didn't fix this right now he was going to be in deep shit when Tiger found out. He tried to arrange his face into a more pleasant expression, not quite creating anything better than tortured, then pointed to the vacant chair.

"Sit there. Touch nothing. I'll be right back."
Evie did as she was told, too intimidated to do anything else, and everyone else stayed far away, in case more shit hit the fan.
Jamie headed straight for one of the soundproofed offices they used when they had client calls or confidential meetings, closed the door and dropped the blinds. He didn't see Evie take off her glasses, give her eyes a quick swipe and put them back on, tucking her black short-bobbed hair behind her ear.
And luckily, no-one heard what he called himself, but it started with 'You stupid—'.
Five minutes later, looking much more composed, he returned. Evie was over the shock and sat with her hands in her lap, swinging the chair lightly. Jamie perched on the edge of the desk, right in front of her.
"Evie, I'm so sorry. That was completely out of line. Please forgive me." No excuses, no reasons, only a simple apology.
She lifted her chin with as much dignity as a twenty-two-year-old could have, when she barely reached his shoulder, and coolly replied, "I'll consider it."
"Is there anything I can do to make you consider it on a shorter time frame?"
"Hmm." She twisted her mouth to one side, deep in thought. "Well, maybe."
"What is it?"
"Show me what you're doing."
"I can't do that without the proper security clearance."
"Then get me it."
"Jesus, kid, you drive a hard bargain!"
She leaned forward with sudden incalculable maturity

on her youthful face and lowered her voice. "If you really want my forgiveness, you'll go a long way to get it."

Tiger's words from the other day floated back to him as an echo of Evie's: *You'll go to the ends of the earth...* They'd been discussing Lori, and Jamie's heart squeezed. But he had a twenty-something young woman to deal with, who was right in front of him and could end his career if she wanted.

"If clearance is granted, I'll do as you wish. Agreed?"

"And if not?"

Jamie spread his fingers. "Whatever's in my power to do." He offered his hand to seal the bargain, which Evie shook solemnly.

"Can I have tantrums like you when I grow up?" she asked with a cheeky grin, and Jamie chuckled under his breath.

"You've got a bloody nerve, Evie," he said, and abruptly became serious. "Don't lose that sharp edge, ever. You'll need it to get along in this industry."

And around the office, the whispers started: *What the hell happened there??*

*

By Tuesday mid-morning, Jamie had an answer for Evie. He didn't like it, but he understood the reasons. Christ knew what she was going to come up with instead, but he sought her out and found her at the shredder.

"Evie, you got a minute?" He waved her over to a quieter part of the office.

"What's up?" Evie looked up at Jamie, hands in her jeans pockets, completely casual.

“I can’t get you clearance for the project. I’m sorry.”
“Oh, I already know.”
“What?”
She shrugged with a lopsided grin. “I’m not permanent staff. I have an NDA, but not a locked-down tight contract like you do.”
Jamie blinked a few times in confusion. “So when did you know?”
“Before I asked you for it.”
“What? Why did you ask, if you already knew?”
“To buy myself some time to think up something sufficiently evil.” She laughed in imitation of an on-screen villain. “Mwahahahaha!”
Shit.
Jamie had no clue what was coming and he heaved a massive sigh.
“OK, what’s your evil retribution?”
Evie rubbed her hands together with glee and giggled before she dropped two words that made Jamie’s stomach nosedive into his shoes.
“Karaoke duet.”
*
Jamie was still focused on finding the error in the project Wednesday morning, but he had an added complication. The threat of the karaoke duet that night loomed as large over his head. And every time Evie went past his desk, whether with coffees or doughnuts or paperwork, she looked over and gave him a wink, or a little smirk.
But a bargain was a bargain, and no-one had forced him to offer it to her. He’d done it to save his own arse, sure, but he’d seen the way her eyes lit up when he was

talking about quantum harmonics, and she hung onto his every word. He even wondered if she had a bit of hero-worship and had wanted to show her he was human and accepted he made mistakes, then took action to fix them.

He also wanted to encourage her to look at the world differently. As somewhere you could ask for something and get it – or negotiate for a decent compromise. And he knew she'd gone through university on a bursary, like him. She had the potential and the slightly devious mind needed to succeed in the industry, and the setup they had was the perfect testing ground to see if she could hack it.

Lunchtime came and went, and this time there was no knot of people curious about how Jamie could stay in such intense focus for hours at a time. Everyone was way too busy making sure all the loose ends were tied up before Tiger came back into the office. And Jamie had no awareness of anything outside the project.

At two, he stopped for a pee break and a drink of water, frustrated that he still hadn't solved it. It wasn't that he hadn't been thorough – he'd been through every line with a fine-tooth comb. The code itself was fine, but something still didn't work.

He scrolled idly from top to bottom, bottom to top, back and forth repeatedly while he relaxed the focus of his eyes, letting his gut instinct come out to play. That was when he spotted something. A specific measurement seemed to jump off the screen at him. It should've been a quantum state, but it'd collapsed to an eigenstate – it was fixed when it should've been variable.

Something tickled inside Jamie's mind, and he shivered lightly. Yeah, definitely felt like it was the wrong state. He rubbed his eyes, feeling like they were full of sand, but he couldn't stop when it was possible he'd found the key.

Ten minutes later, Jamie's hunch had evolved into cautious excitement. He took a full backup in case he was wrong and waited for it to process, then tweaked the eigenstate to a variable. He ran it through once, watching everything it did, waiting to see if it broke. It didn't. Trying to keep things under the radar, he ran it again. Second time, also a pass.

Jamie clenched his fist under the desk and whispered, "Yes." It was a massive step forward. He could leave it to run on soak testing for a while, and perhaps grab something to eat. He looked up at the clock – ten to four.

Jammy little shit. Just in time for the meeting.

He followed the others into the meeting room, taking a seat near the window. As his eyes wandered round the room, he was struck by everyone's appearance. Evie was nervous, biting her thumbnail. Barry looked exhausted, and worry creased his forehead. Meg gazed out of the window, but flipped a pen over and over in her fingers. John was tapping his foot on the floor. Everybody looked tired. And there was an undercurrent of – he wasn't sure what. Indecision? Insecurity?

When had he started reading things like that about people?

Tiger walked in then, greeting everyone collectively and taking his seat at the top of the table.

"OK, people," he said, "Reports please."
The team updated him one at a time, while Jamie listened with half an ear, wondering if the program was still happy in test mode. He thought it would be, but he couldn't get up to check.
"Barry?" Tiger queried. "Any progress? You know Friday's the deadline, don't you?"
Barry shrugged. "I don't know. I handed it over to Jamie."
"And?"
Jamie wanted to drag it out, but couldn't hold back his grin. "Yeah, I think I found it. I've now had two full passes, and it's running the intensive test right now."
There was an outburst of comments, and Jamie felt the energy in the room rise to something more like relief.
"Does that mean we get the early implementation bonus?" Someone asked from the back. Tiger let a smile cross his face.
"As long as the soak test completes successfully, we'll go for install Friday morning. The deadline's Friday COB, so I'd say we can argue the toss for it – we'll be about eight hours ahead," he said. "Great news, Jamie. Well done. And welcome back."
"Thanks." Jamie allowed himself a sigh and stretched out his legs. It was going to be OK.
"And finally Evie," Tiger concluded. "You're approaching the end of your first three months now. How are you finding it?"
"Oh, it's great!" Evie enthused. "And Jamie's doing karaoke tonight."
"Really? That'll be a first. How did that come about?"

Every single pair of eyes in the room turned Jamie's way. He dropped his head into his hands and muttered "shit" under his breath.

Evie's eyes widened in horror, having realised what she'd done. "Well, uhh..." She swallowed hard, not knowing how to answer.

Jamie sighed and decided honesty was the best policy. He flashed a reassuring smile at Evie, who still looked like she wanted to crawl under the table. "I lost my rag with Evie when I was elbows-deep in code, I misunderstood something she said, and... I shouted at her. I apologised, but I thought the situation needed more than that and I wanted to make amends. An apology wasn't enough." He stopped and cleared his throat, knowing his next few words were going to cause him some embarrassment. "I couldn't give Evie her first choice of what she wanted, because it wasn't something I had control over. I said anything that I *could* do, I would. She chose karaoke."

The entire room broke into laughter, speculating what Evie would pick for Jamie to sing, but Tiger waved them into quietening down.

Jamie gave a rueful shrug. "I suppose I'm lucky, really. She could've asked me to run round the block in just my boxers."

Laughter pealed out again, and there was a high-spirited discussion of whether Jamie's boxers were suitable for public viewing. Under the cover of it, Tiger leaned forward intently, catching Jamie's eye. "And would you have done it?"

Jamie looked him squarely in the face. "To make things right, yes I would." And watched as Tiger sat back in his chair with a small, satisfied nod. It was like he'd passed a test of sorts.

"OK everyone, you've had enough of this place for one day," Tiger shouted above the racket. "Go home early, get your party frocks on. We'll be meeting in the bar at 7 for Jamie's karaoke debut. Remember it's midweek mocktails, so no alcohol allowed. Make sure your phones are charged. I get the feeling this is going to be epic."

Jamie rose with everyone else, but as he filed towards the door, Tiger waved a hand at him. "Not you, Jamie. Sit back down."

Oh shit, what now? He was barely starting to feel like himself again, like what he did mattered.

"Evie, shut the door behind you, please."

Jamie squeezed his eyes shut. This was not good. He heard Tiger take a chair nearer to him.

"Jamie, what actually happened?"

"What do you mean?" He looked at his boss.

Tiger's gesture was dismissive. "I know what you said to Evie, because a number of people informed me."

Great. Just what he needed. Jamie groaned, accompanying it with an eye roll.

"It's not what you think," Tiger said. "I've had people watching you all week, to see how you were doing. Making sure you were OK. So now, tell me, what actually happened? Because everything in the client call rooms gets recorded and reviewed, then deleted or flagged to me if it's of concern. You know that. And I know what you said in there."

"Yeah, I forgot about that. But I didn't want to take it out on Evie again so it was the only safe space I could

think of. I thought she was going to cry, and I've seen enough..." Jamie's words tailed off.
"Enough what?" Tiger prompted.
"Enough tears that I've caused lately," Jamie snapped. "Lori's one thing, but Evie's a kid. She didn't deserve that."
"Do you think Lori did?"
Tiger's question took Jamie aback, and he didn't have an answer ready.
"Maybe something to think about, lad." Tiger clapped him on the shoulder. "Come on, karaoke awaits."
Jamie wanted to lie, to say he had a headache, an upset stomach, anything to get out of it. But he'd made the agreement in good faith, and the only way past it was through.
*
Christ, the place was packed for a Wednesday. Jamie quailed. As well as the seventeen people on the team, including him, there were at least thirty others from the office. And everyone had a drink in their hands. Were they all drinking mocktails?
He spotted a sign above the corner where the karaoke equipment was being assembled, which read, "Are you brave enough to sing without Dutch courage? Sign up here!"
Evie sidled up to him and tucked her hand into the crook of his elbow. She nodded at the sign. "We're up second. I've got us a good one."
He noticed she wore a white rockabilly-style dress with thin red straps, covered in large red spots, but her usual black platform boots and black lace choker.
"You look great," he told her and watched her cheeks

flush. "What have you picked?"
"It's probably a bit early… but I wanted maximum impact."
"For…?"
"Well, no-one else is likely to be singing Christmas songs tonight. We're only just into November."
Jamie's knees weakened. "We're doing a Christmas song?" he asked in a croaky voice. She nodded, a bright smile crossing her face.
"Yeah, Mel and Kim, 'Rockin' Around The Christmas Tree'."
"As in, Mel Smith and Kim Wilde?" A Christmas staple on radio stations every year since its release the year before he was born. Fantastic.
"You know it, don't you." A challenge rose in her eyes. He nodded, with a resigned expression on his face.
"Good. Now, what are you drinking?"
It looked like he wasn't going to be let off the hook last minute. Shit. "You can get me an Espresso Martini. I'll need the caffeine."
"Coming right up… Oh good, it's starting. That means we're next!"
Jamie wanted to throw up. He never sang in front of people, only in the shower. He didn't think his voice was dreadful, but he was the only one listening to it. It was certainly scratchy sounding at the lower end, and he was better at mid-range notes. But he could only try.
"Evie," he hissed as she returned with his drink, "Are we done, after this?"
"Done?"
"Will you be happy I've made things up to you

enough?"
She lobbed him a cheeky grin. "Depends on your performance. I might make you go again if you're not putting in full effort."
"Christ..." Jamie was doomed.
But when it came to it, he gave it his all. In the instrumental middle part of the song he twirled Evie round at the ends of his fingers, and even grabbed her waist, swinging her up so he could bring her down again either side of him – although he drew the line at letting her legs go around him. By the end of the song, they could barely keep up with the lyrics, hamming it up for the rest of the team, and Jamie realised he was actually enjoying himself.
When was the last time he'd done that? The last week and a half had been almost constant torment and pain. He couldn't even cast his mind back far enough to find a happy memory. Even the peach video, validated as a memory, had assumed a faded quality since he'd left Littlehampton, as if it belonged to a previous life. Which, in a way, it did.
The cheers and whistles from his work friends as they left the mini stage felt so good, he took a quick bow. Then he leant down to murmur in Evie's ear.
"Are we good now?"
Her face was flushed and her eyes sparkled. "You're really good. You should do something on your own."
"But am I forgiven?"
She pretended to look serious for a moment. "Yeah. But don't do it again. It wasn't nice."
"I'm sorry."
"I accept. And... Jamie?"

"Yeah?"
"People care, y'know. What happened to you was horrible. I hope you get all your memories back, 'cause you deserve to be happy. Everyone does."
Jamie found a lump lodged in his throat, and he wasn't sure she heard the "thank you" he forced out past it, but she gave him a thumbs-up.
Just like that, the feisty intern had handed him back a piece of his self-respect.
"I can collect my bonus now!" she exclaimed.
"Your what?"
"My bonus. I can't get the same perks as the others looking out for you, but Tiger said he'd sort me out some cash. I can let him know I think you're coming back to us."
"Evie?"
"Yeah?" She turned back to where he'd paused.
"What did you read at uni?"
"Computer Science with a side of psychology. It's why Tiger took me on. No-one suspects the intern of being able to see the ins and outs of people's minds. That's a mahoosive secret, mind, so don't tell anyone." And she gave him a wink and disappeared to find Tiger.
Jamie followed more slowly, thinking, but the enthusiastic comments and praise from his workmates about his singing lifted his spirits a little more. And they'd been so happy that he'd cracked the project's minor problem, too. Right then, whatever else was going on, he belonged.
It seemed like karaoke was the thing for the team that evening. Evie went up by herself and sung "Teardrops on my Guitar" in a sweet little voice, a couple of the

guys did some rock stuff, but, funniest of them all, Tiger got up and did "Gangnam Style", including the iconic prancing dance moves. Jamie was laughing so hard that he nearly wet himself. Lori would've loved it. His mood popped like a bubble at the thought. He couldn't share it with her.

"Jamie," Meg, the redhead from reception, called from a couple of tables away, "I've got £20 here that says you don't have the guts to sing by yourself." And she waved the note at him, having already had a go at a Madonna track and mangled it.

"No, I'll pass thanks."

"How about fifty?"

"No." he growled.

"How much, then?"

"Yeah, go on Jamie, how much?" The others joined in.

"I've got a ton!" John called, and Jamie looked around at their eager faces. They supported him, and they deserved something back. Their confidence in his singing gave him a warm feeling, and the exultation of having cracked at least one of the problems in his life coalesced with it.

"OK, but I pick the song," came out of his mouth before he could stop it.

"Bloody hell," John said. "I didn't think you'd take me up on it!"

"Out of money?" Tiger grinned at him. "I'll sub you if Jamie does it."

Before he could bottle it, Jamie went and put his name down on the list. He'd find something to suit when it was his turn. And when the time came, he listened to his gut and allowed it to pick what he needed. He was familiar with the track it pointed out to him and thought he'd be able to fit his voice into it. He'd listened to it often enough after his last relationship had broken down in the way it had.

The backing track was queued up, and Jamie launched into a heartfelt version of "Forget You" by CeeLo Green and he got the rest of the team involved as well, letting them sing, or rather, shout, as most of them were doing, "Forget You" or "Fuck You" as they wished, while he stuck to the more polite version.

As Jamie left the stage, they rose as one, and mobbed him, all talking at the tops of their voices. Amidst the din, Meg whispered in his ear that she'd pay double the stake John had to wedge up, for a private performance.

And Jamie, more raw and vulnerable from the song and the lyrics than he'd expected to be, said yes.

It was a silent walk, Meg hurrying him along by the arm so no-one from the team saw them. Jamie had said his goodbyes and, although they'd pleaded with him to stay, he'd refused with a smile. He'd waited out of sight, already feeling like a thief in the night, for Meg, but as they walked Jamie sensed something else was not quite right.

She let them into her place, and Jamie hung up his coat where she pointed.

"Something to drink? I'm so glad we're done with those mocktails. I think I'd have made a better Madonna with half a bottle of wine in me."

"Thanks, but I'm not drinking alcohol at the moment. I'll have coffee if you have it."

Meg yawned. "Too late for coffee, I think. Well, if you

don't want a nightcap I hope you don't mind if I do."
"Go ahead." Jamie shrugged.
She poured a large glass of red wine and downed half of it in one gulp, then set it on a table. She looked Jamie up and down, lingering over his groin area, and moved closer.
"Well, here we are," she said in a sultry voice as she ran a finger down his chest, "I hope you don't mind if I don't pay you until afterwards."
Jamie managed a smile. "No, that's fine. I've already had to wait on how my performance was judged earlier. It seems to be the thing for me today – well, tonight."
"Ahh, Evie, bless her. I thought you did very well, throwing her around like that."
"You didn't think I could?"
"Oh... not that. Just that there might be a few bruises left after the accident."
"There are." His black eyes had faded down to yellow and green, but there was still a slight lump on his forehead.
"I meant ones I can't see – yet." Meg started to unbutton Jamie's shirt, keeping eye contact the whole time. "Well, don't just stand there. Kiss me."
He took her face between his hands and lowered his mouth to hers, kissing her lightly, but that wasn't what she wanted. She fisted her hand in his hair, sliding her other hand into his shirt and squeezing his nipple. Jamie kissed her harder, recognising that she wanted the thrust of tongues and clash of teeth, and felt himself detach. Yet he continued with what Meg wanted of him because it was easier than processing

anything.
She had his shirt fully open by then, and was working her way down his chest, nipping at his skin, her hands going lower to his belt. That was when he saw it.
“Is that a sex swing?”
Meg looked up from where she was tugging his belt undone. “What? Oh. Haven’t you seen one before?”
“No.”
“Well, that’s a shame. I thought you’d have been the type to try it out. You have to be pretty fit to get good motion in it. And flexible.” Meg’s smile was victorious as she finally got the belt undone and pulled it from the loops. “Let’s see how strong this is.” She pulled it apart between her hands, and the leather made a snapping noise. “I think it’ll do. This way.”
She had a surprisingly firm grip for a woman, Jamie found, as he was dragged through into a dimly lit room.
He was still struggling to get his head round the sex swing. Something about it was bothering him, nagging at his memory. A few words trickled through his head: *Maybe with the right partner,* said by a woman with a soft and distant voice.
He tried to chase the memory down, but Meg took advantage of his distraction and shoved him hard in the stomach. He fell backwards onto the bed, and she was astride him in a moment, her hands everywhere... including somewhere no woman had touched him in over two years.
Her rapacious groping slowed below his waist. “Hmm, it seems we have a bit of a problem. You do realise in order to earn what I promised, you’ll have to

perform?"
Jamie looked at her. He wasn't stupid, but things were definitely not happening down there.
"I know."
"Well, deal with the situation. I expect you hard and ready by the time I've finished my wine."
Jamie's brain scrambled for a solution as Meg sauntered out of the room, and he noted she was still fully dressed, while he was half-naked. The whole scenario was... off somehow. He should've had some sort of reaction because Meg was an attractive woman, yet... nothing. He didn't want to hurt her feelings, but equally he couldn't stay.
The sex swing creeped him out, and the dimly lit room he was in made him feel like it had revolving walls and there'd be manacles and other methods of restraint hanging on the other side. And as his dick wasn't cooperating, it gave him a decent excuse to leave.
He reached for his belt and walked back out to the main room, which was brighter but still felt uncomfortable. And as he fed his belt through the loops, seeing his bruised ribs, he had a brainwave.
"Sorry Meg," he said apologetically. "I was hoping everything would be fine, but the doctors did say after the concussion it might be a while before I could..."
Meg tutted. "That's disappointing. It's a shame you didn't mention it earlier, I would've got something in to help with it."
"It's hardly something I'm going to mention in front of work colleagues."
"It's not hard at all, Jamie, that's the issue. I thought you'd be a bit of fun, but you're boring me now. I hope

you're single and not letting some pretty woman down at home."
No, only himself right there and then. For not being able to get it up – and for lying to her about the reason.
Meg yawned and refilled her glass. "It's not the first time someone's been all sing and no shag. I guess I should be used to you men all being lacking in the bedroom department. Go on, get out. Shut the door behind you."
"Meg—I'm sorry—"
"I said OUT!" She threw the empty wine bottle at his head. Jamie, caught off-guard by her sudden mood change, didn't duck in time and the bottle hit him squarely on the lumpy bruise still on his forehead. The pain was incredible and he swore, grabbing the back of a chair to steady himself as dizziness swept over him. A full minute passed before he could snatch his shirt up from the floor.
"Jamie, I didn't mean—"
"Save it. Goodbye, Meg." He stormed out of the apartment into the chilly night, closing the door behind him as she'd asked. It was only when he was more than halfway back to the hotel that he was able to stop shaking. The lump still pounded, but the nausea had mostly receded, although it still came and went.
He had to find somewhere that had painkillers. He'd finished the ones from the hospital and had thought he was well enough not to need them when he left the coast. Clearly, he was wrong.
As he turned the corner towards the nearest all-night

pharmacy, he thought he heard footsteps, but looking back over his shoulder, no-one was there. He continued on, unnerved, his mind trying to remember the last time he'd got into trouble when he was out on his own.
It'd been about a year ago, in a different area of town. He could remember the phone snatch, the chase, the fall. The pain of the fractured wrist. The weeks off work and the rehab to get his wrist back to full strength after the operation. But he couldn't remember what he'd been looking at on his phone.
His head throbbed once, harder, and Jamie shook it. No, it didn't make him feel any better trying to grab for something that wouldn't come easily. He'd have to wait.
Distracted, he nearly walked into someone lurking at the edge of the dark cut-through he was using.
"Oh! Sorry." He peered into the gloom and recognised the face of a colleague. "Pete?"
"Hi Jamie."
"What are you doing here?"
"Having a piss, do you mind?" Except Pete wasn't having a piss, unless he was letting it run down his leg.
"C'mon, really? You want me to fall for that? Spit it out." Jamie grinned. "Wait, have you been *following* me?"
Pete heaved a loud sigh. "I used to be quieter. You weren't in there long."
Jamie went on his guard. "In where?" he asked, although his mind gave a guilty start.
"Don't shit me, Jamie. You were at Meg's."
"How'd you work that out?"

"You didn't see the look on her face when she left, like she had a new victim to play with. Want to talk about it?"

Jamie's mind flashed back to the apartment: the sex swing, the off-feeling of the dim room, his inability to get it up. "No thanks."

"Please yourself," Pete shrugged. "You're bleeding, though."

Jamie put his hand up to his forehead, touching stickiness.

"Did she throw something at you?"

A curt nod was as much response as Pete got.

"And you're still on your feet? Shit, man. You're lucky. She knocked me out and when I came to I was spreadeagled on the bed with a gag."

Jamie's skin crawled. His instincts had tried to protect him, knowing something wasn't right. Pete hadn't been so lucky.

"What happened?" The question came out before he could stop it.

"I was so scared I pissed myself. She threw me out, haven't spoken to her since. But I had to check on you, knowing her."

"Tiger's orders, keeping track of me?"

"No, man. He'd sack her if he knew. You're a mate and I saw her looking at you while you were on-stage. She's fine at work, but outside of it..." Pete shuddered. "Do yourself a favour, steer well clear."

"Thanks."

"No probs. So where are you headed?"

Jamie pointed. "The chemist, for some tablets."

"Did she offer you any?"

Jamie gave a short laugh to deflect a stab of unease. "No, I was OK until she threw a bottle at me. *Now* I have a headache."
Pete grinned. "Fair enough. Let's get your pain relief sorted. What time's your train?"
"My train?"
"Don't you live on the south coast?"
"I used to."
"Ah, OK. So you're in the hotel then."
"I'd have been safer if I'd stayed indoors."
"But Evie would've been devastated. She's still young, and she was so happy to get one over on you after Monday."
"Yeah... Wait, what makes me think you already knew about that?"
Pete winked as he opened the pharmacy door for Jamie. "She's my niece. I'll wait here for you."
*** suspend(altPOV) ***

CHAPTER SIXTEEN

31st October 2022

I switched my phone back on Monday morning. I didn't want to, because I didn't want any more messages from Rod, but I had to... just in case. I wanted to text Emily, but I didn't know if she knew that Jamie and I weren't speaking, and I wouldn't throw him under the bus with his own sister.

A message popped up: *Hey Lori, any news?*

Why didn't Rod leave me alone? He could get in touch with Jamie himself, couldn't he? Why he was using me as a go-between?

Jamie had left without saying goodbye or leaving a note, and I could understand that, but I didn't even know if he was alive. Did no-one except Rod and me know he'd disappeared?

Archangel Uriel's voice drifted into my head: *You must let him go...He has to move on.*

I tried to work. I really tried, but nothing would flow. None of the readings made sense. I kept hearing Jamie's voice in my head from when he was ranting at me about my "weird shit". I recalled every card I'd ever pulled for him. He'd even chosen my personal deck for his in-person reading. Didn't that count for something?

Apparently not.

My phone buzzed in the late afternoon. Rod:
Bet it's quiet...

Stupid bastard, of course it was quiet. I lived alone. Then it hit me – I lived *alone*. Jamie had gone.

And Rod *knew*.

I didn't answer, but across the evening my phone buzzed again with four separate messages:
Bet he didn't say goodbye.
Bet he didn't leave a note.
I'm sorry he treated you that way.
I'm here if you need to talk.
I had to turn my phone back off. It was enough to know that I'd caused it without rubbing my nose in it, too.
I had to issue a couple of refunds on Tuesday. My work on Monday hadn't been my best, and my clients knew it. I made no protest. I didn't offer to read for them again for free, just sent them their money back. It was the easiest thing to do.
A message came in:
Hey, I heard from Jamie today. He said keep feeding the cat, he doesn't know when he'll be back.
Like I'd ever mistreat Sid, but the fact that Rod had heard from Jamie, and I hadn't, stung. They'd been friends for years, but Jamie had lived here.
I messaged back a single word: *OK*
Wednesday was a week since the "weird shit" confrontation, and it was still ringing round in my head on and off. Every time I picked up the cards and tried to read them, it felt wrong. I hadn't been this unguided since Mother had gone, like my head was wrapped in cotton wool, and everything was deadened.
There were more refund requests. I put a note up on the website that said I wasn't taking any new bookings at that point, but I hoped to be back soon.
Rod didn't message me at all.
I had no-one to talk to. Not even the creepy guy who'd

sent me vile texts, although he'd been kinder the last few messages.

I didn't bother getting dressed on Thursday. Rod messaged me early:

Do you blame yourself for Jamie's absence?

Of course I did. But I didn't reply.

A few minutes later:

You shouldn't, you know. He's in the wrong here.

An hour passed, then:

He's letting you think it's your fault.

That hurt.

Friday, I spent most of the day in bed. I felt thick-headed, like I was coming down with something. I'd had a message first thing:

I didn't know he had it in him to be so cruel. I'm so sorry x

And in the evening:

I wish I could help you x

I left my phone downstairs that night. It was my only link to the outside world, but the further away from me it was, the better.

It was a week since Jamie had left. My world had shrunk to practically nothing, and I didn't even want to go to the beach. The angels seemed absent, too. I tried calling Jamie, but the call wouldn't connect, so there was no way to leave a message. What would I even say?

I guessed he'd moved on with his life, without any more drama from me. Maybe he'd heal, maybe he'd find answers. Silently, I wished him well. Saturday night TV was crap. I found the bottle of wine I'd bought the day I met Jamie for the first time and he'd been called away to work. I opened it, had one glass, and watched the rest pour down the sink.

Rod didn't text me.

Sunday morning, as I had my hands round a mug of instant soup, because the cupboards were looking empty, a message came in from Rod:

Hey Lori, hope you're feeling better. I gave you some space yesterday – I don't want you to think I'm trying to muscle in x

Then, a few hours later:

LMK you're OK, please? I'm worried about you x

I thought about it. I should tell him to leave me alone, because I wasn't OK. Or I could text back and say I *was* OK. But then he could call me a liar, which would've been true.

Damned if I did, damned if I didn't.

The week before, I'd been better able to project the image of being fine, and could tell that lie, but I no longer had it in me. So I did nothing at all, and didn't answer.

Monday morning. More messages in a similar vein:

I know you're hurting. You can talk to me xx

It doesn't have to be this way xx

Just reach out, I'm here for you any time xx

It was getting harder to ignore. I tried tuning into my guides and angels, but silence was the only sound.

Evening fell, and I'd spent all day on the sofa with Sid on my stomach. He hadn't left me alone, and I'd only moved to feed him and use the bathroom.

"You miss Jamie too, don't you, sweet boy?" I whispered, scratching behind his right ear. He laid his head on my chest, and his soft purr eased the tightness of my throat for a while, until my phone buzzed and Sid leapt off me as if affronted.

Lori, I'm hurting because you're hurting xx

I drew a shuddering breath, and turned my phone off.

*

I wanted to leave it off on Tuesday, but in the end I decided not to. There might be some sort of emergency I hadn't considered that I'd need to make a call for. I didn't expect any texts or other kinds of messages. Everyone else was getting on with their lives, so why wasn't I?

Simple answer: I couldn't. I was stuck in a deep pit with no ladder, and I couldn't even see daylight above me.

A message pinged in straight away:

You must be so lonely. Me too :(Talk to me, please xx

Later in the day:

This isn't like you. You don't normally hurt people, why are you doing it to me? :(

I didn't know any more. Why was I still keeping him at arm's length? It was obvious Jamie didn't care, but it seemed like Rod did. And he was right: I *was* lonely.

Wednesday lunchtime my phone buzzed. I knew who I expected it to be, and I wasn't surprised that it was Rod:

Hey Lori, I'm over your way on Friday. Let me pop over and make sure you're alright. Please? I don't need to come in. Just let me see you, to reassure myself xx

Two weeks previously, Jamie had called me a coward, and weak, and soft. Cowards ran away from their problems, and they didn't deal with them head-on. I'd

refuted it then, and I would again if I had to.
I wasn't a coward and, before I could second-guess myself, I messaged Rod back a single word: *OK*
Thursday trudged past. I couldn't settle to anything for long. My cards didn't want to shuffle, they were all sticking together in clumps. I couldn't be bothered to talk to them and find out why. They probably needed cleansing or something, but it didn't matter enough to do it.
I did some housework and had a shower, then deliberated what to wear the next day. Joggers and a hoodie, with a long-sleeved t-shirt underneath, would be fine. I had a fleeting sense of something not being right, but I couldn't put my finger on what it was before it vanished.
Right before I went to bed, Rod messaged me:
10am?
I should've said no. I should've said I'd changed my mind, because I didn't feel right about it. But I ignored my instinct and sent back a thumbs-up.
I didn't sleep much that night.
*
Rod was prompt. I could say that for him. A silver 4x4 pulled up in front of my car at two minutes to ten. I'd been hovering by the window, waiting, since quarter to. I felt sick. This was a bad idea. But I didn't have to let him in, did I?
As he got out of the car, I went to meet him at the front door.
"Hey Lori," he said with a tired smile. "How're you doing?"
"I'm OK," I said. "You look like you've not been

sleeping."
"I've been worried about you. How was I supposed to sleep? And you look exhausted."
Thanks for that. I didn't answer.
Rod yawned. "Sorry, I've been out and about for five hours already. I needed lots of coffee to get here on time."
I nodded. "So what got you out of the house at 5am?"
"Just some business I was doing at Worthing. It's done, so I'm on my way home."
I didn't know where he lived, and I wasn't interested enough to ask. "Oh."
"Look, I know I said I wouldn't come in, but would you mind if I used the bathroom? I could really do with... letting out some of this coffee."
I managed a frown. "I'd rather you didn't."
"That's not nice. After everything I've done for you this week? Checking on you, messaging you, telling you you're not alone. How many times has Jamie messaged you this week?"
I made no reply.
"Why *is* that, Lori? Can you guess?"
"Because he doesn't care."
"That's right, because he doesn't care. I *do* care. I'm right here, right now, as a *friend*. I've done everything I can for the last week to show you that I'm here for you. Is it really too much to ask?"
I sighed. He had a point. "I suppose not," I said, and stepped aside. "Up there, it's the first door you come to."
I watched him go up the stairs and open the door to the back bedroom, where all my cards and crystals

lived after their exile from the front room – courtesy of Jamie. “Not that one,” I called, and pointed to Rod’s left. “That one.”
“Thanks!”
I waited at the bottom of the stairs until he came back down.
“Better?”
“Much, thanks.” He stretched his arms behind his head. “You look really pale, though. Have you been eating enough?”
“Probably not.”
“You should go and have something. I wouldn’t want you to keel over.”
“Yeah, I will. After you’ve gone.”
“Ah c’mon Lori, I haven’t even been here five minutes. I need to know how you really are.”
I swayed a tiny amount on my feet, and he caught my elbow gently. “Where’s the kitchen? At least have a cup of tea if you’re not going to eat ’til later.”
I lowered my head. “It’s through here.”
“Do you want me to make it?”
“No it’s OK, you don’t know where anything is.” I watched him warily while the kettle boiled.
He looked round the entire room. “You done much to the house since you bought it? Looks like it’s still stuck in the last century.”
I bristled at his words. “A few things, but I was on a limited budget.”
“Ah, the tarot business. Does it pay well?”
“Well enough to keep going.” I raised a mug in query at him, but he shook his head, so I only made one for myself.

"You know, your life could be a lot easier if you wanted."

"Yeah, if I had more money."

He looked at me as if he was talking to a child. "I have money. I've worked with Tiger a few times, you know how well that pays."

"I'd rather pay my own way, thanks."

"And look where it's got you. You're alone in a family-sized house. I bet you thought you'd have a family by now, but you don't. You're not even seeing anyone."

I glanced away, and he took a step closer.

"You could have everything you wanted, if..." He stopped speaking and watched me for a moment.

"If?" God, why did I ask that? I didn't want to know his answer.

"If you were with me."

There it was, his cards on the table. That was why he was here.

He put a hand on my shoulder and squeezed lightly. "I'm not a bad bloke, Lori, you know that."

No, I didn't, and I shook my head slightly. The grip on my shoulder tightened.

"I think you'd find pretty quickly I'm better than Jamie. You'd always know where I was. I'd message you a few times a day. Send you gifts, buy you clothes, whatever you wanted. Jamie doesn't measure up – literally." And he held his thumb and index finger two inches apart at most.

A laugh sputtered out of my mouth. "Are you saying—" But I didn't get any further because he bent towards me and pressed his mouth against mine.

Ugh!

I didn't want that *at all* and shoved at his chest. "Let go of me!"
"Come on Lori, I thought you'd be happy to see me after I've driven all this way."
"Not happy enough to kiss you, no. You need to go now."
"But you invited me in. So maybe you want what I want."
"I doubt it."
"But you've been lonely. I've been lonely. It's comforting to have someone to talk to when you've been alone for... what, two weeks?" His thin smile chilled me. "It's a long time to be silent when you've lived with someone for five months."
I knew that but I lifted my chin, trying to act calm although my insides were behaving like a jelly at a kid's birthday party.
Jelly on a plate, jelly on a plate, wibble, wobble, wibble, wobble, jelly on a plate...
I wished I could go back to my childhood right then, to when my parents were still alive, years before my dad got ill. When we were happy. When I wasn't alone in a house with a man I barely knew, whose behaviour filled me with dread.
"I want you to leave. Now."
He shook his head and eyed me pityingly. "That's gratitude for you. OK then, I'll go. But you can kiss me goodbye."
"No bloody way!" I bared my teeth.
He grabbed my wrist. "I wasn't *asking*, I was *telling* you. Maybe you need persuading." He drove me back against the kitchen wall, one leg pinning me in place

while he mashed his lips against mine, trying to force his tongue between my clenched teeth.

I slapped at him with my free hand and caught the edge of his cheek with my fingertips, but he snatched my wrist out of the air before I could try again and transferred both of my wrists to his right hand, gripping them so tightly my fingers tingled through lack of blood flow.

"That was stupid," he said in a conversational tone, and backhanded me hard across the mouth and nose.

My knees gave out and he dropped me, then pushed me over with one foot before kicking me once in the ribs. I was too numb and uncomprehending to react.

Why has he done this?

"I expected better from you, Lori," he said, "But maybe you're just like all the others."

An odd jingling kind of noise sounded above my head as my vision swam and I struggled to hold it together.

He stalked out without another word, and as I heard the front door slam shut I brought my trembling fingers up to my mouth.

They came away bloody.

I didn't know how long I lay on the kitchen floor, too shaken and feeble to move, but eventually Sid came in through the cat flap and approached me. He sniffed round my mouth and nose and began to lick me clean.

I whimpered. His tongue was rough, and my lip was so raw I couldn't tolerate it.

"Just settle down with me, baby boy," I whispered, wondering why I wasn't crying. Then I realised: I was too afraid to make a noise in case Rod came back.

It felt like a few hours before I could wriggle into a

seated position. My ribs ached, my lip stung and my nose was crusty. I probably looked a mess. But as I oriented myself, I had a horrible revelation which closed my eyes as I tried to deny it, yet it was impossible.

I was in the exact place on the kitchen floor where Jamie had collapsed, barely two weeks before. Rod couldn't have kicked me as hard as that did. I wrapped my arms around my knees and rested my forehead on them.

Jamie... forgive me...

There was no point trying to do anything. I went round the house and made sure all the ground floor windows and doors were closed and locked, checking each one three times in case they'd somehow become unlocked the second I walked away.

I washed the blood from my face as gently as I could, surveying the damage in the bathroom mirror. My nose was still its normal shape, and I'd had fatter lips from falling in school playgrounds as a kid, but I'd never been struck across the face before.

And when I'd done all those things, I wandered around the house, picking things up and putting them down again until I wanted to scream at myself, but I stayed silent. The only noise came from my inner voice, which was stuck on repeat:

Should've seen it coming. Should've seen it coming. Should've seen it coming.

I did something that I rarely did because it made my head fuzzy and disrupted my intuition. But with that already lost to me, what harm could it do? I took two each of ibuprofen and paracetamol to try and ease my discomfort, and went to bed.

*

A few hours later, I woke. There was something wrong – I could sense it. What was it?

It still felt like night, but I could feel light falling on my eyelids. I cracked my eyes open, my mind still hazy from the painkillers I'd taken earlier. My bedside lamp was on. That's where the light was coming from. And Rod was standing by my bed, making some sort of rhythmic movement with his right arm.

"What are you doing?" I asked, my voice a little indistinct as I tried to clear my head.

"What—does—it—look—like?" Rod said, and I shut my eyes tight.

Oh God, that was gross! I realised what it was, but my brain didn't want to process it.

"How did you get in?"

"For—fuck's—sake—let—me—fin—ish—first!—Stu—pid—ques—tions!" Rod grunted through his release and I thought I was going to throw up. The noises he was making disgusted me, and I squeezed my eyes tighter shut. I didn't dare let go of the duvet in order to plug my ears. I was wearing pyjamas under the covers, but I didn't want to add fuel to his fire by letting him see them.

"Now, what shall I do with this?" Rod's voice neared, and something wet, warm, and sticky was smeared across my cheek. I froze, horrified and nauseated beyond anything I'd ever imagined.

"I've marked you. Now you're mine." he said in a smug tone.

You're sick.

I didn't realise my revolted thought had somehow become audible until he uttered a hollow laugh.

"Yeah maybe, maybe not. You should ask Jamie what his kink is. I like to twist things a little, that's all. You'll soon learn, and if you don't—" He let the sentence hang in the air. "Well, that's for next time. Anyway, I'll wash my hands and leave you to your thoughts."

As he left the room, he turned back. "By the way, I left something for you. It's in the back bedroom."

I didn't move. I couldn't. I couldn't say anything, shout, scream, or make any further noise. He'd stolen my ability to function with his chilling words:

That's for next time.

If I'd thought time had passed slowly after his first visit, it seemed like a lifetime before the front door closed with a bang. On silent feet, I dragged myself to the window, able to see well enough through the curtain, until the silver 4x4 drove away.

I flew down the stairs, the semen drying on my face like the most repulsive face mask you could ever think of. There was no sign of a forced entry. I had to check – were my keys still in my pocket? Where was the single spare? My brain stuttered to a halt. There was another set of keys that'd been hanging up in the kitchen, and I recalled the jingling noise from after he'd hit me.

Oh no!

I couldn't move fast enough to prove myself right, and as I clung to the kitchen door frame, my worst fear was confirmed.

Jamie's keys were missing.

The sight of the empty hook stole the air from my

lungs and the warmth from my blood, and I wondered whether I'd be able to get someone out to change all the locks before Rod came back.
But one thing was certain – I wouldn't be going back to bed.
*
On Saturday afternoon, I closed the door behind the locksmith with a sigh. I had new anti-bump, anti-pick, anti-snap locks on the front and back doors, and all three sets of keys were currently in my hand. It'd been hugely expensive to get it done the same day, but it was worth it a million times over for my peace of mind.
I tucked one set into my bra, hid one in my underwear drawer inside a box of ladies' things and debated what to do with the third. Jamie didn't need it. The smartest thing to do was leave it in the back door in case I needed to get out fast because the house was on fire.
That done, I could breathe for a moment, until I glanced at my phone. Rod had sent me a message:
Bet you dreamed about me last night xx
Then another:
Something came up, otherwise I'd be back with you already. See? I told you I'd always let you know where I was xx
Did Rod think I'd *enjoyed* what he'd done to me? He had absolutely no right to do something I wouldn't even allow a lover to do! I fumed as I paced back and forth in the hall. And did he really think I *belonged* to him, like a pair of shoes??
How the actual hell had I got into this? Why hadn't I followed Jamie's advice from a month ago? I didn't

even know, at that point, why I hadn't done it before, but I wasn't going to let anything dissuade me now.

I blocked Rod's number.

It was only then that it came back to me – he'd said he'd left me something. I dragged myself up the stairs, my heart pounding against my ribs like it was trying to flee, to avoid whatever was coming. Whatever it was, I knew in my gut that it'd be contemptible, and I braced myself before I opened the door to the back bedroom.

Every single one of my tarot and oracle cards were out of their boxes, scattered round the room like confetti. More than 5000 of my dearest friends were bent and crippled as if they'd been tortured, defiled, then discarded. The boxes had been ripped open in Rod's eagerness to remove the cards.

And as I crept further in on unsteady legs, I saw the wooden box that had housed my personal deck – the one which held all my secrets – smashed on the floor, its lid on the other side of the room. I faced the likelihood that its contents, too, had become a victim. I pivoted slowly, unable to believe someone had done this deliberately.

Then cards laid out on the table caught my attention and blood-curdling horror swept over me.

I didn't want to look, and a sob lodged itself in my throat, but I knew I had to. To honour my fallen friends.

Fifty three distinct versions of the Queen of Swords, my tarot significator, lay on the desk, each torn in half, and one—

Something inside me split apart, and ice flowed in to fill the gap.

The Queen of Swords from the Gilded Tarot, the deck I'd kept private and secret for thirteen years until Jamie had asked me to read with it for him, was in the middle. Untorn, but with the heart of the Queen cut out, and the card impaled on the wooden desk, through her throat, with a flick knife.

I moved around the room like an automaton, too overwhelmed and grief-stricken to do more than pick them all up. Kneeling, collecting, straightening, over and over again, until all the empty boxes and ruined cards were off the floor and placed with tender care into bags for recycling. I could never use them again after the abuse they'd suffered.

There'd been rare decks amongst my collection. Ones that had never made it into production, ones I'd commissioned, ones that had been hand-coloured by the artist. I couldn't even cry – the pain went too deep, to the innermost workings of my soul. I felt like the Gilded Tarot Queen, silenced by a knife through the throat, and my heart slashed out of my chest.

Half of my lifetime spent with them, and countless thousands of pounds gone, especially on the decks which hadn't made it into print. I was almost grateful that I'd never been able to stretch to anything really rare, because they would've met the same fate and there'd be fewer of those almost-lost-to-memory decks in existence. There were hardly any surviving as it was. That was the risk you took, though. One-of-a-kind items could never be replaced.

The rubbish bags were heavy and threatened to split open as I pulled them out of the back bedroom, so I fetched a clean shirt and manoeuvred it underneath.

Each bag felt as I imagined a dead body would, as it bumped down the stairs. It seemed entirely appropriate, as they no longer held the energy I'd lovingly poured into them over the years. They *were* dead – reduced to lifeless pieces of trees felled long ago.

But what could I do with the "murdered" Queens? They deserved a funeral pyre.

I had a fire pit I'd never used. It'd be ritually symbolic: the first use of the fire pit would be the last use of the Queens. An endless cycle of birth, life, death and rebirth. Archangel Uriel would've approved.

I set it alight with kindling I found in the shed, feeding each Queen's two halves in, one at a time, saving the Gilded Tarot Queen for last. I held her in my hands for a long moment while I studied her face for the final time, and pressed her to my heart to bid her farewell.

"Be free, my soul," I wept, and threw her into the flames. Her smoke enfolded me like a brief embrace, telling me she was leaving, then she was gone.

Taking Rod's knife from my pocket I turned it end over end above the dying heat, trying to cleanse his presence and ownership from it with the purity of fire, before making the tiniest cut on the end of my finger to bind it to me with a blood ritual.

I watched until the last flickers of flame extinguished, and the only things left were ash and desolation, then turned away to walk back through the kitchen, locking the door as I re-entered the house. I took the kitchen scissors from the drawer and hauled my feet up the stairs to the bathroom, closing the door.

As I stared at the bruised and abused reflection in the

mirror I wondered who she was without her cards, without her sense of self. No answers came, so I raised the scissors and hacked off her hair. Each chunk that fell into the sink felt like shearing away part of her identity, until it was all gone and there was nothing left.

I mourned my losses, fully alone, with none to see, and even fewer to care that Lori still breathed automatically, but life no longer pulsed through her.

As the evening drew in, I needed the healing power of sleep, but the memories of Rod's depravity were still too powerful in my bedroom. I bundled the duvet up in my arms to take it somewhere less tainted. Not downstairs, he'd been in the kitchen and Jamie had shouted at me about my 'weird shit' in the living room. Even though all the cards were gone, the memory of his contorted face in that moment lingered.

Not the back bedroom, because some of the smoke from the burning had seeped through the window and I could still smell it, and there wasn't enough space in the bathroom. And I wouldn't disturb Jamie's studio on the top floor, whether he ever came back or not. It almost felt like a shrine to something lost.

There was only one room I could realistically use, and it had nothing in it. No furniture, no storage boxes, no memories, nothing except plain walls and a neutral carpet. It was a blank slate. It'd do well enough. I wound the duvet round me, curled up next to the radiator for warmth because I was still chilled to my core, and was asleep in seconds.

*

I woke Sunday afternoon, my mind clouded with too

much sleep at once, and I shook myself free from the duvet. Poor Sid had to be starving, and I was chagrined to find a mouse tail in the kitchen when I went downstairs to feed him. Well, at least he'd found himself something to eat, but I sent up a prayer for the mouse and thanked it for giving up its life to keep my cat going while I slept.

I paused in the kitchen to drink something. My mouth was parched, and I could still taste the smoke of the previous day's pyre, but the water from the tap didn't quench my thirst so I chugged some milk directly from the bottle in the fridge, swallowing three times before I noticed it was sour. Hanging onto the edge of the sink, I brought it all back up, the bitter lumps passing through my mouth for a second time.

That hadn't been the smartest idea.

My phone notified me of an email. I frowned at it. Who'd be sending me an email on a Sunday evening? When I saw it was Jamie, I flew to my laptop in desperate hope that it might provide some resolution to how things had been left between us.

How wrong I was.

Thought you'd like this, the email title said, and I clicked it open.

Hey Lori, the body of the message said, *It's time you stopped playing with the tarot shit and followed something with a more sound financial business model. You need the extra money now I'm not living with you. It's been a while since we last spoke, so I thought I'd make it up to you and give you a helping hand to start. Have a look here.*

It contained a link to my website, with Jamie's name

below.
I was willing to overlook the 'tarot shit' comment if he really had attempted to help me, especially as I no longer had any cards, but when I clicked on the link and it redirected me to an OnlyFans page, I was confused.
It was called Lori's PENIS, which apparently stood for Private Entertainment and Naughty Image Services, according to the caption.
As I looked over the pictures, a seeping sense of horror flooded my body like an inexorable tide. Photo after photo, all with happy memories attached, imprinted themselves one by one on my vision then into my mind. And they were all... pornographic.
Not as I remembered them, on days out or in silly moments. But all doctored. Adulterated. Contaminated.
Depictions of me with semen on my bare breasts, with what looked like more semen dripping through my fingers into my open mouth, which had actually been a melted ice lolly that had slid off its stick, a picture of me being spanked as an animated GIF looping through again and again, spread-legged with my private area on full display, and even a graphic shot of three men taking me every which way they could, one man obviously buried halfway up my—oh God. And there was a video.
I closed my eyes for a moment, unsure if I could take any more, but knowing I had to see the worst he could throw at me. So I clicked on it, certain it'd be deepfaked.
I was right.

"Hi, I'm Lori!" it said in my voice. *"Want to book a call with me? Message me on the number below and we'll have a face-to-face session... with props."* The deepfake leaned closer to the camera, with plenty of cleavage on show – at least three cup sizes more than I had.
"I GUARANTEE you'll be satisfied. And if you're not? We'll do it again...and again... until you are. Your happy ending is my definition of good customer service. Thanks for 'coming' on my page. See you soon!" And "she" blew the camera a kiss.
It was my phone number below the video and I half-laughed in sheer disbelief.
Then messages started to ping up on my phone.
"Oh Jamie..." I whispered, as tears trickled down my cheeks. "What have you done?"
*

Jamie had torn my business and my reputation to shreds with the OnlyFans page. Rod had excised my self-identity and self-worth when he'd slaughtered my tarot and oracle friends.
I had nothing.
I was nothing.
And I couldn't see a way out.
I would never forgive Jamie for what he'd done.
As for Rod...
If he ever tried to touch me again, I'd find a permanent way out. And I had that dratted knife he'd left behind to do it with.
The clarity of the thought calmed me for a short while. I went back online, set up cat guardianship for Sid in the event of my passing, and printed out a DIY will. I

filled it in, put it on the kitchen table, and photographed it, uploading it to Jamie's and my shared pictures folder in the cloud. I had no-one to witness it, but it'd show what my intention had been: to leave my house and belongings to Cats Protection, to be sold for their funds, and to find Sid a new home. That done, something rose from the very depths of my being. I was incredulous that I still had any life in me after all that I'd been through, but there was no holding it back. A shriek ripped free from my soul, an unstoppable torrent of primal force and rage. I leapt to my feet and ran into the front room, still screaming, and snatched up the laptop. I had no control over my life, except in that one moment. I was going to make full use of it.

And I smashed the laptop against the wall, into a million pieces.

CHAPTER SEVENTEEN

14th November 2022

*** enable(altPOV) ***

Jamie was humming to himself as he strolled into work Monday morning.

"Morning everyone," he said in his usual way.

He was halfway across the floor to his desk before he realised anything was wrong. The normal Monday chit-chat about weekend doings had ceased, leaving a noticeable gap in the atmosphere. People were staring at him, and the way Meg glared at him made an unexpected tendril of concern tighten in his gut, Barry stood with his arms folded, John wouldn't look in his direction, and Evie, huddled within the circle of Pete's arms, looked like she'd been crying.

Jamie's steps slowed.

"What's going on?"

Tiger approached from one of the soundproof rooms.

"Jamie, follow me."

"I'll just—" Jamie jerked his thumb at his desk, but Tiger shook his head.

"No, bring your things. Now!"

Oh shit.

Jamie followed Tiger's silent stride back to the soundproof room, and Tiger closed the door behind him, dropping the blinds.

"Put your bag there," Tiger said curtly, and Jamie complied. "And your phone. And your access tag. Now step away from them."

"OK, what's this about?"

"Now present in the room are Tiger Kwon and Jamie

Brightfield. This is Tiger Kwon speaking. Jamie Brightfield, do you confirm that you are present in this room?"

Jamie was immediately wary and confused.

"Y—yes."

"You have the right to have someone with you during this interview, either a colleague or a trade union rep. Do you want either of those?"

He swallowed hard. He'd never faced anything like this before. And he still had no idea what was going on, but it sounded serious as shit. His mouth opened and closed a couple of times.

Who would he even ask?

He eventually forced a few words out. "No, thank you. I'll speak for myself."

"Jamie, do you accept that for this interview all our conversation is being recorded and will be reviewed by management and HR under UK Law, the UK Data Protection Act and GDPR Law?"

He nodded and then realised the recording wouldn't register that. "Yes."

Tiger continued. "All data collected during this interview will be processed according to official company policy and other legal requirements. A record of this conversation may be used in any subsequent disciplinary proceedings."

Disciplinary? Jamie's brain scrambled. *WHAT?*

"OK," he said in a solemn voice. Whatever it was, he'd face it. He wasn't afraid of taking responsibility for his mistakes, and he couldn't think of anything he'd done wrong.

Tiger sighed. "Jamie, you're being interviewed as part

of an investigation into allegations of transmission and distribution of explicit content via the company servers. The outcome of this investigation could result in disciplinary proceedings or immediate termination of your contract."

Explicit content? Jamie didn't even have any porn on his desktop PC at Lori's house. His audiobooks got him where he needed with that sort of thing. And possible termination?

Fuck.

His knees weakened. "Can I sit down?"

Tiger waved him into a chair.

"Is—is that why everyone was looking at me funny when I came in?"

"They all received the content in their emails when they logged on this morning. It's company-wide. And the women in particular are extremely distressed."

"I don't understand. How am I linked to it?"

"It's all come from your email address, Jamie."

"You think *I've* sent it?" Jamie was grateful he was already sitting down, because otherwise he'd have been on his backside on the floor.

Tiger shrugged. "I don't know what to think, Jamie. It seems so. That's why we're doing an investigation. IT are already looking into it."

"I wouldn't do something like this!"

"Well, maybe not. But the content is linked to you directly."

Jamie's blood ran cold. "How?"

"The images and video are of someone that none of us know personally. And I've only spoken to her once or twice, so I can't say whether or not this is her sort of

thing. But—" Tiger spread his hands.
"That's by the by. Until the investigation is concluded, you're suspended. You may not use company property, including your phone, your laptop, or your login credentials, and you may not stay on company premises. Security will escort you back to the hotel, and you'll collect your personal possessions. Then you're on your own."
Jamie's brain was still trying to catch up. "How—how many images? Three, four?" He needed numbers to cling to.
"Over a hundred."
The number meant nothing for a moment, then it landed with a punch. "WHAT??" Jamie launched to his feet, his hands fisted at his sides.
"Sit down. Right now. You have bigger problems than quantity here."
"I do?" He couldn't see how. What could be bigger than dismissal?
Tiger sighed again. "Yes, Jamie. Because unless the subject of the pictures can confirm she gave you permission to use them, the next people asking you questions won't be me or HR. It'll be the police."
"Why? Who are they of?"
"Lori Archer."
Jamie thought his heart had stopped for a moment, as the air turned suffocatingly thick, then he lowered his head into his hands. He was fucked. He wished he'd followed Tiger's advice and made amends with her before he left, but she wouldn't have given him the time of day. "Does—does everyone think I did it?"
"Pretty much." Tiger's cold expression wavered, then

returned to impassivity. "There are processes to follow with something like this, and we have to do it according to what the company handbook dictates."

"Is there anything you *can* tell me?"

"Not really, and I can't let you see the images because it might prejudice the investigation." Tiger leaned forward in his chair. "Jamie, if you have online storage for your pictures, do the smart thing and let IT have the link and any passwords. If there's a chance they can prove you didn't do it, you'd better take it."

*

The interview was over, and two burly security officers flanked Jamie to escort him off the premises. He was tall, but he felt dwarfed by them – and he knew they had concealed firearms. He kept his gaze firmly on the floor in front of his feet, because he didn't want to see the expressions of his co-workers.

"Jamie!"

He turned his head to see Evie struggling to get free of Pete's arms, but Pete was having none of it.

"No, Evie. Leave it!"

"Uncle Pete, I'm an adult. Let me speak to him."

"If your mother found out what he's done and knew I'd let you, she'd kill me! It's not worth it."

Evie stamped with all her weight on Pete's foot, and he was off balance for a moment, but it was long enough. She sprinted across the room and stopped right in front of Jamie.

"Tell me the truth," she demanded, her long dark eyelashes clumped together with moisture. "Did you send them? Because—" She gulped, "Because I don't think you did. But tell me honestly. I know I'm young, but I'm not naïve. And I don't see this in you."

Jamie's throat closed at her unexpected loyalty.

"Evie... I didn't. I swear."

"Good." She straightened her shoulders. "I've got some friends. They know about this sort of thing. I'll see if I can help IT prove your innocence."

"Evie, please stay out of it. I appreciate the offer, but—"

"Don't be stupid. I've *already* viewed the pictures. I know deepfakes when I see them." Evie smiled sadly. "By the way, your friend's beautiful. If I was a bit older I'd definitely do her, but I'm already with a special girl."

He almost had to pick his jaw up off the floor at the casual way Evie had outed herself.

Jamie didn't have enough thinking time on the train to Littlehampton, or at least it didn't feel like anywhere near enough. And his thoughts wouldn't go in a straight line either. They looped, darting in and out of one another, over and around until he was disoriented and tied in mental knots.

The images – over a hundred – were of Lori. And somehow it was his fault.

Evie thought they were deepfaked, and she'd seen them herself.

But how could anyone have got them to deepfake them?

Had they also gone to Lori and, if so, why?

He'd have to face her.

He'd tried to call her from a payphone before he got on the train, but it went to voicemail. He couldn't even warn her.

And it seemed the pulse in his head beat one word for the entire journey: her name.

Lori, Lori, Lori.

*** suspend(altPOV) ***

I'd had a rough night. I didn't really understand why Jamie would've done what he did, because generally he was fair-minded. Maybe I'd pushed him too far, and he'd found a way to get back at me. After two weeks of having time to stew over the injustices I'd dished out, he'd thought of a way to retaliate.

As if I hadn't already lost enough.

Maybe he knew all of that, via Rod, and wanted to drive the last nail in the coffin? I laughed bitterly. Good luck with that. I felt like chunks of my soul were missing, but I was still breathing. "I am in control of this moment" had become my mantra, although I stood on sanity's knife edge with bare, bloodied feet.

It was a grey and drizzly sort of day, but it didn't make any difference to me. I wasn't going anywhere and its glumness suited me.

The first knock sounded on the front door at about quarter to twelve. It was timorous rather than forceful, but I still wouldn't answer the door. There were another two knocks, and I made sure I'd locked the back door. I wouldn't be taken by surprise again.

A shadow passed the front window: tall, male-looking, unidentifiable from where I stood. Were they headed for the side path? The gate to the back garden was locked from the inside with a padlock, so the only way in was over the gate or the wall.

I couldn't even use my phone to call the police. Every

time I tried switching it on, it blew up with messages from OnlyFans sickos. And the broadband didn't have VoIP, because I'd had a usable mobile when it'd been installed.

I crept to the kitchen doorway, where I could peek out into the garden but couldn't be seen from outside, and watched in horror as a bag came over the wall then an arm followed it.

Jesus, this time he's prepared to break in!

Things weren't likely to go well, but I had my mobile in my left hand and the knife I'd claimed in my right. I could probably buy myself enough time with the phone, if I threw it well enough, to escape permanently, so I did the only sensible thing I could think of.

I hid.

*** enable(altPOV) ***

Jamie rubbed his nose, thinking, as he looked at the front door. If he'd been unsure of his welcome before, the changed locks confirmed it: Lori didn't want him anywhere near her. And he'd tried calling her again. He'd even bought a burner phone and Pay-As-You-Go SIM once he'd got to Littlehampton so that he wasn't incommunicado, in case it was caller ID that alerted her to him trying to reach her.

For fuck's sake!

What a shitty Monday it'd become! But Emily hadn't been an option. She'd crucify him for the suspension and not even let him explain he was innocent.

Lori would probably do the same, but his PC was inside and he had some research to do, on subjects like revenge porn sentences. He shuddered. How had things come to this?

Then clarity inserted itself into his thoughts – she might also know about the pictures, which made him feel sicker than anything so far: that she might've seen them – and believed he'd done it. He had to talk to her, to see if he could convince her it wasn't him. But how could he get in, if she wouldn't open the door?

He still couldn't get a call through to her phone. She could've been out, but the car was there and he thought he could hear the TV. Well, at least she hadn't smashed it. He was fond of that TV.

Maybe Lori was in the kitchen and hadn't heard the door. He could go round the back. He'd probably scare her, because she wasn't expecting him, but as long as she didn't hurt him immediately he might be OK. But the gate was locked.

Scrubbing at his hair, he assessed the wall. It wasn't too high – about six inches taller than him, so he could probably get over it. But his bag had to go first, as he couldn't quite recall what was on the other side. If it was a pond he'd hear a splash, and his bag had mostly clothes in it which could be washed.

The bag went over, and he listened for its landing. The soft thud meant it was probably safe, so he got an arm over the wall and scrambled up, keeping low in case the neighbours were watching.

Once in the garden he looked in through the kitchen window, but he couldn't see her. He tried the back door but it was locked. He wouldn't break the glass, because she'd make him pay for it, multiple times. What other options were there? Then he spotted the

cat flap, and an idea formed.
He couldn't get in through the cat flap, but if the key was on the inside and he could somehow turn it, he might gain entry that way. Without breaking anything. It'd mean lying on the ground for a while, but if he could find something of the right length, he could try. He pressed his face to the glass. Was that a key? He couldn't tell, but he remembered the hand mirror in his bag, which he used if he needed to shave when he was out. He fervently hoped it hadn't smashed as he'd put the bag over the wall but luck seemed to be with him in that, even if in nothing else.
He rummaged in the shed, grateful that it wasn't padlocked, and emerged with a dusty litter picker-type tool. He could turn the key with it – if there was a key. Jamie rolled his eyes at himself as he knelt at the back door, with his hand through the cat flap, trying to angle the mirror enough to see if there was a key in the lock.
There was. OK, he could try his trick. And as Jamie lay outside the door, his neck craning to see the mirror and getting progressively more sweaty, he laughed at himself. Certainly Lori would've laughed if she'd seen him going to these lengths. But what else could he do? In theory at least, he still lived here. So he was entitled to be inside, apart from the whole locks scenario. If she called the police on him, he'd be done for breaking and entering, as well as the potential revenge porn charges. And Jamie's efforts intensified – he needed to speak to her. Before more shit rained down on his head.
There was a click, followed by a rush of relief. He

extracted his arm, with the litter picker still in his hand, and went back for the mirror, which he tucked into his pocket. Gingerly, he tried the door handle and pushed it down. Cool, he was in. He needed a shower – he'd broken a heavy sweat stressing about everything.

"Lori?" he called, not seeing her in the kitchen or the hallway outside. The atmosphere of the house pinched him hard, and his gut told him something was wrong. He stopped dead and listened, his eyes scanning the kitchen, and drew a slow breath in through his nose. Something smelt off, and he followed the stench to the sink: spoilt milk. It was unlike Lori to leave it like that, and he ran hot water down the drain and squirted some washing-up liquid after it. That would do.

But he was more cautious, and the hairs on the back of his neck prickled. Something had happened in here, and it didn't feel like a good thing. "Lori?"

There was a piece of paper in the middle of the table. Jamie picked it up and scanned through it.

What the actual fuck?

Lori was only thirty four; why would she have written a will? No, she was likely a year older than that. He didn't know when her birthday was.

That struck him as peculiar in itself – they'd known each other for over a year, he'd lived here since before the middle of June, and he still didn't know her birthday. It was something else he needed to address, on top of the mountain of apologies that he owed. Because most of his memories, especially around Lori, had returned.

There were some things that hadn't come back, but they were fewer now than the things he *did* remember.

And if he could only get to his PC, he could try and get some more of the past back. But it was on the top floor, and his gut was telling him – even the atmosphere of the house was telling him, and he didn't remember having felt that before – that something was dreadfully wrong and dangerous here. He didn't know if the danger was to himself, or to Lori.

He decided against calling her again, but moved on tiptoe to the dining room, opening the door carefully, standing well back in case of nasty surprises. No, she didn't appear to be in there. The living room was next, and he'd been right. The TV was on, and Sid was asleep on the sofa. Jamie smiled and ran his hand along Sid's fur, waiting for the inevitable purr. Sid wouldn't be sleeping if there were colossal problems. But she didn't appear to be here either.

Jamie surveyed the room. Apart from the obvious missing tarot and oracle decks and all the crystals, which squeezed his heart painfully even as he knew himself responsible, there was something slightly off about the furniture. The armchairs were in their normal places from what he recalled, but there was something not quite right about the position of the sofa.

He closed his eyes for a moment to conjure up the room's picture in his mind. He turned it this way and that in his mind to check every angle, then caught something else. There'd been a tiny noise, like a stifled breath. Whoever was in here might be dangerous. But he had nowhere else to go, so he did the first thing that came to mind.

He met it head-on.

"Sorry, Sid," he said as he grasped the end of the sofa and swung it away from the wall.

He was unprepared for the screaming fury that came at him with a knife in one hand and a phone in the other. They battled for a moment and, through sheer instinct, Jamie managed to get his hand round her wrist. He hung on grimly, using fingers grown strong through fifteen years of constant computer use to make her drop the knife.

She cried out at the pain and collapsed to her knees. "No—don't—please—let me go—don't! Please! Don't—please—I can't—don't hurt—not again!" Her breath came in ragged gasps, making it hard to understand what she was saying.

And Jamie had to confront the realisation that the woman whose wrist he held so tightly was the one he needed to talk to.

Her hair was shorn ragged, and he could see a bruise across one cheek and a mark on her lower lip. His heart clutched then ached for her. "Lori..." He spoke softly and relaxed his grip a little. "What happened to you?"

Her head was lowered, and she shook it. "Don't. Don't pretend to care. You've destroyed me between you. There's nothing left now."

What the actual fuck did she mean? Jamie was speechless. He could see something had happened, but he had no explanation. "Lori, talk to me. Tell me what happened. Who did this?"

She sank closer to the floor. "Nothing. No-one."

He didn't buy it for a minute. Sure, she had her clumsy moments when she was tired or emotional, or Sid

tripped her up, but the marks on her weren't consistent with accidents. "Lori… I just want to help."
He almost didn't catch her reply; it was so quiet. "That's what he said too."
Jamie closed his eyes and realised he could hear two things in the room: her irregular breathing and the silent despair that went with it. His throat closed so tightly that he could only whisper, "What do you want me to do?"
"Get it over with."
"Get *what* over with?"
"You came back for something. Your final retribution, or to see what you'd wrought so you could gloat. Given the pictures, I'd expect—you know. So please… do it. I won't fight you. I'll—keep still, and—you can take… Then you can give me the knife back, and it'll be over."
Nausea hit Jamie like a tidal wave. She'd seen the pictures, and she believed he'd sent them. And his brain still hadn't connected what she expected him to do, but when it did, he couldn't hold in a quiet groan. *Christ!*
He couldn't even think about it. And what did she mean by it being over?
It was only as he looked everywhere in the room except at her, that he noticed the smashed laptop in the corner. "You broke your laptop?"
She uttered a brittle laugh, which chilled his blood. "What, you thought I'd just let it go? Didn't you think of the consequences before you set up the OnlyFans page?"
OnlyFans? This was getting worse by the second. "Lori, I don't understand."

"Good, that makes two of us. If you're here to—to take what you want from me, why are you still talking? I've had enough now." She sounded defeated, like there was no fight left in her.

As Jamie watched her chest rise and fall, he felt his heart break into jagged pieces. He slowly released her wrist, letting her sink to the floor, then moved away to a chair, making sure he picked up the knife. She still held her phone in the other hand, but Jamie could see it was off.

"I'm not here to do anything like that. I've been suspended from work. Everyone on the team got the photos this morning."

Lori shifted on the floor, her shirt rising a little, revealing a dark bruise on her ribs. "Bully for them. I got them last night. I've been replaying them in my head ever since. And the messages don't stop. I can't take it. Everything's in ashes. All I want is some peace, and now you've got my knife, I can't get it."

Jamie turned the knife over in his hands. "Where did you get this?" he asked, as his instinct tried to work out what to do with something of her words that jumped out. Ashes. He'd barely glanced at the fire pit in the garden, but maybe there was a clue there.

"It doesn't matter if you won't give it back."

"I don't suppose you'd believe me if I said I hadn't done it, and I didn't create them."

"I don't think it's safe to believe anything anyone tells me any more. It seems pretty much everybody lies. People say one thing and do the opposite. Everyone's only in it for their sordid, sick little perversions. And right now I don't know who's worse, you or him.

You've both done too much to me."

Jamie shook his head. "I've never hit you, nor would I. You used to know that, you *believed* that." He smiled sadly. "That's why it was so difficult when—Never mind, it doesn't matter now. But tell me about the ashes in the garden."

She rolled over, facing away. "I... can't. I can't talk about it." Her voice broke. "Your pictures destroyed my business, but what he did... destroyed me. Like I said, there's nothing of Lori left, just a body that's of no use to anyone."

Jamie knelt on the floor and placed a tentative hand on her back. She went rigid under his touch, and he took it away again. "I know it hurts," he said with compassion, "But please tell me. I want to understand."

"You can't," Lori was silent for a good few seconds, then, "Maybe you can. When you came round after the accident, and your memory was damaged, how did it feel?"

Jamie's breath caught. It was still so recent, and every day he woke up and could remember who he was, where he lived, and what he did was a blessing. "Like I'd lost myself."

She nodded. "Multiply that by over five thousand."

"I can't even comprehend that, Lori. Please explain."

"My cards. He let himself in Friday night, did something – I don't even want to tell you what. Then he said he'd left me something." She drew a long, shuddering breath. "I can't. I can't even say it. It hurts too much."

He couldn't help himself. He reached out to her again

and slowly rubbed her back. Not speaking, just empathising. And eventually, after a long while, he felt her soften a touch under his hand.

Apologies and explanations could wait. Right then, he had a friend going through a crisis. And he could do nothing, say nothing, to aid her. All he could do was be present. For a man of action, as Jamie often was, it was one of the hardest things he'd ever done.

He thumbed out a text with the other hand:

Hey Evie, it's Jamie. This is my new no. Pls text me when you can.

He would need some backup.

He'd thought Lori was asleep; she was so quiet next to him on the floor. But as he messaged backwards and forwards with Evie, trying to work out how best to help Lori without knowing what had happened, she fidgeted a little and spoke.

"Who are you texting?"

"A friend," Jamie said and, without thinking, added, "You'd like her, Lori. She's kind, funny and smart – and she makes me see myself differently. More clearly. She made me do karaoke."

"Oh." And Lori turned her head away, falling silent again.

*** suspend(altPOV) ***

My heart had taken on another ten tons of lead. He'd moved on with his life while I'd been living my nightmare. At some point, if she was the woman I'd seen in the cards for him, he'd move out. I'd be alone again.

And Rod would be waiting.

I struggled to my feet. I didn't know how many hours I'd been on the floor, with Jamie rubbing my back, but it was like the warmth in his touch had dissipated with his words.

I felt less likely to believe that he'd sent the pictures and set up the web page, but I'd been fooled before. When Rod had pretended he cared to get me to let my guard down, so he could strike. But it didn't seem to matter which way I turned; it was always wrong. The opening few lines of The Cure's lyrics from "Never Enough" roared through my head.

"I'm going for a bath," I told Jamie. He looked up briefly and nodded, then returned to his texting.

Deep in the bubble-covered water, with the intense vanilla-scented candles I preferred around the bath and red lights slowly fading in and out, I tried to ground myself. If Jamie moved out, I'd need to go straight to the police. Because Rod had taken something from me that couldn't be replaced and, for all I knew, was waiting until I was lulled into a false sense of security before making his next move.

And things could get so much worse, because losing my life didn't scare me any more. I'd accustomed myself to that possibility. No, far worse was the thought that Rod could do things to me and deprive me of the decision to leave it all behind.

There had to be a better way. I was still me, underneath it all, wasn't I? Did Lori still exist?

My mind became calm, and I relaxed. Yes, I was still inside me somewhere. And I had control over the moment. With a soft smile and a gentle sigh, I slid beneath the surface of the water and inhaled.

I surfaced again almost immediately, choking and trying to clear the water from my airways so I could breathe. I couldn't even get that right. What the hell was with *that*??

And between pained gasps and vomiting water, I almost saw the funny side.

*** enable(altPOV) ***

Single-minded focus could be a blessing or a curse, as Jamie had found out with Evie. He was so intent on working to find a solution with the limited phone in his hand that he was unaware of his surroundings. But Sid heard.

The cat lifted his head, waking from a sound sleep. There was an unusual noise, and he went to the door to listen. It was coming from upstairs. He returned to Jamie, still sitting on the floor, and nudged him hard.

"Hey buddy," Jamie said, not fully paying attention but giving him a brief stroke.

Sid was more attuned to Lori than any other living being at that point, and he did something he never had before – he bit Jamie.

"OW! What the fuck?" And Jamie got to his feet, chasing Sid out of the door. The cat shot up the stairs, and Jamie followed, more pissed off than in pain.

Then something unexpected reached his ears.

Lori was coughing her guts up.

In one long stride from the top of the stairs, he was at the bathroom door, rapping urgently. "Lori? You OK in there?"

She didn't answer. Jamie scowled and tried again, listening for words between her coughs and splutters.

"Lori? Is the door unlocked? Can I come in?"
She made some sort of reply, but Jamie didn't understand what it was.
"I didn't get that. I'm coming in, OK? If that's not what you wanted you can kill me afterwards." He'd started to learn how to respect her boundaries, the more he recalled of his life before the accident. He hoped he was going to survive, if he was crossing another boundary with her, and he swung the door open enough to go in.
He found her covered in bubbles and spitting water as she clung tightly to the edge of the bath, where most of her was still submerged.
"I said, can you get me a towel?" she wheezed.
Jamie complied, and she waited until he held one up for her before she rose from the water. He closed his eyes to preserve her modesty. He'd reacted strongly enough to the whole incident with Sid back in August. It wouldn't be appropriate for something to come up right then.
"What happened?"
"I slipped under."
He narrowed his eyes as he thought, aware of her fragility. He wasn't sure if he should ask, but he did. "On purpose?"
Lori glanced at him, then away, and he had his answer. He smiled sadly at her. "This isn't the Lori I know," he told her in a soft voice. "She's a fighter. Lori never gives up, and she knows what she's doing with her life. She's not... self-destructive."
A soft sigh issued from her lips. "That Lori doesn't exist any more. I keep trying to tell you that. The Lori

you left behind when you ran away to London to escape her cruel words has been obliterated. Wiped off the face of the earth. She's never coming back."

She thought he'd run from *her*? Jamie bowed his head. It'd been so hard trying to fit into a life that hadn't felt like his own, because he couldn't remember it, and the only part he could recall, could control, was his work. He hadn't tried to explain because he thought she wouldn't listen. And something had occurred in his absence that had shattered her.

"Lori, what happened while I wasn't here?"

She shook her head, water dripping down her face. "I can't tell you. Too many things. But you can see some for yourself. Just go – in there." And she jerked her thumb towards the back bedroom.

Jamie, recognising that it was a crucial piece of the last two and a half weeks, crossed the landing and opened the door. It was empty, totally gutted of all her tarot decks and oracle cards, but Jamie could've sworn the distant screams of over five thousand lost souls shivered in the air. He returned to the bathroom, pale and with his hands fisted, and Lori looked up at him, sharing a glimpse of what had happened in her agonised eyes.

"You see, Jamie?" she told him, a catch in her voice. "Wherever this thing with your friend goes, please remember: if you let someone in, they have the power to destroy you. I learnt too late."

*** suspend(altPOV) ***

CHAPTER EIGHTEEN

*** enable(altPOV) ***
Jamie had spent an uncomfortable night, restless in his own bed. He'd forgotten how it all felt – or he'd shut it out – while he was at the hotel. And he'd been up very late, researching what the worst-case scenario was with everything. He'd heard nothing regarding the investigation, but it was barely 24 hours since that had all started, so it wasn't overdue. Yet he still had a gnawing sickness in his stomach when he pushed himself out of bed. He showered and dragged on clean clothes before he was dry, leaving them sticking to his skin and feeling like they didn't fit.

He made his way down the stairs, the smell of coffee drawing him onwards at a faster pace, to find Lori in the kitchen – wearing the same towel as the night before. Undeniable relief at the fact that she was still breathing flooded him. If she'd been intent on ending it she could've done it overnight, and he'd have been none the wiser until the morning. A trickle of anguish ran down his back at that thought.

"There's no milk, but I've got whitener if you want, or you're stuck with it black. Your choice."

"Whitener's fine, thanks," he answered, watching her spooning sugar into the two mugs. Her hand wasn't quite steady. "You'll need to get dressed. My friend Evie will be here about ten."

The sugar crashed to the floor, spilling everywhere, and Lori's gaze turned to something on the wall. Jamie's eyes followed hers but didn't know what she was looking at.

"I can't." She turned enormous eyes in a suddenly pale face towards him, and he offered her a reassuring smile before he fetched the dustpan and brush to sweep up the sugar.
"She's not scary, Lori. I meant it when I said you'd like her," he told her, looking up at her from the floor with kind eyes.
"Not that," Lori whispered. "I can't—go in my bedroom."
Jamie was on his feet before he'd even thought about it, but felt like he'd been punched when she flinched back. Seeing her fear, he tried hard to calm himself. He was desperate to know everything that had gone on, but maybe it was impossible to tell him all at once. It was like a jigsaw puzzle he couldn't see the picture of, that he was only being given one piece at a time, and he was trying to complete it in the dark.
He struggled with his mounting frustration, his inner knowing of something that had happened separate from the cards, and his urge to smash the entire kitchen to pieces to try and break through to her. None of those things would help her right then.
He took a deep breath. In, out. And again. In, out. And when he spoke to her, his words were gentle. "OK, I'll get you clothes. What do you want to wear?"
He received Lori's instructions, and he had an excellent memory for specifics, but he wasn't expecting the emotional surge that hit him as he put his hand on the doorknob. If he closed his eyes, he could picture the room from the last time he'd been outside it like this: Lori lying asleep on the bed, with a tear-streaked face. He'd probably caused those tears, but he put the

thought aside. There was a job to do.
She'd said to get the blue sweatshirt from the hanger in the left-hand wardrobe section, and a t-shirt and joggers from the shelves beneath. Then Jamie's brain ran into a roadblock.
She'd want underwear, too, which meant he had to find which drawer it was in. And handle the items, which seemed almost intrusive, even though he had permission.
He had a few false starts before getting the right one, including finding a photo of himself face down in one of the desk drawers. He studied it, smiling. That was the last big breakthrough he'd had on the quantum harmonics project, a couple of months back. He replaced the photo and closed that drawer.
He took a couple of steps back and looked at the storage in the room. Where would she keep things like underwear? But as the end of the bed touched behind his knees, he turned slowly, frowning. Something wasn't right: there was no duvet on the bed.
She wasn't sleeping in the room. His hunch whispered it was because an event had violated her safe space, and it struck Jamie anew how fragile, isolated, and alone Lori must've been feeling. It had to be grim, whatever had gone on.
Focus, Jamie. If she wants you to know, it'll be in HER time, not yours.
He caught sight of something bright and knew he'd found the right drawer. A tiny corner of shocking pink stuck out. As he pulled it open, a party popper of memories hit him deep in the chest and exploded. The emerald green set, from when she'd done six readings

in a row, sitting tense at her laptop for five hours, and the back massage he'd given that'd left him aching with desire. His own favourite orange set, which he'd taunted her with on a laundry day and she'd fled through sheer embarrassment. He chuckled, his fingers sliding over the silks and satins and cottons. The candy floss pink sleep set she'd been wearing the first time he'd gone to the model yacht racing at Poole, to meet Rod in the spring. And the thought of him brought Jamie to an abrupt halt.

Rod had been sending Lori texts, ones that were far from innocent. They'd got worse after Three Tumps, when Jamie specifically told Rod to stop. He finally remembered it. Rod had been dismissive, asking what it was to Jamie, unless he was screwing her himself. And Rod had found out about the accident when Jamie had called him late on the following Thursday, so he knew about the memory loss – Jamie had revealed it himself.

His departure had left Lori exposed.

His breathing accelerated, his vision blurring, while his fingers furled tightly around a light blue camisole top with a lace edging.

If it turned out that—

Lori's voice floated up the stairs. "I'm getting cold down here!"

He shoved his thoughts aside. Her welfare was way more important right then. He handed her the clothing, including a flowered bra and brief set he'd snatched up when she'd called him. She smiled her thanks, a bare glimmer, and he politely turned his back.

"Jamie?"
"What?" He clenched his jaw at the rage he was trying to suppress.
"Can you help me please? I can't do it," Then in a lower voice, "My wrists are hurting."
He whirled to find Lori with her back to him but looking anxiously over her shoulder, while she struggled to get her bra done up. She already had the briefs and joggers on. He took the ends from her and noted the livid bruises on her wrists that were causing her grief, amongst other things. He hooked the fastenings before trailing a slow finger down her spine, and her light cream skin pebbled as she shivered.
"Jamie, seriously?" Her exasperated tone thumped him over the head – she hadn't been that much like herself since before the accident. Then the doorbell rang, and Lori pulled the rest of her clothes on.
Evie had arrived.
*** suspend(altPOV) ***

I didn't know what I expected in Evie, from Jamie's description of her character, but I was astonished at the petite, black-haired, bespectacled young woman that he introduced me to. If she was his special friend, she didn't match what I'd read for him in the tarot. If I could get it that spectacularly wrong, maybe Rod had done me a favour with the card decks.
"Lori, I need to do some shopping. Sid's nearly out of his special treats, and I don't know how long it'll be before I'm summoned back to the office for a reckoning, so we're going to need a few days' worth of meals. I'm happy to cook. Is that alright? May I take a

key?"
I murmured my assent, and Evie and I regarded each other. There was awkwardness after Jamie left the room, and we didn't speak until the front door closed behind him. I tried to smile.
"I don't really know why Jamie's asked you here, Evie. He just said you're a friend of his."
She rolled her eyes. "He's not always great at explaining himself, is he? He felt it might help you to talk to another woman."
Then she smiled and reached into her backpack.
"I have these to share with you," she said, showing me a microwave carton with what looked like cakes in it, "But I understand if you're too wary to trust me."
She saw right to the heart of the problem straight away. I knew immediately why Jamie said she made him see himself more clearly.
"Maybe later."
"Chocolate's supposed to make everything better. Even this." She reached over and squeezed my hand for a moment, then started the story of how Jamie ended up doing karaoke. I watched and listened, marvelling at how wide open she was. And the more she talked, the more I felt it was safe to trust her.
I shook myself. I'd trusted before, and it'd directed me up shit creek, but Evie was female, and Jamie's friend. Then I clenched my fists – Rod was also Jamie's friend.
Evie tilted her head to one side, a small crinkle of puzzlement between her brows.
"What triggered that?"
"Nothing." I sat back, feeling idiotic. Stupid reactions.

Evie shook her head.
"You might pull that on Jamie, but not me. That's not a 'nothing' response, Lori."
I tried to straighten my fingers. "It'll pass. How did you and Jamie meet?"
"At work, about three months ago."
"Oh."
So he'd known her all this time and my joyous summer, when I thought we'd become so close, had been an illusion. Maybe I wasn't even a friend. I was only the woman he rented a room from.
Rod had been right.
I hated that. A breath escaped from between my teeth that was more like a hiss. Evie leaned forward, her expression intent.
"I know that look," she said. "My sister went through something a couple of years back. Want to tell me about yours?"
"No."
"OK, fair enough. How about some bonding over brownies?"
"Are those my only two options?"
She laughed. "I'm sure you can think of more, but these will do for now. Heads or tails? Heads you spill your guts, or tails we eat the brownies."
Unexpectedly, I laughed with her.
"Can I use your nuker? They always taste better warm."
I waved Evie towards the kitchen and microwave, and she was back quickly with the container and two plates.
"I raided the cupboards for these, 'cause they're too

hot to pick up right now. And forks."
I mentally scratched my head. How was I OK with her rifling my stuff? But the more I thought about it, the more I understood: if Jamie liked her enough to be a special friend, then he trusted her implicitly. And he was usually a smart man – apart from the recent doughnut incident.
God, I hoped I wasn't making more mistakes on top of the others.
"Right, I need to warn you now," Evie said solemnly. "These are weed brownies."
Weed brownies? What the hell? But Evie seemed so... normal. I mentally smacked myself round the head. It could be normal. Lots of people benefited from medical marijuana. Some countries in the world had legalised it completely. I looked at her with a raised brow.
"What'll it do?"
"Ever tried weed before?"
I shook my head. I'd barely even tried a cigarette in my teens.
"OK I won't go into all the ins and outs because you don't need to know that. It will do nothing for the first hour or so. Then it's likely to make your words run like water out of your mouth, you'll feel like your body might never move again and you're probably going to get the giggles. And the other side – the comedown. You'll want to eat everything in the house, and you might sleep for a week."
I exhaled hard. "I could do with some decent sleep right now."
"One more thing."

I waited for her to continue.
"Jamie doesn't know I've got them. This is your choice, Lori. I can talk you through what's happened, try and get some external feedback for it that isn't so deep down your throat that you want to throw up. Take a step back, maybe, then go on with your life."
"Who the hell are you? Really, Evie. Please don't lie to me."
Her eyes widened behind her glasses. "I don't lie to people. Ever. Because how does that build trust?" She crossed her booted feet on the small table within her reach. "Everyone is a living puzzle to me. Not to be solved, but to observe and experience and internalise. I grow from each encounter. And some people I meet are the rare ones. Ones who've been through some shit and need a little nudge onto the healing path." She grinned at me. "And don't try to say you don't know about that. I know what you do for a living."
I corrected her. "I did. Until... things happened."
"Ahhh." Evie nodded. "The hair hack. Which culture inspired you?"
"I have no idea," I answered with a shake of my head. I hadn't even given it a thought. It'd been the right thing to do, that was all. And my brain was struggling to keep up with Evie's directional changes.
Evie narrowed her eyes to scrutinise me. "Probably got a Lakota guide coming in to help you through this. I have ancestors in that tribe."
"They don't talk to me any more." I looked at my nails, avoiding her gaze.
"Bet you shut them out first."
How had she seen that?

"Seriously, Evie, who the hell are you?"
She gave what I expected would be a typical wink for her – cheeky and disarming. No shock, it worked on me too.
"The intern at Jamie's work. I act like an intern, I fetch the coffee and doughnuts and do all the shit errands no-one can be arsed with, and I keep my eyes and ears open. In the evening I report directly to Tiger if I have something to tell him. My Computer Science degree and a hefty chunk of a second degree in psychology means I'm a useful asset."
Her face turned serious. "I'm studying grief and trauma counselling at night school, which nobody knows *at all,* so that's my sister-secret-sharing with you. So you're gonna need to share a secret in return. And I'm twenty two, because I know that's the next question you're gonna ask." She sat back in the chair and took a big bite of brownie. "Mmmm, this is so good. You're missing out."
"Am I just a case study to you, then?" I asked, a bitter tone to my voice.
"No, Lori, you're a friend in the making. Now, are you going to let me in or not?"
"I don't know if I can, but I'll try."

*** enable(altPOV) ***
Jamie returned to find the house quiet. Peaceful, almost, like the clean air after lightning. He carried the shopping through to the kitchen and began putting things away until he heard the living room door open and close again, and watched Evie walk through, glasses in hand, wiping her eyes.

"Evie!"
She waved him off. "It's not for me, I'm fine. But Lori's been through a lot. And I'm amazed she's still fighting to be here," She pulled her shoulders back, looking more mature than her years. "Jamie, do you realise she's lost every single person she's ever cared about?"
"I knew about her parents, but—" He shrugged. "Not the rest. And she didn't lose me."
"Yes, she did, although it wasn't your fault you forgot her. And," Evie paused, "I know this is tied up tight with her beliefs and I don't know what you think about all that sort of stuff, but I'm going to throw it out there. She said Archangel Uriel told her she had to let you go because you needed to walk a different path."
Jamie wanted to laugh, but remembered the white feather he'd found next to him on the kitchen floor after he'd collapsed. Sudden chills slid down his arms.
Evie hadn't finished. "And what did you think you were doing, letting her think you and I were a couple?"
"I didn't... did I?"
"You told her about me and said I was a friend, and you gave her just enough information to let her think the wrong thing. You'll have to straighten that shit out yourself."
She grinned and then sobered. "Good luck with that. But I can tell you, she's utterly terrified of being here by herself right now. She thinks he's waiting, and will come back to do something else. And when she saw your bag come over the wall, she thought it was him."
"How did he get in before?"
"The first time, she let him."
"Of all the stupid—"

"Cool it, Jamie. Have some compassion here!" Evie gentled her voice. "She'd already lost everyone important to her. It was easy for someone to prey on that, to manipulate her, to gaslight her into thinking he cared when no-one else did."
He nodded, accepting that but hating it, and Lori's words came back to him: *Don't pretend you care.*
"And after that?"
"He let himself in."
"How? No-one else had keys that I know of."
"He took yours."
Jamie doubled over as if someone had punched him in the gut, and Evie grabbed his arm. "Sit down quick before you pass out. You've gone white as a sheet." She folded her hands round his face and forced him to meet her eyes. "Don't think for a moment that this is your fault. There's some sick bastard out there that's brought our Lori so low she's barely functioning. Don't waste time on guilt. We need to help her first, *then* find him."
Jamie nodded. He loved the way Evie thought of Lori as theirs. This firecracker, so full of vitality and essential *life spark,* would be good for Lori to get to know. "What happens now?"
"Forensics. Like on the TV." Evie's eyes gleamed. "I know what Lori said, but we probably need proof." She made to leave the room, but Jamie caught her arm.
"Evie, how bad was it?"
"It could've been a lot worse. Go sit with her. I left her asleep." And Evie shooed him with her hands. "Oh, and Jamie?"
He turned back.

"I think you'd better paint over this, or at least wash it off," And she gestured to the mark on the wall that Jamie knew had held Lori's attention that morning. "She's going to be reminded every time she sees it. It's at her eye level."

"What is it?"

"Her blood."

Fifteen minutes later, Evie was back and beckoned Jamie out of the living room, her expression stony.

"Did you find anything?" Jamie kept his voice low.

"I need to ask you two very personal questions. May I?"

Jamie chuckled low that Evie had even asked his permission. Normally, she went straight in with the direct attack. He gulped. He didn't want to think about attacks. Verbal assault. No, that wasn't any better. He gave up. "Ask me anything."

"Have you and Lori ever been together?"

"No." Only once in his head, and that didn't count.

"That was the easy one, Jamie. This one's harder. Don't think that I'll think less of you if you say yes, but I need to know. Have you ever been in her room when she wasn't here and—" She gestured with her hand and wrist.

"Christ, no! I'd never do that. That room's her sanctuary." His mouth twisted.

"Jamie, the room *was* her sanctuary, but not now. Someone – a man – has been in there. She told me about it and the evidence was there, which I've collected."

"Evidence?" The penny dropped. "Oh, shit."

Evie exhaled slowly. "Yep. This isn't just about

manipulation and gaslighting, which are horrible enough, or the fact that he hit her, which is totally unacceptable." She shrugged. "I'd say take it to the police, but she's so delicate right now I don't know that she'd let us, and we can't without her consent."
"What are we going to do?"
"I'm throwing you under the bus, Jamie. You need to get me her phone."
*
"Lori..." Jamie called her name, keeping his voice low. She made a soft noise in her sleep.
"Aww, isn't she cute? She's probably shattered. It's a shame to wake her, really."
"Why don't you take the phone off her?"
"Because it breaks her trust in me, you idiot. I've already asked her for it once, and she wouldn't give it to me. I tried to take it when she first fell asleep, and she wouldn't let go. She's so attached to it, it's like it's become part of her identity."
"What makes you think she'll give it to me?"
Evie's eyes challenged Jamie. "Because I think you can get through to her where I can't. She trusts you. Even if it doesn't look like it on the surface, because she's buried it deep. That's why the photos did as much damage as that sick bastard did."
She gave a sad little smile. "I'm very glad it wasn't you. But Lori can't see that yet, and this can't wait for her to get over it. The evidence won't be useful for long and we need the contacts from that phone. Call lists, texts, emails, WhatsApp messages. And if you can get it from her right fucking now, I have some friends..." She spread her hands wide with a grin.

"Do you have friends for every situation, Evie?"
"No, only morally grey things. Stop procrastinating and wake her up."
"Ooh, big word for such a little girl."
Evie rolled her eyes. "Even size four steel toe caps can do a lot of damage to a man's crown jewels."
"I'll do it! I'll do it!" Jamie reached down and touched Lori's shoulder. "Lori? You need to wake up for me."
Lori mumbled something and shifted onto her side, still clutching the phone in her left hand. Jamie knelt next to the sofa and shook her lightly. "Lori, wake up."
Evie watched with a smirk on her face. "You're going to have to try harder than that. Maybe be Prince Philip to her Sleeping Beauty."
He swivelled to look at her. "What?"
"Kiss her. You know you want to."
"Shut up, Evie. What do you know about it?" He was immediately defensive.
"I've seen you. I'm not the eyes and ears of the office for nothing, Jamie. I know what the picture on your lock screen is. You touch it when you think no-one's looking, like she's special to you. A talisman. And if she is, we need that phone to help her get over this. Phrase it to her differently if you're not ready to tell her."
"Tell me what...?" Lori asked, stirring and stretching. "Sorry Evie, I fell asleep on you."
Jamie quirked a brow at Evie, who mouthed, "What?"
He shook his head. He didn't want to know if it was a figure of speech, or if Lori had actually fallen asleep on Evie's shoulder, or... some other part of her.
"Lori, we need you to give us your phone."

She blinked sleepy eyes. "No."
"Why not?"
"It's mine."
"Lori," Jamie reached a hand out to her, and watched her shrink back into the sofa. He sighed. "OK, I get it. You trust Evie, though, don't you?"
Lori's eyes moved across the room to Evie, then back to Jamie, but she said nothing.
"Evie has some friends, Lori, that might help with all this. But we need the information off your phone."
"You can't make me."
"Yes, I can, because I'm stronger than you. But I don't want it to be that way, Lori. I want you to hand it over, of your own choice."
"You'll hate me when you see—" Her bottom lip trembled.
"Lori, there's nothing you can do that will make me hate you, I promise. We're friends forever. Besides, if he's done things to you, what if he's doing them to other women, and you have the key to solve it? You can help *them*, even without your cards." He knew it was a low blow, and it twisted his gut in knots, phrasing it that way. "I know you, Lori. It's part of your nature to help people, however you can. Your heart is the best part of you. Don't ever change, lovely girl."
Lori's face crumpled, tears rolling down her cheeks, but she held the phone out with a shaky hand, and Jamie took it gently from her. Evie touched his shoulder in gratitude as she pocketed it.
"I gotta go, clock's ticking. Any PINs, pass codes, passwords on it? Fingerprint recognition?" She looked

at Lori, who had her hands over her face.
“Not unless she put them on while I was away. Lori?”
She shook her head.
“OK cool. Gotta run, my friend’s lab is an hour away. Lori, thank you. My sister would’ve been so proud of you.”
“What do you mean?” Lori asked, raising her eyes to where Evie stood poised by the door.
“I told you she had something similar happen. I didn’t say earlier, and I’m only telling you now so you can carry it safe in that enormous heart of yours. She took her own life, and I was too late to save her.” And Evie was out of the door before either Jamie or Lori caught more than a glimpse of her tears.
*
Jamie had left Lori watching TV. Not because he wanted to, but because she’d insisted. The emotions of the day had left him wrung out, and he had no idea what was next. He needed some time to let his mind wrap around everything that had been going on. And thinking of that brought a useful idea to the forefront. What if he did a mind map, like he had when trying to piece everything together from the accident? He still had a piece of the puzzle that didn’t fit, but he had to let it go. Lori’s situation was where he needed to focus. He pulled his largest notebook over, which was blank-paged, and picked up a pen.
But his head clearly wasn’t in the zone, because he started doodling instead. Why was he doing that? He wanted to help Lori, to ease her through what had occurred. Why wasn’t she asking her guides and angels to help her? Curious, he wrote it on the paper.

The white feather on the windowsill was poking at his attention. He fetched it, and ran it through his fingers a few times, straightening the barbs and unfocusing his eyes as he looked at it, as if it was a coding problem.

"What can I do to help Lori?" he murmured, not expecting an answer. "How do I help and not make it worse?" He placed the feather down on the desk and closed his eyes. He was so tired, and fraught with tension. She wouldn't even let him near enough to hold her, and he desperately wanted to, as much to reassure himself that she was still breathing as to offer comfort like he had before. Especially after what Evie had said about her sister.

How was it not even two days since he'd come home?

He felt guided to move the pen over the paper. Slowly at first, and his eyes stayed mostly shut as the lines swirled and swooped on the page. He had no inkling of what he was doing, but he wasn't thinking about that.

I want to help Lori. What can I do?

Eventually it felt like the pen was getting heavier and harder to push, and he laid it carefully down. He could look at whatever was on the paper in the morning.

*** suspend(altPOV) ***

CHAPTER NINETEEN

16th November 2022

*** enable(altPOV) ***

The following day, Jamie contemplated how he'd got a hangover when he hadn't been drinking. His head felt stuffed full of packing peanuts. He scrubbed his hands over his face and propelled himself out of bed and into the bathroom. Regarding himself in the mirror, he laughed under his breath. He looked rough as shit. Sure, he needed a shave, but he wasn't certain if he looked like he'd done ten rounds with a heavyweight or had had an entire night of debauchery. There were similarities: both were too much for him right then. He brushed his teeth and splashed cold water on his face; he could shower later. Intrigue drew him first, to see what he'd created the night before.

Picking up the pad, he turned it this way and that. There were lines all over it. Some of them crossed over, some went back and forth, and some even looked a bit like writing. He peered closer. What did that say?

Choice

How odd. He didn't remember writing anything, although he could recall the movement of the pen. He continued studying it. There was another one:

Release

Jamie put the pad of paper down onto his desk and, beginning at the edge where the line left the page, followed it along with his finger. As he encountered more words, he was impelled to write them all down.

Boundary

Forgive

Unicorn
Worship
Love
Seven words. His lucky number, and Lori's. The hair on his forearms rose, and his heart rate doubled. Somehow, those words were significant. Did they fit together, or were they separate? More puzzles. He'd heard of unicorns, but knew little about them. He could look them up on the internet.
A symbol of purity, innocence and power, he read. OK, he accepted that. But he didn't see how they fit into the picture. Shaking his head, Jamie concluded it could wait until after he'd had coffee. He opened the door and nearly slipped on a piece of fabric that hadn't been there the night before.
Curled up in a duvet and leaning against the wall, Lori slept. He eased himself down next to her and cast his eyes over her face. Pale as cirrostratus clouds and thinner than when he'd left for London, she looked as if she was made of porcelain and not quite real. He reached out slowly and brushed the back of his finger down her warm cheek, watching a hint of a smile bloom at the corner of her mouth. He speculated about what she might be dreaming and hoped it was something nice.
Evie's words came back to him: *You deserve to be happy. Everyone does.*
Lori's happiness had been poisoned by what someone had done to the photos, by the car accident, by his dismissal of her work – when he was struggling so much he couldn't keep his incomprehension of the world around him bottled up. And everything that had

happened since – well, it'd be better not to go there. But she deserved happiness too.
Jamie bowed his head and shook a few tears from his eyelashes. He'd do anything and everything he could to help her reach that place. Tiger had been right: Lori had done nothing to justify Jamie making her cry.
"There'll be new happy memories, Lori. I promise," he whispered, his words so soft he wasn't even sure he'd spoken them aloud. He didn't want to wake her, but their utterance sank them deep into his chest, and they dropped anchor.
Sombre yet hopeful. They were two strange bedfellows, but they were the right words for his feelings. Sliding carefully past Lori, down the stairs, it was his turn to make coffee.
*** suspend(altPOV) ***

I was dreaming about my favourite coffee shop, Creative Heart, and the highs and lows I'd experienced there. Through the dream haze, a few words appeared: something about memories, and a promise. And in the peculiar way that dreams have, it twisted from something bright into something dark.
My precious memories had been destroyed, and the promise was actually a threat.
I came awake, or thought I did, struggling to breathe, my instincts shrilling at me. Someone was nearby. I tried to inhale, ready to scream, but water rose from my lungs and drowned me. I was out of time and tied up, paralysed while Rod leaned over me, leering. Then hands grabbed at me from everywhere at once and began to tear me apart.

"Lori!" I heard my name.
"Jamie – help!" I didn't even know why I was calling out to him. He didn't care; he'd left me, and he was with Evie. He'd said we'd be friends forever, but how could that even be possible?
"Lori, wake up!" I felt myself being rattled like a dried pea in a box, my head snapping backwards and forwards on my neck, and I was surprised it hadn't come off. Then everything stopped, and a gentle warmth seeped in, like the bathwater I'd slid under. But this time I didn't want to die, and flailed my arms and legs to try and swim, but I'd forgotten how.
"Lori, wake up now! We'll fall down the stairs if you don't!"
That was a strange thing to hear, even in a dream, and I opened my eyes to discover I was on the tiny half-landing outside Jamie's door. He had one arm tightly round my waist and was clinging onto the handrail for dear life.
"Lori?"
"Yeah, I'm awake."
He blew out a breath, turning me slowly to make sure I wouldn't tumble down the steep flight. His hands were shaking. "I was calling you. Didn't you hear me?" He shuffled backwards to give me some space.
"I wasn't sure. I was dreaming. You said we were going to fall down the stairs."
"Yeah, I thought we were. When did you get so strong?" He managed a tremulous smile.
"Fear is a powerful motivator."
"Aww, Lori," Jamie closed his eyes for a moment. "Clearly not a pleasant dream."

"No."

He helped me to my feet and untangled me from the duvet. "Come in, and let's talk. I have coffee."

"Bless you," I said, and followed him through the doorway.

I hadn't been in the room since he and Sid had moved in, back at the beginning of summer. And he hadn't moved any of the furniture, but it felt different somehow, and I stopped to consider why.

Jamie handed me a mug of coffee, watching me intently. "Not what you expected?"

"No. I didn't even know you'd redecorated. When did you find the time?"

He grinned. "A perk of working from home," He perched on the edge of the bed. "Sit wherever you like."

"May I look around?"

He waved a negligent hand. "Have at it."

The shower room was as I remembered it, with blue and white mosaic tiles. But where the bedroom had been a cool blue-grey before, the walls were now a pale orange, like sorbet. I drifted across the floor to the window, looking out for a moment, feeling the curtains. He'd upgraded them to a heavy navy damask with a silver pattern, and sudden envy flooded me. They'd look gorgeous in my room, which was directly below where I stood.

I chopped that thought back ruthlessly. I wasn't ready to spend time in that room, and the curtains gave off a vibe that insisted you stop to admire and appreciate them.

I wished I gave off that vibe.

I continued my slow tour while Jamie sipped his coffee and watched me, unspeaking and unsmiling.

"You're quiet, are you OK?"

I plucked at the black and white duvet cover, which was something he hadn't changed. "I feel out of place, like I'm trespassing."

"I invited you in."

It felled me so quickly that I landed on my hands and knees to stare at the carpet. Jamie was at my side in an instant.

"Hey, hey, easy now. Here, sip this." He steadied the mug he'd pushed into my trembling hands to allow me to drink, and I realised it was his own mug he'd given me, not the other one.

"You're shivering. Get into bed." He folded the duvet back, then frowned when I didn't move.

"I'll be OK in a minute."

"Not buying it. In." And he pointed, his brows still drawn together. I did as I was told, and he propped me up with pillows, tucking the duvet round me. I could still feel the remnants of his warmth in the bed, and I drew in a long, shuddering breath, releasing it slowly. Jamie passed me my mug.

"Want to tell me?"

I shook my head as he sat cross-legged next to me, but his expression was of such kind concern I thought I should try and be an adult about it.

"I made the wrong decision."

"With what?"

"I—invited him in. You saying that... I guess it triggered something."

"Oh, Lori..."

“It’s alright, you can say it was a stupid thing to do. I accept that, and I’m not making excuses,” I looked down into my coffee. “It happened, life moves on, and I’m still here. Evie’s sister isn’t.”

“Would you have done anything differently, if you’d known?”

“Oh, I might have kicked him in the nuts before he even got over the threshold. But then... who knows? He could’ve got more violent.” I raised my right shoulder and dropped it as a half-shrug. “We’re always clever with hindsight.”

“Yeah. Lori, will you tell me what happened?”

“Maybe at some point.” I yawned. The bed was warm, and the coffee comforting. I leaned back against the pillows. “Is it OK if I stay here for a bit?”

Jamie smiled. “Let’s get you settled.”

*** enable(altPOV) ***

Jamie had been playing with the seven words’ mind map for nearly an hour. He’d started off drawing simple connections between them, with Lori in the centre, then somehow the connections had become tendrils and he’d drawn leaves on them, because it made him smile. He rolled his eyes at himself because he knew they all connected to Lori, but he wanted to go deeper into *why* and what they meant.

He stole a peek at her over his shoulder. She was still asleep where she’d settled, her arms around one of his pillows and the duvet tucked tight down behind her. She’d probably lost a lot of sleep over the past few weeks, and if she felt safe enough to sleep in his bed, that was a good thing. And better for her than sleeping on the floor in the spare room. He wouldn't wake her. He looked at the words on the large pad again. Maybe he should go into them one at a time. That seemed like a brilliant idea, so he began with 'choice'.

Underneath it, he wrote: *How does this relate to Lori?* He thought of all the ways she'd made choices recently. She'd chosen to hand over her phone to Evie, to potentially help other women, even though he still thought he'd been a bit of a dick for the way he'd persuaded her. She'd chosen to shut out her own guidance, which had left her in an isolated place, after eighteen years of developing it, of honing her skills. She'd chosen to let her assailant into the house – and Jamie still believed there'd be clues why on her phone. She'd chosen to smash the laptop because—Here Jamie stopped. Was it because of the pictures themselves, or was it because she believed *he'd* sent them and it was an enormous breach of trust? He wasn't sure.

She'd chosen to try and drown herself, because she felt like she no longer existed – and some part of her had chosen *life* at that point, not death. And she'd chosen to sleep outside his door. Why hadn't she knocked, and said she couldn't sleep, or whatever the reason was? She'd chosen not to. Perhaps he'd ask her why when she woke.

Where had she had *no* choice?

Jamie swallowed hard. When he'd gone to London because trying to fit into his life from before the accident was too hard. When some sicko had taken advantage of her naturally trusting nature, and willingness to see the best in everyone. When Jamie

had swung the sofa away from the wall, spurring her into fatalistic action.
He rubbed the back of his neck. Yes, she'd made some mistakes, but that didn't give anyone the right, including him, to take choices away from her. He'd need to keep that in mind. And somewhere in there was a duality of choice / no choice with the tarot and oracle cards. He knew they were gone, but she wasn't ready to tell him why or how. That was OK – he wasn't in a rush. And he made a mental note to remind himself that Lori did things she chose to, in her own time. She wasn't passive. She didn't sit and wait for things to come to her. But it had to be at a time of her own choosing.
He tapped the pen on the paper, to the rhythm of a song in his head. He was sure there was more to it than that, but perhaps it'd come later as he worked on the other words.
Release was the next word, and part of Jamie's mind headed straight down a dirt track. He yanked it back hard, reminding himself of the "evidence" Evie had found in Lori's bedroom.
Focus, Jamie.
He was trying to help Lori, not spend time and effort being smutty. So, what did Lori need to release?
A massive lump of the recent past. Not to forget it, but because it could hold her back. Ahh, and stop her from making different choices for herself. If she thought she'd made too many wrong decisions, she'd get herself stuck somewhere she didn't want to be, and she'd hate that. Because she'd been there recently, when she'd felt her path had narrowed to only one

option.
What else could release mean? And Jamie flicked himself on the side of the head. It meant letting go. Evie'd said Lori had mentioned something about Archangel Uriel, and that Lori had had to let Jamie go. Why?
To walk a different path.
Was this the "different path" that was meant – one where he came out with strange words in writing that he didn't recognise? Or was it something else? He didn't have the answers. Maybe Lori would, or maybe he'd have to discover them for himself.
At that thought, the white feather on the edge of his desk seemed to quiver. OK, he wouldn't argue with that. Looked like he'd have to find out for himself. It was leading him somewhere interesting, whatever.
"Jamie?" Lori's voice seemed to come from far away, soft and dreamlike. He turned, but her eyes were still closed.
"Right here, Lori."
"'K, just checking..."
Anguish clutched at his heart, that she'd felt that need. He thought she'd probably drifted off again, but she might have some helpful information for the mind mapping.
"Lori?" he said, his voice barely above a whisper.
"Mmm?" Her voice was even fainter as if she drifted in and out of slumber.
"What do you know about unicorns?"
There was silence for a while, and he guessed she'd fallen back asleep, but her voice surfaced again.
"They only come to those who are pure of heart..."

Jamie wrote it down. It might be important later.
Onto the next: *Forgive.* He already had, but what if she hadn't? What could he do to make it right?
Ask for what you want.
Where had that come from? Oh, in the aftermath of the doughnut incident. He grinned at his subtle coaching, not twigging at the time he was being played by an expert. Evie would have some tips... no. Because this was between him and Lori, and nobody else knew the depth of hurt they'd caused each other. He'd need to do it. Maybe he could throw himself at her feet and profess – what, exactly? Everlasting companionship? Lori still thought he and Evie were together, and he hadn't fixed that yet either.
He exhaled slowly. This was bloody difficult, the self-reflection stuff. He questioned how Lori made it look effortless, then shook his head. Probably years of practice, and he was only beginning, at thirty four, but at least he was starting. Some people never did and went through life completely oblivious to any pain and suffering they caused others. What had Lori called them, months ago? Poor blinkered souls, or something like that?
Worship was next. So maybe he was supposed to throw himself on her mercy. Could he do that before he'd proved his innocence in the photo distribution? She'd said she no longer believed what people said to her any more, but that could've been her shutting everyone out, because there was too much hurt already inside. And she'd turned up on the half-landing. Was that because he was a man and could protect her physically, or she felt safe with him personally, or

something else?
He uttered a sharp sigh. He was getting off-topic. What did worship mean? When did you worship? And what? He drew his brows together. It meant you had faith in something.
Had Lori *lost* hers, and that was why she shut her guidance out? It was possible.
And what about him? What did he have faith in? Jamie went through all the things he could think of, logical and provable things such as numbers, formulae, computer code. And then one other thing crept up behind him and smacked him round the head.
He'd had faith in *her*. With the tarot readings.
Holy fucking shit!
More to the point, did he still have it? He'd have to come back to that one later. He really wanted to get it finished before she woke.
OK, so, *boundary*. Jamie cringed, thinking of how many times he'd crossed Lori's over the past few weeks. That needed addressing, and he'd ask her to be more clear about where they were. He didn't want to keep pushing and pushing if she wasn't ready to give back – he'd drive her further away into mistrust, and he definitely didn't want that.
He wanted what they'd had before the accident. The uninhibited laughter, the banter, the shared popcorn in front of a film. The play fights, which left him so hard his dick demanded he retaliate by giving her rear a good smack, so every time she sat she was uncomfortable, the way he was. He'd never done it, though.

If her boundaries had moved because of the attacks, he wanted her to feel safe enough to tell him so he didn't go too far.
He stretched, and his neck clicked, but he was nearly halfway through. Stirring noises came from behind him, and he turned to see the sunlight was falling across Lori's face, illuminating her from within, or so it seemed. He crouched next to the bed, watching as she cracked her eyes open the smallest amount.
"Hey," he said with a smile, "How do you feel?"
"Hey you," Lori slid her hand under her cheek, "I'm OK. Is there any more coffee?"
"Shit, I left the machine on. It'll be like tar in the bottom of the jug, sorry." Jamie shrugged with his hands in apology. He'd completely forgotten about it, he'd been so focused on mind mapping those words.
She gave a soft laugh. "Just as well it wasn't the good stuff."
He waited for what was coming next.
"What?" she asked, shading her eyes to look at him.
A teasing smile tugged at the corner of his mouth, but he shook his head.
Ask for what you want, he said in his head. *Trust me.*
"Ugh! Do I have to go make it myself?"
He sat on the floor and crossed his arms, and watched her slither across the bed so they were nearly nose to nose. He kept his gaze firmly on her bright blue eyes, the mischief in them warring with irritation.
"You're already out of bed. I'm not."
"So?" His tone was deliberately provocative.
She frowned, trying to work it out, until at last a brilliant smile burst across her face. "Please will you

make some fresh?"
He reached out slowly to touch her cheek, and she squeezed her eyes shut, her face twisting in distress even as she permitted the contact.
He hoped that reaction would fade in time.
"Oh, there you are, beautiful girl. Welcome back." He unfolded himself from the floor and walked away whistling. Her reaction told him what he most needed to know right then: she accepted he'd told the truth about the pictures.
Downstairs, Jamie contemplated the state of the filter coffee jug, wrinkling his nose at the intense burnt aroma. He'd need to soak that.
He did, however, remember they occasionally used a cafetiere, but he wasn't sure if they had enough of their normal filter coffee for it. They'd been getting low for a while. He checked the usual cupboard and grinned to himself. There on the top shelf, where Lori would never have found it, was a pack of Tales of Napoli ground coffee. He'd break it out as a special treat.
He was halfway up the second flight of stairs, with the cafetiere, sugar, milk in a small jug and two cute turquoise blue espresso cups on a tray, when it hit him. He was taking premium coffee upstairs. To a woman. In his bed.
And she was a friend. A good friend. But... it wasn't enough, for him, to be friends any more.
It felt bigger than that.
The last of the seven words came to him unprompted: *Love.*
Oh shit. Did he...? Jamie's brain promptly ran into a brick wall. It was all he could do to get up the last few

steps and put the tray on his desk without dropping it. "Be right back, it has to brew for a minute."

"Jamie, what—?" Lori's puzzled expression followed him out of the door.

He flew down to the first floor and ran into the bathroom, locking the door. He thought his head was imploding.

What the actual fuck?

Was this some sort of joke, or a test? He flopped onto the toilet lid, clutching his hair with trembling hands.

Try to breathe, try to think. Rationalise it.

Anything to get back to logic, instead of where his memory was gleefully reciting all Lori's characteristics that matched the woman she'd described for him in his tarot reading, except the one unknown: her birthday. His incredulous laugh was followed by a sharp pang. He'd forgotten. He'd put it together back in April, but with the turbulence of the redundancy, the job change, then moving house on top, and general life stuff, it'd become buried. Until the right time for him to remember. It was perfect timing.

Divine timing.

The hairs on Jamie's arms bristled with the thought, and his stomach fluttered. The feather, the writing, the nudges of something he felt when coding. Especially when he'd deliberately opened himself to it, to solve that tricky variable state problem. He'd been evolving, day by day, until he'd been ready to see it.

Sneaky little minx. She'd been under his nose for months.

He'd never considered her as more than a friend, until recent events had reshaped their dynamic unnoticed.

She was the woman on the Eight of Swords card, blindfolded and stuck, but she didn't need rescuing – only a helping hand to show her she wasn't stuck at all. And there was so much more to the world than she could perceive through the blindfold.

OK, he could just about accept the transformation of his feelings to something considerably more than friendship, although it made him retch with nerves. He couldn't even, in his head, bring himself to name the emotion, but he touched his finger to his chest in acknowledgement.

I know you're in there.

And Evie had called him on it, too, without knowing Jamie hadn't clocked it himself at that point. He'd thought she was needling him, because it was funny to her, but she'd helped him see Lori in a different light: as a woman and not only as a friend.

Or rather, Evie had given him a size four boot in the arse, because she saw things people didn't, or refused to.

Jamie lurched to his feet, his wrath rising. Someone had hurt his Lori and she couldn't even accept friendly affection, like they used to share, without withdrawing from him. When he found out who it was, he'd obliterate them.

He brought himself up short. She wasn't his, she was her own person. Not an object to be owned, but an individual in her own right to be respected and treasured. Which meant she'd have to show him she wanted this, too. He couldn't take what she wasn't willing to give. Which gave another layer to his understanding of *choice.*

Jamie swore he'd never take advantage of her. Lori *was* the unicorn, the symbol of purity and innocence, and he needed to be deserving of her. He wished that she'd choose him, some day in the not-too-distant future.

But the coffee upstairs was getting cold and stewed, and he had some hard thinking to do. While there was a gorgeous woman that he knew he wanted and – that word – in his bed, in skimpy pyjamas that showed off her curves.

Meanwhile, she thought he and Evie were together.

I'm completely fucked.

*** suspend(altPOV) ***

CHAPTER TWENTY

It'd been an odd day so far. Jamie had come back up with the fresh coffee, disappeared for five minutes to have some sort of crisis, and had returned with his face as a mask. We'd had the coffee, but the disconnect was back between us: on his side, this time, not mine. So I'd left him to it.

I couldn't pretend it didn't hurt, but I wouldn't poke the bear. If he lost his temper, I'd feel like I was back to square one again with no safety net. I still had trouble reconciling the Jamie I knew with the one who had blown his top at Evie. My mouth twisted in a wry smile. I would've loved to hear that exchange. Evie had told me it word for word. I tucked it away in case I needed it, either for future ammo or entertainment.

By four in the afternoon, I felt stifled indoors. The sky was overcast, and it looked like there was more rain coming in, but it didn't matter. I hadn't been out into town or to the beach since before Jamie had left. I went up and knocked on the door. "Jamie?"

There was a brief pause before he answered. "Yeah, what's up?"

"I want to go walk on the beach for a bit. Will you come with me?"

"Hold on."

"It's OK, I can wait downstairs. Just wanted to know if you'd come, or not."

"Yeah, I'll be with you in a few."

"Thanks."

We set off ten minutes later in the drizzle, walking side by side in silence. I stole glances up at him as he strode along. His jaw muscles were tight, and he was brooding over something. The light was fading rapidly, and as we neared the beach I drew in a comforting salt-laden breath. I dropped the waterproof blanket on the shingle and sat, knowing from my deep connection to the sea that the tide had not long turned, and felt the waves' spray caress my cheeks like a friend.

"Want to talk about what's bothering you?" I asked.

"Not really." He was closed in on himself. "You?"

It was hard to identify his expression. "I think so, yes."

"Are you sure you want to do this now? Today?" I had his immediate attention.

"Is there a reason why not?"

"No, but if you tell me everything there might be emotional fallout."

"You're telling me you think I'll cry? It's likely."

"That, or I might want to kill someone and I'll verbally lash out at you through anger, frustration, pain... I've done that before, Lori, and not faced up to it for days afterwards. I don't want to do it again, and I'm sorry I put you through it. Forgive me."

Just as well I was already sitting down. That was heartfelt and humble and brought me close to tears.

"On one condition."

"Name it."

"You forgive me too. Or at least, try. For what I said, and this, and—all of it."

He shook his head slightly in the deepening gloom.

"You don't need to ask, you have it. Didn't you realise?"

"No, because you didn't tell me. You're very black and white with things sometimes, and I can't always follow how you feel. You slam the door in my face and I'm on the outside. If you explain, I'll understand."

"I'm not always good with words. I guess I do see things more in black and white. Ones and zeroes. Fixed and variable. But that doesn't mean I won't try harder."

"Thank you." Then I added in a soft voice, "I forgive you."

"Thanks," He dropped his head and breathed slowly for a few moments. "OK, I'm as ready as I can be. But if it's too hard you don't have to go all the way, all at once."

I was already taut as a bowstring, so I wasn't surprised at my nervous snigger, "And how does that chat-up line work for you normally?"

"Lori! I'm being supportive." A glint of light reflected off his teeth as he failed to repress a grin. "Seriously," he said in a softer tone. "I'm right here. If you want to hold my hand at the difficult bits, here it is." He placed it within reach on the blanket.

"OK." I told him what had happened, trying to stay detached, but it was impossible and I cried. And when I told him about the fallen Queens, I took him at his word and clung to his hand while my tears fell harder than the rain which surrounded us. I couldn't tell him who'd done it – it was too soon for that – but I covered everything, all the way through to when he'd come home on Monday and I'd gone for him with the knife. After I'd finished and silence had fallen between us, he squeezed my hand once and released it before rising to his feet.

I'd only had my best friend back for a few hours, but I

was sure I'd lost him again.
"Jamie?" My voice still wavered.
"Give me a minute," he answered in a short tone, then more gently. "Stay here. Please."
I followed him with my eyes until he was barely visible, further along the beach. I couldn't tell what he was doing. Every so often he'd bend down like he was picking something up, and I'd see his arm go back then forward, time and time again. Whatever it was, it took a while, ten or fifteen minutes, and by then it'd grown so dark I couldn't see him at all.
He was dragging his feet when his outline emerged from the early night that enshrouded him and, as he grew close enough for the lights to catch his face, I saw his cheeks were wet. He stopped to wipe them on his sleeve before approaching closer, and let himself drop back onto the blanket next to me.
"Can I ask what you were doing?"
He put his hands over his face, and I thought he wouldn't answer, but eventually something dragged his voice out.
"A stone into the sea and a prayer into the wind, to go with your funeral pyre. One for each. Fifty four in all."
I choked back a sob and laid my hand on his arm.
"That's beautiful, Jamie. Thank you."
He covered my hand with his, and we sat quietly for a while before he said, "I want to kill him for what he's done."
"You can't do that. Maybe he has an entire collection of broken-down women that he uses when he feels like it, because he gets off on the power? What if Evie's sister was one of those, but she couldn't take the

humiliation? What if there's another woman, or women, whose lives are hanging on by a thread because of it?" I stopped and gulped, wanting to share my thoughts but my throat was blocked.

"One more piece of recrimination, one wrong word, and they might feel suicide is the only option they have left. It goes round and round in your head, on an endless loop, becoming a holding pattern, literally. It binds you. You get stuck in thinking that's all you're worth." I looked down at my hands. "I did."

"Christ, Lori, you're worth so much more than that! All women are."

"Yes, but what if he preys on those who have no-one to remind them? It was nearly successful with me because I'd already lost faith in where my life was going. I'd spent part of every day for the last five months with you. You were always there – until you weren't."

I took a deep breath and continued. "And then—he stepped into that gap. Once it starts, it's almost impossible to stop. It's relentless pressure. Take my word for it, Jamie. When you hit that point, dying feels like a better choice than living that way."

He shuddered, and I had no more words to express how it'd felt.

"I hope Evie's friends turn up enough useful info on your phone that the police can do something."

I knew most of what they'd find already, but I couldn't tell him. He had to let the knowledge of what had happened in our home settle first, then his deep intellect could process it. After that...

He rose to his knees, tugging me up with him. "Let's

get fish and chips on the way home."

Neither of us were particularly hungry, so we shared one between us on a bench outside the chip shop. The air felt much cooler and, as we continued up Pier Road and past the station, I shivered a few times. Maybe it was the rain causing it, but it didn't take long for Jamie to notice.

"Plenty of space in my pocket for an extra hand," he offered, and I took him up on it.

When we got indoors I turned the heating up, and he fed Sid the few bits of fish we'd kept him, on top of a normal meal. I went to make some hot chocolate for us both but couldn't reach where he'd put it away.

"Jamie, would you please...?" I waved my hand at the jar and, without thinking, he reached over me to get it down.

I stiffened, clutching the edge of the worktop so hard my knuckles creaked.

"Shit, sorry. I didn't mean to." He backed away to give me plenty of space and leaned against the far end of the table. I took a deep breath and released it excruciatingly slowly, counting as high as I could with one exhale.

"I know." I continued with the hot chocolate, trying not to spill too much with my trembling hands.

"Shall I take over?" he asked gently, and I shook my head.

"No, it's OK. You never stir mine enough and it's always lumpy at the bottom."

"Nobody likes a lumpy bottom." He caught my eye, and a smile tugged at the corner of my mouth which drew a sigh from him in response.

"I guess we're both pretty fragile with everything. I'll try not to screw up, and make you feel you're trapped."

"You do that, or face the consequences," I teased, my paralysis lessening, and passed him a mug. He raised it in a toast.

"What sort of consequences are we talking? Because FYI I'm not into spanking."

I knitted my brows together. Rod had said to ask Jamie about his kinks, and I nearly asked him what he was into, except I remembered in time: Evie. Knowing he had someone special, it was none of my business. I turned away to hide my fear of the future, when things got serious between them.

I could already guess what would happen, but I wouldn't borrow trouble and my reply didn't reveal my worries.

"I guess it'll take a while to learn what we're OK with, and where we need to be careful for a while. I don't want to be like this forever, I want a normal life. I want to feel like me – whoever that is now."

He smiled. "Give yourself some time, lovely girl. I think you're doing great, all things considered."

I opened my mouth to thank him, but paused when I heard the buzz of his phone. He pulled it from his pocket and read something on it, then nodded.

"I have my meeting with HR and management tomorrow morning at work and I might be gone all day. What will you do while I'm not here?"

Panic. Pace the floor. Cry. Fret. Jump at every noise. Be afraid of shadows. Say goodbye to my sanity and my safety. All at once.

I screwed up my courage. "Can I come to London with

you?"
"Of course." Relief flooded his face. "And if they sack me we'll get extremely drunk in the West End, and catch a train to somewhere we've never heard of, just for fun."
"Sounds like a plan." And neither of us would have to face scary things alone.

*** enable(altPOV) ***
"Jamie?"
"Lori?" He was at the table with a notebook and pen, Thursday morning, trying to put together as much information as he could in case he needed to defend himself in the meeting. He clicked the pen's button in and out to help him stay focused on the task.
She fluttered her eyelashes at him. "Will you please get me some clothes?"
"Sure. What does madame require today?"
She sniffed, and spoke with a posh voice, "Mademoiselle, actually. Besides, I have no trollops to command, so I can't be a madam."
Jamie touched his forehead. "Beg pardon, miss."
She went to swat at him but held her hand and exhaled abruptly. Her reaction saddened him. She didn't seem to feel safe enough to play around the way she used to, and he missed that. He wanted to help her get that bit of herself back. He *would* persuade that Lori out of hiding.
She picked up the A4 size whiteboard they'd got off Amazon for the purpose and wrote:
Hangers 7 and 12 – labels around the hook bit
Black suede ankle boots on bottom shelf

Full length purple slip – looks like a nightie
Black leggings - folded below the hanging rail
Undies – no preference, but matching please
Thank you x

Jamie's heart lurched. Something that looked like a nightie? That was going to cause him some mischief. Or maybe, if he was feeling wicked, he could turn it round on her. "I'll be right back."

"I'll wait outside the bathroom."

A few minutes later, Jamie passed the things over to her, keeping a straight face. He'd enjoy this.

She rolled her eyes. "I gave you a list and you still didn't get my underwear?"

"Au contraire, mademoiselle," Jamie produced the fiery orange bra and brief set from his pocket. "I like this one best. Remember?"

"Ohmygod." Lori flushed up to her ears. "I can't believe you reminded me of that! You rotten beast!"

"Need help with your bra today?"

"Not after that!" she said, a half-shriek of laughter falling from her mouth, and her cheeks looked like they were hot enough to fry an egg on. But as she disappeared into the bathroom as suddenly as a magic trick, he glimpsed her smile.

That aspect of her, the one who liked to be teased and tormented and got flustered with things he said, was still in there somewhere. It made his day five times brighter.

He changed clothes then sat on the bottom stair to wait, and when she emerged he leapt to his feet. Christ, she was stunning! Her dove-grey tailored silk blouse with pearl buttons and long sleeves, with a high collar, gave her elegance, and a bright red velvet brocade ankle-length skirt lifted the overall vibe. That was a confidence-inducing outfit if he'd ever seen one, and knowing his favourite set of her underwear was underneath—

Oh shit, not now...

She looked him up and down with appreciation – he was suited and booted.

"Nice to see you standing to attention when a lady enters the room," she quipped, mischief sparkling in her eyes. Then she ran down the stairs while Jamie lingered, goggle-eyed and hard, until he could go downstairs under full control of himself. He'd get whiplash from her abrupt mood changes at the rate she was going.

But in his heart he knew she was trying to find where they fit together, if they still did. And if she could cope with it.

*** suspend(altPOV) ***

CHAPTER TWENTY ONE

*** enable(altPOV) ***
As they approached Jamie's office, an inconspicuous brick and tinted glass two storey building five minutes' walk from Victoria station, Lori caught Jamie's arm and pulled him to a halt.
"Jamie, you know that whatever happens in this meeting I have faith in you, don't you? That I know you wouldn't do anything like that?" Her voice was small with worry.
He took her hand and squeezed it. "Relax. I'm nervous, obviously, but I know I didn't, you know I didn't, and everything else is a technicality. Even if I get fired I know enough now to find more contracting work." He'd already considered that.
Lori nodded dumbly.
"But I'd better call Evie and tell her you're here too. You'll need to go through security before you can go in."
"OK."
Bloody Evie this, Evie that. Lori liked the girl, and trusted her, but Jamie and her...? No, she wouldn't go there. Instead, she listened to Jamie's side of the conversation to try and get a hint of anything useful.
"Hey Evie, can you let Tiger know I'm here for the meeting? And I've got Lori here too, in case he wants to speak to her." He winked at Lori while Evie said something that Lori couldn't hear. "OK, I'll let her know."
He put his phone in his pocket and turned to face Lori. "Evie says, no-one knows she came to see us the other

day because she took a sick day. So don't be surprised when she seems not to know you and calls you Miss Archer, OK? Act as if you'd never met."

"I can do that."

"And I thought it best if Tiger believes you're here in case you're needed to provide something for the investigation, as a character witness maybe." He smiled down at her. "It's no-one's business but ours that you didn't want to be at home by yourself."

*

Evie strolled over to Tiger's office and knocked, putting her head round the door. "Tiger, Jamie's here for his meeting and he has someone with him. I think it's Miss Archer." Evie cleared her throat. "I recognise her... from the pictures."

Tiger nodded, too professional to show surprise. "Go down to meet them please, Evie. I'll send a security guard down to take her through everything before she comes up."

"Sure." Evie nearly took the shortcut like she normally would when no-one was around, but there were too many people in work that day to get away with it. She huffed under her breath: it was way more fun when you could slide down the wide handrail and leap off at the bottom.

She descended the stairs like a grown-up and waited at the bottom for the security guard, who nodded at the two stationed discreetly by the door, then one of them pressed a buzzer and the door unlocked. Evie motioned to Jamie and Lori.

"Hey Jamie, good to see you. Good morning, Miss Archer."

"Lori, this is Evie Mackenzie," Jamie said, as if they hadn't met earlier in the week. "She's our intern."

"Hello." Well, she could be polite, couldn't she?

"Miss Archer, you'll need to clear security before you go up. This way please." And Evie pointed after the security guard, who was making his way to a small room up ahead.

"Can someone call me if Lori needs a strip search, please?" Jamie begged.

Lori whirled back to him and, with intense eyes, hissed, "You couldn't handle watching a strip search. All your blood would rush to your dick and you'd faint." She winked, then turned on her heel and followed the guard, leaving Jamie open-mouthed in shock – and awe, at the way she'd diverted his nerves with the barb. He grinned to himself. Yeah, he was going to do his damnedest to be worthy of her. She really was something special.

He followed standard procedure for colleagues without access tags and gained admittance to the first floor. He had to walk past Meg on reception to get to the waiting area and gave her a brief nod.

"Meg."

She blanked him, and Jamie didn't care a bit. He took a seat until the meeting started.

Lori and Evie came up together, and he could almost feel the tension radiating off Lori. She was worried about the outcome of the meeting, and as her eyes darted to him when she walked past, he wanted to run after her and hug her, yet he couldn't for too many reasons right then.

"They're all staring at me," Lori whispered to Evie,

holding a tissue to her nose and pretending to blow it. Evie nodded almost imperceptibly.
"They all think they've seen you naked, and screwed six ways to Sunday," she answered in an undertone, then in a normal voice. "This way please, Tiger wants to meet you before the meeting."
Lori had at least spoken to Jamie's manager before, so it wasn't as bad as being gawped at. It was like she was in one of those hellish dreams where she'd forgotten her clothes and everyone was staring.
"Hey Lori," Tiger offered his hand to shake. "Nice to meet you in person at last. Shame it's not under better circumstances."
Lori smiled. "I hope when this is resolved I'll be invited to karaoke night. I'd be very happy to see a repeat performance of what you did."
"Ah. You heard about that."
Evie sniggered, and Tiger caught her eye, giving the tiniest shake of his head. She straightened her face at once. "Can I get you some coffee, Miss Archer?"
"Yes, please."
"What would you like? Our machine can do pretty much anything barista-style."
"Cappuccino, please, with extra sugar." Lori wouldn't let her guard down for a moment, even to have the drink she really wanted, which was a mocha. Too much was at stake.
"We also have some doughnuts that were freshly cooked about an hour ago, if you'd like one?"
Lori's smile was so rigid it was almost a snarl. "Thank you, no. I'd have preferred a doughnut that somebody hadn't licked the sugar off before it was offered."

Fucking hell, thought Evie admiringly as she left the room, trying to hold in her laughter. *Who's set her on fire today??*

She had to walk past Jamie, still waiting, to get to the coffee machine. "You didn't tell her yet, did you?" She hissed, her dark eyes alive with mischief behind her glasses. "That we're not together."

"I haven't had a bloody minute, Evie. There's been so much happen since Tuesday. She told me everything, yesterday night, including what he did to her cards."

"Well, that was faster than I expected. Brave girl. But she took me down, thinking you and I are an item. You're so dead later when she finds out..."

She continued on, and Jamie sat open-mouthed. *Christ, what did Lori say?*

*

"I must get the meeting started, Lori," Tiger told her. "You're welcome to wait here in relative privacy until it's over." He grinned. "I don't know anyone will dare come and indulge their curiosity about you, or your OnlyFans page."

Lori laughed, her tension ratcheting down a notch. "Let them. If Jamie had any explicit pictures of me he'd be smart enough to keep them on an encrypted hard drive."

"You believe he didn't do it, then?"

Lori leaned forward in her chair and looked Tiger full in the face. "Of course I do. I've known him well over a year, and he's been my housemate since June. We've had our differences, especially through the amnesia after his accident, but I know in my heart he wouldn't have done this. So let's hope your IT guys have come to the same conclusion and HR throws it out. Because if not, your team is going to be distinctly poorer for it."

Tiger privately agreed with her.

A few minutes later, Evie returned, calling out so those loitering to see what was going on could hear. "Here's your cappuccino, Miss Archer. Sorry for the delay. I got waylaid to do someone's shredding." Once inside Tiger's office, she hurried over to Lori with a large paper cup in one hand, and two items of mail in the other.

"This one's yours. Read it then hide it," she said under her breath. "I suggest you don't let Jamie see it. You'll know why when you read it. I have to go deliver this."

"What is it?"

Evie was halfway to the door but turned back, moisture brimming in her eyes. "Exoneration."

Lori deflated like a balloon. Evie clearly had deep feelings for Jamie, and Lori couldn't blame her for that.

She opened the letter and scanned it. The words flowed past her eyes, but she understood enough jargon to get to grips with the information:

...Technical fingerprinting indicates the origin was consistent with the Basingstoke area...

She couldn't think of anyone she knew who lived in Basingstoke, but the next line made it crystal clear:

This location aligns with that of the assailant – the individual who had sent you coercive and manipulative messages via mobile on prior occasions.

Shit. When she'd blocked Rod's number, she'd thought there might be repercussions, but she hadn't expected this.

...It further supports the likelihood of a targeted campaign intended to isolate, humiliate, and discredit you, possibly to induce self-harm.

So he'd taken his rejection badly, had deliberately destroyed her business, and tried to extinguish her sense of self, because she wouldn't have him in her life. He'd wanted her powerless and submissive, and she refused to become that.

She'd been willing to take her own life if he came back, and she still was. Better that than suffer further at his hands.

He was utterly despicable.

But Evie was right. Jamie would go ballistic if he read the report.

*

The meeting hadn't long started, but the waffle and legalese that IT and HR were droning on about was already boring Tiger. Why couldn't they simply state the decision and whether he was about to lose a valuable team member – and someone Tiger respected as a man of integrity? It was ridiculous. The company handbook, whose rules they were all following, needed simplification and streamlining.

He assessed the others around the table – the HR manager, Claire, the IT manager, Robert, and Jamie himself. Jamie looked preoccupied and like it didn't matter to him what the outcome was.

A slight movement at the edge of the nearest blind attracted Tiger's notice. There was an unwritten rule about the soundproofed meeting rooms being sacrosanct for confidential meetings and conversations, so no-one could knock unless the building was on fire – literally or metaphorically. So that wasn't it, but there was a person out there trying to get the attention of someone inside. He held up a hand.

"Can we pause for a minute, please?" He was grateful for the respite. In his limited capacity as Jamie's line manager, the balance of power in the room wasn't on his side. HR didn't understand how important it was to have people like Jamie on the team, because the other side of that was his skills being extremely useful to industry competitors or – God forbid – the criminal underworld, and IT were only interested in making sure any breaches had been addressed before things became catastrophic and client data security was jeopardised. If the ICO got involved under GDPR law, there'd be hell to pay.

He went to the door and opened it to see Evie bouncing up and down, waving an A4 envelope.

"Oh good, you saw me. I'm sorry to interrupt, Tiger, but this has arrived by courier and it's relevant to what's going on in there." She handed him the envelope, and Tiger could see the internal case reference on the label. What was it? Something unexpected, certainly.

Evie didn't hang around, but when Tiger read through the report, he hissed out a breath to relieve the pressure in his chest. So that was why Lori was present: she'd provided evidence to help clear Jamie's name.

And from the look of the summarised information, it was at considerable personal cost.

Armed for battle with the report, whatever the

outcome, Tiger re-entered the meeting room.
*** suspend(altPOV) ***

I was refolding the letter when the door opened, and a middle-aged redhead with a fantastic figure walked in. I offered a small smile and a nod.
"If you're looking for Tiger, he's in a meeting."
"Yes, I know. I'm not."
"OK..." I was a little anxious at her regarding me the way she was.
"So you're... Lori."
"I am. And, contrary to popular belief around here, a relatively normal human being." I didn't mean to be sharp, but knowing that Rod had caused the entire wreckage of my life made me defensive.
She perched on the edge of a chair, almost as ill at ease as I was. "My name is Meg."
"It's nice to meet you, Meg. What can I do for you?" I reined in my attitude. There was something at play here, and I didn't know what it was. I'd go cautiously.
"Jamie really went to town on those pictures, didn't he?"
"No. You actually think he did it?" I scoffed.
"Why wouldn't I? I saw them all."
"So did I. They're not me."
"What is he to you?" Meg's voice was a little unsteady.
"A friend. He lives in the studio apartment at the top of my house, why?"
"Aren't you worried?"
"About what?" I was becoming concerned about the torrent of questions.
"Well... image-based abuse often isn't the only thing

going on. There's frequently physical or sexual abuse that goes with it." Meg's hands were trembling. I watched her for a long moment before I spoke gently.
"Meg, may I be completely candid with you?"
She nodded, her eyes wide.
"I can see this is harrowing for you. Yes, you're right, there was physical and sexual abuse associated with the images. But Jamie did none of these things. It was someone else known to me." I watched her reaction and had the presence of mind to whip a clean tissue out of my bag when her eyes filled with tears. I passed it to her and moved my chair closer, letting her mop her eyes before I laid my hand over hers.
"Meg, did something like this happen to you, too?"
She lowered her head, shredding the tissue between shaking fingers.
"I'm so sorry," I said. "I have some idea of how hard it is when someone we trust turns on us. Especially us women."
She burst out, "How can you sit there and be so strong?"
"Because I have faith."
"So you put your trust in God, and all that rubbish?" She practically snarled at me. "Divine retribution and all its associated warblings?"
"Not at all," I replied. "I have faith in myself to find a way, somehow, to make sure that the man who abused me can't do it again. Not for my revenge, but to protect other women." I stopped and drew a shaky breath in, letting it out again before continuing.
"I have a dear friend currently being raked over the coals for something he didn't do, because of this sick

bastard. Yes, I want him brought to justice, but I'm not prepared to let other people get hurt in my pursuit of it, or to become a vigilante. There's only so far I can go, and still sleep at night. I've done all I can for now."

I smiled slightly. She was listening intently, but my next words somehow flowed through me rather than coming from me.

"I'm not judging all men by what that pervert is like. I won't take matters into my own hands and inflict pain and torment on innocent people because *I* was hurt and tormented. My peace of mind – and myself – are worth more than that, Meg. I still have my self-respect, but it was a hard fight to keep it. Some women probably lose theirs, then turn on others."

I patted her hand. "Just know, in this moment, that whatever happened to you wasn't your fault. And if you choose to get help to allow you to deal with your experiences in a better way, it's out there. In case you haven't already."

She leapt to her feet and fled the room, and I didn't see which way she went, but I hoped she'd at least think about what I'd said. Even though not all of the words had been mine.

I tucked the letter away in my bag. I'd make very sure that Jamie didn't see it until I felt strong enough to weather his reaction. He said he'd forgiven me for everything, but I didn't know how this was going to affect things between us. I would wait.

And in that moment, I'd drink my coffee and wonder how much a machine like theirs cost, because I fancied one for at home. Whatever coffee Jamie had put in the cafetiere the day before needed treating with respect.

As we all did.

Another ten minutes passed before I got out of my chair and paced across the room. Why was it taking so long? Corporate rules and that sort of crap, I guessed. Then I heard an indistinct murmur of conversation in the open plan part of the office. Something was going on out there.

The door opened, and Tiger held it for Jamie while both men came into the office. Jamie looked tired, like he'd gone through the wringer.

"...So if you want to take your things with you today, that's fine." Tiger was saying.

I almost lost it there and then. Had what I'd done been unsuccessful? But I was learning to hear people out instead of jumping to conclusions, so I kept my mouth shut.

Just as well in this instance.

Jamie rumpled his hair. "I think so. Then I can drop you a text if I feel like working on the S7-A before then, right? To let you know it's me accessing it."

Thank God for that.

I sank into a chair and Jamie rushed to my side, crouching next to me. "Are you OK, Lori? You look like you're going to faint."

"What's the outcome?"

He grinned. "It's all sorted. I told you everything else was a technicality, didn't I? But Tiger," he waved his hand at his boss, "Has suggested I take some emergency leave to 'recover from the process' or whatever company bullshit he's calling it."

Tiger inclined his head in agreement.

"Isn't that the same as running away until the fuss has

died down?"

A bark of laughter emanated from Tiger. "You have your hands full with this one, don't you, lad?"

"I bloody wish," Jamie muttered, and I shot him a sharp look.

"What was that?" I arched a brow.

"Let's discuss it later. We have a lunch booking I want to get to, and then... I have a few other things planned." He waggled his brows at me, and my cheeks flamed.

Oh my God!

Why would he tease me that way in front of Tiger? It wasn't like that between us!

"Just winding you up, Lori. Because I can."

Tiger shook his head, struggling to keep a straight face. "Get out of here. And take your charming friend with you." He bowed over my hand. "We'll get you back up for karaoke soon, Lori."

"You won't get me doing it though. Last time I sang along to something on the radio Jamie thought I'd stood on the cat's tail."

We all laughed, and Jamie held the door for me. Evie was loitering by the photocopier, watching as we exited the office, and Jamie went over to have a few words with her. I saw him put his hand on her shoulder, but I couldn't see his face. I turned away and pretended to be looking at the pot plant near me. Nope, still wasn't any of my business.

"Let's go," Jamie said. "My work stuff's downstairs with security. I can pick it up on our way out."

"What did you say to Evie?" I blurted, before I could stop myself.

“I thanked her. We’re meeting up for drinks later not far away before we head back. Is that OK with you?”
Whatever I thought, however I felt, I owed Evie thanks too for what she’d done. “Yeah, it’s fine.”

*** enable(altPOV) ***
Jamie bowed Lori through the restaurant door after a light lunch. He’d asked her not to go over the top with food or she might regret it later, and it piqued her curiosity enough that she’d agreed. He offered her his arm as they wandered up the street, and she tucked her hand into the crook of his elbow.
“So... I may have done something that you’re going to be annoyed at,” he said, and Lori flicked her eyes up to his then blew out a breath.
“Fabulous. Just another normal day in the Brightfield-Archer household.”
A windmill-shape of joy whirred in his chest at how she’d put their names together, and he came nose-first up against a lamp post because he wasn’t paying attention.
Lori squealed with laughter. “Go on then, shine a light on what you’ve done!” she chortled.
Jamie rolled his eyes. “Yeah yeah, whatever. But...” He could see the lighter aquamarine spikes of colour in her eyes and had to drag himself back to the conversation. He touched the back of her hand with a fingertip, careful of her sensitivities. “I know you hacked off your hair to honour the Queens, and I fully respect that. But, if you’d like, and only if you’d like – I’m not pressuring you, it’s your choice, Lori – I thought... you might like to get it shaped into

something... else."
Christ, he couldn't say something that suited her better, because she was 'knock your socks off' gorgeous anyway, and he didn't want her to think he was objectifying her. He squeezed his eyes shut, expecting her to actually slap him, and stood unmoving for almost a minute.
Had she stormed off?
No, surely not. He could still feel the back of her hand under his finger. He risked opening his eyes – she'd shut hers and tears trembled on her eyelashes.
"I know, it was a stupid idea. You must think... I don't know what I think you think. I'm sorry. Just forget it."
She raised her hand, and he thought there was trouble coming, but she dashed the tears from her eyes and gave him a wobbly smile. "I think it's a great idea. You're right, I look like a badly stacked heap of twigs, waiting for someone to set a match to it."
He risked a grin in return. "Well, something lit a fire under you at the office, handing out banter like you give out cat treats."
"You mean about the strip search?" She smirked. "I figured it was the perfect thing to settle your nerves. You needed a distraction. So where are we going for my hair chop? Did you book something?"
Jamie couldn't keep up. One minute she had him looking in one direction, then the next he was arse-about-face. He shook his head. Tiger was right – if Jamie could ever get her to see him like that.
"We've got to catch a bus. C'mon."
*

Two hours after Lori's haircut, which gave her a Julia

Roberts' Tinkerbell-type vibe, Jamie had decided that in his next lifetime he was *not* coming back as a lady's maid. And since when had he believed in reincarnation?
Must be because he detested the thought of all the women driven to suicide after being assaulted. He couldn't accept that they'd been snuffed out like candles. He had to hope they'd come round again some time.
Back to this lifetime, though. He'd thought it was a great idea to let Lori try on various costumes in a hire shop, but he'd been clueless how long they took to put on and take off, or how many petticoats and underskirts and all the other stuff there was to deal with. Bustles? Crinolines? Panniers?
Apparently, they didn't wear undergarments back then. Knickers hadn't been invented, according to Lori, who was having the time of her life while he was stuck outside the massive changing room with his arms full of reject dresses to put back onto hangers, waiting to see how she'd torture him next.
"Longest day ever..." Jamie groaned quietly and heard her giggle. It was as well she was in there by herself, because he'd have found it hard to resist discovering how authentic she was being with the costumes, by putting her over a chair and—
Yeah, better stop that train of thought before it runs away with me and something comes up.
She stepped out of the changing room at that point, and the train crashed into the buffers.
"Oh!" He swallowed hard. "Oh Lori..."
She had her eyes cast down, watching where she put

her feet. Her cornflower blue dress had a wide neck, a boned bodice, and was off the shoulder, with chiffon round her upper arms and no sleeves. The skirt was wide and full, with ruching at the hem. Part French fashion plate, part Southern belle, 100% Lori Archer. And she looked so regal, Jamie wanted to fall at her feet.
"I thought maybe this one, but... I wasn't sure if it was close to what you had in mind. Is it good enough?"
"Stand still a minute, I have something to top it off." He dumped the dresses on the nearest chair and took a slender gold coronet with leaves wound round from the shelf next to him. He placed it gently on top of her head, then tried to fumble his phone out of his pocket. His hands were shaking.
He had to get a grip quick, or he'd never be able to video the moment and the rest of the surprise would be spoilt. "Lift your chin... a little more, beautiful. Now look at me." And he tapped record, hoping what he captured would be good enough.
Lori's eyes were sparkling, and she turned her head as he moved round her, videoing from all angles. A smile touched the corners of her mouth, and she leaned nearer to him, her expression changing to a blend of wicked temptress and ice queen. He had no idea how she did that.
"I had to take my bra off for this one, it's still in there." She jerked her thumb over her shoulder, and Jamie's mind went straight in that direction.
"You're a torment." He knew that when he sent the video off for the next part of the surprise, it'd have the audio track removed. "OK, we're done. Need help

changing?"
"Nope." An impish grin crossed her face. "But I'll have my bag back now, thanks."
He handed it to her and retreated, with no clue what she had in store for him next.
*
Jamie's brain hadn't fully rebooted from the costume hire shop scenario when they arrived at the club where they were meeting Evie. Not only had Lori looked incredible in that dress, she'd come out of the changing room like a woman on a mission in killer-heeled knee-high black patent boots with a skin-tight pair of black crushed velvet leggings, a gold bustier top and a shimmering gold overshirt.
He was finding it hard to breathe. He couldn't even be certain he hadn't let out a little whimper when she'd revealed her outfit.
Were those boots known as fuck-me heels? And was it a 'take me now', or a 'Christ, these are killing me' type thing? He was completely adrift, and Lori was clearly loving his discomfiture.
She, meanwhile, had come equipped for the job at hand. She knew they were going out on the town at some point, either to drown their sorrows or to celebrate, and hangers 7 and 12 had given her all she needed except for the boots, but they lived in the cupboard under the stairs, anyway.
She'd wanted to give Jamie something to take his mind off recent events, but he hadn't been able to hold much of a conversation for the last hour. Maybe he was tired.
Evie waved at them from a table she was leaning on

over to one side, and they headed in that direction. She'd changed from her typical workday outfit to a frilled white shirt, red choker and red skinny jeans, but kept her usual platform boots. Lori, nearly as tall as Jamie in her boots, was about ten inches taller than Evie.

"You've cut your hair!" Evie said in surprise. "I was loving the boho bitch chick vibe of this morning."

Lori grinned. "Sometimes you have to show the world who you are. What are you drinking?" She took their orders and headed to the bar.

Evie looked across at Jamie and saw the stunned look on his face. "Well, look at you all gooey-eyed and ready to take her... home." She sniggered, and Jamie shook his head.

"She keeps surprising me, Evie. She's unique. I thought she'd slap me when I suggested the haircut, but she just sort of shrugged and agreed, and then went all-in. I get more neck ache from her shifting moods than from eight hours' coding."

"And? What else did you do this afternoon?"

"I'll tell you where we went, if you tell me how she took you down this morning."

"That was priceless! I've only known her a couple of days but fuck me, she's not afraid to fight for what she wants."

"Right now she wants to stay living," Jamie replied in a voice tight with worry. "I hope it lasts. I know she's fragile underneath, I can feel it between us, and all I can do is show her that I'm safe to be around and I won't hurt her. That I care about her and want her in every part of my life."

Evie's eyes softened. "That's lovely," she said. "She's amazing, Jamie, and she seems good for you. I'll do what I can to ease her through all the shit, but she's withdrawn from where we were Tuesday. I reckon she thought she was safer, with you home, then she misunderstood about us. Be a man, Jamie, and straighten it out." She rose to her feet. "I will if you won't. I'm going to dance."

He frowned at her retreating back. There was no way Evie was going to best him again before the end of the month. He'd meet that challenge.

Lori came back with a tray of drinks and slid it onto the table. "There's a cute guy at the bar asked for my number," she smirked.

Jamie ground his teeth. Of course, guys were going to chat her up. She was hot as hell.

"He didn't believe me when I said I didn't have a phone, so I gave him your number." She lowered her eyes and took a long swallow of her drink – something that looked like a tequila sunrise, but he could see her smiling round her glass.

"What the actual—"

"Your burner phone, obviously. I wouldn't do anything to harm your professional reputation." She had another swig of the pink and orange concoction and licked the rim of the glass so it didn't drip.

Jamie wasn't sure what she was playing at. "Lori, you're going to kill me one of these days..."

She put her glass down and took his loosened tie between her fingers before leaning over the table, affording him a good look down her top through the transparency of her shirt. "I hope it's 'une petite mort',

instead of the real thing," she whispered.
"What? What's that?"
"Look it up! I'm going to dance with your girl. See you in a bit."
He searched on the net for the expression and had to grin. It was a French term for an orgasm. Yes she would, when he was alone. He caught the tail end of the song playing, recognising it as Lionel Richie's "All Night Long". All night? No, more like 30 seconds with the way she'd gifted him a view down her cleavage. Then a Take That song came on and Jamie burst out laughing. "It Only Takes a Minute"? The universe, or whoever was keeping watch over him, was clearly having a joke. He took it to mean he was heading along the right path, even if he hadn't worked out yet where it was going.
*** suspend(altPOV) ***

The first thing I did when I got to the dance floor was tell Evie about the cute guy and the phone number, and we both shrieked with laughter. It felt good to laugh at something without using it to hide deeper emotions.
We danced and chatted, and every so often I slid my glance across to Jamie to make sure he was watching. But it'd been so long since I'd let my hair down – not really since I'd left London to move home – that after a while I let myself feel the rhythm as much as listen to it. My moves became more sensual, and Evie matched me, even taking the lead with some things and dancing the male steps to my female.
"You really get into it, don't you?" Evie said, and I

nodded vigorously.
"Music's always been a big part of my life. You're a fabulous dancer yourself."
"Thanks! I'm dancing for Helen. I always do." She saw my blank look. "Helen's my sister. I dance for her because she loved it so much, and she's not here to dance for herself."
"I bet she is, and she loves that you do this for her."
We shared an understanding smile, then she framed my face with her hands and kissed me lightly on the mouth.
"Thank you."
I pulled back sharply. Not to hurt her feelings, at what I took to be a sisterly kiss, but because the last time someone had kissed me it'd been against my will.
"I told Jamie everything." I said to Evie.
"That's so brave of you, Lori. So powerful for your healing."
"I didn't tell him who, yet, and I don't know if I can." I knew Evie would've looked at the messages on my phone.
"Does he know him, then? I realised it was someone you knew."
"They've known each other since university."
"Shit, he's gonna take it bad, but I'm so proud of you for it. I want to be you when I'm older." She said something then that stole my breath. "I'm still a princess, or maybe a page. But Lori? You're a queen." She wrapped her arms round my waist, and I laid my head on her shoulder, feeling a tiny rekindling of happiness in my soul that I'd survived the crucible again.

We circled to something slower for one song, then Jamie approached. "Excuse me, ladies, can I cut in here?"

"Of course," I murmured, and took a step backwards. Evie laughed her head off, which confused me. I had no idea what was so funny, but she left the two of us on the dance floor and made her way back to the table with our drinks on. I tilted my head to regard Jamie with perplexity.

"What's with her?"

He shrugged and drew my arms round his neck, his hands dropping to my waist. "Who knows? I want to dance with you, though, Lori."

"You should dance with Evie. That's what couples do."

"We're not together, silly. I meant what I said Monday night – she's only a friend."

"But I thought—" I stopped and Jamie's eyes gleamed with mischief, even as we swayed to the music.

"No, Lori. She might be into you if you were closer in age."

I stared at him, open-mouthed with surprise. "You mean—?"

He laughed at me, and I hid my flaming cheeks in his shoulder.

"Oh...my...God. I did *not* see that coming. She kissed me, as well!"

"I think she did it to provoke me, but I want to know what you said to her earlier in the office. She didn't tell me, although I asked her."

So I told him and we laughed about it, and other things, for a while until my colour returned to normal. Jamie kept me close to him, his arms round me as if to reassure me he was there, and I allowed myself to feel safe.

A while later, the three of us were sitting at the table with our drinks, chatting about the strangeness of the day and what we'd done in the afternoon. Evie, sensing a lull in the conversation, suddenly piped up.

"So if I'm your little sister, Lori, and Jamie's my big brother, will it be incest when you two get it on? Because that'd be illegal, in case you didn't know." She cackled, then jerked her thumb over her shoulder towards the door. "Time to go. Therese is waiting for me so I'll leave you to it."

She headed off, leaving awkward silence sitting in her place.

Jamie broke it. "Do you think of me as a brother, Lori?" A shadow moved across his eyes as he kept them trained on my face.

Definitely not but I couldn't categorise how I *did* think of him, so I went with humour.

"You're more of a bother than a brother." I teased.

"I'd like to get you hot and bothered," he muttered, so quietly that I wasn't sure he meant me to hear.

Probably not, so I ignored it and exhaled, half-sigh and half-tired moan.

"I've had enough emotional pinball for one day, Jamie. Let's go home."

CHAPTER TWENTY TWO

18th November 2022

Early Friday morning, a lurid nightmare crossed my sleeping brain. Rod, my wrists held tightly in his grasp, was backhanding me repeatedly across the face, and each time he did it, I felt a little more of my face tear off and my identity shrink.

I woke, already feeling sick and shaken, and with the acrid stink of fear in my nostrils, to find that there were fingers around my wrist.

My body reacted before my mind could process anything, and I was out of the bed and three quarters of the way down the stairs before my surroundings even made sense.

I'd been on the top floor, in Jamie's room. In his bed. Unless my life was even more of a train wreck than it had been lately, they'd been Jamie's fingers round my wrist. Probably something instinctual in his sleep, as he dreamt, but it'd still triggered me.

I dropped onto the bottom stair, its wooden surface cool beneath my bottom, and covered my face with my hands. Moving on from what had happened seemed as distant as the moon right then.

*** enable(altPOV) ***

Jamie roused slowly, his hand sliding across the bed as he reached for Lori, but she wasn't there, and alarm shook him upright. She'd fallen asleep on the sofa the night before, already in pyjamas and with hot chocolate next to her on a table, and he'd carried her to bed. In her sleep she'd tucked her head into his shoulder with her arms around his neck, the way they'd danced, and he'd loved the feel of her in his arms, accepting her deepening trust.

It'd been a risk bringing her upstairs, but he wanted her to be more comfortable than the sofa allowed. Then he'd been a complete idiot and got in next to her. With boxers and a t-shirt on, true, but she would've woken at some point and realised she wasn't alone in the bed. Sudden doubt clutched his heart.

Have I ruined everything between us by taking that choice from her?

Mentally crossing his fingers, he wandered over to his desk, hoping he was still in enough of a receptive frame of mind to try the writing trick. If ever he needed guidance, it was right then. He picked up the pen and smaller notepad, letting his mind quest for Lori's. She was likely somewhere in the house, not too far away... and his hand started to move the pen.

When it stopped, and he opened his eyes, it was to see the bittersweet drawing of a heart, with one word written across the middle:

Patience.

He hung his head, knowing he needed more of that. He'd made the mistake of thinking, because she reacted less to unexpected things while she was awake, it'd be the same in sleep. It obviously wasn't.

As he stood and processed the word, feeling the indent of the pen on the paper, something pressed itself into his awareness: the writing wasn't his. It never was. But it wasn't the *other* writing, either. He recognised it, and the knowledge soothed the stinging pinch of remorse.

It was Lori's.

Somehow, he'd tapped into her higher self. Maybe he hadn't ruined everything. He needed to find her, to see how she was after a few hours in a proper bed, and perhaps they could talk.

If not, at least there'd be coffee.

*** suspend(altPOV) ***

I heard the door open at the top of the stairs, and turned to see Jamie, typically bed-headed and not looking fully awake, but dressed. He came halfway down the stairs and sat.

"Hey," he spoke in a soft voice, "If I share my bed with a woman I prefer it if she's still there to say good morning to when I wake up." And he gave me a sleepy grin. "So what was that, sleep and split?"

I knew he was teasing me, and I was grateful, but I still felt nauseous, so didn't smile.

"What happened?"

"A nightmare."

"Why didn't you wake me?"

"You've been through so much recently, I didn't think it was fair." And I knew the next thing I said would upset him, but I wouldn't conceal it. "And I think you triggered it."

His shoulders slumped. "What did I do?"

"You were holding my wrist in your sleep. Unless there's anyone else up there, and we were three in a bed?" I tried to be funny, but the look in his eyes told me it hadn't worked. I moved up the stairs, so we were only two apart, and laid my head on his knee. He raised his hand to touch me, but let it drop instead.

"I'm sorry. I can't face sleeping back in my room yet, I can't kick you out of your bed, and sharing it is problematic. But the sofa isn't for sleeping on, really, either."

"Yeah." He scrubbed his hand over his face. "So we need another solution. And I may have one."

"Care to share?"

He extended his legs to walk down the rest of the flight, then crossed the landing and waited by the door to the spare room, beckoning me to join him. I did, and he opened the door.

"You're not using this room for anything particular. Why don't we get another bed, and set this up as your second bedroom? We can kit it out like it's a proper healing sanctuary. You've even got the whirlpool bath with LED lights right next door."

I leant against his arm. "Why didn't I think of that?"

"See, I'm useful sometimes. Not just a nightmare trigger. Get dressed, we're going shopping. And you're driving."

I looked up at him, seeing a touch of vulnerability before it faded, and he smiled.

"I trust you more behind the wheel than myself right now."

"How do you know I'm not still drunk from last night?"

"Because I carried you to bed, and you smelt like Lori, not alcohol." And he looked vaguely guilty, but I didn't press him. If he was more sensitive to it since the accident, I wouldn't blame him.

"Well, I wouldn't do," I retorted, "I didn't *have* any alcohol last night. Did you really think I could walk

round town in those heels if I was tipsy?"
"Suppose not," he conceded. "Wait, that means – oh shit."
"What's the matter?" I looked up at him, all wide-eyed pretended innocence. "Oh, you thought I didn't know what I was doing when I had you by the tie, because I'd had a drink? Or giving your phone number to the guy at the bar? Or... any number of things that happened last night before I conked out? How about dirty dancing with Evie? I bet you thought that was hot."
Jamie looked at me, his jaw set. Eventually he ground out, "I really want to put you across my knee right now and give your peachy backside what for."
"Thought you weren't into spanking?"
"I'd make an exception for you!" he said and lunged at me. I squeaked and darted into the bathroom, expecting him to follow. He didn't disappoint – and came face to bra cup with my drying lingerie, hanging from a temporary washing line strung across the room. He threw up his hands in resignation.
"OK, I'm done. You'll have to wait for me now. I need a time out." He stamped back up the stairs, slamming the door behind him. I giggled softly as I dressed: he'd said I was a torment.
Poor Jamie.

*** enable(altPOV) ***
Fifteen minutes later, when Jamie was back in full control of himself, they set off. He'd needed so few things for the flat he'd rented that this kind of shopping was a novel experience for him. He hadn't

ventured far beyond the edge of town when he'd driven, except for that fateful trip on the M1 motorway, but Lori knew her way round.
"What sort of bed do you want?" he asked while they waited at some traffic lights.
She wrinkled her nose. "Nothing flashy. A standard double divan, I think. I mean, I got you the super king size because you're tall."
"You know, the duvet doesn't really work on a super king if you're not sleeping solo. Two bodies take up more space under the covers so it doesn't reach the edges."
Lori glanced across at him. "I'm hoping we can find something they can deliver this afternoon, so I don't have to steal any more of your sleep."
Jamie said nothing. She stole his sleep whether or not she was in the bed. He wanted her as a permanent fixture, not an overnight guest, or for an hour here and there. But he'd been told he needed patience, and he'd work on that.
"So we're doing that first?"
"Yes, because anything else we can get home by ourselves. Much as I love my little car, it won't take a double mattress or divan."
"That makes sense."
Once they'd organised that, with a sneaky extra £20 cash that got them same-day delivery, they moved onto the fun things.
"How long did it take to repaint your room?" Lori asked.
"I didn't do it all at once," Jamie replied. "I was supposed to be working."

They both laughed.
"I want some kind of deep purple colour, I think." She mused.
"What, like aubergine?" Jamie asked and immediately regretted it as the colour drained from her face. "Sorry, poor taste after the WhatsApp stuff. What shade did you have in mind?"
"I have some lovely Uruguayan amethyst. It's dark enough for what's in my mind but doesn't have the red undertone of that other one. Let's see if we can find something close enough."
They bickered about it for a while. Jamie liked Purple Pout, and Lori preferred Regal Purple.
"I think your one sounds more like a lipstick than a paint colour," she said.
"Do you even own any lipstick?"
She rolled her eyes. "What sort of question's that? Of course I do."
"Why don't you wear it?"
"You know why it was invented, don't you?" She gave him a deadpan stare.
Jamie shrugged. "No, I'm a guy."
"Oh for God's sake, do I have to teach you everything? Yesterday it was historical facts about knickers. I thought you were a guy with experience."
"Not with lipstick."
"Well I suppose I should be grateful that I'm not living with a secret drag queen and you're raiding my underwear drawer—No, actually, I take that back. You tried to take my orange set and I caught you at it."
He spread his hands. "Guilty as charged. But if you recall, I didn't want to *wear* them."

"Ohmygod, I walked straight into that." Her cheeks flamed.

"That's the first of many paybacks you have coming, lovely girl. Now tell me the origin of lipstick."

Lori grabbed him by the shoulder and pulled him down to her level, whispering, "It's supposed to make men think of lady garden lips."

"Ahh," Jamie nodded, "Yeah, I can see that. But why don't you wear it, if you have it?"

"Oh I sometimes wear a nude pink shade, and you wouldn't notice that. But I don't really like being noticed through wearing make-up. I'm all about the clothing colours, because—" She stopped and lowered her eyes with a shy smile. "I'm not vain, but hey, I'm not what I'd call ugly, either." Then she looked away. "Even if I wanted to wear a brighter shade, right now I'd rather not draw more unwanted attention to myself."

Jamie squeezed her fingers. "You were stunning yesterday without it, so I'm not arguing with you."

"Flatterer." The light sparkle of amusement reappeared in her eyes. "What are you after?"

He leant close to her ear, and whispered, "I'm not telling you. You'll have to guess."

"I'm not playing that game with you." She folded her arms, her mouth set in a straight line.

"Spoilsport. Look, there's someone at the paint counter now. We can get your Regal Purple mixed."

And like that, he was back in her good graces.

They had coffee and a snack while they were out, and Jamie wanted to lick the froth Lori had on her nose, but was a gentleman instead and handed her a napkin.

She'd laughed, and he was content. Laden with cushions, candles – Lori's favourites were still drying out after the bathroom incident on Monday – and a couple of vases for fresh flowers, they packed themselves back into the car.

"Do you think we have everything?" Jamie asked, looking at the boot load they'd bought.

"Hmm," Lori thought for a moment. "Well, I didn't see anyone while we were out that'd scrub up into a nice enough masseur, so I guess I'll have to make do with you rubbing scented oils into my skin. Are you up for it?"

Fuck. Yes, he definitely was. He needed another time out.

They got most of the painting done before the bed arrived, which was good timing. They manhandled it up the stairs between them, and she surprised him with her strength as she tugged on the mattress wrapping. When he mentioned it, she grinned.

"Don't forget I did a lot of things here myself, including shifting all my boxes and cards. I'm allowing you to help. I got both beds up here by myself, although I had the delivery guy help me with your mattress."

A shadow dimmed her sunlight at the mention of her cards, but it passed. Jamie wanted to wrap his arms round her, but he couldn't think of anything to say that'd be helpful or comforting. She had to grieve their loss in her own way.

Eventually it was all done, and Lori threw herself backwards onto the bed. "Sumptuous!" she declared, surrounded by jewel-toned cushions and other pretty

things. “Even though it stinks of paint in here.”
“We’ll air it for a few hours,” Jamie suggested. “That’s all I did with mine. And it’s that special paint that isn’t supposed to give you a headache. I’ve got painkillers if you need them later.”
“Thanks.” She squinted up at him, because he was standing where the light was visible over his right shoulder. “I’m really glad you came up with this, Jamie. Thank you.”
“Welcome. Are you hungry yet? I thought we’d get pizza in. My arms ache so I don’t feel like spending any time stirring a saucepan.”
“You could be the first guest of the sanctuary, if you like? I’m not bad with my hands.”
“I bet you’re not.” He winked at her.
“Oh my God, Jamie! How am I supposed to answer that??”
“Actions speak louder than words?”
“Get out, filth monster!” Lori leapt up and shoved him towards the door. “Go order pizza. You know what I like.”
Not yet, Jamie thought, *but I hope to find out one day.*
*** suspend(altPOV) ***

It’d been a day that didn’t start well, but ended on a higher note than I’d learned to expect of late. Stuffed full of pizza and fizzy cola, we’d watched something trashy and squabbled over the remote control until about 10. Then I said goodnight, and Jamie came up with me.
He settled the duvet round me with a smile and turned off the light.

"You know where I am if you need me," he said. "I'll be awake a bit longer yet."

I felt safe, snuggled under my own duvet in my new sanctuary, but sleep refused to come. It was a new bed, too, so I wasn't used to it. And the leftover paint fumes were pinching at the sides of my head.

Pain in the arse.

Jamie had said he had some painkillers, and I wondered if he was still awake. I crept upstairs, and as I neared the top, I saw his light was still on. I tapped on the door and waited.

Nothing.

After a few minutes, I tapped again, louder. This time he came to the door, rubbing his eyes.

"I'm sorry I woke you. I thought you were still up because the light was on."

"No matter. Are you OK?"

"You said something about painkillers earlier. Are they decent strength? I've only got normal ones downstairs: ibuprofen and paracetamol."

"I think that's what I've got, but I'll check. Come in."

He swung the door open wide enough for me, and I realised he was still dressed, just barefoot.

"You fell asleep before you went to bed?"

"I was reading and couldn't be arsed to get up and take my things off. I'd have woken up in the night anyway and done it then." He rummaged through his bedside table. "No, I only have normal ones, sorry."

"It's OK, sorry I woke you for nothing." I turned to go.

"Lori?"

"Mmm?"

"I'm awake now. You may as well take my pills and

stay up here until your headache eases."
"I'm stopping you from getting back to sleep."
"I don't mind. I've got some apple and elderflower in my fridge."
Damn. That was one of my favourites, and he knew it.
"OK." And I perched on the edge of the bed while he fetched me a drink and passed me the tablets.
"Get comfy, they may take a while to kick in."
I took two of each, and the memory of the last time I'd taken painkillers – the Friday before – jolted me. It was exactly a week, pretty much to the hour, since Rod had let himself in with Jamie's stolen keys.
I lowered my head. No wonder I hadn't been able to sleep.
"Lori?" Jamie's voice was careful. "You look unsteady. Want to talk to me about it?"
"Yes... no... I don't know." I turned where I sat, and he was watching me from a reclined position with his arm behind his head. "It's been a week."
"Yeah, you're not kidding. So much has gone on it's not funny."
"No, Jamie, you misunderstand. I meant, it's been a week since he was here and... it happened."
He closed his eyes for a beat. "Oh Lori... Sweetheart." He patted the space near him, not so close that I'd feel smothered, but close enough that we'd be face to face.
I put my glass on the desk and stretched out next to him.
"I'd hug you, but I don't think you'd let me."
"Not right this minute."
"Talk to me. I want to understand why not."
"I'm not even sure I know where to begin."

Jamie frowned, then a gentle smile formed on his lips. "Start with this morning, when you left me."
I exhaled. "As you've realised, I have a few triggers. I'm able to control them better when I'm awake, but it still happens."
"OK, with you so far."
"If I initiate touch, I seem to be better. But—well, the wrists thing." I regarded mine, then held out one for him to see. "You remember I freaked when you grabbed me on Monday."
"Vividly." He shuddered.
"You see here, you can just about make out the bruising? The left one was the worst of the two, because I'd already tried to slap him when he—he tried to kiss me. He had both held in his right hand when he hit me across the face, and he made sure I couldn't get free."
I stopped for a moment and cleared my throat. "So any restraint around them triggers me. I'm sure you didn't mean for it to happen, but I'd already been reliving it in the nightmare. When I woke and I was still being held, my body reacted before my brain had time to think. It was survival instinct, I reckon."
"So I can't tie you up with silk ribbons right now?" he teased, his voice gentle.
I shook my head, unable to smile. "I think I'd have a panic attack. And that won't be pretty."
His smile broadened. "That's something that must be consensual, in my book."
I lowered my gaze. "Mine too."
"OK, I understand. Do you want to continue, or do you need a minute?"

"I need a minute," I admitted, meeting his eyes. His gaze was steady, warm and open. He wanted to learn how *not* to hurt or scare me. That meant so much.

I looked at the distance between us on the duvet, and Jamie's hand lying passive while his other arm held him up. His hand wouldn't harm me. I could see it in my memories: stirring something for dinner. Stroking Sid and scratching behind his ears, immersed in the moment with his cat, forehead to forehead. Typing at 100 miles an hour on his keyboard in coding mode, oblivious to everything around him, including his rapidly cooling coffee. Wet with my tears, when I'd told him everything.

He wanted to know how much touch was OK, and where the line was. I reached out and laid my hand over his. Grounded and solid, my best friend. I closed my eyes, trusting him, and he remained perfectly still. *Thank God.* I let out a shaky breath, and the contact imbued me with courage. Maybe I could carry on.

"Following on from that one, you won't be surprised that being trapped or boxed in also causes..." I shrugged with a half-hearted smile, "Problems."

"Yeah, I saw that."

"So if I ask you to reach something down for me, can you please let me step out of the way first?"

"Of course. I just did what I usually would." He looked past me, over my shoulder. "It was so great to be thinking like me, reacting like me, after the whole concussion thing. To be somewhere that felt familiar again, almost like I hadn't been away, once the memories came back." He slid his hand out from beneath mine.

Had I hurt his feelings, saying it like that? I didn't think so, but he might have been remembering everywhere things had gone wrong over the previous few weeks – God knew there'd been enough of them. "It sucks, doesn't it?" I said to draw his attention back to the present.

"Yeah. Anything else I need to know?"

"Everything's easier if you move slowly, let me set the pace if we're doing something together, at least for a while. It gives me time to assess what's going on, rather than the instinct stuff kicking in."

"You were fine dancing last night."

"Yeah, that felt *so* good. Because music is there to be experienced. It's not trying to take anything from me. But next time we dance, I want lower heels on."

"Are we talking vertical dancing or horizontal?"

"Oh my *God* Jamie, is there even an entire hour of the day when you're not thinking about sex?"

He grinned. "Probably not. Unless I'm coding. That's the trouble if you don't get any, it preys on your mind more."

"Can't say I've ever had trouble ignoring it."

"Now, is that a Lori thing or a woman thing? Shall we ask Evie? The way she and Therese were when they left, their sex life must be fantastic."

"Nope. Don't want to know. None of my business. Besides, everyone's different. For example, if I was a nympho, your idea of plenty might not be enough for me."

He flopped onto his back. "Yeah, thanks for that. I've never had any complaints... Well actually, that's not true."

"Oh?"
"The only time I've left a woman dissatisfied was because...nothing happened."
"What, nothing?"
"No. I thought it was a good idea before I got there, then..." He raised his shoulders as best he could from his position. "Well, never mind."
"Do you want to talk about it?" I asked in a soft voice.
"No, I'll pass. It wasn't my proudest moment."
"OK, I won't ask again. But remember what you said earlier about knowing where you were? That goes both ways. If you want to talk about anything, I'm here for you."
"Can we talk about me having you on the kitchen table?"
What...the...hell?
I fixed him with a stare, incredulous at his question.
"Guess not. So you've already spoiled it, haven't you?" His grin was a mile wide.
I rolled my eyes. "I meant serious things."
"Oh. Well, I suppose having you on the table would be fun, so it doesn't count. I'll let you off."
"Thanks, I think."
"Might think about it later instead."
"Jamie!"
"Seriously though, don't you think about it?"
"I've been burnt by you before with questions like that. Are we talking general thoughts about sex, or specific ones? I want to know before deciding whether to answer you or not."
"Aww Lori, where's the fun in telling you which it is? I love seeing you get flustered."

"You said something last night about getting me hot and bothered, you beast!"
"Oh, you heard that? Good. I don't need to repeat myself, then."
"I'm going now. Goodnight." I scrambled off the bed and he chuckled.
"Goodnight, Lori, come again any time!"
I put my nose in the air. "I hope you'd be a *little* more observant if I had, while I was here."
"It depends. Are you a screamer?"
"I'm out of here. See you tomorrow."
His laughter followed me down the stairs. Drat him, I couldn't see any way I'd win. He was far more comfortable talking about sex than I was, which meant he'd always have the advantage there. I'd have to find something else I could beat him at.

CHAPTER TWENTY THREE

24th November 2022

The days that followed, with Jamie still off work to get over the emotional fallout from the deepfake pics accusation, were like a second summer – although the weather was doing its usual double-digit days and single-digit nights, as November often did. We unearthed new-to-us places to visit, made happy memories to replace unhappy ones where we could, prepped and batch cooked meals together and loaded the freezer, and relaxed back into our best friendship, which I'd sorely missed. It was easier to be around Jamie once he knew more about what triggered me, and he did his best not to overstep the boundaries I'd asked for.

Thursday morning, quite early, Sid was round my feet and being a bit of a pest. He didn't need feeding, and he let himself in and out through the cat flap when he wanted, so it wasn't that. I remembered Jamie had some treats in his bedroom, so went up to ask for them, knocking at the door.

No answer.

I knocked again, but silence reigned, even when I put my ear against the door. That was irritating, as I was pretty sure he was in there – his footsteps had creaked the floor above my head before I got up. Maybe he was in the shower and couldn't hear me, because he'd never slept through when I'd knocked twice before. I shrugged to myself and went in, and as I did so I could hear the water running. OK, no problem. I was sure the last place I'd seen the treats was on his desk.

As I looked for them, there was a noise from the shower that had a kind of rhythm to it. A dull thud. Was he OK in there? It wouldn't hurt to make sure, in case something had happened, like he'd slipped and banged his head and was having a seizure. As I peeped round the edge of the open door, I saw him silhouetted behind the frosted glass. And he was... relieving some tension.

Flashbacks to the night of the 11th came flooding back – waking to find Rod in my bedroom doing the same thing – and I couldn't get out of there fast enough. How I made it to the bottom of both flights of stairs without breaking my neck I had no idea, but Sid was going to have to wait for his treats. I was *not* going back to get them.

When Jamie came downstairs ten minutes later, hair still damp but fully dressed, I couldn't look at him.

"Did you come up while I was in the shower? I thought I heard the door."

"Don't talk to me, please." I wasn't sure whether my face was red or white. It might have been alternating.

"Oh, you did. Yeah, sorry I wasn't there to greet you. My self-care routine's pretty important."

"I don't want to know!"

"What's the matter, Lori? Are you uncomfortable with knowing that about me? Figured you'd already worked it out." Jamie grinned.

"God, it's not that! Not at all. There's no way I'd have come in if I'd known you were... enjoying yourself."

He poured some coffee and slathered butter on a piece of toast. "So what's the problem?"

"It should be done in private and I intruded on your

session, which was embarrassing enough. But it threw me right back to when I was here alone. I was so upset when Rod—"

Shit. In my efforts to be honest with him about things that triggered me, I'd let that slip.

"You—what?" Jamie spoke in such a soft voice that fingers of worry ran down my spine.

"Sorry, I have somewhere else to be. Talk later?" I leapt up from my chair. I had to get away fast – I hadn't meant to tell him that way.

He reacted in less than an instant and flattened my hand on the table so firmly with his strong fingers that I had no avenue of escape. I didn't even have time to register he'd moved before I was stuck, but at least he wasn't hurting me.

"Sit—the fuck—down." His voice was implacable.

There was no option for me to do anything but comply.

"Explain. Right now. Is it true?"

My teeth snapped together so hard on my lip that I tasted blood, but I nodded.

"You've been keeping this a secret the whole time? You couldn't tell me?"

"What did you expect me to do, Jamie?" I answered, sarcasm biting through my words. "Drop it into our morning coffee chats? Yeah I can picture it now. 'Hey Jamie, you know your friend who sent me those disgusting suggestive texts? Well guess what, he's even more of a sicko than we both thought. All the things I went through that you've been wanting to kill someone for, the photos that destroyed my business, the email that impersonated you, for Christ's sake, was all him. Is this the sort of friend you want in your life?'"

I filled my lungs and then shrieked at him, "*HOW WAS I SUPPOSED TO SAY THAT TO YOU??*"
"I don't believe you!" Jamie's face was a granite mask.
"Jesus! Pass me my bag." I removed the letter I'd had from Evie's friends. "You really think I'd lie about something like this?? That hurts, Jamie, as much as being hit across the face does." I shoved it across the table at him with my free hand. "Read that. Get your damn head round it. The guy's sick."
He skimmed through it. "I don't understand. Why didn't you tell me?"
"Because I *knew* you'd be furious, Jamie! You'd already said to me you wanted to kill whoever had done it. This is someone you've known for *years* longer than me!"
He loomed over me, his jaw tight. "Yeah, it would've been difficult, I get that. But keeping it from me, Lori? Concealing it? Deceiving me over it? That's much worse. What were you doing, protecting him from me?"
"How is this my fault now? That's not fair!"
"Fair? Life's not fair! I placed my trust in you! I've done everything I can to help you move past it, and this is how you repay me? I thought we were best friends, open and honest with each other. This—" He gestured at the letter, his voice straight from the Arctic yet pitched low, and it was all the more painful for that restraint.
"Your actions tell me otherwise. I've been so fucking stupid. Have I been a pawn to your little scheme the whole time? Have you been laughing at me behind my back that I was so gullible? Did you make it up so I'd

feel sorry for you, and the whole time you were leading him on, or even screwing him? Then it's all 'oh poor me, look what the nasty man's done' bullshit!"

The pulse in his temple beat double-time as he took a deep breath. "I thought you were different, Lori. I expected better of you." And he turned on his heel to drag his steps along the hallway, shoulders bowed.

"If you're really that disappointed in me, try using your own words instead of parroting what Rod's already said!" I flung at his disappearing back, but I didn't know if he'd heard me before the front door slammed shut behind him.

My dearest, closest friend felt I'd betrayed him.

I wanted to cry. I wanted to scream. I wanted to smash the kitchen into pieces.

But I did nothing. I sat in the chair like a statue, while snow flurried through my veins to form a glacier that covered my heart, and sank my entire world into its own private ice age.

*

I didn't know how long I sat there. I knew Jamie had come home after however many hours it was, because he came in the back door and walked right past me without speaking, without looking at me, like I didn't exist in his eyes any more. And I didn't try speaking either. The weight of his disbelief pulverised me.

I wanted to be numb, but the closeness we'd had, over the previous week, had made me feel alive – properly alive – for the first time since before his accident. I had to be breathing, because surely death couldn't be as excruciating.

I went to bed about 7. I didn't bother with dinner, but I

made sure Sid was fed and had some cuddles before I retreated. The man might hate me, but at least his cat didn't. No surprise, I didn't sleep. But as the clock moved on towards 10pm, I thought I heard something outside.

I was already hyper alert from the events of the morning, and my lack of eating had left me untethered. I didn't even use conscious thought before I slipped from the bed on light feet and made my way to the window. There was a slight shimmering outside, near ground level, of a reflective flat object being lowered to the ground, and the figure of a man.

My blood ran cold. Our town was a quiet seaside resort and rarely saw serious crime. Not like a city, where there was all sorts going on. You were more likely to get a dust-up over the last cream cake at a café in town than anything else, but I couldn't deny the evidence in front of me.

I suspected I knew who it was. And I needed to be certain before I did anything about it – or as certain as I could be. And if it was him, why was he breaking in when Jamie was here? Then it became clear. If Rod had seen Jamie leave but not come back, or believed him to still be in London, avoiding me because of the photos, he could've waited until after dark before doing anything.

Rod must've gained access over the side wall like Jamie had ten days before. He wouldn't know there was a way you could enter the garden unobserved if you had a dollop of ingenuity, catlike stealth, and crossed fingers. But we did.

Nausea oozed through me, thinking it was probably

him, but fear wasn't a good enough reason for ignorance.
I slipped out of the sanctuary and across to my old bedroom. I hadn't been able to set foot in it since Rod had been in it, because it didn't feel like my space any more. It was tainted. And I didn't want to go in it but I needed to, to confirm or refute that Rod was breaking into my house.
I steeled myself and opened the door.
Memories assaulted me – Rod's behaviour, the ritual to release Jamie, Sid sleeping on my bed the nights Jamie was in the hospital. So many emotions, and most of them negative. My breath caught in a quiet sob, which I quickly choked back. I forced myself over the threshold and towards the window, drifting on silent tiptoe, avoiding the two floorboards I knew would give me away.
The bay window gave me a perfect view of the street, and up by number 13 I could see what looked like a silver 4x4 that wasn't usually there. I closed my eyes for a moment, praying for strength. I knew what I had to do, whatever the consequences, but I was afraid that Jamie wouldn't listen to me. He'd said horrific, hurtful things earlier.
I had no choice.
Leaving my room, trembling with fear and apprehensive of my reception, I sneaked up the stairs. I didn't dare knock because sound carried throughout the house at night. I turned the handle and went in, to find the room in total darkness.
"Jamie." I whispered.
Nothing.

"Jamie." I said again, at the same volume.
"Go away."
"It's important."
"I don't care."
I knew where he was, lying on the bed, on the side he let me use if I was talking to him, nearest the desk. I tiptoed across the floor.
"I need to tell you something."
"I'm too angry to listen. Go away and leave me alone."
"Jamie, I can't explain how important this is unless you listen."
He sighed, but didn't switch a light on. "Five seconds, then get out. Five...four...three..."
"Someone's broken into the house. They're downstairs."
He swore under his breath.
"I think it's Rod. I thought I could see his car, parked up the road. Will you check, and see if you agree?" I kept my voice at a whisper.
"But why now?"
"It's Thursday. You're often at the office. I don't know how long he's been watching the house, but I'm pretty sure he won't know you're here."
"Suits me fine." Jamie's voice was low and controlled. I shivered. He didn't sound like my laughing, teasing bestie at all.
If he even still was.
I quashed that thought and waited. Jamie moved silently in the dark to the window and looked out before making his way over to me.
"I can't see the reg from here, but it looks like it. Stay here."

"What are you going to do?"
I felt his burner phone being pushed into my hand.
"Sort this shit out. If it gets noisy, call the police."
I grabbed his arm, but he wrenched it out of my grip.
"Jamie."
"What *now*?"
"Be careful."
He didn't reply, sliding down the stairs in socked feet, and I did what I was told.
I stayed put.

*** enable(altPOV) ***
The room was dimly lit from the street lamp outside, but Jamie could see well enough after hours of sitting in the dark. He took his phone from his pocket and set it on the desk to record, and hoped it'd be good enough. Fire ignited throughout his nervous system in anticipation.
He wanted to pace, feeling caged, but he didn't want his footsteps to give away that he was there. And he was pretty sure that Rod, if it was him, didn't have any idea of his presence. He stationed himself behind the door, where he wouldn't be seen immediately, with one finger poised above the lamp switch, and waited. The darkness amplified every single sound in the house, and he could hear his own breathing, even though he was trying to keep it slow, to keep control. His heart felt engorged with blood, ready to fuel him into what needed to be done. And in that moment, he heard it: the door handle going down.
He readied himself. Things could get ugly.
The door opened and Rod came in, making his way

over to the bed with the familiarity of someone who'd been there before. Jamie watched from the gloom, his eyes narrowed. He hadn't wanted to believe Lori's letter. Hadn't thought his friend would actually stoop so low, but it was looking more irrefutable by the second.

One final chance to redeem himself. Jamie flicked the lamp switch.

Rod whirled, and Jamie smirked.

"Not who you were expecting?" He glanced down at the objects Rod held: duct tape, a flick knife and some braided line from the DF95 boats. Disbelieving, he barked a laugh. "What were you planning on doing, kidnapping her?"

"Fuck, no," Rod answered with a shrug. "Just having a bit of fun. She's too whiny to have around all the time. I thought she'd be better than the others, but I was wrong. Doesn't seem to matter what I do to them, they all end up the same." His tone was almost wistful, and Jamie's blood ran cold.

"They don't want what I want to give them. And that hurts, y'know?"

Jamie did know, but he thought his way of giving, and Rod's, were very different. He took a measured step towards him.

"You stole my phone," Jamie confronted him. "You took the happy memories of us building a life together and turned them into something hateful. And if you'd do something like that, it's probably not a massive leap to think you tricked me somehow into drinking alcohol that night at the meet, too."

"Nah, I wouldn't call it a trick, as such. You don't really

notice a shot of coffee liqueur in a mocha. I thought it might free up your tongue to get you to be honest. If you were banging her, or not, as you said. If you weren't, I didn't see what the problem was if I showed interest."

Rod laughed, a hard mirthless sound. "Seriously, if you're living with that and not balls-deep, what the fuck is wrong with you?"

"It's called respect, which I'm beginning to think you know little of."

"It's called being pussy-whipped – and you've not even sampled the goods. I have. Be prepared for disappointment."

Jamie folded his arms. "You manipulated Lori when she was already vulnerable. You gaslit her into thinking you cared, and that I didn't. All while I was trying to put the pieces of my life back together after the accident."

"Can you even hear yourself? Don't you get it? She's never going to want you. She'll never come to you of her own accord. You'll *never* be able to give her what she needs. But I can." Rod's mouth twisted into a nasty grin. "She needs a real man in her...life."

"It won't be you!" Jamie retorted and jabbed at him with his fist, dancing back out of the way as the blade of the knife appeared.

Rod wiped his bleeding nose on his arm. "That wasn't friendly," he said. "After all I've done for you, we fall out over a woman?"

A red mist filtered down over Jamie's eyes. "No, Rod," he answered, unable to comprehend Rod's attitude. "Not just a woman. *All* women. They're not toys, to be played with and broken, then discarded."

Rod shrugged. "Don't agree. The strong ones don't break straight away, so they're more fun. Look at your Lori, she's a prime example. But if you want a fight over opinions, let's get on with it."

"Put the knife down first."

Rod rolled his eyes. "Everyone knows you should never give up your advantage. It makes you weak." He sprang at Jamie, the knife in his hand catching the lamp light.

Fists flew back and forth a few times as they circled and closed, grappled and separated, neither inflicting much damage on the other with untrained blows, until Rod caught Jamie with the knife tip twice in quick succession – across the chin and between the eyebrows. Maddened by the sting, Jamie descended fully into the red mist. He'd had enough.

He flew forward and, heedless of the danger, blocked the knife blade with his forearm, the sheer momentum of their combined body weight driving them towards the far wall. Rod's lungs emptied of air at the impact, and Jamie knocked the knife from Rod's right hand with his left before he gripped Rod's throat with his fingers and punched him hard in the face with the other hand.

"Fuck you, Jamie, and your stupid bitch!" Rod spluttered through a mouthful of blood and Jamie hit him again as the door burst open, then drew his fist back for another blow.

Lori flew in, her face white. She hauled back on Jamie's arm and hung on grimly.

"Jamie, please. Not this way. Please." Her voice was

steady, at odds with her expression and how tightly she grasped his arm.
“What’s wrong with you?? I can’t believe you’re still protecting this sick bastard!” He raged at her. She lifted her chin.
“Not him, us. You and me, Jamie,” She stopped speaking and shook her head, “Cross this line and there’s no going back.”
A heavy silence fell, broken only by Jamie’s ragged breathing, then he exploded.
“FUUUCK!” he roared, driving his fist into the wall, rather than Rod’s face. The intense pain brought him partway back to himself, and he let Rod’s throat go, staggering back and falling to his knees as his ex-friend slid down the wall into unconsciousness.
Lori caught Jamie’s face between her hands, her touch gentle yet forcing him to look up at her. “Jamie. Focus on me now. Breathe with me, in... and out. Slowly now. That’s it. You’re doing great. The police are on their way.”
*** suspend(altPOV) ***

The paramedics made sure that Rod was still breathing and patched him up a bit before the police carted him off. It looked dire for him. The police also took evidence from my old bedroom and, when I saw what Rod had brought with him, I had to turn away, heaving.
Jamie handed his phone over to the police, and I heard him talking with the officers quietly, but I retreated to the bottom of the stairs out of the way. I wasn’t convinced my legs would keep me up anyway.

One of the attending officers came to speak to me.
"Lori Archer, right? Do you want to give me your version of what's happened tonight?"
So I related how the day had gone, from first thing in the morning to that moment. Then I answered questions about what had happened on Friday 11th, and they took the letter Evie's friends had sorted out for me. I explained that HR at Jamie's work had the full report if they needed a copy of it. The officer smiled.
"We know about these guys, we've had dealings with them before. They've still got your phone?"
"Yes. I don't want it back."
"We'll be in touch to get you to sign a release form for it so we can look over those messages. OK?"
"Sure."
Then they asked whether I wanted to press charges against Rod. I did, and we went through what they all were. Being inside the situation rather than outside, I hadn't considered how many there were, and it disgusted me. Partly because I'd allowed things to go that far, but mostly at the deranged individual that had done it.
But my heart hurt most for Jamie. Losing a friend of fifteen or so years would be devastating for him.
A paramedic came over to check if I wasn't injured, and for the first time I noticed there was blood spattered up my arms. Probably Rod's from when I'd restrained Jamie, but there were larger drops on my pyjama top: they were Jamie's. My bottom lip quivered, but I refused to cry in front of all those people doing their jobs. There'd be time enough for

that later.
"You're probably in shock," the paramedic said. "Have you got any brandy in the house?"
"No, we don't drink it. I'll make myself a hot drink in a minute." I didn't think the kitchen had been trashed, but I'd find out soon enough.
"Can you have a word with Jamie? The way his hand's swollen up so fast it may be fractured somewhere."
"I'll try."
Jamie sat on the end of my bed, his right hand cradled in his left. I could see what they meant about the swelling. I touched his shoulder, and he flinched.
"Hey," I lowered myself down next to him, trying to make eye contact. He was having none of it, and turned his head away. "Thank you for what you did. I'm so glad you were here."
He said nothing and kept his face averted.
I sighed and hoped the fracture between us would heal, but if there was one in his hand I was powerless to help.
"I think you should go to A&E and get your hand looked at."
He made no response.
"It's probably going to hurt more in a few hours. Right now it might not be too bad, because your system's full of adrenaline, but it could swell up further. If there's anything broken it'll need setting or whatever they can do for it. I can't help you with that, but I can take you up to the hospital. Or you can go in the ambulance, and I can come get you when you're done."
His shoulders stiffened. "I don't want or need anything from you."

"Take the phone with you, then. Call a cab to get home."
"I'll make my own way back, when I'm ready." And he rose, walking away to let the paramedics know he'd go with them.
He didn't say goodbye.
I waited until everyone had gone and the house was quiet, then went into the kitchen. Rod's bloodied face and Jamie's blind rage alternated on repeat in my head. In the heat of the moment, I hadn't even stopped to think whether it was a good idea to try and stop Jamie from going further than he had. I didn't know where I'd got the strength from, but it didn't matter. Rod was still breathing, even if I hadn't decided whether he deserved to.
I wasn't a fan of violence by any stretch of the imagination.
It was chilly in the kitchen, and for a minute I wondered why. Oh, the window! I'd have to stop it up until I could get it fixed. More bills I could've done without, with no money coming in. I was pissed off and heartsick, and there was a flip switch between them. One minute one would be at the forefront, then the roles were reversed. It was exhausting, but I couldn't think of a way to turn it off.
Then something overruled both at once: I owed Jamie my life, and he didn't want to be anywhere near me. I crumpled to the floor, sobbing, and I was no longer heart *sick* – it'd gone from ill to broken in zero seconds flat.
A wet patch had formed under the window where the rain had got in. How much more would there be? I had

to find something to block the window with, in case it poured. I tried to restart my brain to think of what I could use, but all I came up with was one of my half-finished paintings. They were stashed in the small understairs storage cupboard on the first floor. It wasn't important which one I used, only that it was a good enough fit for the window, so I grabbed the first one at hand.

It was of Brookfield Park. I remembered the day I'd gone up there with a picnic, before Jamie had moved in. The foxgloves had been in flower, extending their purple blooms outwards from the tall spikes. I'd been quite pleased with how it'd turned out, but it was more use keeping the rain out than as a landscape.

I was indecisive after that. An enormous chunk of me wanted to sit in Jamie's room, where I still felt relatively safe. Or even curl up on his bed and hope to Spirit that he came home.

When he was ready, he'd said.

It could be hours, until the hospital had done what they needed.

It could be days, with him staying somewhere else until he felt able to walk through the front door again.

It could be weeks, with him buying new clothes instead of coming back for his things here, and living in one of the company suites up town.

It could be never.

And I had to accept that it'd be his decision.

The day dawned after an eternity. Jamie wasn't home, and it crossed my mind that he could still be at the hospital. I hoped not, for his sake. He'd be pissed off and bored by now, with no phone, nothing to do and a

bomb load of pain in his hand.
There were drops of blood – it didn't matter whose – on the landing, down the stairs and in the hall. It was sickening. I wanted to look up ways the net suggested getting it out of the carpet, but Jamie's burner phone wasn't cooperating with our Wi-Fi and I hadn't replaced my laptop. There was no way I was going to use Jamie's. It had all his work stuff on it, and his own PC had personal things, and it'd be a massive invasion of privacy.
There was no other option: I'd have to go to the library and either use their computers to look stuff up, or borrow books on household tips.
While I was out, the burner phone rang, and I cautiously answered it.
"Hello, is that Miss Lori Archer?"
"Yes, that's me."
"It's DS Sharon Walker from Sussex Police."
"Hello, how are you?"
"I'm good. Thank you again for your cooperation last night. Am I OK to call you Lori?"
"Yes, that's fine."
"I just wanted to follow up on a couple of points from your statement, Lori. It's nothing to worry about, we're simply reviewing everything fully now that Jamie Brightfield's recording has been logged."
Jamie had recorded what had happened? Oh, that was why the police had taken his phone.
"OK, how can I help?"
"There's a couple of things we'd like to clarify, specifically about what occurred on Friday 11th. In our conversation last night, you mentioned about the two

visits from Rod Corland: one in the morning, one late that night or maybe early morning on the 12th, when you said you experienced sexual assault at his hands. Are you OK with going further into some details around that? Do you have someone there who can support you?"

I shuddered because I didn't want to, but I could if it made it easier for the police to do their job. "I'm alone, but I can answer. What do you need to know?"

"You mentioned this involved Rod Corland masturbating in your bedroom then depositing his semen on your person. But in the recording, there's a comment from him saying that he had already 'sampled the goods'."

"What?" I said faintly. "Did I hear that right? He said he'd sampled the goods?"

"Yes, Lori. It's unpleasant to hear, sorry about that. We understand that it could be posturing or bravado, but it does directly contradict your account. So I need to confirm, were there any further sexual interactions between you and Mr Corland? Even if you didn't feel comfortable disclosing them last night, it's important for us to have all the relevant information in one place."

"No, there was nothing else. What he said is not true at all! There were the two incidents I told you about last night. Before that it was solely the texts, and no direct contact since. Just the photos and website I mentioned. I'd already blocked his number on my phone and had the locks on the house changed prior to the deepfakes." I was shaking, and it stemmed from anger, not fear. How *dare* he say that?? Lying bastard.

"Thank you, I appreciate that. We're treating it as part of the formal charges, and it helps us solidify the timeline."

"OK, I understand."

"There's one other thing. On the recording, Mr Brightfield makes a reference to 'building a life together.' Can I confirm, have you and he been in a romantic relationship at any point?"

I thought about it. I supposed we were building a life together, as friends. Jamie had only ever kissed me on the cheek or the top of the head, and that rarely. Sometimes we hugged or cuddled up on the sofa to watch TV, but it never went further. We both knew where the best friend line was drawn. "No. Not previously, and not now."

"That's great, thanks. I'm only asking to rule out that motive. The CPS will want to be certain he acted for protective reasons, not in retaliation or through jealousy."

So Jamie wouldn't face prosecution for what he'd done. "OK, I understand." I said again.

"Thanks again for your time, Lori. If you need support – emotional, legal, anything – our victim liaison team can help you directly. They'll be in touch soon to go through what they do, and to set you up with a specific officer."

We said our goodbyes and hung up.

Just as well Rod was already in the hospital - for lying like that I'd have wanted to put him there myself.

But my head dropped into my hands as it all clarified at once. He'd been talking to Jamie, who'd already accused me of deceiving him. Of having a "little scheme" and laughing behind his back about it all. Of making it up.

Jamie had also accused me of screwing Rod.

Quite possibly, he would never believe another word I said.

CHAPTER TWENTY FOUR

The rest of Friday passed with me up to my elbows in stain extraction. It appeared each time I diluted and removed one bloody spot I saw another, which added to the list. I hadn't even contemplated how much there'd be in my old bedroom to clean up. I almost got up the nerve to look, but grief and fear at how overwhelming it'd be stole what little courage I had. When I came over light-headed, I didn't have the heart to cook or make myself something. I found Jamie's leftover toast from Thursday morning and ate that. It'd tide me over, and maybe I'd feel like eating something the next day.

I had another 15 hours or thereabouts before someone would be out to replace the glass in the kitchen window. Chances were, nobody would try and enter the house overnight, but I couldn't take the risk. I sat up all night, TV on but muted, with a knife in my hands.

And Jamie still didn't come home.

*** enable(altPOV) ***

By the time Jamie had been triaged, x-rayed, splinted and sent on his way, until a week later for reassessment of his two fractured metacarpals, it was light. He wasn't sure of his emotions about anything: part revulsion at himself for the violence, fury still at Rod, and a weary yet unrelenting nausea at Lori. She said she'd told him everything, but she'd lied. It was almost her proper name – Lorelei sounded very similar to 'Lori lied'.

Or maybe Rod lied, his heart whispered, but he ignored it. He couldn't deal with any of it right then. He wanted – needed – to get some sleep, but he didn't even know where he was. Not in Littlehampton, that was obvious, but which hospital they'd brought him to was a mystery.

He hung around outside the main building for a while, trying to do Lori's trick of being able to feel which direction the sea was in, to orient himself, but failed. He closed his eyes, seeing if he could feel anything that might help. Guidance, a gentle tug in a particular direction, a hunch.

Nothing. He was painfully alone. The sun was rising, and he squinted at it. It was too bright. Birds were singing, and they were too loud, and it was like someone was rubbing sandpaper over his mind. At least the sun told him which direction was east. Compass points, OK, but he didn't know which way home was, and people were staring at his bloodied clothes.

Yeah, fair enough. They made him feel sick, too. He'd better deal with that. The pain in his hand and the whole shitshow had drawn heavily from his reserves, and he'd have to refuel, but it was shitty to make other people see him in that state. Nobody deserved to witness the aftermath of what had gone on in the front bedroom.

Lori was inside the aftermath, his heart reminded him, and he wasn't there with her. He told it to fuck off and leave him alone.

She'd lied to him about Rod. If there had been more to it, which Rod had said there was, it made a mockery of it all and he'd be facing charges for GBH. He knew Rod could be a litigious little bastard when crossed – he'd seen someone else run afoul of him some years back. He groaned and went to scrub his hand down his face, only to smack himself in the eye with his new cast. Agony shot from his fingers to his shoulder in response.

"For fuck's sake," he muttered under his breath, and used his left hand instead to rub some of the fatigue from his eyes. And it began to dawn on him how bad things were.

They'd called it a boxer's fracture, and the splint immobilised his outer two fingers. He might be able to hold a pen if he was lucky, but they'd said any pressure on his hand from normal activities would likely make him nauseous for a few days until the worst bruising receded.

He couldn't hold and steady a mug of coffee. He couldn't tie shoelaces. He'd even found it difficult taking a piss. And he couldn't type with his right hand, which meant he wouldn't be able to code.

Great.

Tiger was going to kill him. He was supposed to be back at work Monday.

As he ran through things in his head, he discovered how many of them required his right hand. Cooking, showering, reading, dressing. Pretty much existing in general. This was so much worse than when he'd broken his left wrist. As a right-hander, that had been tough, but he'd coped. There was a special word for this situation, wasn't there?

Yeah, fucked.

No, a proper term. He paused in his ruminations to breathe a little deeper, trying to centre himself.
Focus on me now, Lori had said. *Breathe with me... You're doing great.*
She'd put herself directly in the path of his hurricane fury to try and reach him. To touch his inner self, the one she knew. The man she trusted.
Not for him – us, also drifted across his memory. *Cross this line, and there's no going back.*
He hadn't crossed that line, but there was no going back, anyway.
Maybe she'd only said it as part of her ploy for believability. Maybe she didn't care about him at all. A sour taste flooded his mouth at the thought, and he was overwrought enough to want to spit it out, but his parents hadn't brought him up that way.
It boiled down to a simple thing: should he believe Rod, who he'd known for sixteen years since university, who had sometimes been evasive in the past but never outright lied to his face, to Jamie's knowledge? Or Lori, who had? Was she lying again about everything between her and Rod? Was it actually consensual, and through her manipulations she'd cost him Rod's friendship?
It wasn't a tangle to unravel at home, if it even *was* home any more. He needed some space to think.
First, where the fuck was he? To find that out, he'd need to speak to someone, or find the hospital name and hope it told him where it was. He detested having to ask for help, and he didn't want to interact with people, but he had no other options – the police had his phone.

He went to the main reception at the hospital. He was mentally familiar with the order of towns along the Sussex coastline, west to east, from when he and Lori had been having days out the week before. Bognor, Littlehampton, Worthing—

Brighton? He wasn't even in the right county: he'd crossed into East Sussex. Absolutely fucking brilliant. Could Jamie walk into the city centre from the hospital? He had no idea and asked the person at the main desk. He could, they said, but it didn't look like he was currently up to it. There were regular buses that'd take him there.

The sling was already chafing at the back of his neck after only a few hours, riding above the collar of his t-shirt. He needed something that gave him more protection.

An underground bunker would be a useful thing right then so he could isolate himself from the world, never mind a hoodie.

Just as well he had his wallet in his pocket, though. It looked like he'd be exploring Brighton for the next however long, until he came to some sort of decision.

The shops were opening by the time Jamie reached the centre of the city. He'd need clothes he could get into and out of without clouting his hand often – and the sooner the better. People must've thought he'd been out all night on the piss and had got into a fight through drunkenness. It was hard to admit to himself that he didn't have that excuse.

He couldn't put names right then to the emotions he was feeling, but they weren't ones he'd experienced often.

He found most of what he was looking for in Primark. It didn't matter what his clothes looked like, all he was concerned about was comfort and looking more presentable. And being able to dress himself.

Christ, it was like being a toddler! Not that he remembered being that young, unless... Was that a memory of Emily's first day of school and how much he'd howled when she wasn't there? He was three years younger, so it'd be about right.

Thinking about Emily, it was a good job he didn't have a phone on him. His sister had an uncanny knack for picking up when he was in trouble and giving him hell about it. He didn't need the aggro.

Once he had replacement clothes, it was easy enough to duck into the public toilets at the Churchill Square shopping centre and change. He struggled to get the massively oversized shirt sleeve over the splint but achieved it at last, although the agony twisted his stomach into knots. Feeling a little more human, the next thing was to try and secure himself a hotel room. He wanted to be as distant from people as possible to process everything.

Especially the Lori problem. That was going to take some sorting out. There was an easy way, which was to ask her. But he already doubted her word, and she might lie to him again – and he'd be none the wiser. This sucked.

If he could take what she'd said as truth, she'd been justified in withholding that info from him, because once he'd known he'd lost his shit. Twice: once with her and once with Rod.

He was getting fucking nowhere. Nothing was true,

everything was true, some of it was and some wasn't. But broken trust and betrayal lay right at the heart of it, and it didn't really matter who'd done what, who'd said what – it was even more of a mess than 24 hours before.

Except it did matter.

He couldn't check into his hotel room until the afternoon. In the interim, he'd seen a Waterstones on his wandering. He could lose some time in there.

He emerged a few hours later, already regretting the coffee and slice of cake he'd had in its café. Instead of having its normal effect of focusing his mind the coffee had made him jittery, and the cake had given a sugar rush followed by a crash. He needed to eat something more sensible. Making sure he tucked his new books securely under his left arm, he began a search for sustenance.

Meandering down towards the sea, he came across a Wetherspoons and decided that was his best option. Choosing a sirloin steak and Mediterranean salad, he sat in a corner with his back to the world so he could hold the steak in his left hand and gnaw on it like a dog, with no one being the wiser. He lingered over the meal with an orange juice, feeling fatigue settle in after his dessert of a warm cookie dough sandwich. He could probably switch off for a bit after that.

Jamie disappeared off the streets of Brighton and checked into the hotel, taking some painkillers with a bottle of water he'd bought. He fell into bed and slept for 16 hours straight through.

When he woke, the first thing he did was curse at the torturous pain in his hand. Either it was more swollen or he'd been squashing it in his sleep. There was no clock in the room, but he switched on the TV to see the time. Knocking back twice as many painkillers as he should, because he'd missed more than one dose while asleep, he was vaguely curious what day it was.

They'd have come to bang on the door if he'd slept past what he'd paid for, wouldn't they? He flicked through various channels, trying to get his bearings, and found a programme he knew to be a weekend edition. Well, at least he hadn't slept through until Monday. So it could be Sunday, but he thought probably not.

What was he going to do next?

He'd hoped his brain would've had some solutions for him with that amount of sleep, but he couldn't come up with anything. His hand throbbed. His neck felt twisted. He tried to put the sling back on, but it took him a while to work out which way up it went, and by the time he'd washed a bit and dressed he was ready to either throw up or pass out.

Or both, which he considered.

He'd thought sleeping it off would help, but all it seemed to have done was delay the inevitable. He wanted his own bed and Sid: someone who couldn't lie or betray him. And cats often chose their owners. As long as *she* had been feeding Sid, the black cat would be waiting for him at home. A loyal friend. Uncomplicated by any ulterior motives – apart from wanting more treats.

Jamie could handle that level of relationship and set off to the train station, with home and Sid in mind.

Upon arrival at Littlehampton station, he was astonished at how normal it felt to be walking along

Terminus Road, heading for Sainsbury's in the high street. But the initial normality wore off quickly when he worked out that if he wanted to avoid *her*, as he did, he'd need simple food like tins of soup and microwave meals: things that he could prepare in his kitchenette. Well, at least he had a fridge, but it wasn't easy to pick things up, and that was before he tried to open tins. But he refused to be reliant on *her* for anything. She'd probably gloat and rub his nose in it, all the while worrying about her boyfriend in the hospital, and speculating when the police would come and arrest Jamie for assault.

He growled out loud, and the elderly lady next to him looked at him in consternation, then moved further away. Fuck that. He had enough food for a couple of days, which might be long enough to work out what the fuck he was going to do. Less than ten minutes walk and he'd be home. Maybe *she'd* be off visiting her boyfriend and he wouldn't encounter her at all.

As Jamie turned the key in the front door with his left hand as usual, the bags hanging off his arm swung against the door with a thump. So much for a quiet entrance. He hoped his luck would hold, and she'd be out. He pushed the door shut with his right shoulder and gave an involuntary gasp as a dagger-like pain ran down his arm. Something had to be damaged further up, as well as the injury to his hand. Then the living room door opened, and he came face-to-face with *her*: the one person in the world he least wanted to see.

Lori took a half-step towards him, and his reaction was immediate recoil. His left hand shot up to shoulder height, palm facing her.

"Stop! Stay away from me." His voice was rough with the memories pummelling him from Thursday night. Balancing his shopping bags and himself as best he could without using his right arm, he headed up the stairs to his room on the top floor, and didn't look back.

Lori stood open-mouthed at the bottom of the stairs, and accepted that her worst fears had manifested. Her bestie was gone. Not through memory loss that time, but deliberate withdrawal. She still owed him her life, but before they'd probably have talked about silly things to do to make up for it. This wouldn't be like that. She pressed her lips together in a thin line. Without friendship, what she owed was only a business transaction.

Half an hour later, she slipped a piece of paper under Jamie's door.

When he disinterestedly picked it up an hour later, he unfolded it to see she'd written a message, in clear individual letters rather than her usual untidy cursive script. He read it through, barely registering the words:

To: J. Brightfield

From: L. Archer

I O U 1 life.

Please advise preferred payment method below and return to Bedroom 2 by Monday 8am

----

Signed: L. H. Archer

Date: 26th November 2022

He would've laughed if he hadn't been feeling like everyone and everything in the world was total shit. It was so typical of her to phrase it like that. He left it on his desk for a couple of hours, hoping some of the desolation that flayed his heart would ease.

It didn't, so he screwed the note up and chucked it in the bin.

*

Jamie woke Monday morning with a fuzzy head. He wasn't sure if he hadn't slept enough, or too much. It didn't matter either way, but he still had to let work know he'd be late.

He'd have to retrieve the burner phone from *her* to do that, but when he opened the door to go and look for it, he didn't need to. It was right there, waiting for him.

She anticipated me. She knew him too well. That was how she'd been able to deceive him so easily.

He picked the phone up with his left hand and took it to his desk, trying to wedge it still against something heavy while typing a message to Evie.

It was utterly ridiculous that he couldn't even do something as basic as texting, but he finally got a string of characters assembled:

Can u let Tigr no ill b in @ 12. U free 2 tk notes – need ally – def. need sndprf mtg rm

It took him ten minutes to type because he kept pressing the keys the wrong number of times with his left index finger, and he was sweating and nauseous afterwards. He had no idea how he was going to do anything.

This is all HER fault.

He couldn't even dress in his normal smart casual for work, because he hadn't worked out how to do buttons, and he definitely couldn't tie shoelaces. So he did what he could and dressed in a polo shirt, hoodie, joggers and a pair of trainers with elastic laces. At least the shirt collar would protect the back of his neck from the sling and he fought the zip into submission with his left hand while his right remained fixed against his shoulder.

Thank fuck for velcro! He'd never have coped with the intricacies of an old-style calico sling by himself, and a shuddering breath escaped him that he'd avoided that.

Evie messaged back: *What u done now?*

Tel u l8r, he sent. Even those few key presses made him break a sweat.

And Evie, concerned in the office, took her phone straight to the boss. She knocked on his office door and went in, barely waiting for his permission to enter. "Tiger, I think we have a problem. Something's happened. Jamie doesn't text like this – he usually only shortens a few things, and I'm worried." She showed him the messages.

Tiger rolled his eyes. "Let's hope you're wrong, Evie. We don't need anything else going on right now. We'll see what happens when he arrives."

*** suspend(altPOV) ***

I waited until the front door closed before emerging from the sanctuary. There were some things I had to do, and I didn't want to risk running into Jamie either coming in or going out. I hoped he'd made the sensible decision of going up to London to let Tiger know in person about his injury.

Tiger wouldn't be expecting Jamie to come back from two weeks emergency leave with his hand immobilised

and unable to work.
It wasn't my problem. He'd shown that by not returning the IOU. Even if the cast or splint meant he couldn't hold a pen, he could've tried to talk to me. But I hadn't seen him except for that one brief glimpse on Saturday.
I hmphed. He could get on with it. I had a life to rebuild without him, and I needed things to do to keep me occupied. I had some money stashed away so I could replace some of my tarot decks if I wanted but each time I considered it my mind shied away, still aching with grief at the bereavement.
Sainsbury's in town had an Argos collection point, and I already had a replacement SIM card for when I got a new phone, with a new number. If I got myself back online, connected to our Wi-Fi...
Shit. My Wi-Fi. That'd take some getting used to.
I rolled my eyes. A little under two weeks before, I'd thought Jamie and Evie were together and he'd move out to be with her. My misunderstanding, and I'd got over it. This time the rug pulled out from under my feet had put me on my arse, and the daggered pain of it stole my breath again.
I'd already lost count of how many times that bitter slice had cut me.
No going back, I'd said to him on Thursday night. How very prophetic.

*** **END OF BOOK ONE** ***

ACKNOWLEDGEMENTS / ADDITIONAL

THANK YOU FOR READING!

This is the FIRST book in a romance SERIES – I hope you weren't expecting a happy ending yet because there isn't one, obviously #sorrynotsorry. But I promise there WILL be one when the story concludes.

My grateful thanks go to my entire ARC team – you're such wonderful people! I'm so happy you took a chance on the story!

Thanks to CP, the first person to read the initial few pages. Her "I need more!" response told me the characters were ready to share their lives with the world, but they had to wait for me to catch up. Sorry I was slow – I needed more development time than they did LOL.
Thanks also to MA for suggesting the plot twist that causes so much growth across the characters' arc. He'll probably never see this, but I don't need him to.
Thanks to LB and SG for believing in me when it was hard to believe in myself, and to everyone who's had a hand in birthing this creation.

And as always, most importantly, my deepest gratitude and service to Spirit for choosing me as the medium for the story. Thank you.

I believe we're all here to learn and grow as people, as souls, but that's *my* truth. You're entitled to your own truth as much as anyone is.

I would never force my beliefs on another, but if you feel you have touch points in common with mine, or with what's in the book, I'm always open to heart- and soul-led discussions.

You can email me (address in the About The Author section) or feel free to drop into www.tarotfortwo.com. There's some fun stuff planned for the website and elsewhere (no spoilers lol) – sign up for the mailing list if you want to be kept in the loop! Plus there's a little special something as a way of saying thanks for giving the book your time. I hope you didn't get through as many tissues reading it as I did while writing it.

And if the book didn't resonate with you, that's OK too. Maybe you're not part of the intended audience, or you might not be ready to look down this path... yet.

In any case, I wish you happiness, and thank you for spending the time with us.

ABOUT THE AUTHOR

Ella Hamilton lives in South East England with two spoilt cats, and the challenges of trying to wear All. The. Hats. while being a creative and author with ADHD – and not having enough spoons in the drawer, or hours in the day, to do it all at once.

The story came to her in 2021 when the world was a little mad, and she decided to write her own version where she could be the sort of "crazy" that suited her best, i.e. NOT someone else's label. The title came first, unexpectedly, then the plot, and finally the two main characters turned up with Lori's frequent eye rolls and Jamie's banter already front-and-centre.

But it took an ADHD diagnosis and Radleigh Valentine's Certified Angel Tarot Reader course, both in 2024, plus a vision board workshop with Colette Baron-Reid in early 2025 before the author was ready to see past the plot twist that had hamstrung her for 2.5 years.

When not wrestling with plot twists and plummeting down whichever research rabbit hole is right in front of her, you can often find Ella under a heated throw, reading tarot cards, having in-depth and often filthy discussions with the book characters in her head, and staying up well past her bedtime.

It's just as well this is her full-time job, as she wouldn't thrive under someone else's rules now. Once you taste creative freedom, you can never go back to society's constrained boxes without feeling your wings have been clipped and your true voice muzzled.

You can contact the author at ella@tarotfortwo.com or visit www.tarotfortwo.com

COMING SOON

Tarot For Two Book Two – <no title spoilers lol>

Release planned for Spring 2026

Want to be on the ARC team? Tell Ella!
ella@tarotfortwo.com

Printed in Dunstable, United Kingdom

76581679R00231